RESISTANCE

POWER PLAY

CAT GRANT - RACHEL HAIMOWITZ

CW00606745

RIPTIDE
PUBLISHING

Riptide Publishing
PO Box 6652
Hillsborough, NJ 08844
http://www.riptidepublishing.com

Power Play: Resistance
Copyright © 2012 by Cat Grant and Rachel Haimowitz

Cover art by Imaliea, http://imaliea.deviantart.com
Cover design: L.C. Chase, http://lcchase.com/design.htm
Editor: Carole-ann Galloway
Layout: L.C. Chase, http://lcchase.com/design.htm

ISBN: 978-1-937551-33-9

Printed in the United States of America
First edition
April, 2012

Also available in ebook
ISBN: 978-1-937551-28-5

RESISTANCE

POWER PLAY

CAT GRANT - RACHEL HAIMOWITZ

RIPTIDE
PUBLISHING

TABLE OF CONTENTS

For everyone who's ever felt shame at their desires. Don't. Be proud; you are perfect the way you are.

CHAPTER 1

"Cognac, please."

Bran looked up from his beer at the preppy little moron who'd just sat down beside him. *Fucking tourists.*

Jian Li blinked twice and went back to cleaning glasses behind the bar.

The moron cleared his throat. "Pardon me? Sir?"

Jian Li kept ignoring him. Tourists tipped for shit anyway. Bran took a sip of his beer—warm like the Chinese always drank it; wouldn't that throw Mr. Tourist for a loop—and decided to take pity on the man.

He was kind of cute, after all.

Bran planted his elbows on the bar and raised an eyebrow at the guy. "Lost?" he asked.

Mr. Tourist blinked at him like he hadn't already checked Bran out—though he obviously had, else why invade his space at an otherwise empty bar—and flashed him a bright smile. "Not anymore."

Strange diction. Not quite New England, not quite old England. Certainly not California. The tourist cast his eyes about the crowded room, and Bran could see the exact moment when he registered the lack of white faces in the bar. "No cognac, then?"

Bran chuffed into his beer. "Don't get a whole lot of call for it in this place. Jian Li," he said, raising his hand to catch the bartender's attention. "A beer for the *Gweilo*, please." Jian Li gave him a small nod and an even smaller smirk, and Mr. Tourist turned to him with a quizzical glance. "That's what everybody here calls me," Bran said with a shrug. "Beer's warm, by the way."

Jian Li placed a mug in front of Mr. Tourist with a curt nod.

Mr. Tourist took a sip and tried very hard not to grimace. Bran stifled a snort.

"Yes, well . . . much obliged. Next round's on me."

This time Bran didn't bother hiding his amusement. "Who says there's gonna be a next round?" He drained what was left in his mug, then nodded at Mr. Tourist's. "Since it looks like you're not gonna drink that . . ." Bran scooped it up and saluted him with it. "Thanks, pal." Then he nodded at Jian Li, got up, and sauntered over to the nearest table.

He felt Mr. Tourist's gaze burning a hole in the seat of his jeans on the way. Even thought about inviting him over for second. After all, the guy was cute in a scruffy puppy sort of way—if totally fucking clueless—but Bran really wasn't up for company tonight. He took a swig from Mr. Tourist's beer. Took another. Sank down and put his back to the guy. He wasn't nearly drunk enough for . . . well, *anything*.

Fucking tourist looked made of money. *Bet his hands are soft.* Fucker.

But of course, Mr. Tourist couldn't take a hint. He pulled out the chair opposite Bran as if he owned the place, then asked, "Mind if I sit down?"

Bran sighed. "Would you leave if I said no?"

Mr. Tourist shrugged, smiled with the kind of confident swagger Bran imagined lawyers flashed at juries. "What's bothering you?"

"Besides you, you mean?"

"Ouch." Mr. Tourist sat down. "I did let you steal my drink, after all." He held out his hand. "I'm Jonathan, by the way."

Bran stared at the outstretched hand, contemplating spitting into his palm before shaking it. *That'd scare him right off.*

For some reason, though, he didn't. And yup, Jonathan's hands *were* soft. "Bran," he conceded.

"Short for Brandon?"

Bran's gut tightened the way it did every time he heard his given name. Old habits and all that. "Just Bran," he said curtly. "So, you're obviously not from around here. Slumming it tonight?"

Bran tried to pull his hand back, but Jonathan held on for a few more seconds, a sardonic smirk tugging up one corner of his mouth. His very, very pretty mouth.

Pink, like a girl's.

"Just wanted to get out of the house. I've lived here five years now and there's still so much of the city I haven't seen." Now Jonathan was grinning in earnest. "How about you?"

For a moment, Bran nearly gave in to the urge to spill his whole stupid story. He'd never see this guy again anyway, right? But all he said was, "Getting drunk, actually. Isn't that what people do in bars?"

Jonathan's grin turned downright filthy. "Among other things."

Shit. Bran drained the beer in one long gulp—Jonathan's eyes zoomed in on his throat and stayed there—then banged the empty glass on the table. "Buy me another, and maybe I'll tell you."

"Fair enough." Jonathan nodded and went to the bar for another round.

Bran most definitely did *not* check out his ass while he walked away.

Jonathan came back a minute later with two whiskeys and that same stupid, cocky grin plastered to his face. Bran took a sip. It was the expensive stuff—the kind people only bought him when they were trying to get into his pants. *Still not in the mood, pal, but I'll drink your liquor.*

Jonathan held up his glass. Bran clinked it, then knocked back his double in one go. It burned the whole way down, but damn if it wasn't good.

Jonathan's eyebrow arched high and perfect over one blue, blue eye. "We're not running a race here, you know."

"Good thing, cos I'm getting a little too drunk for that."

Jonathan laughed, genuine and carefree, loud enough to turn disapproving heads in the bar. If he noticed, he didn't seem to care. "What's the occasion?"

"Lost opportunity."

"Can I help you find it?"

Bran snorted and grabbed the still-full shot glass from Jonathan's hand. "It's not in my pants, you know."

Another laugh. "Maybe it's in mine?"

Touché, sir. Bran leaned over the table and eyed Jonathan's crotch. "I dunno, looks a little small to be hiding three million dollars."

There went the other eyebrow. "What do you need three million dollars for?"

"My boss is selling his business at the end of the year. Wants me to buy it—*I* want me to buy it. Little matter of scraping up the money, though. No fucking clue where I'm gonna get it, but once I sober up tomorrow I'll figure it out."

"I hear banks are pretty good for that kind of thing."

"Not for guys like me. I'd have better luck with the Triad."

"Don't they break your legs if you miss a payment?"

Bran smirked and downed Jonathan's whiskey. "One more drink and I won't even feel it."

A hand slid onto Bran's thigh, and he jumped at the touch. "Do you feel this?"

Now it was Bran's turn to raise an eyebrow. Among other parts of his body. But he held perfectly still and said, "Bit handsy, aren't you?"

The hand slid up his thigh, fingers brushing his swelling dick through his jeans. "Let's just say I'm used to going after what I want."

Bran nearly choked on his next breath as those questing fingers squeezed his dick. "Guess you rack up a lot of restraining orders?"

Jonathan laughed. "I like you. Let's get out of here." He pulled his hand from Bran's crotch just long enough to slap some money on the table—*A fifty? Jesus fucking Christ*—then grabbed Bran by the wrist. Bran's first instinct was to dig his heels in and shake the guy off, but his dick was practically poking a hole through his zipper, whiskey be damned.

Jonathan pulled him toward the front door, but Bran jerked his head in the opposite direction. "This way." They marched toward the back, past the men's room, which of course Jonathan tried to tug him into. Bran tugged him back. "Don't disrespect their space."

Jonathan's eyebrows shot up again, but he didn't argue.

They stumbled out the back door, into the alley. It'd rained earlier, which helped to drown out the stench of piss and rotting garbage at least a little. Too-bright sodium lights on the bar's back façade glistened off the damp pavement and burned halos through the humid air.

Not the nicest place he'd ever fucked, but he kinda liked it exactly for that reason; twenty bucks said Jonathan was appalled that even the soles of his shoes had to touch this filthy ground. He backed Jonathan against the brick alley wall, a little harder than he'd meant to in his urgency, but Jonathan only smiled up at him.

Bran wanted to ravage that smile right off his smug little face.

"I wanna fuck you," Bran growled into Jonathan's neck. He had four or five inches and twenty pounds on the guy; he could pick him up, fuck him right against the wall. "I wanna—"

Fingers closed over his wrist as he reached for Jonathan's zipper. A sharp flash of pain, and next he knew, he was on his knees in a fucking puddle, cold water seeping through his jeans, wrist still clamped in Jonathan's hand.

"What the *fuck?*" Bran tried to pull away, couldn't. *Fuck,* that hurt. Tried swatting at Jonathan with his other hand, but ended up grabbing the wall to keep from toppling over. The first stirrings of fear cut through the pleasant haze of liquor and lust he'd been dumb enough to let himself sink into.

And yet he couldn't quite shake it off. Didn't want to—too fucking horny. And how fucked up was that?

No more fucked up, he supposed, than Jonathan, who caught his eye and smirked that self-satisfied smirk as he worked down his zipper with his free hand and pulled out his dick. He was already rock hard, and surprisingly well-endowed for such a short guy. Longer than Bran's, actually, straight and thick . . . and sprinkled with freckles, just like the bridge of his nose. Bran's mouth watered.

"Suck it."

Was he *serious*? "You're out of your fucking mind. Let go of my hand."

Jonathan let go—and grabbed hold of Bran's hair instead, tugging his face into his crotch. That impressive erection slid right past Bran's shock-slackened lips.

For a split second, Bran considered biting him, but . . . damn, he tasted good, felt even better, firm and heavy on his tongue. His hand drifted down, cupping his own dick through the confines of his jeans. He was already so fucking hard he knew he'd come if he touched himself skin to skin.

"That's right," Jonathan said. "Hands on *me*. Take that cock—you know you want it."

The hell of it was, he *did*.

Jonathan's fist tightened in his hair until it felt like he'd rip it right out, shoved his head forward until his chin hit Jonathan's nuts. He gagged, tried to pull back, but Jonathan held him firm.

"I said *suck it*," Jonathan growled, yanking Bran's head back until only the tip was in his mouth, then jerking him forward again.

Bran's hands came up to Jonathan's hips, grabbed hard, but whether to shove him away or drag him closer, he couldn't quite tell. All he knew was his balls were hot and tight, his dick pulsing with every rapid beat of his heart, every thrust of Jonathan's dick down his throat, every painful tug on his hair, and if he let go of Jonathan's hips he'd touch himself and come until he passed out in this filthy fucking alley and he didn't want it to end yet, didn't—

Jonathan groaned and came, flooding his mouth with salty bitterness. He tried to pull off, but Jonathan held him there, fingers tightening until his eyes watered and the pressure in his belly, back, and balls fucking *exploded*, set the world to swaying, and only Jonathan's hand in his hair kept him upright as his chest hitched and his muscles spasmed with the force of it.

"Swallow it." He did, since Jonathan was giving him no choice. It tasted fucking disgusting, but he felt too good to care very much.

Jesus, like a fucking teenager again, coming in my own pants. He wiped his mouth, looked up at Jonathan's smug smile. *How did he fucking* do *that to me?*

Bran wobbled to his feet, hand flailing out to catch hold of the wall. Jonathan stared at his lips—no doubt red and swollen from their recent punishment—and licked his own. He leaned in to peck Bran on the cheek, then ducked his head to refasten his pants.

"So . . ." Jonathan said. He fished into his pocket, retrieved his wallet, snagged a business card and handed it to Bran. "Perhaps you'd like to see me again sometime? Dinner maybe? Do it right?"

Do it right? What was he, some blushing virgin? But he had to admit, he *was* feeling better than he had all day. Hell, better than he had in the last couple of months.

"Yeah, maybe." He took the business card, stuck it in his pocket. "Don't get lost on the way home, *Gweilo.* This neighborhood's a little rough at night."

Jonathan laughed, winked at him. "Oh, don't worry about me," he said. "I can take care of myself."

Bran didn't doubt that for a second.

Bran landed face-first in his pillow the moment he got home, and slept like the dead. Didn't stop him waking up with a monster hangover, though, his eyes burning in his skull like a pair of boiled eggs. That's what he got for being stupid enough to get shitfaced. Usually one beer was his limit.

He dragged himself out of bed and stumbled to the kitchenette for a glass of water, realizing two steps in that he was still wearing his jeans—and they were fucking disgusting, knees still damp with alley slime, crotch stiff and crusted with last night's loss of control. Jesus, what the fuck had come over him?

Jonathan, apparently. Or whatever his name really was.

He knocked back his water in one huge gulp, then unzipped his jeans and peeled them off. They stuck to him, pulling at his pubes. *That's what you get for having casual sex in an alley, idiot. Probably have herpes now.*

And I'd fucking deserve it.

. . . But damn, it really had been kind of hot. *Fuck "kind of." Try "insanely."* He chuckled, and his headache spiked.

Gritting his teeth, he gingerly disengaged his pants from his pubes, dropped them where he stood, and headed for a shower. He stayed under the hot spray until his skin stung, toweled off, threw on clean boxers and an undershirt, and trudged back into the living room. He scooped up his dirty jeans and was about to toss them in the laundry basket when his wallet fell out of the back pocket. A business card fell out along with it.

Oh, right. Mr. Bossy had given it to him. Bran hadn't even bothered looking at it before. *Jonathan S. Watkins.* Name and phone number. Nothing else. What the hell kind of business card was that? He flipped it over, but the back was blank.

Watkins . . . Jonathan Watkins . . . Why did that sound so familiar?

He fired up his ancient desktop, drumming his fingers on the desk while he waited for Google to load.

17,400,00 results? What the fuck? Who *was* this guy?

Ex-CEO of the world's largest computer empire, apparently. And current Chairman of the Watkins Foundation, charitable organization extraordinaire. Yup, the photo matched. Jesus, the guy didn't even look thirty.

Holy shit. I blew a fucking billionaire.

Bran picked up the plain white business card again, flicked it with his thumb. Did this guy really want to see him again? What for? Last night was a little fuzzy, but he didn't actually recall Jonathan drinking more than a sip. But he had given Bran his card—his *personal* card, from the look of things.

Bran fingered his cell phone. Looked back at his computer screen. Surely a guy like Jonathan wouldn't answer his own phone. A secretary maybe. Or a personal assistant. Whatever guys with more money than God hired.

Eh, he probably didn't really want Bran to call him, anyway. Probably just felt bad leaving his bit of rough on his knees in an alley with cum dripping down his chin.

And yet, he had invited him to dinner, hadn't he? Or had Bran been so drunk he'd imagined it?

Only one way to find out. Bran flicked on his phone and punched in Jonathan's number. It rang twice before the line clicked on.

"Hello, Brandon. How's your headache?"

What. The. Fuck? "How did you know it was me?" Who was this guy, some kind of fucking stalker? Bran went to the window and parted his drapes, feeling ridiculous even as he did so.

Jonathan chuckled. "Do you know who *I* am yet?"

Bran hesitated. "Uh, yeah."

"Well, there you go. So, dinner tonight?"

"You sure you got time for me? Sounds like you're pretty busy."

"I managed to squeeze you in last night, didn't I?"

"Fuck you," Bran replied, but his words lacked the bite he'd intended.

Another chuckle. "Eight o'clock, then? I'll send my car to pick you up."

The line went dead before Bran could even tell him where he lived.

Bran's doorbell rang around four in the afternoon, jarring him from his concentration. He eyed the door, eyed the numbers he was crunching for his business plan, eyed the door again. He wasn't expecting anyone, and the mailman had already come. Unless it was . . . No, Jonathan wouldn't show up four hours early. Would he?

Fuck it, the plan was more important if he had even the slightest hope of getting a loan. He went back to his numbers.

The doorbell rang again.

Bran sighed, scrubbed his hands across his face. The lingering remnants of his hangover flared at the noise. "All right, all right, I'm coming," he called, pushing up from his desk. Whatever. He'd been sitting in the damn folding chair too long anyway.

He swung the door open to find a uniformed courier holding a black leather garment bag. "Delivery from Mr. Jonathan Watkins for Mr. Brandon McKinney?"

Bran blinked. "What is it?"

"No idea, sir. We're not allowed to inspect the packages." The courier handed him the garment bag and turned to go.

"Wait a minute." Bran dug in his pocket, but all he came up with was a crumpled dollar bill and a handful of change. Still, better than nothing.

The delivery man shook his head. "Don't worry about it, sir. It's been taken care of." He headed off before Bran could reply or give the bag back.

The hell? This guy thinks I can't dress myself?

He thought about leaving the bag in the hallway. But then, he supposed wherever Jonathan was taking him, he probably *didn't* own a nice enough suit. Might as well see what he'd sent.

He took it inside, laid it across the bed and unzipped it, breath catching at what was inside. At first he thought the three-piece suit was black, but subtle navy tones shone in the light when he lifted it up. Soft, soft wool from the feel of it, maybe even a wool/cashmere blend. The pristine white dress shirt underneath was definitely silk, with stiff French cuffs. Last time he'd worn anything even half this nice was to his mother's funeral. He didn't even own cufflinks anymore.

But of course the pretentious asshole had thought of that too: silver, or maybe platinum, nestled in a little velvet box along with a matching tie clip. Simple and elegant. *And probably a month's rent, too, the ostentatious little shit.*

There were shoes and cashmere socks, leather belt and a tie, too. The shoes so polished he could see his reflection, the belt supple as suede, the tie the exact same shade of green as his eyes.

One last thing in the garment bag, too dark to discern until he pulled it out and saw . . . underwear?

Are you fucking kidding *me?*

He wadded the black silk boxer-briefs with the intent of hurling them across the room, and found a little handwritten note pinned to the waistband: *Boxers ruin the line of the suit —J.*

Oh, fuck this, and fuck him too. He knocked the whole ensemble onto the floor with one furious swipe. What the hell did Jonathan think this was—*Pretty Woman*? Just because he'd sucked the guy's dick didn't make him a whore.

Still, the attention *was* strangely flattering. He bent down, picked the clothes up off the floor. Shook out the suit, smoothed a hand along one sleeve. God, it was so fucking soft.

Couldn't hurt to try it on before he sent it back with a "Fuck you." Just to see what it felt like to stand—literally—in a billionaire's shoes.

He stripped off his T-shirt and jeans—and after a moment's hesitation, took off his boxers too. The black silk whispered over his skin. He pulled on the pants next, then the shirt. He'd never worn anything so nice in his life. Or so perfectly fitted. Like it was made for him. Probably was, actually; he hadn't seen a single label on anything.

His fingers felt clumsy as he put on the cufflinks, the tie, the vest and the jacket, then sat down on the edge of his unmade bed to slip on the socks and the shiny black brogues.

Jesus, this was creepy. Had Jonathan had his credit card statements hacked? How else would he know what size Bran was? Know *exactly,* too—enough to custom tailor, because this sure as shit hadn't come off some rack somewhere. No labels in anything. Even the shoes fit perfectly.

He studied himself in the full-length mirror on the back of his bathroom door. Barely even recognized himself. He looked like a fucking executive or something, despite his shaggy hair. *No, like a business owner.* Stupid as it was, it kind of made him feel like maybe it was possible to buy Sung Integrated Design. Rename it, maybe: *McKinney* Integrated Design.

Jesus, Bran, what are you, five? Playing dress-up? Really?

Apparently so, because long after he stepped away from the mirror and returned to his P&Ls and his five-year plan, he still hadn't changed out of the damn suit. Hadn't even loosened the tie. Maybe he'd go out with that arrogant little fuck after all. Just once. Just to see what the high life was really like.

CHAPTER 2

Jonathan sipped his green tea and glanced at his phone. Five minutes till eight, and no sign of Brandon. No word from him, either, and the suit had been delivered hours ago. Had he pushed too hard? Overstepped his bounds?

Jonathan waved off the head waiter, who'd come over to refill his cup, and toyed again with the notion of calling his driver. But no . . . He was so rarely surprised—so rarely *denied*—it was actually quite delicious to remain in suspense. He loved being uncertain what Brandon would do. What an intriguing man Brandon was turning out to be. So defiant on the outside, and yet so submissive deep down. God, he'd come in his pants on his knees at Jonathan's feet. All Jonathan'd had to do was pull Brandon's hair and shove himself down the man's throat.

Upon consideration, maybe that was the problem. Big tough construction worker, on his own since he was fifteen. Not the kind of man to admit he liked being dominated. In fact, despite the obvious submissive bent, he seemed to have a rather toppy vibe himself. A switch, maybe? Well, wasn't that just half the pleasure of getting him on his knees?

Jonathan smiled and shifted a little in his chair. Thank goodness for dimly lit rooms and long tablecloths.

Forget the tea. He needed something stronger.

He picked up the wine menu, and the sommelier virtually materialized at the table. Jonathan knew little of Chinese liquor, so he let the man recommend a Wuliangye baijou nearly as old as he was. The sommelier left, returned with the bottle a few minutes later. Poured Jonathan a taste. It looked like white wine . . . and tasted like soy sauce mixed with Everclear.

Ah well. He supposed it would settle his nerves.

And clear out my sinuses.

He sipped his baijou—very, very slowly—and cast another glance at his cell phone. 8:03. Perhaps he should call his driver.

Patience, Jonathan.

Brandon sauntered in at last—eight minutes late—completely worth the wait for the sight of that long lean body in jacket and vest, wavy ginger hair combed back and curling softly at the nape of his neck. Jonathan's fingers itched to card through that silky length again. To grab a good handful and yank.

God*damn* he looked good in that suit. And judging by the smirk on his face, he knew it.

Not *just* a smirk, though. The lines around the eyes and the stiffness in his shoulders held anger, irritation. Maybe even a touch of trepidation.

Interesting.

"I'm glad you came," Jonathan said. He made to stand but thought better of it; no need to give Brandon the upper hand by letting him see how . . . *powerfully* he was affecting Jonathan. "But I have to say I'm not quite sure why you did if you're so upset with me."

Brandon's smile froze uncomfortably on his face, just for a moment, before his swagger reasserted itself. "It's not every day a guy sends me a three-piece suit. Or takes me to the most expensive restaurant in Chinatown. In a limo."

"So I'm just a meal ticket, then?"

"I can buy my own dinner, thanks. And I'm sending the suit back tomorrow."

Jonathan grinned at the flash of fierceness, but couldn't quite resist replying, "Eating cold chili out of a can over the sink is hardly what I'd call a decent meal."

This time Brandon's smile fell clean away and he took a single step back, as if to flee from Jonathan right then and there. "How did you—?"

He clenched his jaw, but too late; the question—the *confirmation*—was already out.

And yet he's still here. Curious after all, then.

No, not just curious. *Compelled.*

"Please"—Jonathan waved at the chair opposite him with his wineglass—"sit."

Brandon hesitated, hand poised on the back of his chair. Studied Jonathan for a long moment, jaw working, before he finally sat down. And wasted no time pouring himself a big glass of the baijou.

"Careful—" Jonathan began, but Brandon waved him off and said, "I'll drink your damn $3,000 Wuliangye if I want to."

Interesting. Jonathan gestured with his glass again—*By all means.*

"Shit," Brandon said after another sip, "this stuff is *good.* The sommelier has good taste."

As if I don't. But Jonathan decided to let it pass—this time.

Brandon fidgeted with the imperfect knot of his tie, and Jonathan's eyes zoomed in on those long thin fingers, nicked and calloused but clean. "So how the hell did you know what size I wear? This suit fits like I ordered it myself."

Jonathan smiled. "I have a good eye. And you have a great body. I enjoyed dressing you up."

"What, like I'm some kind of doll?"

"Please," Jonathan drawled, "don't pretend you're not enjoying the feel of that fabric against your skin."

"I *do* have my own suit, you know. Picked it out myself and everything," Brandon added, dry as the Wuliangye.

A dozen different replies rose to Jonathan's lips, but there he kept them; best to let the man have his pride, at least for now. He smiled. "Yes, well, how about we order?"

The waiter, ever attentive, took that as his cue to join them with menus. It seemed all the wonderful things he'd heard about this place were entirely justified. But then he opened his menu, and his smile faded. Chinese. Every last word. "Hmm," he said, "Perhaps we should ask for recommendations?"

But when he looked up, Brandon was studying the menu with feigned interest. "Hmm," Brandon drawled, in what struck Jonathan as a deliberate imitation. "Have you ever had stuffed lotus leaves?"

Two can play at this game. "Why not. What are they stuffed with?"

Brandon consulted the menu again, then said, "Sticky rice, Chinese sausage, shiitake mushrooms, chicken, and sun-dried shrimp."

Everything he'd stopped eating a long time ago. Too bad. "Very . . . creative. Unfortunately, I'm a vegetarian."

Brandon's brows furrowed. "You don't eat meat? How about fish?"

"Afraid not."

Brandon turned back to the menu, forehead crinkling. "Okay. Guess we can get them to substitute tofu. That all right?"

Jonathan shrugged, curious to see how far Brandon would take this. Brandon turned to the waiter, and began speaking—in rapid-fire Chinese.

Seriously?

Jonathan pushed back in his chair, closed his open mouth as the waiter nodded, said something back.

How on earth had his investigators missed this? True they'd only had a day, but they'd dug up everything from his shoe size to his eating habits, for God's sake; surely a Chinese education would've been easier to find than that?

Brandon turned to him with a feral grin—all teeth, *far* too many teeth, and humor at Jonathan's expense—and said, "They're making yours with tofu and seitan. Hope you don't mind me taking the liberty."

Mind? Delighted, more like. It'd been a long time since anyone had surprised him quite so often, and it was wonderful to confirm there was more to Brandon than a hot body and a gorgeous face.

Good. Beautiful faces got old fast, but beautiful *minds* . . . well, that was an entirely different story. A beautiful face to go with it was just icing on the cake.

Brandon was still grinning at him with a million teeth. "I thought you knew everything about me," he said. "Investigators miss a bit?"

"I suppose they did."

"You should fire them."

Jonathan laughed, and Brandon joined him. "So how does a construction worker learn Chinese?"

That seemed to be the wrong thing to say; Brandon stiffened, put his teeth away. "Fourteen years in Chinatown. How could I *not*? You think I'm an idiot just 'cause I work with my hands? 'Cause I never finished high school?"

"No, I—"

"I did get my GED, you know. Even got my associate's. Okay, so maybe it's not MIT, but *fuck you* for thinking you're better than me for having money."

Brandon shoved away from the table so hard he nearly tipped his chair, and Jonathan reached across, grabbing his wrist. The look Brandon shot him was downright dangerous, but he didn't let go.

"That's not what I meant," Jonathan said slowly. "Do you really think I'd bother with you if I thought you were stupid? I have better things to do with my time."

"Like pick up strangers in dive bars?" Brandon jerked his wrist from Jonathan's hand. "A little blue-collar rough and tumble, a face-fuck in an alley, and back to your limo and your Ivy League pals, is that it?"

"MIT isn't actually an Ivy League—"

"Oh *shut up!*" Brandon whirled toward the door, took two steps, whirled back again. "God, you're *infuriating!*"

Jonathan's lips quirked into a grin. "And yet you're still here."

"If either of us goes, it's gonna be you." Brandon reached for his wine, glaring daggers at Jonathan over the rim of his glass. Positively adorable. "Haven't eaten yet."

"Thought you could get your own dinner."

He drained his glass and sat back down on the very edge of his seat, body language screaming, *Push me again and I'm outta here.* "Fuck you. I ordered it, didn't I?"

Jonathan leaned forward, planted his elbows on the table and smiled over his laced fingers. "Have you any idea how badly I want to kiss you right now?"

Brandon rolled his eyes. A step in the right direction, perhaps; exasperation was better than anger. "Think you're pretty funny, don't you?"

"Are you going to tell me to fuck myself again? Because honestly, it'd be a lot more fun if you joined me."

Brandon snorted, shaking his head like he couldn't believe Jonathan's audacity. And was that a smile fighting its way onto his face? "This time I expect dinner first," he said. "Wouldn't want you to think I'm *too* easy." Another flash of white, white teeth. "Takes more than a five-thousand-dollar suit to get into my pants."

"Eight, actually."

And worth every penny.

Watching Brandon eat was sheer pornography. He'd ordered himself some beef dish which he wolfed down with relish, licking drops of plum sauce off his long fingers. Surely he had to know what that was doing to Jonathan's . . . *appetite.* Jonathan could barely keep his attention on his own plate, superlative as the food was. One of the best meals he'd had in months—and he had a private chef.

Slightly tipsy, he leaned back in his seat and enjoyed the view. How on earth did Brandon keep that body with such an obviously prodigious appetite? Well, he no doubt did a lot of heavy lifting at work. And after work, too; a man like that must beat off prospects with a stick.

Soon the waiter cleared away their dessert plates and left them staring at each other across the table. Brandon's eyes looked positively post-coital—a little sleepy, a little tipsy, a lot sated. God, to put that look on his face every day . . . and not just from food and wine.

Every day? Getting a little ahead of yourself there, aren't you, Jonathan?

No point denying they both wanted it tonight, though. So why were they still sitting here? He cleared his throat, hitched a thumb over his shoulder toward a row of windows. "My driver's in the parking lot."

Brandon stood with a grin and took off toward the exit, leaving Jonathan, with his much shorter stride, to jog behind him.

He'd have to pay for that later, Jonathan thought with a grin.

Brandon stopped short at the curb, gazing around the parking lot. "Uh, which limo is yours?"

Jonathan smiled and signaled to his driver, who started up a black Mercedes and drove it over. Jonathan had never much been one for cars, but this one, elegant and guilt-free with its emissionless hydrogen fuel cell, got him every time. He waved off the valet and opened the back door himself, then ushered Brandon in with a flourish. "Age before beauty."

Brandon snickered and slapped him on the butt before sliding in. Jonathan climbed in after, knocked on the divider, and off they went. His gaze followed Brandon's to the bottle of Veuve Cliquot in the silver ice bucket in front of them. "Care for a glass?" Jonathan asked.

"Think we've had enough, don't you? I mean, I want to make sure your dick still works by the time we get to your place."

Jonathan laughed and slid closer. "Fair enough. But why wait?"

He grabbed Brandon by his tie and dragged him in for a kiss.

The tie clip popped right off and landed God knew where. "Hey—" Brandon said, but Jonathan cut him off with another kiss.

"Forget it. I'll buy you a new one."

Brandon pulled back, lips twisting into a scowl. "Or we could just, you know, *look* for it."

Jonathan shrugged, smiled, undid a shirt button peeking out over Brandon's vest and slid his hand inside, all smooth fabric and smooth skin and *God,* he had to have this man. "Or we could just, you know, do this instead." Questing fingers found a nipple, pinched gently.

Brandon's head tipped back on a moan, irritation forgotten.

Jonathan's free hand traveled up Brandon's throat, slid round to the back of his head. He cupped Brandon's skull in his palm for a few precious moments before seizing a handful of hair. Brandon gasped, but didn't try to pull away. In fact, he leaned into it, head lolling back into Jonathan's grasp.

Impossible to resist that sleek, smooth expanse of throat, pulse throbbing visibly, clean line of ginger scruff beneath the chin. Jonathan locked his lips on it and sucked hard, Brandon's breath catching as his teeth nipped hot flesh. He tightened his fingers, yanked Brandon's head back and held him there, trailing lips and teeth along the underside of Brandon's jaw. When he'd taken his fill—*for the moment, anyway*—he pushed Brandon's head back down until their lips met, then guided Brandon's mouth to his own throat.

"If you shove my face into your crotch again," Brandon rumbled, teeth flashing, "I'm gonna fucking *bite* you."

Jonathan chuckled, fingers tightening past the point of pain in Brandon's hair—Brandon gasped against his throat, teeth scraping again—and said, "I didn't hear you complaining last night, Mr. So Turned On I Came In My Pants."

"Oh, you *fucker* . . ."

Brandon's hands reached up to tangle in Jonathan's hair. "Ah ah ah," Jonathan said, very deliberately taking one of Brandon's wrists, then the other, and laying them across Brandon's lap.

"What, I don't get to touch you back?"

"You have to *earn* it first."

Brandon snorted, shook his head—or tried to, anyway; Jonathan's fist in his hair held him fast. "You think awfully highly of yourself, don't you."

An insult on the surface, but the man was smiling, smiling, endless rows of straight white teeth on display. Jonathan jerked his chin at Brandon's crotch and said, "Your cock seems to think pretty highly of me too. Perhaps it'd like a kiss?"

"Well, fuck," Brandon said.

Exactly.

As if on cue, the limo rolled to a halt. A few seconds later, Jonathan's driver opened the door. No shock at the sight that greeted him; he'd been with Jonathan long enough to expect far more salacious things than a simple kiss.

Brandon gave a nervous chuckle and whispered, "Planning on letting go of my hair, or are we just gonna fuck in the back of the limo like a couple of teenagers?"

Jonathan smiled and gave one last hard yank on Brandon's hair. Brandon winced, made a face at him and rubbed at his head when Jonathan let go.

"The limo's nice, but my bed's much nicer."

"Must be a damn nice bed. Lead on, then."

He couldn't help but notice how Brandon's eyes widened when he got a look at the building—clearly dazzled, almost slack-jawed. But Brandon didn't try to linger; they hurried through the lobby hand in hand, Jonathan nodding at the doorman and security guard as they greeted him, pulling Brandon along behind him to his private elevator. As it started the long slow climb to the penthouse, he turned to Brandon, backed him into a wall and bracketed that narrow waist in both arms. "So," he said, leaning in to nuzzle at his throat. "Thirty-four floors. Whatever shall we do in the meantime?"

Brandon smirked. "You could suck *my* dick this time," he said, putting his hands on Jonathan's shoulders. But when he tried to push him down, Jonathan refused to budge.

Brandon sighed. "So I can't touch you, you won't blow me . . . remind me again what I'm doing here?"

"I just thought this time you'd like to come with your pants *off.*"

"You're never gonna let me live that down, are you?"

The elevator dinged before Jonathan could summon up a suitably pithy reply, the doors gliding open on his foyer. He slipped an arm around Brandon's waist and led him inside.

Brandon took two steps and froze, eyes tracking from the marble tiles to the crown molding to the floor-to-ceiling windows overlooking the bay. "*Jesus,*" he whispered, pacing slowly toward the nearest wall, running reverent fingers over a seascape mural, a framed Tomasz Rut original. "Jesus," he said again, and then, turning to run those fingers over Jonathan's smooth cheek, "Bedroom. Where is it?"

Jonathan took his hand and tugged him down the hallway. Lights flicked on ahead of them and blinked out behind them as they stumbled toward the bedroom. Brandon looked back at the living room, now lit only by the built-in reef tank that divided the living room from the office, and said, "Fancy," but seemed to give it no more thought.

They crossed into the bedroom and Brandon started to pull off his jacket. Up came Jonathan's hands to stop him.

"What *is* it with you?" Brandon demanded. "I can't touch you, can't undress myself. You won't blow me. What d'you want me to do, just stand here and let you yank my hair out of my scalp?"

The smile slid off Jonathan's lips to be replaced with something softer, more sensual. "Relax," he murmured, stepping forward to smooth his palms up Brandon's chest. "Let me take care of you."

Brandon bristled beneath his touch. "I don't *need*—"

"I know you don't." Jonathan dropped one hand to Brandon's crotch, cupping him gently. "But isn't it fun sometimes?"

Brandon half-whimpered, half-moaned, and dropped onto the edge of the bed, legs splayed. Jonathan leaned in to straddle his lap, dusting a kiss across his lips before reaching down to unbutton all those layers. *God, why did I buy him a* three-*piece suit again?* "See? Isn't this better than some back alley?"

Brandon's lips twitched. "Better than kneeling in a puddle."

Jonathan pushed Brandon's shirt, vest, and jacket as one down to his elbows, exposing miles of farmer-tanned skin sprinkled with freckles almost the same shade as his hair. Hard to resist the urge to play connect the dots with his teeth; he settled instead for running lips and tongue over flat planes of muscle—the top of a pec, a bared shoulder, a beautiful triceps. Michelangelo's David.

Perfect.

He slid the top layers off completely, then nudged Brandon in the chest until he got a clue and lay down. Jonathan followed with his lips, tasting the ridges of Brandon's stomach, the sparse ginger happy trail, the impressive bulge straining at the suit pants. Brandon's hands settled in his hair—not pulling, not threading, just resting there—but Jonathan shook his head and said, softly, "No."

Brandon returned his arms to his sides. Jonathan had known he would.

Back to Brandon's pants. Jonathan pulled the tongue of the belt from the buckle with his teeth, fingers busy tickling tracks up and down Brandon's flanks. Brandon gasped, squirmed beneath him. *"Fuck, Jonathan,"* he moaned, hips thrusting up as Jonathan rubbed his cheek against Brandon's trapped cock. "Come *on . . .*"

"Patience." A smile as he pulled Brandon's belt through the loops. It slithered into his hand, and for a moment he couldn't help but imagine the sound that soft Italian leather would make against the pale expanse of Brandon's back, that perfect ass, Brandon gasping and writhing and begging beneath him.

God, what lovely marks it would make.

But not now. Not yet.

It would probably help to get him out of his pants first. Button undone, zipper down, he hooked his thumbs in Brandon's belt loops and tugged them down, silk boxer briefs and all.

Brandon flashed him a crooked smirk. "I just got this suit, and now you can't wait to get me out of it?"

"What do you think I bought it for?"

Eyes back on task. As if the rest of him weren't impressive enough, Brandon's cock alone—a healthy handful, thick but not impractically long—would've made Jonathan drool. For once, he was actually tempted to bottom. But tonight he had other plans.

He slid his palms up Brandon's bare thighs, brushed teasing fingers through his pubic hair. Brandon moaned again, angled his hips, but Jonathan was careful not to touch him where he so clearly craved it. "Up," he said, pulling one hand away to tap at Brandon's leg. "You're half off the bed here."

Brandon rose up on his elbows and scooted fully onto the bed without a second's hesitation, back coming to rest against a pile of pillows, head against the headboard. He spread his legs, watched as Jonathan crawled up between them. So gorgeous, so hungry for something Jonathan had an inkling he'd never experienced before. Hard to believe no one had taken the time to enjoy every delight this beautiful man had to offer.

All that lovely skin, just begging to be kissed. Jonathan started in the middle of his chest and worked in circles, painting wet little curlicues with the tip of his tongue. Brandon let out a startled moan and brought up a hand to tangle in Jonathan's hair. Jonathan's first instinct was to shake it off again, but it was such a gentle touch he allowed it this time. Nothing wrong with a little give and take—within reason.

"Jesus, you trying to tease me to death?" Brandon choked out. That strangled sound went straight to Jonathan's cock. He could imagine Brandon making that noise again with his hands around his throat. It might frighten Brandon at first, but he'd love it, the loss of air, the rush of blood, the dizzying delight at the first stolen breath when at last it came. The *ecstasy* of it all, a pleasure unveiled the likes of which he'd never known—

Honestly, Jonathan, not exactly first-date material. Try not to make him think you're a serial killer.

He nuzzled into the hollow beneath Brandon's collarbone, then glanced behind him with a smile. Eyed the handcuffs he always kept there, dangling discreetly from the bedposts.

But maybe just a little taste . . .

Lacing their fingers together, he slid Brandon's right hand up the pillow, pressing a kiss to his parted lips, darting his tongue inside. Brandon arched up beneath him, fingers tightening around Jonathan's own.

Distraction achieved, Jonathan grabbed the loose end of the handcuff and snapped it over Brandon's wrist.

CHAPTER 3

ran jerked from his lust-induced stupor at the first touch of cold steel on his wrist. "What the *fuck*?" he shouted, shoving at Jonathan with his free hand and giving the cuff a hard tug. It didn't budge. "Get this shit off me right now. I'm not kidding, pal."

"Easy, easy." Hands out and open, Jonathan sat back on his heels. "Look, do you trust me?"

"I don't even *know* you! I never saw you before last night. First you shove your dick down my throat, now you're chaining me to your bed?" He rattled the cuff again, jerked it so hard he hurt himself. Shit, still not budging.

Jonathan swung his legs over the side of the bed and reached into the nightstand, pulling out a little silver key. He laid it on the edge of the table, within easy reach of Bran's free hand. "Go ahead and unlock yourself if you really want to. I won't stop you. But . . ." Jonathan pointed at Bran's crotch, and to Bran's utter chagrin—*What the* fuck*?*— he realized he was still hard. Throbbing, in fact, a bead of pre-cum dribbling down the aching crown of his dick.

Jonathan leaned in to lick it off. Bran gasped, bucked his hips, and Jonathan parted those pretty red lips and swallowed him to the root.

He threw his head back so hard he banged it against the headboard.

Headboard . . . something about a key . . .

Fuck it. Who could think anyway with Jonathan swallowing around his dick like that? Jesus, didn't the guy have a gag reflex?

Jonathan sucked him until black spots danced in front of his eyes. Another second and it would've been all over, but Jonathan pulled off just in time. Bran cursed, reached out for that thick dark hair—

And the handcuff rattled against the bedpost.

Fuck.

Jonathan sat back on Bran's thighs and licked his swollen lips, his grin as smug and filthy as a porn star thrusting out a twelve-inch dick. He scraped one hand up Bran's chest, fingernails first, to tweak a nipple, and said, "Not yet, Brandon. I'm not finished with you yet."

Why the hell did he keep calling him that? "Bran, *not* Brandon. I told you before."

"I refuse to call you something that gives me the runs." A pause, "Even if you *are* kind of—"

"Okay, okay! Don't say it or I'm walking."

Jonathan leaned over him to reach for the nightstand again, and for one hot-cold moment, Bran thought he was calling his bluff, grabbing the handcuff key and sending him on his way. But instead he opened the drawer, pulled out a condom and a squeeze-bottle of lube.

"*Fuck* yeah," Bran said, eyes darting from the lube to the curve of Jonathan's thighs. "Ride me."

The look Jonathan threw him at that could best be described as *Disapproving Schoolteacher.* Didn't even bother to correct him. Just: "Spread those lovely legs of yours, if you'd be so kind."

Suddenly that hot-cold feeling went completely cold. "Uh, wait a minute. I haven't bottomed in, like, *years.*"

Jonathan flipped open the lube and squeezed some onto his fingers. "Don't worry, I'll be gentle."

"Yeah, right." Bran rattled the handcuff. "This looks real gentle to me."

Jonathan nodded toward the nightstand. "There's the key."

Yup, there it was. But no way was he going home tonight without getting off first. This smug little fucker owed him that much.

Which must have been permission enough for Jonathan, because he elbowed Bran's knees apart and thrust what felt like his entire fucking *hand* up his ass.

"*Ow!*" Bran jerked back, cracked his head against the headboard again. Jonathan's fingers followed, still lodged firmly inside even as he closed his legs, kicked at him. Jonathan captured his ankles one-handed and pinned him with his body.

Bran struggled until he wore himself out. Couldn't free his legs, couldn't even dislodge Jonathan's fingers from his ass. Demanded instead, "What happened to being gentle?"

"Sorry," Jonathan said, batting completely un-sorry eyelashes at him over his stupid fucking un-sorry Bambi-eyes. Then he pulled out a fraction, crooked his un-sorry little fingers, and *pressed.*

Bran suddenly forgot what he was so upset about.

Holy fuck I'm gonna come, he's not even fucking touching my dick and I'm—

The fingers disappeared, and from a thousand miles away, a smug little "Ah ah ah" floated round his head. "I *said* I wasn't finished with you yet."

"Finish, then," he growled. "For fuck's sake, *please*."

"Ah, there's the magic word." Jonathan hoisted up Bran's knees, settled his hips between them, and plunged inside.

Bran clenched his jaw on his shout—*I won't give the smug fucker that.* But Jesus, it hurt—for about thirty seconds, and then the sharp stab of entry faded to a slow burn. He gritted his teeth until the sensation eased into an ache that actually felt good. Too good. Every thrust teased his prostate, made his own neglected cock bounce against his belly.

"Jesus, *touch* me."

"You've got a free hand," Jonathan huffed, not even breaking rhythm, "Go ahead and use it."

He would have, but it was wrapped around the other bedpost, right beneath the dangling handcuff. How the hell had that happened?

Before he could think too hard about that, Jonathan's fingers wrapped around his dick and drove all the thoughts right out of his head. One stroke, two—

And he came so hard he splattered his own chin.

Jonathan never broke stride, pounding into Bran's ass and carrying him through the orgasm, on and on and fucking *on,* milking him so hard he couldn't breathe, milking him *raw,* and "Okay, enough," he panted. Peeled his fingers from the bedpost, shoved at Jonathan's shoulder. But his muscles had gone all limp and liquid, and yeah, it hurt, but no more than the fingers had, and fuck if it wasn't kind of . . . well, not *all* bad, anyway, and the sight of Jonathan's eyes fierce and boring into him as intently as his dick, lips pulled back with the force of his pleasure, was crazy fucking hot—

Jonathan stilled, hands tightening painfully on Bran's thighs—and what was *with* this guy and hurting him, anyway?—then pushed in deep and let go with a strangled gasp.

His dick slid from Bran's abused ass, and he collapsed on top of him, slick skin to slick skin, panting into Bran's chest. Bran wasn't much of a cuddler, but he had to admit he liked the feel of Jonathan atop him, the heat and solidity of him, the gentleness of his kisses a shocking contrast to what had come before.

When their breathing settled, Jonathan rolled off, sat up, and grabbed the handcuff key.

Shit, he'd forgotten all about that. Odd, since now that he thought about it, his wrist was stupidly sore and his hand was tingling, half numb.

Jonathan peppered it with kisses as he freed it. "So lovely," he said, drawing Bran's wrist down to where Bran could see it, running a single fingertip over the redness there.

"Uh." Bran pulled his hand away, used it to push his hair off his face. "Yeah. Sure. But look, next time? Maybe we skip the cuffs, okay?"

Jonathan fixed him with a steady gaze. "Look me in the eye and tell me that wasn't the best orgasm of your life."

He opened his mouth to say exactly that, but then closed it. He was too fucked out to lie.

CHAPTER 4

"That's what I thought," Jonathan said into Brandon's reluctant silence, but the truth was, he hadn't been so sure a moment ago. Had he gone too far? Brandon had certainly seemed to enjoy himself, but was he starting to regret it now?

Brandon swung his legs over the side of the bed and said, "Where the fuck did you throw my pants?"

Jonathan hesitated a moment before sliding his hand onto Brandon's shoulder, then up to his neck. He resisted the temptation to grab his hair again and simply let it rest there, fingers skimming over Brandon's still-throbbing pulse. "Stay," he murmured.

At first Brandon stiffened, head turning, eyes averted. "I, uh . . ." He cleared his throat, stood, took a step away, toward where his pants lay crumpled on the bedroom floor. "I should go home, shower."

Jonathan stood, reached out, touched Brandon's forearm with his fingertips. "Please. Stay."

Brandon looked up sharply, as if he couldn't parse Jonathan's gentleness now, or maybe just because Jonathan had said "please." He'd not intended to throw Brandon quite so off guard with his request, but he might as well make the best of it. "Come on," he said, stepping close, sliding his arm through Brandon's, pressing shoulder to shoulder and hip to hip. He led Brandon back to the bed, guided him down onto his back. Brandon followed mutely, strangely stunned. Had he never stuck around after sex before?

How terribly sad.

"Here." Jonathan pulled the comforter up to Brandon's waist. "Stay here, I'll be right back."

He padded into the bathroom to wet down a washcloth, then brought it back to bed. Brandon had curled onto his side, breathing slow and calm, watching Jonathan through heavy lids. At least he seemed a bit more relaxed now.

Taking care not to jolt him, he put a gentle hand on Brandon's arm and rolled him onto his back. "Nice and warm, I promise," he murmured, wiping a streak of cum off Brandon's chest with the washcloth.

Brandon huffed softly, already half asleep. "What happened to your evil twin?" he mumbled.

Jonathan laughed. "I drowned him in the tub."

A mischievous little smile curled up Brandon's lips. "Too bad. He was great in bed." Jonathan smiled back, absurdly pleased, and nudged Brandon to roll over. The washcloth was cooling, but Brandon might appreciate that now; he wiped it gently between Brandon's cheeks to wash away the lube, and Brandon hissed. "On second thought, maybe I won't miss him after all."

Liar.

Jonathan gave him a playful slap and finished cleaning them both off, then tossed the washcloth in the hamper and came back to bed. Brandon's breathing had slowed again, so Jonathan merely tugged the covers up over both of them and switched off the light.

Impossible, though, to ignore that lovely body, even in the dark, and besides, he was feeling rather oddly fond right now. Rolling over, he slid an arm around Brandon's waist, but Brandon jerked away, ended up curled with his back to Jonathan on the far, far edge of the bed.

"I'm sorry, I didn't mean to startle you," Jonathan said, but Brandon was breathing deep and even again, asleep or maybe just pretending to be. Jonathan wasn't sure which he'd have preferred.

Either way, message received, loud and clear.

Bran awoke to find himself alone in a soft warm bed the size of Chinatown. Early-morning sunlight streamed in through far too many windows, sounds of traffic so muffled and distant he wasn't even sure he was in the city anymore.

What the hell . . .?

He sat up, realized he was naked. And holy fuck did his head hurt. Not to mention his ass.

Jonathan.

Where was the little fucker anyway?

And where the hell were his clothes?

Something black and shiny lay across the foot of the bed. A robe. Since he had nothing else to wear, he slid it on, warm silk gliding over his skin. He found the bathroom, gulped water straight from the faucet, then took a piss. Shower next, using Jonathan's ridiculous boutique soap and shampoo. He put the robe back on once he'd toweled dry.

So what now?

"Jonathan?" he called. Had the guy left him alone in his bazillion-dollar home? Seemed unlikely. Wishing he'd paid more attention on the way in, he stepped out into the hall, called Jonathan's name again.

No answer. Maybe he was in the kitchen, wherever that was. Stomach rumbling, Bran wandered through the living room, taking stock of the vaulted ceiling and minimalist furniture, all clean lines, dark wood and natural fibers. It was a huge room, cavernous, even—a thousand square feet at least, with a spiral staircase at the far end leading down to another floor. Skylights directly above let in the sun, scattered rays poking through the thick March cloud cover.

Through the built-in saltwater aquarium taking up almost the entire left wall, he could just discern the rippling outline of an office. He peered through the tank, half to see if Jonathan was in the other room, half because the coral reef inside was so damn pretty. At last he tore his gaze away and cast it to the floor-to-ceiling windows overlooking a spectacular view of the city stretching out beyond the Golden Gate.

Jesus, a place like this must've cost ten million, easy.

As he wandered back toward the hall, a silver-framed photograph on the coffee table caught his eye. A smiling couple standing in front of a boat with a little boy between them. Obviously Jonathan—same toothy grin and thick mane of hair. Couldn't have been more than twelve. Same age as Bran when . . . well, no point dwelling on that.

He turned away from the photo. Spotted a balcony at the opposite side of the room, its sliding glass door separating him from a familiar figure sitting at the table outside.

Bran's bare toes sank into the decadently plush carpet as he ambled over and rapped softly on the glass.

Jonathan smiled, put down his newspaper and beckoned him outside. No robe for him: he was dressed in clean, pressed jeans and a blue sweater that looked like it'd been knitted by hand. Made his eyes sparkle like the water in the aquarium. "Good morning," he said.

"Morning." Bran hesitated before stepping out and sliding the door shut behind him. The whole balcony was enclosed like a greenhouse, and just as warm and sticky with the morning drizzle fogging up the glass. Potted orchids, birds of paradise, and small orange and date trees clued him in on the reason for it.

An awkward silence, then Jonathan cleared his throat. "Sit. Have some coffee."

Bran sucked in a breath, slid his hands down the robe. Why the hell didn't this thing have pockets? When Jonathan nudged out the other chair with his toe, Bran sat down. Well, why not? The coffee smelled damn good, and he needed something to hold his headache at bay.

He reached for the stainless steel carafe and poured himself a mugful, eyes drifting shut at the first sip. Some freshly-ground dark roast, he thought, though it'd been so long since he'd let himself indulge, he couldn't be certain. A hell of a lot better than the horse piss they served in the trailers at every fucking construction site ever.

"Good, isn't it?" That smug smirk curled the corners of Jonathan's lips. "Are you hungry? I can have my cook fix you anything you like."

Bran's stomach rumbled, but he shook his head. He'd already stayed longer than he'd intended. He still couldn't figure out why Jonathan had asked—hell, practically insisted—he stay over. No one had ever wanted him to stick around once they'd gotten what they wanted.

"That's okay," he said. "I'd rather just get dressed and get going."

"Yes, well, I sent your suit out to be pressed." Jonathan's grin widened. "We got it a bit wrinkled last night."

As if he needed to be reminded. He fingered the mark on his wrist before lifting his mug for another sip. There was a bowl of fresh fruit within easy reach, along with a plate of buttered whole grain toast. Might as well have a bite. He obviously wasn't going anywhere for a while.

Like a fucking mind reader, Jonathan reached for a smaller bowl, scooped some fruit into it, and placed it in front of him. This time he didn't hesitate; he grabbed a fork and popped the first bite into his mouth. Amazing. Kiwi, honeydew, pineapple, blackberries, seedless grapes. Everything he loved as a kid, but couldn't afford now.

"I grow these myself," Jonathan said, waving a bite of kiwi on his own fork. "Good, huh?"

"Hmm," Bran conceded around another mouthful of fruit. Okay, so Jonathan was a weirdo in more ways than one, but Bran might as well enjoy it while he could.

He shoveled more fruit into his mouth.

"So," Jonathan said. He sipped at a steaming mug, eyeing Bran over the rim. By the little smile on his face, he seemed to like what he was seeing, even if Bran hadn't shaved today. Bran scratched at a stubbled cheek, suddenly self-conscious. "How'd you sleep?"

Bran sighed. *This* was why he never stuck around after sex.

Not that anyone's ever asked you anyway.

"Okay, I guess."

A moment's silence. Another. Jonathan looked on like he disapproved of Bran not holding up his end of the conversation. "Not very talkative in the morning, are you?"

"What's there to talk about? Unless"—he hooked his thumb over his shoulder, pointing back toward the bedroom—"you want to have another go?"

Jonathan laughed, shook his head. "It's nice having a conversation every now and then. In fact . . ." He wiped his hands on the napkin in his lap. "I wouldn't mind having dinner with you again. How's tomorrow?"

"Tomorrow's Monday. Some of us have to *work*."

Jonathan pursed his lips. "I didn't inherit all this, you know. But if a work night isn't good for you, how about this Friday?"

Persistent little bugger, wasn't he? But what the hell . . . the sex was good, and so was the food, and he supposed the company wasn't *too* unbearable. "I'll have to check my schedule," he said. "Sometimes jobs run long."

"All right." If Bran had disappointed Jonathan, he didn't show it. He sipped his drink again, buttered a piece of toast. Cut the crust off before he ate it.

God, what a waste. Bran sighed and plucked the crust off Jonathan's plate. "This is the best part."

"See?" Jonathan said, grinning wide. "We're a perfect fit."

Bran grimaced and put the crust back on Jonathan's plate, irritation rising at Jonathan's frown. What the hell did he expect? They'd only slept together twice—or technically, once—for fuck's sake. Not exactly cause for picking out china.

He went back to his fruit. Jonathan went back to the paper. A few minutes passed in silence that looked much more comfortable to Jonathan than it felt to Bran. He picked up his mug, drained his coffee. Flicked the handle with his thumb. Jonathan looked up at him over the paper and arched one eyebrow—*everything okay?*

"I just . . . I don't get it," Bran said, then wished he hadn't.

Jonathan put the paper down. "Don't get what?"

"You. This." He waved around at the greenhouse, the half-eaten breakfast, the silk robe. "All of it. I mean, look at you. Why—?"

Jonathan just smiled. "Why not? You're an interesting man. I'd like to get to know you better."

"You've already gotten to know me about as well as a guy can."

"On one level, yes. But I've a feeling there's a lot more to you than a tight ass and a pretty face."

Bran felt his cheeks heat, but he put on his best scowl and said, "Gee, thanks a lot."

Jonathan flashed him that smug smile again. "You're blushing."

Fuck you, asshole.

"You're very cute when you blush."

With an ice pick.

And damn Jonathan for being so adorable when he smirked. Even worse, he clearly knew it.

"There's more to me than my money, you know. Come, Brandon. One more dinner. I'll even cook."

"*You* can cook?"

"Like I said, I didn't inherit all this. And I much prefer a home-cooked meal to opening a can."

"I'll think about it," Bran said. He picked up his napkin and wiped his mouth, just to have something to do with his hands. Plus, it felt surprisingly good to toss it back to the table. "Listen, I should go. Got anything to wear that won't be six inches too short?"

Jonathan narrowed his eyes—*Ha, hit a nerve, fucker!*—then recovered his composure and shook his head. "I'm afraid not."

Bran didn't doubt it. Everything the guy owned was probably tailored. Even his damn socks.

"But your suit ought to be ready by now. I instructed my maid to leave it in the bedroom. Shall I check?"

Bran shook his head and stood. "Nah, I got it." Bad enough the guy had bought the suit; he didn't need to fetch it for him too. "So, I'll uh . . ." He hesitated, stuck his hand out for Jonathan to shake. Jonathan stood with another raised eyebrow and shook back with both hands—and yeah, okay, maybe shaking hands *was* ridiculous after the sex they'd had.

"My driver will take you home," Jonathan said, still clasping Bran's hand in both his own.

"That's not—"

"I insist." Added, softer, "Please."

"Fine," Bran grumbled. It's not like Jonathan didn't know where he lived already anyway.

Bran showed up at work early on Monday morning. Why not? He hadn't exactly gotten a good night's sleep with his last conversation with Jonathan still rattling around in his brain. So he stood around in the early-morning cold, drinking coffee and checking scaffolding until his crew showed up.

"Looking kinda ragged, buddy," Mike said the second he climbed out of his van. "Wild weekend?" Bastard was smirking, just like Jonathan. He clapped Bran on the shoulder. "She have a sister?"

Bran flipped him the bird. "Won't your blow-up doll get jealous? Get to work, asshole."

"Yes sir, Mr. Foreman, sir." Mike tipped his ball cap with another fucking smirk and poured himself a cup of coffee.

The rest of the crew filtered in, and soon Bran found himself up the frame of the ridiculous mansion they were building for some Chinese broker, nailing down roof joists with a pneumatic gun. Not his usual work, but he liked it just fine, and they were down a man today. He laughed at an image of Jonathan trying to fill in. He'd probably nail his hand to the wall. Or fall off the scaffold.

And so will you if you don't stop thinking about him and focus.

Lunchtime finally rolled around, and Bran and his crew sat out front, eating their sandwiches and drinking cheap coffee. Nothing like the stuff he'd been drinking yesterday. He'd forgotten coffee—hell, food of any kind—could taste so good.

They were all about to get back to work when a white van pulled up, and out climbed a guy in delivery coveralls. What the hell? This was a closed construction site and he hadn't ordered any supplies in today.

The guy circled around to the back of the van, then reappeared with a small potted plant. An orchid. Just like the ones on Jonathan's balcony.

He didn't. Tell me he didn't.

The delivery guy headed straight for them and said, "Brandon McKinney?"

Shit. He did.

For a second, Bran was tempted to tell the guy he had the wrong address, but then Mike piped up with a very amused, "Right here!" Added, quieter, to Bran, "Ain't that backwards, buddy? Aren't *you* supposed to send the flowers?"

Oh, you are so fired, you jerk.

The delivery guy walked up to Bran and handed him the pot. "Here you go, sir." And just like Saturday's courier, he walked away before Bran could tip him.

There was a card, of course. *"Friday at eight? I'll send the car. —J."*

Mike snatched the card from his fingers with an exaggerated, "Oooooooh. Who's J, Bran? She hot? Oooh, 'send the car'? She *rich*?"

Bran reached to snatch it back, but Mike danced out of the way. He'd never shut up if Bran didn't shut him up, so he flashed a smile at Mike—all teeth, no friendliness—and said, "Yes, he is."

For a second Mike just blinked at him, and he regretted having said anything—they might actually *believe* him, and he needed these guys to respect him. But then Mike just laughed and shook his head and said, "You handsome fucking shark, you're dating a Playboy bunny, aren't you," and handed back the card with another friendly pat on the shoulder.

Still, Bran had a feeling he was *never* going to live this down.

CHAPTER 5

Brandon looked amazing. A few days' worth of ginger stubble, neatly trimmed. Dark jeans that showed every plane and curve of those gorgeous legs. Sport coat over a bright green dress shirt that made his eyes pop like spring grass. The top two buttons were undone, revealing a tantalizing hint of throat and collarbone.

Brandon crossed his arms and grinned like a piranha. "You're staring."

Jonathan cleared his throat. "Yes, well, I can hardly be blamed. Please, come in."

He put an arm around Brandon's waist and ushered him inside. Gesturing toward the couch, he said, "Have a seat. Would you like something to drink?"

Brandon's smile softened. "Is your scotch as good as your coffee?"

"Even better."

"I'll have a double."

He poured doubles for them both while Brandon took off his jacket and settled on the couch, then handed Brandon his drink and sat down across from him. For all of Brandon's apparent nonchalance, he really had made an effort tonight.

Maybe he really does *like me.*

"So . . . how was your week?"

"Fine, until your damn flower came," he groused, but without any real rancor. "The guys are still ribbing me about it."

"Yet here you are."

"Well, it was a very *pretty* flower."

They finished their drinks and drifted into the dining room. Brandon stilled, his gaze captured by the view of the Golden Gate Bridge through the floor-to-ceiling windows, lights shimmering in the evening fog. Jonathan couldn't resist stepping up beside him and laying a hand on the back of his neck, fingering the soft hair there. "Beautiful, isn't it?"

Brandon nodded and leaned ever so slightly into Jonathan's side.

They stood there in silence a few moments longer, and then Brandon turned, leaned in, brought his own hand to Jonathan's cheek—

Jonathan clasped gentle fingers around Brandon's wrist and took one step back. If he let the man kiss him now, they'd never get around to dinner. But he brought Brandon's hand to his lips, pressed them there, long and soft. "Later," he promised. "I spent hours on dinner. Please, come enjoy it."

Brandon nodded, smiling gently—no sign of those teeth—and let Jonathan lead him to the dining room table.

His eyebrows rose at the sight of the table: white linen cloth, real silverware, beeswax candles, and two courses laid out in polished wooden dishes.

"Please, sit," Jonathan said, then draped a napkin over Brandon's lap and served him a bowl of salad.

Brandon rolled his sleeves halfway up his forearms, and it was all Jonathan could do not to stare at the casual reveal of lean muscle and tendons and veins, the light scatter of pale ginger hair on tanned, freckled skin. "Um." He gestured with the salad tongs. "Mixed baby greens; I grow them on the balcony. And I made the dressing myself."

"Of course you did." Now the teeth were back. "Did you butcher your own tofu, too?"

Jonathan laughed. "Actually now that you mention it, I did grow the mushrooms"—he pointed to the portabellas on the chafing dish—"and stuff them myself, but I'm afraid the tofu's from Whole Foods."

"Cheater," Brandon said around a mouthful of salad. Then, "Mmm, this is really good."

"Thank you." Jonathan served himself and sat down. "So . . . any luck with your loan application?"

Brandon froze mid-chew, eyes narrowed. "Why do you care?"

Jonathan put his hands up. "Just making conversation. In a roundabout way, it is how we met, after all. I'd love to hear more about it. It's a construction business you'd like to buy?"

"Yeah." Brandon poked at his salad, ate a cherry tomato. "Sort of an architectural firm, project management firm, and construction business all rolled into one, actually. My boss does custom designs for people like you. I help figure out what we need and how to make it happen, then supervise the day crew on-site when we go out and build it."

"You have an architecture degree?"

Brandon's eyes narrowed once more. "Did your investigators fall down again?"

"Doesn't mean I wouldn't like to hear it from you."

"I've taken some classes, got my associate's at City College. Wanted to keep going, transfer over to UC Berkeley, but I haven't managed to scrape the money together yet." He shrugged. "Even if I did, it's tough to make the time. I'm salaried, no overtime, so the boss pushes me pretty hard; most weeks I put in sixty hours. Don't always get evenings or weekends off."

"Well, good to hear the business is doing well, even in this economy. Sounds like a wise investment."

Another shrug. "I've crunched the numbers. Honestly, the margins are pretty slim, but it's been good before and it'll be good again. Thing is, my boss is a nice guy, but half his profitability comes out of our pockets. All those long hours, and the work doesn't pay for shit. It doesn't even have to, because where are we gonna go? It's not like there are construction jobs out the wazoo right now."

"You think you can run the business better than he can?"

Brandon looked right at him. "Yes. I know I can. I'm halfway doing it already."

Nothing sexier than confidence. And well-muscled forearms. Jonathan's gaze lingered on the latter while he pondered the former.

"So," Brandon said, scraping up the last of his salad, "How about you? How'd you get into computers?"

"I had a bit of an unconventional upbringing, you might say. Home schooled." He chuckled. "Even spent three years on a commune, believe it or not, and then nearly as many on a research vessel with my parents—they were marine biologists, you see. Anyway, everywhere we went, I saw problems I thought could be fixed if only there was an opportunity for education, for bringing the knowledge of the world into all those pockets of poverty. I knew by the time I was twelve that I wanted to bring a computer to every classroom in the world. I went off to college at fourteen, and four years later, I'd built a $100 computer for my master's thesis. The idea kind of took off from there. So many of the software and hardware principles were applicable to mainstream consumer culture, so I got my MBA on my way to my PhD, and—" He looked up, realized Brandon was staring at him, empty fork held aloft. "Look at me, I'm rambling. And I've neglected to serve the main course."

He stood to do exactly that, scooping stuffed mushrooms onto polished wood plates and putting one before each of them.

"Wow," Brandon said, but whether to the food or to Jonathan's life story, Jonathan had no idea.

He waited for Brandon to take a bite of the mushroom. The ecstatic look on his face as he started to chew made all that time in the kitchen completely worthwhile.

Brandon swallowed, forked up another bite and peered at it, then looked at Jonathan, delight giving way to utter incredulity. "There's really no meat in this?"

"Not a morsel."

"Wow," he said again. "Learn how to cook on the commune?"

"And out at sea. Although I haven't eaten fish in years."

"Didn't like chowing down on your friends?"

"We're fishing the oceans to death. I want no part of that."

Well, that answer went over about as well as it usually did. Brandon looked more uncomfortable than normal as he went back to his food. They ate in silence for a bit, but at last the awkwardness faded, and Brandon said, "You know, you and I might have more in common than I realized."

"Oh?" Jonathan asked when Brandon took another bite of stuffed mushroom instead of expanding on his thought.

"Mmhm," he said round a mouthful of food. Swallowed, and added, "One of the things I've been focusing on at work is green development. Not just solar panels and geothermal heat pumps—though," he added, "those too. But building to the climate, you know? Skylights and south-facing windows up north, close-planted shade trees and white pavement down south, xenoscaping in the desert, vertical gardening and low-maintenance grass roofs, mycelium insulation and drywall—"

"Mycelium?" Jonathan asked, almost loath to interrupt Brandon when he was clearly so enthused. "Do you mean mushrooms?"

Brandon forked up more stuffed mushroom with a gleeful grin and nodded. "Not the parts you eat, of course, but the root systems. They can be grown into, essentially, foam blocks that insulate better than fiberglass. Plus they're stronger than concrete, totally fireproof and nontoxic, hundreds of times more mold- and water-resistant than standard insulation and drywall, and can be built on the super-cheap because mushrooms eat the empty husks from rice and cotton seed, which, by the way, you can't even use as feed for farm animals—pure agricultural waste."

"Huh. And this mycelium, can it be grown anywhere?"

"Sure. In fact, there's a company right here in California growing them in old shipping containers. And I can't help but think, you know, how much of a difference building design like that could make in people's lives."

Jonathan nodded; he'd seen firsthand how sometimes the simplest innovations could exponentially raise someone's standard of living.

"Habitat for Humanity builds homes for folks in need, but then they're stuck with electric bills and water bills every month that might mean the difference between, you know, buying their kids clothes that year or not. If they just started applying some of these principles, they could design almost entirely self-sufficient homes—places that could literally function off the grid, cutting energy use by up to 90% and water waste by over 50% and—" Brandon blushed, looked down at his cooling food. "And now *I'm* rambling, aren't I."

Jonathan shook his head. He'd have smiled at Brandon, but he was already grinning like an idiot. "No, it's fascinating. My foundation's been supporting green housing development for years, but I had no idea it was so rife with innovation."

Brandon shrugged, wouldn't meet Jonathan's eyes of a sudden. "Well, that's all for the future anyway, I guess. My boss is perfectly happy to listen to me ramble, but he's not so interested in actually making these things happen. 'Why mess with a good thing,' he says. Guess I can't blame him."

For a moment, Jonathan felt terribly sorry for Brandon—so much passion, so many ideas, and no power at all to make it happen—but he shook it off, knowing how much Brandon would hate his pity. They both went back to eating, but at least the silence didn't feel strained this time.

When Brandon scraped the last bite of stuffed mushroom from his plate, Jonathan said, "Want more?"

Brandon thought about it for a moment, then shook his head.

"Dessert? I made mousse."

Brandon's foot touched Jonathan's under the table. "Not the dessert I had in mind."

Beautiful and *smart* and *passionate? Oh God, give me strength . . .*

"Look, about that." He leaned in, laid his hand over Brandon's where it rested on the table. "You've probably realized by now that I have certain . . . proclivities."

Brandon snorted. "Is that a fancy word for 'likes to handcuff guys to the bedpost and fuck them raw?'"

Jonathan chuckled and nodded. "That, among other things." He paused, gauging Brandon's reaction. No surprise or fear—not yet, at least. "And I think that you too have certain proclivities."

Brandon yanked his hand out from under Jonathan's, threw it up like a traffic cop. "Hey, wait a minute, pal. That kinky shit? Was all you, not me."

"True," Jonathan conceded, "but you enjoyed it. Very much so, in fact; I seem to recall cleaning cum off your chin. And you didn't free yourself when given the chance. You *stayed*." Brandon scowled but said nothing. "There's no shame in it, Brandon. Quite to the contrary; embracing your sexuality—a sexuality as deep and delicious as yours— that's a gift. A treasure. It's one I'd like to help you explore."

Brandon looked a little sullen when he said, "That's what I was suggesting a minute ago."

"Not exactly what I had in mind."

"What, so you invited me over here just to *talk*?"

Jonathan laid his hand atop Brandon's again, quirked a smile. "I realize that might come as something of a shock to you, but yes. It's not that I don't want you"—he eyed Brandon up and down and up again just for good measure—"*believe* me. Rather the opposite, in fact. I want you terribly. And I thought . . ." He paused, bit his lip. This wasn't going to go well—*couldn't* go well, not with a man this proud—and yet he had to try. "I thought perhaps I could help you achieve your business goals while pursuing some mutual pleasures."

Brandon's fingers curled into a fist beneath Jonathan's hand. "You mean 'helping me to explore my *proclivities*?'"

"Yes."

"While *paying me*?"

"I never said—"

"No, but what else could it be? God, you fucker!" Brandon shoved his chair back, jumped to his feet. "Just because you picked me up in a bar doesn't make me a whore."

He grabbed his jacket off the back of his chair, turned and stomped away. "I'll mail the suit back, you slimy son of a bitch."

Jonathan winced; this was even worse than he'd anticipated. Still, Brandon wasn't gone yet. One more chance to turn this around. He jumped to his feet and followed Brandon into the living room. "I don't think you're a whore," he said. "In fact, I admire you a great deal. Look how far you've come under your own steam. Taking nothing from anyone. I'm not asking you to take anything from me, either. I'm asking for six months to devote myself to you—come, move in, let me show you a side of yourself you'd never dared to explore until you came through this door. And because I know that's terrifying—because I know how big a chance it is, how big a risk it feels like, how much it might change your life, I'd offer you the power to change it back when we're done." He waited a moment for that to sink in; for all Brandon's fury, he did at least appear to be listening.

"Change it back how?" Brandon demanded, each word bitten off as if he'd tried to stop it from coming out.

"I liked your idea for shifting your boss's construction business over to green housing. You've certainly got the talent, the drive—the *passion*—to make a go of it. So let me help you. Spend the next six months here with me, and I'll give you the money to buy the business."

Brandon glared, stone-faced. "Three million dollars," he said flatly. "For six months of my life."

A bit blunt, but, "I suppose that's the long and short of it, yes."

"And how is that not prostitution, again?"

"Because I'm not interested in *taking* something from you, Brandon! I'm not interested in a transaction. Look at us! We're already fucking for fun—dare I say even growing to care a little? You like me. I like you. I want to get to know you better. This isn't . . ." He shook his head. Now was *not* the time for words to be failing him, damn it. "Think of it as a gift, then. The money's nothing to me. But *this*"—he pointed back and forth between himself and Brandon—"*this* could be something *spectacular*."

Brandon seemed to think on it for a moment, then nodded once and swung his jacket on. "Fuck you," he said, and pushed the call button on the elevator.

"Brandon, wait—"

"What part of 'fuck you' didn't you understand?"

Jonathan swallowed. "At least let my driver take you home."

"I'll call a cab."

He dug into his pocket, reaching for his wallet. "Well at least let me—"

Brandon's eyes flashed murder. "I don't need your money," he growled, each word its own distinct, poison-filled sentence.

Jonathan pursed his lips, nodded. And then, softly, "Have a good night."

The elevator doors opened, and Brandon stepped inside. He tossed one last look over his shoulder as he left—furious, yes, and fierce with pride. And, Jonathan dared to hope—or maybe he was just imagining it?—just as disappointed as he was.

CHAPTER 6

"I'm sorry, Mr. McKinney, but I'm afraid we can't help you."

Bran curled his fingers into the armrest of a chair that seemed purpose-built to discourage people from getting too comfortable. He'd taken the day off for *this*? The urge to punch the false sympathy off the loan officer's face was nearly overwhelming.

"Are you sure I can't convince you otherwise? The business is profitable even now, the client list impressive; we have projects booked well past the proposed sale date, and—"

The loan officer held a hand up, just like the five before him had when Bran had made the same argument to them. "I really would like to help you, Mr. McKinney, and your credit score *is* solid, but you have no collateral, no down-payment to speak of, and you're asking us to fund a purchase in one of the most unstable industries in the nation right now." He consulted the file on his desk—more a courtesy, Bran suspected, than with any intention of changing his mind. "I see the business has collected down-payments on eleven scheduled projects, but these are luxury homes we're talking about; statistically, six of those eleven projects will be deferred for three to five years or cancelled altogether. What would you do then? How would you make your loan payments in the meantime?"

That was in his five-year plan, too, if only the bastard would *look*. "I'd turn focus from local construction to national and international LEED-certified project design and management. The work's more competitive, of course, but we *do* have a strong reputation in both areas both in and out of San Francisco, and green building is *growing*, not shrinking. In fact, I plan to turn a stronger focus on green design and development regardless."

"With only one architect? Or does your boss plan to stay on and consult?"

"Architects are an easy hire. We've brought in freelancers before—people I've worked with and trust. Besides, I've apprenticed under Mr. Sung for years, and I'll have my degree soon."

The loan officer eyed Bran over the file, then tapped a page with his index finger. "I see it took you five years to earn your associates degree—"

"I could only attend classes on Saturdays—"

"And you're not even *enrolled* in a bachelor's program right now. Even if you do, I'm not convinced your time frame would be any different if you owned the business. Harder, even. You couldn't just stay home because you have to study."

"I *know* that—"

"Look, Mr. McKinney. *If* you fit the criteria for an SBA loan, then I might consider it. But without government backing, I'm afraid this is just too risky for this bank." He closed the file: end of discussion. "Again, Mr. McKinney, I'm very sorry. Maybe in a few years, when construction picks back up . . ."

The business would be sold by then, the opportunity gone, and this guy damn well knew it. Bran stood, jaw clenched. Yet he shook the loan officer's outstretched hand; he wasn't dumb enough to burn bridges he might need one day, no matter how much he wanted to squeeze until he crushed the guy's bones. "I understand," he forced himself to say. "Thank you for your time."

The loan officer nodded. "Good luck."

Yeah, right. Six banks, six no's, three million dollars short . . . He was going to need *way* more than luck to figure this one out.

Bran took the bus home and trudged up to the fifth floor of his building, glaring at peeling linoleum tiles and chipped paint, the elevator that'd been broken since 2003, the grease stains and graffiti on the walls. He stopped short in front of his door when he saw a small potted orchid, purple this time instead of white, with a card attached. He didn't even want to look at it. A sigh, then he scooped it up, pocketed the card, and left the flower in front of Mrs. Chan's door. She'd always been kind to him, and maybe it would brighten her day a little. God knew she could use it, living alone in *this* dump.

The dump where he'd been for fourteen years. Jesus, was this his life? He unlocked his apartment door, kicked off his one pair of dress shoes and stood in the entranceway, unsure of what to do next. Was this the best he'd ever be able to do? Threadbare carpet, a jammed window he couldn't get his landlord to fix, milk crates for bookshelves, and an old folding table for a desk? God, even his computer was probably an antique by now. It'd all seemed nice enough when he'd first rented the couch here after half a year on the streets, but his roommates had all moved up and out. Why hadn't he?

His stomach rumbled. He'd skipped lunch bouncing from bank to bank, which in retrospect seemed pretty stupid. His fridge was as sad as the rest of the place, but the milk was still good, and he didn't feel like cooking anyway, so he grabbed a box of Oat-O's and a bowl and ate standing at the counter. Too tired to bring over the desk chair.

Over the rim of his bowl, that damn gorgeous white orchid stared at him. Why the hell hadn't he thrown the damn thing away? He put his back to it; it was like watching Jonathan smirk at him all over again.

Jonathan. Rich stupid fucking rich asshole. Must be nice to have that kind of money.

Would it really be so bad?

Yes. Fuck yes.

But he *was* a good lay. And the food was great.

And you don't need him.

Bran froze mid-chew and threw his bowl in the sink, cereal half-finished. *Yes, you do. If you want to buy this business? You do.*

God, he couldn't believe he was actually considering this.

Suck it up, crybaby.

He'd sacrificed worse for his future, after all. And how bad could it be, anyway? Certainly not as bad as *this*.

Well, if he really was going to consider this, he'd better do his homework.

He fired up his computer, waited for his ancient modem to dial up, and then went straight to Google. Over seventeen million hits. This was gonna take a while.

He scrolled past the first two pages of results—all details about SuperComputing (which had moved from $100 desktops to $100 laptops in the last few years) and the Watkins Charitable Foundation—but did stop to read his Wikipedia page. *Probably edited to high hell by his own staff.* Still, he was able to learn a few things. Like that Jonathan had been *married*. To a *girl*, no less. Divorced five years back. Bran followed a few reference links. From the looks of it, she took half his fortune with her when she left. And cited "some freaky shit" in the bedroom as a reason for leaving, according to GoGossip. Bran smiled to himself; *a trusted source if you've ever seen one, eh?*

Twenty-four pages of results later, he found out Jonathan's real name was—*Are you* serious?—Ocean Windsong Watkins. When he managed to stop laughing five or ten minutes later, he read on about

Jonathan's hippie parents—mom British, which probably explained that crisp proper diction of his—taking him from the commune at age nine to spend nearly three years at sea doing research on sharks. Two years after that—time spent, as best Bran could tell, being home-schooled in Monterey—Jonathan was off to college with a shiny new name, and who the hell could blame him?

Bran sat back, rubbed his eyes, realized the apartment had gone dark and he was starving. Shit, when did it get to be almost ten o'clock? He had to be up for work in seven hours. He looked back at the screen: page 132 of Google results. Probably safe to call it quits at this point. At least now he was reasonably sure Jonathan wasn't an ax murderer. And, though he hated to admit it, the guy *did* sound pretty astonishing. Six months might go by fast with him.

Who knew? Might even be fun.

CHAPTER 7

J onathan's buzzer rang around seven, and Bill, the evening security guard, rasped over the line, "There's a Mr. McKinney here to see you, Mr. Watkins. Says he has an appointment."

Cheeky bugger. Still, quite the relief to know Brandon's anger had finally cooled.

"Send him up." Then, with a smile, he stood and waited by the elevator, hands in his pockets. His grin widened as the doors opened, and out strode Brandon like he owned the place.

Jonathan didn't even get the chance to say hello before Brandon blurted, "So what exactly does this offer of yours entail?"

A moment's hesitation. How best to present this without sending him running again? Then again, perhaps it was better to put everything on the table from the outset, give him the tools to make an informed decision.

"I'd like to show you something," he began, "but it might be a bit . . . overwhelming." Brandon went stiff and narrow-eyed when Jonathan touched his shoulder, so he pulled his hand back. "Yes, well, I'd just, I'd ask you to promise me you won't bolt. Just . . . stay and hear me out. Consider it for a moment, even if you think it's crazy."

Of course that earned him a suspicious glare, but he could live with that if it got him what he wanted. Brandon scowled and scratched at a stubbled cheek with his knuckle, but nodded. "Okay. I promise, I won't bolt." Left clearly unspoken: *Weirdo.*

Jonathan led him to the spiral staircase. They walked down a flight, past the kitchen to the suite of rooms at the end of the hall. Brandon shuffled from foot to foot as Jonathan pulled a key from his pocket and unlocked the door.

"So, is this where you bury the bodies?" Brandon asked with a nervous chuckle.

"In a manner of speaking," Jonathan said, winking at Brandon before swinging the door open. Then he rested a hand on the nape of Brandon's neck and watched his face very, very carefully as he flipped on the light.

As he'd expected, Brandon tensed, froze, and took a step back. He might have taken more, but Jonathan tightened his fingers, ever so slightly, and said, "Remember your promise." He tried to imagine how it must look to Brandon—the black walls hung with crops and paddles, whips and cuffs; the man-sized cages, one dangling by a chain from the ceiling like an empty sarcophagus; the St. Andrew's cross and the spanking bench; the padded restraint tables and the rope spiderweb; a hundred things a man like Brandon probably wouldn't even begin to understand. And those three mysterious doors along the back wall, also painted black. To Jonathan, it was a playground of untold delights. To Brandon, it must look like a torture chamber.

Brandon stood frozen, mouth open, eyes wide. Jonathan turned him physically, by the shoulders, until their eyes met. "Would you believe me if I said this was all in the pursuit of pleasure?"

Brandon knocked Jonathan's hands from his shoulders with rather more force than was necessary and took two huge steps back. "You're sick," he said flatly. "Handcuffs in bed are one thing, but this . . . This is *not* my scene."

"I know it isn't *now*, but I've seen the potential in you. If you could just trust me a little, let me help you awaken to everything you could be, all that magnificent promise." But Brandon was shaking his head, over and over. Best to switch tacks. "You've been taking care of yourself since you were fifteen; rediscover the beauty of *being* cared for again, of *trusting* again. It's all right to let go, Brandon. It's all right to *want*. You don't have to be on guard all the time."

Whether he was getting through or not, he couldn't say, but at least Brandon had stopped backing away from him, seemed to be listening at least a little—gotten over his initial fear, perhaps, that Jonathan would lock him down here against his will. "Aren't you tired, Brandon? Don't you ever wish it could all just . . . *stop* for a little while? You could have that here. I could do that for you; I *want* to do that for you. And I would never, ever harm you, I swear it."

Brandon snorted. "So those whips are just for show, then, is that it?"

"Here," Jonathan said, walking over to his collection of impact toys and pulling a lightweight suede flogger off the wall. "Feel this."

Brandon flinched back when Jonathan held it out, but quickly recovered, reaching for it reluctantly. He ran the falls through his fingers once, twice, a third time. Seemed a little surprised by it.

"Nice, isn't it? You'd be surprised how much pleasure I could wring from you with this. A natural high. Like flying."

"You're full of shit," Brandon said, even as he twined the falls through his fingers once more. Any second now, he'd probably jerk it over his shoulder, try to strike himself. Jonathan would've bet half his fortune on that.

And there Brandon went, right on cue—a halfhearted swing, the falls slapping lightly against the back of his shirt. He probably barely even felt it.

"It feels even better on bare skin," Jonathan said. He took the flogger from Brandon's unresisting fingers, held Brandon's arm by the wrist and draped the falls across his forearm. For a single fraction of a second, Brandon's eyes closed. "See?"

But then Brandon jerked his hand back and folded his arms across his chest. "You're insane," he said—though with considerably less heat than before.

Jonathan shook his head. "No. I promise you." But that didn't help, of course it didn't; Brandon had no reason to trust him at all. "Look . . ." He took a step forward, another, closing the distance between them. Brandon let him. Let him grasp his shoulders in both hands, despite the flogger still occupying one of them. "I know what your father did to you. I know what you must think when you look at all these toys—"

Brandon knocked Jonathan's hands from his shoulders, curled his fingers into fists. "What the fuck do you know about my father?"

Jonathan had suspected that would strike a nerve, but not with quite so much force—not after all this time. He tried on a smile and said, "My investigators didn't fall down on *everything*, you know. Police reports and hospital records don't just go away."

"Who do you think you are! What gives you the fucking right to go snooping around in people's pasts?" He thrust one hand, fingers still tightly clenched, just inches from Jonathan's face. "I'm not a kid anymore. That shit's behind me."

"I know that." A hand on Brandon's shoulder again, miraculously allowed. He was so tense he was trembling. "And part of this is about reclaiming what you lost then. This is *for you*, Brandon. For both of us. You'd be amazed at how much pleasure you'd find in these walls, how much of yourself could unfold before you. That's my only goal here. I said I would never harm you and I mean it."

"Yeah," Brandon said, knocking Jonathan's hand away again. "My dad used to say that too. But at least he didn't fool himself into thinking I'd *like* it."

Jonathan couldn't help feeling a bit disappointed, but still, this was further than he'd ever hoped to get after Brandon had stormed out the other day. In fact, he was amazed Brandon was still here. Clearly the man was intrigued by all this. Maybe the submissive inside him really was stronger than his shame, his fear.

Maybe it was time to leave him alone and let him hash it out for himself.

"Why don't I let you have some time to yourself," he said. "Take as much as you want. Touch anything you'd like. Nothing's off limits."

Brandon nodded warily, and Jonathan handed him the flogger. "When you're ready, I'll be waiting for you upstairs. If you'd rather leave, I'll have my driver take you home."

Still here, still staring at the flogger, its soft falls tumbling through his fingers once more, a strange, hypnotic look in his eyes. Not moving, not demanding to leave. Instead, he brought the flogger up to his face and sniffed, eyes closing, cautious pleasure leaking through his guard. Maybe there was still cause for hope, after all.

Jonathan left the door open when he walked away, and for a long moment, all Bran could think was *Thank God he didn't lock me in here.* Not that he'd *really* believed that would happen, but some small part of him couldn't quite let it go. Not after all he knew people were capable of. Not after all he'd just seen.

And just what *had* he seen, anyway? He realized he was still holding that stupid whip and put it down on the nearest horizontal surface—alongside what looked like a little power unit and a whole array of matching steel . . . *whatevers*, though from the shape of them he had a pretty good idea of where they might get shoved. Even the small ones looked intimidating; the large ones looked like they'd rip him in two. People didn't actually *use* those, did they?

Against his will, his fingers closed around one, hefted it up. Cold. Heavy. Smooth. *Strangely compelling?*

No. No.

He put it down, wandered over to the wall of whips and crops and God knew what else—hundreds, it looked like, all different shapes and sizes and materials and what the *fuck* was he still *doing* here?

He fingered a row of whips. Some velvety soft, like the one Jonathan had handed him. One even seemed to be made entirely of rabbit fur, another of feathers, a third one strips of silk. He spotted a leather one with braided tails and heavy knots at the bottoms. Picked it up. No soft suede here. Hadn't old British naval ships used these to punish mutinous sailors? Seemed like the sort of thing you could cut someone with.

So why was he pushing his sleeve up, thwapping himself on the arm with it? It didn't hurt, not really. The little red marks it made faded almost instantly. He hit himself again, harder this time, and *ow*, that *stung*. He hung the whip back up, rubbed at his arm. The marks weren't fading so fast anymore. Felt kinda warm now, though. Nice, almost.

No, it's not nice at all. *You just want it to be because you need the money.*

Near the end of the wall of whips hung a series of leather straps, one exactly like a belt without a buckle. Bran shuddered and turned his back to it. No way in hell he'd ever let *anyone* do that to him again.

Some strange furniture across the room. Bran left the various implements of torture to go check it out. Some of it was obvious: cages; a big X with straps for ankles, wrists, waist. Beside the X—which, it turned out, spun around like a wheel when he gave it a little nudge—sat a padded leather bench-like contraption with leather straps. He sat on it, gave a little bounce. But surely that wasn't how it was meant to be used. He stood up, took a step back, studied it with a builder's eye. *Ah, like so.* Kind of like a kneeling bench at church, except . . . He put his knees on the pad, slotted his ankles into the straps but didn't fasten them closed. Leaned long-ways over the bench. It held his weight, surprisingly comfortable. He realized there was a strap for his neck when he planted his elbows on the pads near the ground. Handles for him to grab, too. Some morbid curiosity propelled him to buckle the left cuff around his wrist. He pulled it tight, leather soft and snug and very, very secure, and holy shit was he actually getting *hard* from this?

No. *Fuck* no. Must've just reminded him of sex last week with Jonathan. Which, he had to admit, had been pretty fucking amazing, even if the guy had handcuffed him to the bed.

If, or because?

"Shut up, Bran. Just . . . shut up." He unbuckled his wrist from the cuff, stood up. Fuck, he really was hard. He turned his eyes back to the belt-like leather straps hanging on the far wall, stared at them until his erection faded.

"Three million dollars," he mumbled, then shook his head. "Three *million* dollars." For six months of his life. Down here. In *this.*

"Can't be *that* bad, can it?" He'd been beaten plenty and survived. And Jonathan had sworn he'd never harm him. Strange, but he believed the guy. Which was more than he could say for his father. And if he'd lived through *that*, surely he could live through this. And he'd have a lot more to show for it when it ended than a rented couch in the ass end of Chinatown and no prospects for his future.

Bran took a deep breath, another, dragged his hands through his hair and then shook them out. "Come on, Bran. Suck it up. You can do this."

Jonathan's stomach clenched as Brandon's footsteps echoed on the stairs. He'd been down there alone for at least twenty minutes, and the wait had been so nerve-wracking that Jonathan had brewed some tea and forced himself to sit on the couch lest he wander back downstairs.

Brandon came over and sat in the recliner across from him, hands gripping his knees, jaw clenched. "I need a drink."

Jonathan's eyes went instantly to the red marks on Brandon's left forearm; he'd clearly hit himself with something much nastier than the suede flogger. Had he liked it?

"Not tonight," Jonathan said. "This is not a conversation to be had under the influence. I'd be happy to pour you some tea, though."

"No thanks. So . . ." Brandon sucked in a deep breath. "How do we do this?"

"I take it that's a yes, then?"

Brandon grimaced. "For right now, it's a maybe. We need to get a few things straightened out first. Like, how do I know you'll hold up your end of the bargain if I let you do this to me?"

Jonathan resisted the urge to argue he'd be doing it *with* Brandon, not *to* him. Now wasn't the time for that, and Brandon would learn soon enough anyway if Jonathan managed this discussion properly. "Well, it's perhaps a bit crass to think of it this way, but it *is* a legal agreement. We'll have a contract."

"Sounds like you've done this before."

Jonathan nodded. "Once or twice, perhaps."

"And what happened to *those* guys?"

"Their contracts ended and they went on their way. Quite pleased for the experience, I assure you."

"Can I talk to them?"

"I'm afraid not. It would be a violation of their privacy."

Brandon's brow furrowed. "So that *is* where you bury the bodies, then."

But it was said without heat; Jonathan chuckled. "Look, I'm no stranger to the local scene. I'd be happy to give you some references if you'd like."

Brandon said nothing. If Jonathan were in his shoes, he'd assume any references had been bought.

"So this contract . . ."

"Yes?"

"I'd have to live here, right?" Jonathan nodded. "What would happen to my apartment? It's rent-stabilized; I can't afford to lose it."

"I'd pay it off for a year when you signed the contract, and deposit thirty thousand dollars into your bank account then too." At Brandon's suspicious glare, he added, "Well, you'd have to quit your job, after all, and it's important you not feel trapped here. As with my prior arrangements, you could leave at any time. And you'd have a financial net to fall back on if you decided to go before the contract played out."

"Thirty grand," Brandon said, toneless in his incredulity. "Just for signing the contract?"

Jonathan nodded. "Just for signing the contract."

"And if I left in a day?"

"I'd be sad to see you go, but the money's yours to keep. Of course, if you want the three million, you'll need to stay until the end. The full hundred-and-eighty days."

"And what exactly would I be doing here for a hundred-and-eighty days? You gonna keep me locked up in the torture chamber?"

"Dungeon," Jonathan corrected with a tiny smile. "And no, we wouldn't spend all our time down there. Just the more fun times."

"Fun for *you*, maybe."

"And for you, once you learn how wonderful it can be to let go. Once you let your submissive side out of that little prison in which you've been keeping it locked all these years."

Brandon scoffed. "And I'd do that by letting you keep *me* locked in a little prison? I saw all those cages down there."

"Look." Jonathan scrubbed a hand across his mouth, rested his chin on his hand. "I'm not going to pretend this will all be flowers and orgasms. Will there be great sex? Yes. I'd even go so far as to say mind-blowing. For a submissive who's never let himself *be* submissive, it can be absolutely transcendent when he does." *Like our sex last week*, he didn't have to say; he could see the thought stamped clear across Brandon's face—right alongside the urge to argue, *I'm not a fucking submissive.* "*But*, breaking down all those barriers you've spent your whole life building can be a . . . *difficult* process. It won't always be easy, or fun, or even pleasant."

"Hence the whips and cages?" Brandon said, but it wasn't a question, not really.

"Hence the whips and cages, yes. But even *that* can be beautiful. Learning to trust someone like that, so deeply, so completely. Learning to move past your strongest barriers, face your deepest fears . . ." He shook his head, grasping for words to describe something so far beyond mere words. "It would change your life, Brandon. And not just because of the money waiting for you at the end."

"So what do you get out of it?"

"Simply put, I'm a Dominant and a sadist. Which means I enjoy taking absolute control, and yes, I enjoy inflicting pain. But it's not like I go around pulling wings off of flies."

"No, you just go around offering men money so they'll let you beat them. Sounds like a pretty expensive hobby."

"I've actually never paid anyone before—well, excepting living expenses they couldn't meet while serving me full-time. My prior arrangements were all with submissives quite eager to be Dommed by the best. And you must understand, the money . . . I'm not *buying* you. I'm *not*. I just, I see this gift inside of you and I want so very much to bring it out. Don't tell me you'd have considered it without a compelling enough reason."

Brandon shrugged. "Whatever you gotta tell yourself to sleep at night, pal."

Jonathan grinned. "And what about you? What do *you* tell yourself to sleep at night?"

"I'm not a whore," Brandon growled.

"I wouldn't want you if you were."

Brandon sat in silence for a few moments, staring down at his hands. "So do I get any say in what happens to me here?"

"Yes and no. Of course we'll agree on a safeword, and on lines we won't cross. But otherwise, this is— Have you heard the term 'total power exchange'?" Brandon shook his head. "Basically, it means that, within the framework of the boundaries we set, you obey me in all things, 24/7, regardless of what I ask of you."

Brandon's head snapped up. "What, you mean I'd be your slave?"

"I suppose you could put it that way. Although I prefer 'submissive' to 'slave.' It's all part of the process of letting go, allowing me to lead you, show you your full potential."

"Don't you already have servants catering to your every whim?"

"Yes," Jonathan grinned, "but I can't fuck my maid."

"I'll bet she'd say yes for three million dollars."

"Let me rephrase, then: I don't *want* to fuck my maid."

Brandon chuckled, and something unclenched in Jonathan's chest. If Brandon was feeling comfortable enough to *joke* . . .

But Brandon's smile faded quickly, and he opened his mouth, closed it, opened it again. His fingers twined and untwined in his lap. "So these lines we won't cross . . ."

"I told you I'd never harm you, and I won't. Yes, I may *hurt* you—there will be pain, or rather, heavy sensation—but never harm. Never injury. At least nothing an ice pack or a Band-Aid can't fi—"

"No blood," Brandon blurted. "I don't . . ." He dropped his gaze from Jonathan's eyes to his own hands, still fidgeting in his lap. "I don't want you to cut me."

"All right," Jonathan said softly. "That's no problem."

"And what if . . ." He trailed off, didn't finish his sentence.

After what felt like half a minute, Jonathan prompted him with, "If?"

Brandon looked back up at him, a fierce blush coloring his cheeks. "What if I can't . . . I mean, what if—"

"If it's more than you can handle?" Jonathan offered. Brandon nodded, blush creeping right to the tips of his ears. "That's what your safeword is for. If I'm starting to push you too hard or it's getting too bad or you're too afraid, you say 'Yellow,' and I'll slow down. If I've already pushed you too hard or it's gotten too bad, you say 'Red,' and I'll stop. Right away. No questions asked."

"Really?"

Good Lord, was he ever adorable when he'd been surprised. Jonathan couldn't help but smile. "Really. I may be a sadist, but I'm not a psychopath." Brandon's return smile wobbled, but it was there. "Although it's very important you not abuse the safeword. It's there only for when you *need* it, not simply when you *want* it. I will know the difference. If you use it when you *don't* need it, I retain the right to void the contract."

"All right," Brandon said, but he didn't understand yet, not really; he'd spoken with the blithe disregard of a man who had no idea what he was getting into.

Jonathan sat forward, looked him dead in the eye. "Listen to me. I mean it. This is serious, and you *will* need to safeword eventually. I can't stress enough how important it is that I can trust you on this—both to use it when you've reached your absolute limit and to hold your tongue when you haven't. No macho posturing, no childish games."

Brandon met Jonathan's gaze, unflinching. "All right," he said again, and this time his words held weight.

"Good, thank you. Now, is there anything else? If you want to set limits, you need to set them now; once the contract's signed, you'll get no say in anything anymore."

Hmm, maybe he'd put that a bit too harshly; Brandon paled, swallowed hard. "Um." He scratched at his cheek again. Did the scruff itch that much, or was it just a nervous gesture? "Condoms," he said. "All the time."

Of *course* he'd pick the one thing Jonathan couldn't give him. "About that . . ." Brandon looked to be in the process of working up a murderous glare, so Jonathan pressed on, even before he'd figured out exactly how to say it. "If you're not, er, *healthy*, then we can't move forward with this. Part of exploring the Dom/sub relationship necessitates I be able to do certain things with you that can't be done if there's any risk for disease. So if we agree to this, you and I will go— *together*—to be tested at the doctor of your choosing. I'll pay for it, of course, and we'll view the results together too. Does that suit you?"

Brandon thought about it for a minute, then nodded once. "Yeah, I guess."

"Excellent. Anything else? Any other questions?"

"Not right now."

"Are you sure? This is your last chance. I'll have the contract drawn up in the morning with everything we've talked about tonight."

"Yeah. I'm sure." Another deep breath. "So when does this thing start? I'll need to give notice at work."

"How does two weeks sound? We'll go get tested tomorrow."

"All right." He stood, rubbing his palms on his jeans.

Jonathan stood with him, put a hand on his shoulder. Brandon flinched again, but Jonathan supposed he'd expected that after the evening they'd just had. At least Brandon hadn't tried to push him away.

CHAPTER 8

ne bag. Don't bother with clothes; I'll take care of that.

Bran looked around his apartment, battered duffel bag in hand. If he couldn't pack clothes, what the hell else was there? *Toiletries, I guess.* He wandered into the bathroom, grabbed his toothbrush, his razor, his comb, his deodorant. Which still left . . . 99 percent of the bag to fill.

He couldn't decide if it was Zen or just pathetic that he had nothing else in this place he didn't want to leave behind for six months.

Well, okay, *one* thing. He snatched the picture of his mother off his dresser—one of the only things he'd managed to take with him when his dad had thrown him out—wrapped it carefully in his favorite ratty old Henley, and put it in the duffel. Grabbed his dog-eared copy of *Huck Finn* to go along with it. Not that Jonathan had any shortage of books, but his mom had given him this one, and he'd re-read it at least a dozen times in the years since she'd died. He took a long look around the bedroom, but nothing else called out to him. Same in the living room/kitchenette. He felt kind of silly carrying a nine-tenths empty duffel, but one long last look around the apartment revealed nothing else with which to fill it.

He heaved a sigh, told himself he wasn't wistful or worried in the slightest, and walked out the door.

Jonathan's driver was waiting for him in the parking lot, limo idling weirdly quiet at the curb. He climbed into the backseat before he could second-guess himself.

At Jonathan's building, the security guard ushered him straight to the penthouse elevator, then punched the button. Thirty-four floors never ticked by so slowly. Jonathan was waiting for him on the other side of the door, smiling, hands in his pockets. Well, of course—what did *he* have to be nervous about?

He supposed it shouldn't have come as such a surprise when the first thing out of Jonathan's mouth wasn't "Hello" or "How are you tonight," but "Strip."

Bran stepped out of the elevator and dropped his bag to the floor. "W-what?"

Jonathan gestured at him with an open hand. "Strip, please. All your clothes. Leave them where you stand."

Jesus, he wasn't serious?

But that no-nonsense look in his eyes made it clear he was.

Well, it wasn't as if Bran hadn't known what he was getting into, even if he could feel the humiliation burning straight up to the tips of his hair. He took a deep breath, reached up with shaking fingers—*Really, Bran? Trembling like a little kid?*—and began to unbutton his shirt.

And then it hit him . . . "Wait, don't you have a live-in maid?"

"And a cook, and a driver, too. Nothing they haven't seen before. Anyway, they have their own suites downstairs."

"But they don't . . .?"

"Join in?" Now Jonathan smiled. "No, definitely not. I'm afraid I'm really quite selfish; only child, you know." He made another impatient waving gesture and said, "Sometime tonight, please?"

All right, don't think about it, just do it.

Shirt first, then he toed off his sneakers and socks and unbuttoned his jeans. Skinned them down and stepped out of them, leaving his boxers behind.

Jonathan raised an eyebrow in the general direction of Bran's crotch and folded his arms across his chest. "I said *all* your clothes. You're new to this, I know, so I'll try my very best to be patient, but let me make this clear right from the start: I expect to be obeyed, without hesitation or question, and I *do not* like to repeat myself. When you make me do things I don't like, I'm afraid I'll have to do things *you* don't like in return. Do you understand?"

Bran thought back to all those implements of torture in the dungeon and barely repressed a shudder. *You can do this, Bran. Think of the money . . .*

Jonathan slapped his cheek. Not hard, didn't particularly hurt, but *holy shit did he just* slap *me?*

Bran touched his cheek, realized his mouth was hanging open and closed it. Jonathan sighed as if he were dealing with some idiot child. "What did I just say?" he asked, and despite the slap that had preceded the question, the question itself came out infinitely patient.

Which was a good thing, because try though he might, Bran couldn't seem to remember. "I, uh . . ." He cleared his throat, tried to stick his hands in his pockets and realized he had none anymore. It was cold in here; he shivered.

A warm hand landed on his shoulder. Gentle, soft. "It's all right," Jonathan said. "I know how overwhelming it can be at first. So I'll say this one more time. I expect to be obeyed without question or delay, and this is the last time I'll *ever* repeat myself without taking it out of your hide. One demerit for every infraction—more for the particularly egregious ones—starting now."

Bran shuddered beneath that gentle touch, that deceptively gentle voice and the talk of demerits. Jonathan wasn't shitting around, this was for *real*. He glanced back at the elevator door, really *thought* about it for a second, but . . . *Three million dollars, Bran. Suck it up.*

"Take off your boxers."

Strange, how easy it was this time. Not like Jonathan hadn't seen all of him already anyway. He hooked his thumbs beneath the waistband and pulled them down, kicked them a few feet to the side. He met Jonathan's approving gaze and said, "Now what?"

"Now, rule #2. Never speak out of turn. If I ask you a question, I expect an immediate, honest answer. If you need time to think, you may tell me so, but *don't* leave me waiting. If you have something you're dying to say and I've not asked you a question, you may ask me for permission to speak. I may or may not grant that permission. Understand?"

Bran nodded. He'd learned how to keep his mouth shut after his mother died.

Yet Jonathan's gaze narrowed. Fuck, had he done something wrong already?

"When I ask you a question," Jonathan said, "I expect you to answer me out loud unless I've gagged you." *Gagged* him? What the *fuck*? "Understand?"

"Um, yes, sir?"

A little smile broke out on Jonathan's mouth (that *gorgeous fucking mouth*, damn him all to hell), and he said, "And for God's sake, don't call me sir. Jonathan, all right? Just Jonathan."

Bran felt a little smile break across his own mouth. *Or maybe Ocean Windsong, you little fuck?* He held back his snort and said instead, "Yes, Jonathan."

Silence then for a time, as Jonathan looked him up and down, studied him like he'd never seen a naked body before. Kinda strange, but as long as Jonathan wasn't taking him downstairs, he wasn't gonna complain.

Jonathan reached out and brushed fingertips across a two-inch scar high up on Bran's left pec: the one he didn't like to think about if he could help it. Thankfully, Jonathan didn't ask about it. Didn't ask—or say—anything, actually, and really, how long was he gonna leave him standing here, naked and shivering in the foyer?

Or was this a test? Just waiting for Bran to say something right after he'd told him he couldn't? Well, fuck that; he wasn't that stupid.

"You're quite the fidgeter, aren't you," Jonathan said through that familiar smug smile of his, dragging the fingertips of both hands across Bran's flanks.

Well, yeah, when you're tickling me, fucker. But oh, wait, he was supposed to answer out loud, wasn't he? "I dunno," he said. "Guess I never really noticed."

"I don't know, *Jonathan*," Jonathan corrected.

Bran grimaced—*Really? You're really gonna make me do that?*—but repeated flatly, "I don't know, *Jonathan*."

That seemed to satisfy. Jonathan nodded and said, "Well, I can't have a fidgety sub. We'll have to work on breaking you of that habit."

Great. Just great.

"Follow me, then."

He turned and headed for the stairs without waiting for a confirmation from Bran, and for a moment, Bran's feet seemed glued to the floor. To the dungeon . . . he was taking him to the dungeon *already*? Did he mean to start . . . to start *breaking* him now?

"Keep up!" Jonathan singsonged as he headed down the first stair, "Or I'll put you on a leash!"

Smug fucker. Effective, though; next Bran knew, he was hustling after Jonathan like some simpering dog, anxious not to be kicked.

Jonathan led them down the hall to the dungeon, unlocked the door, and beckoned Bran inside. Bran's gaze zeroed in on a set of shiny metal cuffs laid out on a table near the door, one pair slightly larger than the other, four inch-wide O-rings welded to each of them by tiny little U-bolts. Jonathan pocketed the door key and said, "Hold out your wrists."

Bran didn't move. Did Jonathan really mean to lock him in those things? Worse, what would he do to him after? "Uh . . ."

"For the record, I hadn't planned to inflict the slightest discomfort on you today, but now you've just earned yourself *two* punishments: one for speaking out of turn, and one for not obeying immediately. Would you like to make it three, or would you like to hold your wrists out?" A second's pause, and then, "Or would you like to leave? You know where the door is; you're free to walk out of it at any time."

Was that a question? Was he allowed to speak? He raised his hand like some kid at school, felt like an idiot and put it back down. But Jonathan seemed to appreciate the gesture, or maybe his confusion. "Go ahead," Jonathan said, though he sounded kind of irritated about it. "You can speak."

"Um, *punishment*, Jonathan?"

"Yes, punishment. Don't ask any more questions about that; you'll learn soon enough. For now, hands out, or out the door. Your choice."

No choice at all. Bran held out his hands.

Cool metal closed around his left wrist, and with it, a moment's panic. He tried to pull his hand back, but Jonathan's fingers lingered, holding firm, thumb stroking the back of his hand.

"It's all right, see? No pain. Nothing to be afraid of."

The cuffs were kind of comfortable, actually, rounded at the edges like a well-tooled watch band, the fit so perfect he wouldn't have been surprised if Jonathan had measured him in his sleep. The hinge was machined entirely inside the seam, and he couldn't even see the locking mechanism: some kind of tongue-and-groove, as seamless as the hinge, the keyhole tiny. But he could certainly feel the weight of the thing, even if it was only an inch wide and no more than an eighth of an inch thick. He was also pretty sure he'd jingle when he walked, what with those four steel O-rings dangling against the steel cuff.

Why so many?

Jonathan was still holding Bran's wrist. He slowly turned it over, caressed the heel of Bran's hand with the pad of his thumb—a little shiver ran straight down Bran's arm and to his dick, like the two were fucking attached somehow—then placed the other cuff in his hand. "Here, put it on. Push the ends together until you hear the click."

Bran turned the steel cuff over in his hands for a moment, feeling the heft, the coolness, the sheer solidity of it. And more than that, too. It was one thing for him to let Jonathan lock it on him, but to make the choice to lock it on himself . . .

His gaze wandered of its own accord to the dungeon door, down the hall. He couldn't see the elevator from here, but he knew it was there, waiting. Jonathan was waiting too, more patiently than Bran might've thought.

He knows how hard this is for you.

The realization hit him with all the strength and meaning of the steel cuffs. This really *wasn't* all about Jonathan. He *did* care about Bran's feelings and fears.

Bran nodded and locked the second cuff on.

"That's very good," Jonathan said, so soft it was almost a whisper. "Very good. Here"—he handed him the ankle cuffs—"these too, if you please."

Bran didn't hesitate this time. The hard part was already over, after all, and he hadn't forgotten Jonathan's talk of *punishment*.

When he finished fastening the cuffs and straightened back up, Jonathan was smiling at him, all fatherly approval. And didn't that just make Bran want to punch the grin right off his stupid too-pretty face. What kind of idiot had he been to let Jonathan's approval mean a *thing* to him, even for a single second?

"Now aren't you lovely," Jonathan practically purred.

Correction: he wanted to punch Jonathan in the fucking throat.

"Come along," Jonathan chirped, threading a finger through a ring on Bran's wrist cuff before tugging him to one of the doors at the back of the room. Did he even want to know what lay behind those doors? What could possibly be so awful that Jonathan had felt the need to hide it, even from *this* place?

No, he decided, right around the second Jonathan took the choice out of his hands.

But then the light went on beyond the door, and Bran's thrashing heart settled, more or less. Just a bathroom. A really, really nice bathroom, actually: marble sink and vanity, marble tiles, massive heat lamp, full-length mirror. Bright white, all of it, even the curtain on the curved shower rod.

Nothing freaky here at all, it seemed.

"Sit," Jonathan said, indicating the bare toilet lid. Bran eyed it for a second, testicles creeping up into his belly at the mere *thought* of all that chilly porcelain. He half-expected Jonathan to force him when he didn't move, but instead Jonathan merely said, "That's three."

Huh? "Three what?"

"You've forgotten about the demerits you've earned already? And that makes four, by the way. Third for hesitating, fourth for speaking out of turn."

Well, fuck. Apparently all he had to do was *breathe* and he'd rack up another demerit. He stifled a sigh and sank down on the toilet lid, and *holy shit* it was every bit as cold as it'd looked.

Jonathan opened the medicine cabinet and drew out an electric razor. As he flicked it on, Bran realized it had a hair clipper at the end. His gut immediately tightened. "Wait, you didn't say anything about—"

Shit. He clapped a hand over his mouth, cursing his flapping tongue.

"Good effort, but that's five. And I gave you every opportunity to set limits when we negotiated our contract."

"But you never said—"

"Six—"

. "Oh, *come on!*"

"Seven. I can keep doing this all night. I *like* hurting you, remember?"

Bran scowled. *Fucking pervert.*

"Going to behave now?"

Bran gritted his teeth, but nodded. Then he remembered he needed to answer out loud and said, "Yes, Jonathan," before the sick fuck could make it eight.

Jonathan smiled and patted him on the head. "Good boy."

Oh, fuck the throat. Bran wanted to punch him in the fucking *nuts*.

But of course he didn't—three million dollars, after all—and Jonathan grabbed a good handful of his hair and started shaving. Bran watched the first clump of ginger curls float to the floor, wondering what he'd gotten himself into, why he was letting *anyone* treat him like this, if all the money in the world was worth it. If he'd wanted to be bossed around, he would've joined the army. At least they'd let him keep his clothes on while they sheared him like a fucking sheep. The back of his head grew cold as more tufts of hair fell around his shoulders.

"You should consider yourself lucky," Jonathan half-shouted over the buzz of the clippers. "I normally shave my boys right down to the scalp on their first day, but I must admit a certain fondness for your hair."

Yeah, if you shave it all off, what will you grab, you fucker?

Jonathan finished the back and then shaved down both sides. He paused to change the cutting guard before shaving the rest, and much less hair seemed to drift into Bran's lap when he ran the new guard through the top. When Jonathan turned off the clippers, Bran reached up to feel what he'd done, but Jonathan knocked his hands away. "Stand up and take a look."

At first Bran hardly recognized himself. He hadn't worn his hair this short since middle school, when the girls had started trying to touch it, never mind that it hadn't been the girls he'd been interested in. He ran his hand up the close-cropped hair at the back, then ruffled the couple inches Jonathan had left up top, gentle curls spilling through his fingers.

It actually felt kinda nice. And he supposed it didn't look so bad, either. At least it'd be easy to take care of.

He debated asking Jonathan if he'd shaved his initials into the back of his head, but decided it wouldn't be worth an eighth demerit.

"Time for a shower," Jonathan said, pulling the shower curtain back to reveal a jetted soaking tub big enough for two and a pair of waterfall shower heads. Looked heavenly, like something from a five-star hotel. Jonathan turned on the water, waited for it to start steaming, then began unbuttoning his shirt. "Go on, get in," he said. "I'll join you momentarily."

Bran had showered before he'd come over, but now that he had hair clippings down his back—not to mention his ass-crack—another one sounded like a good idea. Besides, no need to ask him twice to enjoy *that* shower. He climbed in, moaning softly as warm spray poured down his skin. He stood there basking in it for a few seconds before Jonathan stepped in behind him and closed the curtain.

Jonathan's arms encircled his waist as he pressed up behind Bran, brushed a kiss to his shoulder blade. Bran tensed; it was impossible to miss that erection pressing up against the back of his thigh. Jonathan wasn't gonna fuck him in the *shower*, was he? It'd been too rough for Bran's tastes in that nice soft bed, and at least they'd used lube then.

"Shhh, relax," Jonathan whispered. "I'm not going to fuck you here," and oh God, was he *psychic* now, too? "At least," he added with gentle humor, "not tonight."

Bran reached for a nearby bar of soap, just for something to do with his hands, but Jonathan took it from him and said, "Let me."

What the hell? Didn't Jonathan think he was capable of washing himself? Still, Jonathan's soapy hands glided like silk over his skin, and damn if it wasn't nice. Better than nice, even, when strong fingers dug into the tension at his shoulders, his neck, the small of his back. He propped his palms on the shower wall and let his head hang between them, closed his eyes and just enjoyed himself. Easy enough to do if he pretended this was two weeks back, before the contract, before the talk, when they were just two guys hooking up, having some fun.

Jonathan leaned in, rested his chin on Bran's shoulder and whispered, "No disappearing on me, Brandon."

Fuck. Was he supposed to reply to that? It wasn't a question exactly, but . . . He took a chance and said, "I'm not, Jonathan."

Jonathan slid a soapy finger down the crack of his ass and said, "Good," so he supposed he'd done right. "Turn around."

Suddenly Bran realized things were perking up south of his equator. *Great. As if the smug bastard weren't smug enough.*

And of course Jonathan went right for it the second Bran turned around.

"Well," Jonathan said to Bran's tight-lipped refusal to moan at that fantastic fucking touch, "it does need washing too, you know." But the slow, steady pump he gave felt *nothing* like washing, nor did the stroke after, nor the stroke after that. Bran stumbled back a step on the fourth stroke—with an added twist and squeeze around the crown this time—and leaned against the shower wall lest his knees go. The shock of cold tiles tamed his arousal a little, and Jonathan, the little fuck, didn't seem to have any intention of finishing what he'd started anyway. One more pump and he pulled his hand away, slid it down to Bran's balls and gave them a too-rough soaping up.

"Hey, not so hard!" Bran said, then realized immediately what he'd done.

Worst of it was, Jonathan didn't get any gentler as he said, "Eight."

Actually, no, Bran was wrong. The *real* worst of it was that Jonathan was reaching for a disposable razor with his free hand, and he didn't really mean to do what Bran thought he was gonna do, did he?

"Spread your legs and hold still," Jonathan said, dropping down to one knee beneath the shower spray.

Well, fuck.

No fucking way.

Jonathan held Bran's dick out of the way with one hand and lifted the razor with the other.

Bran jerked back.

"Brandon," Jonathan said, slow and warning, but hey, at least he hadn't said *Nine.* He sat back on his heels, looked up at Bran, water streaming over his shoulders and falling in fat drops from his eyelashes. Fuck, his eyes were blue. "You're a smart man," he said, and it seemed downright *surreal* to be lectured by a wet man on his knees and yet here they were. "I know you remember my rules."

Bran nodded, unsure of whether he was supposed to speak.

"Tell me what they are."

"Don't speak out of turn."

Jonathan nodded. "And?"

Bran took a deep breath, another, thought about the money. "And obey every order, without question or hesitation. Don't make you repeat yourself."

Another nod. "And what happens if you break my rules?"

"You punish me," Bran spat, lip curling in disgust. He wasn't some fucking child to be lectured, patronized, turned over someone's knee and spanked.

"So you see where this leaves us," Jonathan said.

"Let me guess. On nine."

A little smile, more in the eyes than on Jonathan's lips. "That too, yes. And I won't force you"—he held up the razor in the general vicinity of Bran's crotch—"but this? Is non-negotiable. You have a safeword, of course; use it if you must, but I *know* you don't need it now, and I get understandably tetchy when my subs abuse my trust about something that important. What we have here is a simple case of pride, yes?"

Bran wasn't sure he could answer with anything but *Fuck you*, so he held his tongue.

"That's ten, and yes, I see: pride indeed. Tell me, Brandon, why don't you want me to shave your pubes?"

Bran glared down at him, bit back another *Fuck you*. "Because it's *ridiculous.*"

Jonathan pursed his lips, raised his eyebrows. "Humiliating, you mean? Embarrassing for you?"

No shit. Even *talking* about it brought heat to his cheeks that had nothing to do with the shower. "Yeah, I guess. Won't it itch, too?"

"A little," Jonathan conceded. "Which is why we'll wax next time. But that's a bit much for day one, don't you think?"

Wax? *Fuck* that. No fucking way was Jonathan coming anywhere *near* his crotch with hot wax.

"I see you think you'll find a way out of that one too, but you won't." A statement of fact. Calm, assured, even a little bemused. Like he thought he knew fucking everything. "Do you remember," he asked, "how we talked about tearing down barriers and walls? About trusting me? About breaking you of all the destructive thoughts and habits that prevent you from realizing your true potential?"

"Yeah," he conceded.

"Yes, *Jonathan*," Jonathan corrected. "And eleven, by the way; I've let that slide too much already. Would you care to go for twelve?"

"No, Jonathan," Bran groused. Added, at Jonathan's raised eyebrow, "I remember talking about all that stuff, yes, Jonathan."

"Well, this is part of it. So either you trust and obey me now, or you leave and we call the whole thing off."

Well, that was no choice at all again, was it. Bran let his head thunk back against the shower wall, covered his face with both hands, and spread his legs.

Jonathan soaped Bran back up, gentler this time. Reward for obeying, perhaps? Though he knew it was coming, the first touch of the razor against his groin made him twitch. Good thing Jonathan had started nowhere near the particularly sensitive bits.

"Hold still," Jonathan warned. Another scrape, terribly uncomfortable, tugging some hairs out at the root like when he tried to shave a beard after letting it get bushy. He tensed his ass and thighs and belly to keep himself from squirming, sucked in a sharp breath when Jonathan ripped out yet more hairs. Didn't he know you were supposed to *trim* hair long enough to grab before you took a fucking razor to it?

Come to think of it, he probably did. He had said he *enjoyed* hurting Bran, after all, hadn't he.

Fucker.

Another painful tug, and this time a soft "Ah—!" slipped out between Bran's clenched teeth. Not that it hurt *that* much; it was just a really, really, *really* uncomfortable place to be hurting at all, and fuck, would that stray little sound earn him another demerit?

"Relax," Jonathan said, patting his thigh like he was some fucking skittish horse or something. "I'll never punish you for vocalizing pain or pleasure unless I've specifically told you not to." He looked up from his shaving, flashed Bran an angelic smile and fluttered his lashes at him. "In fact, I rather quite enjoy hearing you suffer."

Jesus, how could he say shit like that through such a bright fucking grin?

Jonathan bent his head back to shaving. More tugging, and this time Bran made damn well sure he didn't let out a single fucking *peep*. Shit, this was itchy already. He wanted to scratch, tried to, but Jonathan hooked his cuff by a ring and pulled his hand away. Wow, that was gonna get annoying fast. Did these things come off? Or did Jonathan plan to leave him shackled for the next six months?

Probably option #2.

It seemed Jonathan had finished with the safe zone, because he took Bran's soft dick in hand, lifted it up, and began to shave beneath it. Bran doubted Jonathan was touching to arouse, and anyway all that miserable tug and pull of razor over very sensitive skin—not to mention the shame of this whole situation—should have discouraged excitation, yet there he was, getting hard in Jonathan's hand again. Great. Just fucking great. But he supposed he was a healthy thirty-year-old guy with a too-long-ignored sex drive, and it was probably perfectly normal to get a little wood when someone that damn good-looking was handling you, no matter how much you wished he weren't. At least there was no hair on his dick, no reason for Jonathan to go near it with the—

Shit. Seemed there *was* some hair on his balls, though. He went so still when Jonathan pulled the skin of his sac taut that he forgot to breathe.

"Easy," Jonathan murmured. "I won't nick you if you don't move."

Oh God, this was *not* happening. Bran's hands came up to cover his face again.

"There," Jonathan said, and then after one more drag of the razor, "Nearly done now. Turn around, please."

Odd to be so polite when he wasn't giving Bran any kind of choice in the matter. Still, Bran turned around without having to be told twice, pressed his forehead to the shower wall and re-spread his legs at Jonathan's gentle taps to the inside of his right thigh. Jonathan worked up a lather on the back of Bran's sac—and *fuck* if that didn't start to get him hard again—and finished shaving him. Soapy fingers ran over his ass cheeks a moment after, and he heard a low, thoughtful "Hmm" before he felt Jonathan stand up behind him.

"Barely any hair on that tight little ass of yours. No point in shaving the stragglers, I think."

How very generous of you.

Jonathan removed the shower head from its cradle, pressed it into Bran's hands, and said, "Rinse off," before reaching for a small stainless steel case on a nearby shelf. Strange, but Bran hadn't even noticed it before. He went back to rinsing the soap from his crotch, running fingers over the weirdly smooth skin there, trying to re-map a part of himself he'd known so well for so long.

Huh, my dick looks bigger now without all that hair in the way.

Jonathan turned back to face him a few moments later, holding the case. He caught Bran touching his newly-bared skin and said, "Nice, isn't it?"

Bran wasn't sure he'd call it *that*, but he needed to reply with *something*, so he said, "I guess, Jonathan."

"Trust me, you'll love how sensitive you are down there now. Speaking of . . ." Jonathan dropped to his knees again, and whatever thoughts Bran might have had about the shaving or the mysterious metal case ran right out of his head when those lush lips wrapped around his soft dick and swallowed it whole.

For a second, he had to fight the urge to push Jonathan off. He couldn't stand much more teasing, and if Jonathan ran true to form, Bran knew he wasn't gonna let him come. But fuck, it felt amazing. He was hard in seconds, and still his whole dick was in Jonathan's mouth. He closed his eyes, let his head loll back against the tiles and gave himself over to it. Why the hell not? Truth was, this was half the reason he'd agreed to this in the first place. Best fucking sex of his life.

Somewhere off in the world beyond streaming hot water and Jonathan's even hotter mouth, he heard a faint click. He thought about opening his eyes to check it out, but decided he didn't want to know. Another click, even fainter than the first, and then Jonathan was parting his ass cheeks with one hand, slipping a lubed finger or two inside with the other. Bran lurched, gasped hard. *Shit,* that was amazing. He pushed his hips back, tried to take Jonathan deeper, desperately chasing the orgasm looming so close—

Jonathan pulled his mouth off and grabbed Bran's hip with one hand. "No squirming," he warned.

Nothing for a moment; Bran realized Jonathan was waiting for an answer. "Sorry, Jonathan," he said, even though he wasn't, not even a tiny little bit. Whatever . . . *Anything* to get that mouth back on his dick again.

Jonathan's fingers started moving in his ass again, and he pressed his palms flat to the tiles, fingers white with the strain of *no squirming no squirming no squirming*, and Jonathan murmured "Good" like a ten-syllable word and sucked Bran's cock back into his throat.

Bran squeezed his eyes closed, bit his lip. He would *not* move, *not* make a sound, because Jonathan obviously expected both and he wasn't gonna give him any reason in the whole fucking world not to let him come. Yet still he couldn't quite stop the little whimper when Jonathan pulled his fingers out, or the one that followed when he pushed them back in—

Not fingers. Hard. Cool. Bran's eyes flew open, but it wasn't like he could see his own ass, now was it, and Jonathan's mouth was still on his dick so he didn't dare move, but then—

Jonathan reached up behind Bran, fiddled with something on the wall, and suddenly—

What. The. Fuck.

Something warm and wet and *too full* flowed up his ass, and he lurched so hard his cock slipped from Jonathan's mouth.

"No squirming," Jonathan said again, entirely too cheerful. "And don't push. Just relax and take it."

"Take *what*?" Bran nearly shouted. "What the *fuck*, man?" He tried to step away from whatever it was Jonathan had shoved up his ass, but Jonathan just tightened his hold on Bran's hip and followed along. "Get that outta me!"

"Twelve," Jonathan said, and seriously, *fuck him*. "Stop being such a baby; it's just a little enema."

"E—" He couldn't even *finish* that sentence, but of course Jonathan filled in his stunned silence with, "Thirteen."

He pried a hand from the wall and reached out behind him, felt for the hose and yanked, but Jonathan was stronger than he looked, the little shit; Bran barely felt the thing move in his ass.

"Fourteen. And *hold still*. You'll hurt yourself."

"Like you care."

"Fifteen, and yes"—Jonathan looked up at him, so deadly serious Bran felt real fear for the first time since he'd walked through this door—"I *do* care." He took his hand from Bran's hip, kneaded at Bran's tense thigh, belly, wrapped his fingers around Bran's still-hard dick—*What the* fuck, *dick?*—and gave it a long, slow pump. "Easy, Brandon, please. I think you'll find this all quite pleasurable if you just *relax*."

Bran closed his eyes, tried to just breathe, to focus on the sensation of Jonathan's hand on his dick rather than the sensation of warm water filling-filling him, like fingers, like a whole fucking *hand,* snaking up where dick and fingers could never reach, putting pressure on *everything* like dick and fingers couldn't possibly, everywhere and all at once and *holy fuck* did he want to come, *need* to come, but not like this, not with a fucking shower nozzle shoved up his ass against his will and this smug fucker's hand on his dick and he clenched his eyes shut and whispered, "Please," half-broken even to his own ears, and the worst thing of all was that he wasn't sure if he'd meant *please stop* or *please don't.*

Jonathan licked the crown of Bran's dick in a single broad stroke and said, "Sixteen. Please what?"

Fucker.

Another lick. "Seventeen. Please what? Answer me."

"I . . ." No lick this time; Jonathan sucked the whole crown between his lips, worked the shaft with his hand. The pressure in Bran's ass was getting unbearable, creeping up into his belly, making his muscles contract and hinting at the promise of cramps. "Stop. Please."

Jonathan's mouth popped off his dick. "Don't you want to come?" he asked, like he already knew the answer was yes.

Bran nodded, even as his mouth said, "Not like this. Please not like this." Even as his hips thrust forward, seeking Jonathan's lips.

The flow of water up his ass stopped, but the nozzle remained, blocking him from pushing anything out. The pressure was still huge, his dick so hard his balls hurt. Jonathan's hand came off his dick and stroked his spasming belly again, strangely soothing. "Do you need to safeword?" he asked.

Bran opened his mouth to do exactly that—it wasn't a cop-out, he had *permission*, Jonathan wouldn't think he was faking—but God he was horny, *unbearably* so, and if he didn't come soon he was pretty sure he'd go batshit insane. It was almost over anyway. He could handle it. He *could*.

"No, Jonathan," he said, then added, soft and scratchy because even *this* much was a blow to his pride, "But . . . yellow."

"All right." Jonathan stood, shut off the water, dropped a soft kiss on Bran's pursed lips. "That's okay, that's good," he murmured, kissing Bran's chin now, his throat, his collarbone. He draped a crazy-plush towel over Bran's shoulders, stepped out of the shower. "I'm going to take the nozzle out now," he said. "Clench shut as I do. Hold it as long as you can. Then go sit on the toilet and just relax. Let it all flow out. No need to push."

That . . . was not the orgasm he'd been hoping for. But he certainly couldn't complain about easing this terrible pressure. Maybe Jonathan would finish sucking him off after?

Fuck, he nearly shot his load just at the sensation of the nozzle sliding free, nearly forgot to clench around all that water, nearly stumbled with the effort of stepping out of the tub. Jonathan held him steady, lending coordination until the spasms in his gut got too strong to ignore. Then Jonathan guided him over to the toilet and sat him down.

"Go on," Jonathan said. "Just let it go."

Bran blinked up at him and waited, teeth clenched against the urge to do exactly as Jonathan had ordered.

Blinked again when Jonathan didn't move.

Was Jonathan really gonna stand there and *watch* him?

"Any time now," Jonathan said.

And Bran couldn't help himself; he asked, "How 'bout a little privacy, huh?"

When Jonathan was done laughing—and really, it wasn't *that* funny, was it?—he eked out between snorts, "Eighteen. And no, you signed away your right to even a moment's privacy when you signed the contract. Now kindly go before I make it nineteen."

Well, no point putting off the inevitable. Maybe if he closed his eyes first, he could pretend Jonathan wasn't—

"Eyes open, Brandon."

Well, fuck you too.

"Nineteen then?" Jonathan actually sounded put out about that, like *he* was the one who'd have to endure nineteen God-knew-whats. Fuck, why was this so hard? All he had to do was relax. Let go. So what if Jonathan was watching?

Yet the blush creeping halfway down his chest put lie to that. Still, wouldn't it be a relief to have it over with? To get this ache out of his gut?

A deep breath, and the pressure flowed out of him along with the water, relief so profound he moaned, reached for himself without even thinking, realizing, until Jonathan caught him by the wrist and said, "Absolutely not." And then, "That was very good, by the way. I know it wasn't easy."

Jonathan flushed the toilet, then handed him a wad of toilet paper and said, "Clean up and dry off. You have two minutes. I'll be outside." Jonathan snagged a towel and his clothes on the way out and most decidedly did *not* shut the door behind him.

Bran wobbled to his feet and took care of himself, shooting a baleful glance at the doorway. *Couldn't even close it halfway, you smug little fucker?* He ran a towel over his skin and through what was left of his hair, then gave himself a quick glance in the mirror. God, he looked absolutely fucking wrecked—tense, exhausted, debauched. Worst of all, he was still horny as hell. And the clock was ticking. Better get out there before Jonathan made it twenty.

Jonathan was standing fully-clothed next to a high table upholstered in leather. "Here," he said, beckoning Bran over. Bran's gaze locked on Jonathan's hands as he slowly pulled on a single fingerless leather glove and flexed his fingers. "Bend over the table, please."

Panic shot through him, but for once he resisted the urge to speak out of turn. Practically gnawing his tongue in half, he stepped over and did as he was told, peeking for nearby implements. Nothing on or near the table as far as he could tell—no whips, no straps, no nothing. Was Jonathan really only going to use his hand?

Except you know damn well how much a hand can hurt, Bran.

"Don't worry, I won't be using any of that today," Jonathan said. Jesus, the guy really was a mind reader—or maybe Bran was just really fucking obvious. "Just my hand." Actually, both of them, since he'd already reached out with the ungloved one and pressed it to the back of Bran's neck. An oddly reassuring gesture, even a comforting one, fingers caressing the damp hair there. "Tell me . . . why are we doing this?"

"Because you like to fucking hurt me."

"No, that's not it. And that's twenty, by the way. Try again. With a little less attitude this time."

What the hell did his guy want from him? "Because I don't know how to keep my mouth shut?"

"Yes, and?"

"I didn't hold still when you told me to?"

"Yes, and what else?"

"Because I didn't answer you immediately? Because I fought back?" *And you obviously can't handle that.*

"Very good. Now, are you ready to ask me to correct you?"

Bran shot up from the table—or tried, to, anyway; Jonathan's fingers went bruisingly tight around his neck, and next he knew he was being slammed back onto the leather cheek-first.

"You are out of your Goddamn mind," he growled. "You've had your fun, yeah? Teased me, humiliated me, groomed me like a fucking *dog*, but there is *no fucking way* I'm gonna *ask* you to beat me." He tried to pull out from under Jonathan's hand again, couldn't; pain flashed up his neck and down his shoulder, so sharp he choked on a yell. How was the little fuck so strong? "Red," he said, but still Jonathan didn't let go. Bran squirmed beneath him, grabbed at his forearm, but Jonathan held him fast, maddeningly calm. "Red, you fuck, I said red!"

Jonathan eased up but didn't let go. "Are you quite finished?"

Bran bared his teeth at him but said, "Fine, yes. Are *you*?"

The fingers on his neck tightened warningly again. "I'm sure you'll recall me saying I get tetchy when my subs abuse the trust inherent in safewording." When Bran said nothing, Jonathan added, low and cold, "Don't say it again unless you mean it."

"I did," Bran growled. Fuck, he felt ridiculous, having an argument bare-assed and bent over a table.

"Pride again," Jonathan said. "Nothing more. One day you'll come to understand that these punishments are meant to help you. For now, I'm content for you to try harder simply because you wish to avoid pain. But you *will* follow my rules, Brandon McKinney, or you will leave. The choice, as always, is yours."

More silence. Bran knew if he opened his mouth before he calmed down, he'd say things he couldn't take back.

Finally he said, "I'm not going anywhere." And, almost as an afterthought, "Jonathan."

"Then in that case, I think you've earned yourself another five for that little display. Misuse your safeword again and it'll be twenty. Now put aside your pride—it has no place here, Brandon—and ask me to correct you."

Silence. Deep, shuddering breaths. The hand on his neck started stroking again.

"You can always ask me for a moment if you need it, Brandon. I may not always grant it, but you need never fear to ask." The hand drifted down to his shoulder, scratched lightly. It would've felt great if he hadn't wanted the smug fucker's hands off him so fucking bad. "Now . . . were you about to ask me something?"

Another breath. "Please, Jonathan," he rasped through clenched teeth, "will you—" God, it was like slicing every word from his throat with a fucking razor blade. "Correct me?"

"Very good. And yes, I'd be delighted."

I bet you would, you sick fuck.

The gloved hand smoothed across his left cheek, then his right. "Remember, now," Jonathan said, teasing with a finger down his crack, behind his balls, "if you can't hold still, I'll have to restrain you."

Bran wrapped his fingers around the far edge of the table and held on tight. He wouldn't give this fucker the satisfaction of tying him down. Every muscle tensed, he put his head down and closed his eyes, waiting for the first blow.

"No," Jonathan said, the hand on Bran's ass going still.

Oh, right. Of *course* Jonathan would want his eyes open for this, even if he couldn't see—and thank God for that—what Jonathan was doing. He stared straight ahead, taking in a lovely view of all the fucking whips and crops and shit hanging on the back wall. Everything he had to look forward to.

The first blow wasn't too bad, even though it landed with a loud smack. For a second, the sound of leather on bare skin tore Bran fifteen years into the past, but he clawed his way back; no way was he letting himself fall down *that* hole ever again.

The second blow hit his other cheek with even greater intensity, a little ball of fire right in the center. He went rigid, hands clenching on the edge of the table, fighting against the urge to squirm. He sure as hell didn't need any more blows added to his count.

"It's all right to squirm while I'm spanking you," Jonathan said. "In fact, I'd be insulted if you didn't. But don't try to avoid my blows. That puts me rather out of sorts."

Yeah, and we wouldn't want that, now would we.

The next couple still weren't too much to take—until the heat started building up. And of course the sadistic little shit was hitting him as hard as he could. Bran gritted his teeth and kept his eyes on the back wall, biting back grunts as each fresh strike fell. He wasn't gonna cry out like some whiny kid over an open-handed spanking. Wasn't like he hadn't taken a lot worse. Still, it'd been a damn long time since he'd let someone do this to him, and shit but he'd forgotten how much it could hurt.

But he wasn't going to yell. He *wasn't.*

He quickly lost count of how many blows he'd taken. What was it now—eight, nine? At least ten more to go, and he already wanted to scream.

"Relax," Jonathan said, and somehow his lips were at Bran's ear, brushing across the lobe. "Let it wash over you. It's easier if you don't fight it."

Easy for you to say. Still, it'd hurt him a lot more to open his mouth. He let out a breath and went limp against the leather padding, tried to peel his fingers off the edge of the table.

The next blow knocked him forward, forced a gasp from his lungs. No mercy, no respite, nothing except Jonathan's leather-covered hand hitting over and over, leaving barely a moment in between to process the pain. Jesus, how could the smug bastard keep it up? Didn't it hurt his hand?

Apparently not, because Jonathan sped up even more, one blow on top of another, until Bran couldn't even tell where they were landing. His entire ass was one huge mass of pain and heat. Tears stung his eyes, but he blinked them back. *No way I'm gonna cry over a fucking spanking. Not gonna give him that.*

The next blow landed on a viciously sore spot. Jesus, had he meant to do that? And another right on top of it—

"Ow, fuck! Yellow, Goddammit, *yellow!*"

Jonathan stopped immediately, the hand at Bran's neck going gentle. "What is it?"

"What do you mean, 'What is it?' Jesus Christ, that fucking *hurts!*"

Jonathan blinked at him like he was a particularly dense child. "Yes. It's supposed to. That's why they call it *punishment.*"

"But—"

"Is that all? Are you feeling ill?"

A choked breath. "No."

"Then lie back down. You still have five to go."

Five? Might as well be fifty.

"Unless you want to—"

"*No.*" Jesus, it didn't even hurt that bad. He was just wound up, humiliated, *furious.* "And stop asking."

"Six more, then," and God but did Jonathan have to sound so fucking *cheerful* about it?

So much for not hurting that bad. Bran cried out when the next blow came down, skin on fucking fire. Every strike hit a raw spot. His stomach roiled, sweat pouring down his face. How many more? He'd lost count again. *Red* sprang to his lips, but he choked it back; this was nothing. Just a spanking. If he couldn't get through this, he was never gonna make it through the next six months, but *holy fuck* it was—

. . . Over?

Bran sniffed, realized he'd been crying . . . Well, not *crying,* but his eyes and nose were running. He wanted to ask if it was over or if Jonathan was just toying with him again, but for the first time in a long fucking time he was honest-to-God afraid to open his mouth.

So he was almost grateful when Jonathan pulled his mind-reading trick again and said, "There now, all over." The hand on his neck moved up into his hair, petting like he was a child or a fucking cat or something. Strange how after all the pain Jonathan's other hand had inflicted, this one actually felt damn good. He caught himself pressing up into the touch and stopped.

"It's all right," Jonathan said. "Come on." An arm around his waist, another at his shoulders. Jonathan stood him up, held him steady as pain washed through him all over again, took his breath away and nearly unhinged his knees.

Jonathan's erection digging into his thigh didn't help matters.

He sniffled, and a tissue materialized in Jonathan's hand. But he didn't pass it to Bran; merely dabbed at his eyes for him, then his nose, then held it there and said, "Blow."

Bran was too sore to argue.

Well, he didn't hurt *that* much anymore, but he felt *strange* now, crazy jittery, heart thrashing like he'd run for miles, like he hadn't slept in so long he'd gone way past tired and out the other side into loopy. Like he'd burst out laughing—or maybe just cry—at the slightest provocation. Not so different, come to think of it, from that time he'd woken up in the hospital stoned off his ass on morphine, if perhaps a little less itchy and nauseous.

"I know you probably don't think so," Jonathan said, hand warm and sure at the small of Bran's back, "but you took that *very* well. I didn't go the least bit easy on you"—*No shit*—"and for your first time . . . Well, to be honest, I thought you might try to safeword again."

Bran swallowed hard but said nothing.

"It's all right," Jonathan said. "You can speak if you'd like."

Bran nodded, once. "I guess I didn't need to, Jonathan," he said. Didn't say *Even though I really wanted to,* or *You would have known I was giving up too soon.* No need to state the obvious.

"That's good—you're a quick learner. I suspected you might be."

Amazing how warm that made him feel. Even warmer when Jonathan smiled at him—never mind that a pretty large part of him still wanted to smack that smile right off Jonathan's face, see how *he* liked being hit.

"And quick learners deserve rewards."

Did that mean he'd finally get to come? Terrible timing; he wasn't exactly raging horny anymore, not after having his ass beat black and blue.

Jonathan cupped the back of Bran's neck again, steered him toward a metal bar hanging from the ceiling. Looked like a trapeze. Jonathan gestured for him to hold up his arms.

What the fuck? This *is my reward?*

"It's all right, Brandon. I'm not going to hurt you now, I promise."

Define "hurt."

Still, Jonathan was *looking* at him like any second now he'd forgo the "reward" altogether and start handing out demerits again, so he did as told, gingerly holding up one arm and then the other for Jonathan to clip to the ends of the bar. Then Jonathan squatted down and tapped the inside of Bran's left ankle. "Nice and wide, please," he said, and Bran obeyed. Jonathan tapped him again—"A little more, if you would"— and Bran shuffled his feet a bit wider, until he was straining just a little and had made himself short enough to take most of the slack out of his arms.

There were hooks in the floor, attached to lengths of chain. Jonathan fastened one to Bran's left ankle cuff, then did the same with his right. Bran tugged experimentally against his bonds, realizing—*of course*— that Jonathan had given him just enough slack to squirm, but not to bring his legs together. Not enough to protect himself.

He clenched his ass, for what little good it would do. Jonathan had been as hard as concrete since the spanking, and what was Bran here for, after all, if not to sate the man's every desire?

Jonathan brushed fingertips across the small of Bran's back, circled around to stand in front of him. Those fingers trailed, tickling along his flank, ghosting over his stomach. Despite the chains, his dick was getting interested again.

"Look," Jonathan said, "I know you think I've been hard on you, that I'm bossy, that I don't care about your feelings. But none of that is true." A crooked little grin, and then, "Well okay, maybe I'm a little bossy."

Bran chuffed. *Yeah, just like you're a little short.*

"I also know you think submission is weakness. Quitting. Shameful. But none of *that* is true, either." He leaned in, lips hovering above Bran's left nipple without touching. A gentle puff of air, a shiver down Bran's spine. Above him, chains rattled ever so slightly.

"Submission is *strength*. Willpower. Iron control." Those lips closed around him, barely a ghost of a touch. Bran's breath caught, held. He fought the urge to push into Jonathan's mouth. "It's trust, and relaxation, and rest, and *pleasure*." Fingers cupped his dick, and Jesus, when had he gotten so hard again? He moaned almost silently, couldn't tear his eyes from Jonathan's fingers. Not squeezing, not stroking, just . . . holding him.

"I'm not going to fuck you now, Brandon. You'd resent it, wouldn't you?"

"Yes," he whispered without hesitation, but the word stuck in his throat. He cleared it, tried again. "Yes, Jonathan."

The fingers around his dick squeezed, hard but just this side of sweet. This time, his moan was nowhere near silent.

"You don't *want* to feel good here. You don't think you should. Is that right?"

Those squeezing fingers began to pump, slow and steady and inescapable. He couldn't have moved his legs, closed his knees, even if he'd wanted to. His hands found the chains clipped to his wrist cuffs, wrapped tight around them. The cuffs were biting into his wrists.

"Answer me, Brandon."

"Sorry," Bran said. "Hard to think when . . ." Jonathan's hand stopped moving. Still hard to think anyway, with his dick in that hot dry palm. Or maybe it was just the question. Maybe he didn't *want* to think about it.

"That's one," Jonathan said, his voice as whisper-soft as his touch, and for a moment Bran couldn't even bring himself to care, but then the fingernails of Jonathan's free hand scraped light across his ass and lit four streaks of fire in their wake. He gasped, jerked away from the touch and accidentally thrust his dick into Jonathan's waiting hand, and there was *no way* that should've felt as good as it did.

"Sorry," he said again. A flare of panic—he'd forgotten Jonathan's question.

"Sorry, *Jonathan*," Jonathan reminded him, and then, "Two." *Fuck.* "Never be afraid to ask me for help. Do you need me to repeat the question?"

Bran nodded. "Yes, Jonathan."

That hand at his dick started stroking again, Jonathan's other hand dropping down low to fondle his balls. Jesus, if he kept that up, this would be over in half a minute. "I said, you don't *want* to feel good here. You don't think you should. Right?"

Truth be told, he was feeling pretty fucking good about feeling good right now. But that was in the heat of the moment, beneath the thrill of Jonathan's gentle touch. He knew damn well he'd be ashamed of it later—pissed, even—for letting Jonathan do this to him after everything else he'd already done. For being weak enough to succumb to it. "Yes, Jonathan," he forced himself to say, because even *that*—even letting Jonathan wring that truth from him—was shameful enough.

Jonathan leaned in close, pressed lips to the shell of Bran's ear, fingers still working-working at his dick, and whispered, "Don't. Shame has no place in these walls. This, here, now? Is all about *your* pleasure. Embrace it. Let it wash over you. Be strong enough to be helpless to it"—a wet tongue darted across the lobe of his ear—"to succumb to it"—teeth now to join it, a little nibble that sent a shiver down the side of his neck and chest—"to *revel* in it."

Bran's eyes drifted shut as Jonathan's hands wandered all over him, taking their time on their way back to his crotch. Nails dragged over his skin, making him shiver and strain in his bonds. Felt good having something to grip, something to struggle against as Jonathan's fingertips traced over every inch of him, stopping to linger at his nipples, worrying and pulling and pinching. And there was that mouth again—that fucking *amazing* tongue—fastening on one nipple, then the other, until they stood up straight and hard.

No one had ever made the rest of his body feel this good. He'd never even imagined it *could* feel this way. Even when he jerked off, he got it over with quickly, racing headlong toward orgasm. Never touched himself above the waist. Never played with his ass. Sought relief but never lingered in the pleasure. Not like this.

Jonathan circled around to Bran's other side, dusting kisses over Bran's arm and shoulder as he went, giving him the barest edge of his teeth. Bran gasped, shivered, tugged at the chain over his head again. Tiny bites along the nape of his neck, across his shoulder blades, then downward, tracing every bump and dip along his spine. Jonathan reached around to fondle the front of Bran's torso, fingernails swirling everywhere, like he was trying to memorize each muscle and rib.

Then Jonathan stopped, palm pressed to Bran's fluttering belly. "You're tensing again," he said softly. "Let it go, Brandon. I told you, I'm not going to hurt you."

Pretty hard to keep in mind—he groaned inwardly at the awful pun—with his own dick throbbing for what felt like ever now and Jonathan's chino-covered erection pressing a hard sore line into his left ass cheek. How the hell did Jonathan hold himself in check when he obviously wanted to fuck the shit out of Bran?

How much more of this fucking torture is he gonna make me take?

The fading heat from his spanking flared to life again as Jonathan stepped back and slid his hands around to smooth over Bran's ass. No pinching this time, thank God, but the skin down there was still so fucking sensitized he couldn't stop himself from jerking.

"Sorry," he rasped through gritted teeth. "Jonathan."

"It's all right." A gentle touch at his hip, and then Jonathan started kissing his spine again. "Go ahead, struggle in your bonds. That's why they're there—so you can *relax*." The words vibrated against his skin, seeped in alongside another warm, wet flick of Jonathan's tongue.

Jesus Christ, any second now he was gonna *explode*, and Jonathan wasn't even touching his dick. Bad enough that those pink, smirking lips of his were reading Braille down his back, gliding to the base of his spine.

But when Jonathan's fingers slipped between Bran's aching ass cheeks and slowly parted them, Bran nearly pulled the fucking bar out of the ceiling.

"Calm down," Jonathan said sharply, the hand still resting on Bran's hip tightening. "I said I wasn't going to fuck you."

Then what the hell are you doing—besides driving me completely fucking insane?

"There's more to sex than your cock, you know," Jonathan said, pressing another kiss to the small of Bran's back. "Then again, maybe you don't. What a pity. Such a beautiful body. Hard to believe no one's taken full advantage of everything it has to offer. Or maybe you simply haven't let them?"

Another thought plucked right out of Bran's head. It'd been years since he'd indulged in more than quick fucks and backroom blowjobs. All he'd cared about was getting off. Taking his time getting there . . . well, what was the point in that?

Then Jonathan sank to his knees and buried his tongue in Bran's ass, and the entire world tilted on its side. Bran's mouth fell open on a loud moan he couldn't have smothered even if he'd had his hands free. Nobody had ever done this to him before—hell, he'd never even considered the *possibility*.

Jesus, and he'd thought giving head was the best thing Jonathan could do with that tongue. It licked, flicked, swirled and wiggled inside him, sending him up on his toes for a moment, until his legs—hell, his entire *body*—couldn't take it anymore. Every bone, muscle, and tendon dissolved and his hands slipped off the bar, leaving him dangling like a puppet on the tip of Jonathan's tongue. His wrists hurt, but it was all so far away he couldn't be bothered to care, to make it stop.

Pleasure, torture . . . it was all running together. He bit back the awful whimper welling up inside him, but one more tongue-flick nearly did him in. Jonathan eased off, and for a second Bran could've sworn the little fucker actually chuckled, but then he went right back to driving him insane.

Jesus, kill me now . . .

Because he wasn't gonna come, not like this, with his poor neglected dick bobbing against his belly. This was supposed to be a *reward*? He'd rather take another fucking spanking. At least it'd be over with quicker.

But then Jonathan started tongue-fucking him in earnest and reached around to grab hold of his dick. He was so close to the edge, all it took was a few strokes before every strained muscle in his body tensed and the black-walled dungeon sheeted white before him and he came with a rattle and a shout so loud the whole fucking building must've heard him. And *shit*, but Jonathan's tongue was still milking him, milking him, even as his fingers, covered in Bran's cum, gentled on his still-hard dick. Bran shuddered bodily, and again, feeling like he'd never be able to catch his breath, make his legs work, convince his lips to shape the *Holy fuck* bouncing around in his head.

From behind him, Jonathan chuckled, a warm vibration against the sensitized skin of his ass. He unhooked Bran's ankles from the chains, then stood, his clean hand smoothing over Bran's hip, lower back, shoulder. Fingers alit briefly on the nape of his neck—he couldn't even lift his head to look Jonathan in the eye, smile at him, maybe say thank you.

"The dungeon's soundproof, by the way," Jonathan said, then brushed a kiss across his neck. "Feet together now, there's a good boy."

Bran tried, he really did, but what Jonathan had just done had robbed him of every ounce of coordination he'd ever had, and nearly every ounce of strength. His wrists were really starting to hurt; he needed to take the weight off, but he just—

Jonathan's arm went around his waist, and the guy lifted him to his feet like he didn't weigh a thing. He leaned into Jonathan and just breathed, eyes closed, cheek pressed to that thick head of hair.

He smells like apples.

"Better now?" Jonathan asked.

Bran *mmm'd*, found the wherewithal to open his mouth to mumble, "Yes, Jonathan." A tuft of hair slipped past his lips. He didn't care. "Thanks."

Jonathan let him go, and he kept his feet. The buzz was starting to fade a little, but he was high and sleepy and so sensitive he could practically feel each individual molecule of air as it bounced and skipped against his skin.

Jonathan reached up for his left hand and said, "Stay sharp. This might wake you up quick."

The clip came undone, and Bran's arm dropped like a rock at his side. A very, very *hot* rock covered with fire ants. He shook it out with a hiss as Jonathan freed the other one, and then strong arms were around his waist again, guiding him to the padded table. He debated sitting on it—he still had *no* idea how his legs were working—but in the end just propped his hip against it, let it take his weight. He lifted his hands in front of his eyes, flexed his fingers. The cuffs slid down his arms a quarter-inch or so, exposing the marks they'd made when he'd struggled.

From barely a foot away, Jonathan watched him study himself, then plucked one of his hands from the air and kissed the base of his thumb, where the red marks were the worst.

"Are you back?" Jonathan asked, gaze intent on Bran's.

Back from what? "Sure? Um, Jonathan."

Jonathan chuckled again, his thumb rubbing absently over the wrist he was still holding. Felt kinda nice.

"Another shower, perhaps, then? You've worked up quite a lather."

Sure, why not. He nodded mutely, remembered the rules in a flare of panic and hastened to say, "Yes, Jonathan, please." Froze two steps later and said, "Um . . . permission to speak?" because as much as he really didn't want to be hit again, he also *had* to know . . .

Jonathan nodded, and Bran asked, "You're not, um . . . going to . . . you know." He pointed with his index finger in a manner he was pretty sure indicated *enema*. "Again?"

Jonathan chuckled softly, no malice. "No, no, you're quite clean enough there, I assure you." He dropped a hand on the nape of Bran's neck again, led him to the bathroom. "Water the grass if you need to," Jonathan said, and it took Bran a moment to interpret that as "Take a piss," but once he did, he realized he had to badly enough to empty his bladder even with Jonathan standing there. Not like Jonathan was watching anyway; he was busy fiddling with the shower knobs, adjusting the spray until it was barely lukewarm.

Bran flushed the toilet, let Jonathan guide him to the shower. "In you go," Jonathan said. He didn't strip to join Bran this time. Didn't try to wash him.

Bran didn't bother with soap, just let the water sluice the sweat and cum off. The water tempered the tingling in his ass, his nipples, his *everywhere*, cooled what heat remained from the spanking. Or maybe the pain was just fading on its own. It *had* only been a spanking, after all. A stupid little spanking. He was just out of practice with the whole getting-his-ass-kicked thing.

After a minute or so, Jonathan turned off the spray, wrapped Bran in an enormous towel, and guided him from the tub. Bran followed, grabbing the edge of the vanity to hold himself steady. Jesus, if he was this wrecked after the first fucking *afternoon*, he didn't even want to think about tomorrow, let alone the other 178 days to come.

CHAPTER 9

"**S**omething to eat now, perhaps?" Jonathan asked, studying Brandon for a moment. He'd done well. Better than Jonathan had expected, given his earlier resistance. Jonathan had been worried there for a minute during the spanking, when Brandon called "yellow." Afraid Brandon would give up too quickly or even that he'd pushed Brandon too far, especially for his first day.

But rules were rules, and God knew Brandon needed them. He was wild, undisciplined, too full of stubborn pride. Much as Jonathan might want to, giving Brandon even an inch of slack would just make this all the harder for the both of them.

Though, he might need to get rid of the steel cuffs if Brandon was going to struggle like that even during the *fun* play.

Brandon nodded, then quickly added, "Yes, Jonathan. I'm starving."

Jonathan grinned. It seemed Brandon had already learned—albeit the hard way—the proper way to address him. Was already correcting himself without being reminded. Good. *Very* good.

Not, mind, that Jonathan wouldn't have liked the excuse to beat him again.

"Let's see what we can find in the kitchen," he said, ruffling Brandon's hair before leading him out of the dungeon and down the hall. Brandon tensed, hanging back before they entered the kitchen, but Jonathan's hand closing gently over his elbow calmed him. "Don't worry, I've given my household staff the day off. It's just you and me today."

Jonathan pulled out a tall stool from the center island and sat down, waving Brandon over to the fridge. "Get us some water and grapes. There should be a cheese tray as well."

Brandon just blinked at him for a second, all that orgasmic bliss slowly draining from his face. "Oh, uh . . . you want me to—"

"Yes, I do. And that's four. Do you know why?"

Brandon winced. "Um, one for hesitating, one for speaking out of turn?"

"Yes. Very good. Now go on, get the food."

Shoulders stiffening, Brandon turned to the fridge and rummaged in it for the items Jonathan had requested. What a nicely reddened ass, the color so symmetrical on both sides. He'd done a good job, even with Brandon squirming like he'd taken a cane to him. *Later.* He could hardly wait. And with the way Brandon was racking up fresh demerits, he wouldn't have to wait long.

Brandon shuffled back to the table and set everything down, eyeing Jonathan warily. "Um, can I ask a question, Jonathan?"

"Feel free." Jonathan plucked a cube of cheese off the tray, relishing the way Brandon's famished gaze followed it all the way to his mouth. At least Brandon was smart enough not to take any for himself without asking.

"Can I sit down?"

Jonathan held Brandon's gaze, then very slowly and deliberately grabbed the cushion off a nearby stool and dropped it on the floor at his feet. "By all means. Please sit."

Brandon's eyes flashed pure murder, but he sucked in a breath and lowered himself onto the cushion, grimacing as his reddened ass made contact.

"If you'd prefer to kneel," Jonathan said, taking a cube of cheese, "I have no objections."

"Yeah, I'll bet you don't," Brandon mumbled.

"What was that?"

Even Jonathan could see the effort it took Brandon to unclench his jaw long enough to say, "Nothing, Jonathan."

Jonathan cocked an ear toward Brandon, raised his eyebrows. "Are you sure? Because it sounded rather suspiciously like *five* to me."

Brandon chewed his lip, but was wise enough to hold his tongue this time. "May I ask you something else, *Jonathan*?"

Jonathan let him sweat for a moment, plucking up a few grapes and eating them before he said, "Go ahead, but I suggest you watch your tone."

"May I fix myself a plate *please*, Jonathan?"

So much for watching his tone. Still, it was kind of amusing. "That's six. And no, you may not fix yourself a plate. Here." He pulled a couple of grapes off the stem and lowered his hand to Brandon, but when Brandon tried to take the food from him with his fingers, Jonathan shook his head. "No. In this house, if you want to eat, you eat from my hand." When Brandon didn't seem to get it—or maybe just didn't *want* to get it—he added, "With your mouth. You don't get to use your own hands."

Brandon jerked his head away and clenched his hands, white-knuckled, in his lap. "May I ask you *another* question, Jonathan?"

"You are perilously close to seven, but go ahead."

"Do I really have to behave like an animal here?"

Jonathan's mouth tightened, but he did his best to conceal his irritation. Brandon wouldn't learn a thing if Jonathan reinforced his negative behavior by letting the man visibly affect him. Besides, Brandon was new to this world. He didn't understand yet. And he never would if Jonathan didn't keep his patience.

So he reached down to stroke the top of Brandon's head before he answered. Brandon allowed it, but no doubt only out of fear; Jonathan could practically see the smoke coming out his ears. "Honestly, Brandon, that's not what this is," he said, ironically in the same tone he might use to address a spooked pup. "I'm not interested in dehumanizing you. Quite to the contrary, believe it or not. But to answer the question you *should* have asked—and that *is* seven, by the way, for your lip—yes. If you wish to eat, you'll eat from my hand. If you don't wish to eat, then don't. I won't force you, and I won't punish you. The choice has to be yours."

He pulled his hand back, used it to pluck up another cube of cheese and popped it in his mouth. "Now if you'll excuse me," he said, "if you're not going to eat, I certainly will. This is a *very* good aged gouda."

Jonathan finished his meal with as much gusto as he could muster, trying to tempt Brandon into eating half a dozen times before giving up. He hadn't expected anything different; a man that proud wasn't going to give in on an issue like this so quickly. Let hunger settle in first; it would win in time. At least he'd coaxed the man into drinking some water. Sipping through a straw wasn't quite as humiliating as eating from his fingers, he supposed. Besides, thirst was a much more merciless master than hunger.

Brandon shifted restlessly on the cushion, ass obviously sore, too stubborn to get on his knees instead. Jonathan let him for now, but he'd have to address the man's posture soon, not to mention his propensity to fidget. The next few weeks would likely end up being one never-ending patience training session—no doubt that'd go over about as well as a whole herd of deer in his vegetable garden. He smiled, shook his head. *It's your own bloody fault for taking on such a raw sub.*

"Well," he said, at least half to himself. It'd been over a year since he'd had a live-in; he wasn't used to giving quite so much of his focus to another human being these days. "Some of us have to work"—and yes, it *was* satisfying to throw Brandon's own words back in his face and watch them land with such delicious force. He handed the dishes to Brandon with a casual, "Here, wash these."

Brandon's gaze drifted to the dishwasher, his mouth opening, then closing. *Good boy.* He gathered up the dishes he hadn't eaten from and took them to the sink. Jonathan had deliberately left a cube of Gouda on the tray, and as he'd suspected, Brandon snuck it into his mouth as soon as his back was turned.

"I saw that," Jonathan said. "And that's eight, by the way." He made a tutting noise. "Your poor ass. What did it ever do to merit such flagrant disrespect from its owner?" Brandon's back went tense—and wasn't *that* a lovely sight?—but he ran the water, rinsed off the plates, and set them in the drainer with practiced competence. *No dishwasher in his apartment.* Then he turned around and waited, hands at his sides.

Well, maybe he was learning something after all. Jonathan smiled, nodded. "Upstairs, then. Follow two steps behind me at all times. And pay close attention; I may direct you with my hands."

Jonathan set off at a brisk stride toward the staircase, glancing behind him once or twice to make sure Brandon was keeping up. Just barely, and no wonder, with the morning he'd had. Still, best to begin as they meant to go on. No point in coddling him, or he'd start expecting the same treatment every day.

They reached his office, and Jonathan sat down at his desk, opened his laptop, grinned to himself at the riding crop lying beside it. Brandon simply stood there looking at him, shifting from one foot to the other, shivering a little. It was a bit colder up here—comfortable for Jonathan, but he was fully dressed—and Brandon hadn't eaten anything. Not exactly any extra fat on that body to insulate him. Probably had a bit of adrenaline hangover, too. Still, teaching him to hold still was definitely in order.

Jonathan pointed to Brandon, then to the cushion on the floor beside his desk.

Brandon blinked at him as if he didn't understand. *Oh, please.* "Yes, Jonathan?"

"Nine," Jonathan sighed. "Even *dogs* understand pointing."

Brandon's whole face scrunched up, teeth flashing in a snarl. "What happened to not treating me like an animal?" he demanded, yet even as he spoke he was stalking over to the cushion, dropping to his knees.

"If you insist on acting like one," Jonathan said, calm as he could make it, "then what else am I to do? You may not believe this, Brandon, but I'd really rather you not make me punish you like this on day one. And ten, of course; please tell me you're done."

For a second, it looked like he wasn't—he glared up at Jonathan, opened his mouth, but then settled for baring his teeth again. Almost as intimidating as a snarling dog—or probably would've been, at least, if he weren't naked and kneeling.

Speaking of kneeling . . . "Back straight, hold your head up, eyes on me at all times." Brandon looked up at him—still steaming, but obedient at least. "Good, now spread your knees— that's it, a little more, if you please. Shoulder width apart, always." He leaned over in his chair, reached down and gave the head of Brandon's flaccid cock a little pinch. A sound choked and died in Brandon's throat. "You must never deny me access to what's mine, after all." Brandon's hands, on his thighs, curled into fists. "And hands behind your back. Shoulders nice and square. You can lace your fingers together, or hold one wrist in the opposite hand—whichever you prefer."

Brandon did as told, bringing the muscles of his chest, stomach, shoulders, and upper arms into stunning definition. Jonathan just took it all in for a second, reached out to touch, tweaked a nipple hard enough to make Brandon jump and hiss. How tightly coiled he was, how ready to spring up with his fury. But he wouldn't dare now, and time and exhaustion would wear down the urge soon enough, let his gentler urges, his deeper ones, shine through.

"Beautiful," Jonathan whispered, skimming his knuckles across Brandon's cheek, catching his bottom lip with his thumb. Brandon held so still he trembled with it. Probably resisting the urge to bite. "One last thing now: sit back, ass on your heels. Yes, I know it hurts, but you've brought that on yourself. Do it anyway."

Again Brandon obeyed with only half a second's hesitation, the tension in his thighs not so much lessening as just shifting—going from holding himself a hair's width above his heels to bracing against the pain of putting weight on his well-spanked ass. Jonathan couldn't see it, but he rather liked to imagine that Brandon's hands were fisting behind his back.

"Very good," he said. He picked up the crop by his laptop—Brandon's eyes followed, widened at the sight of it. "Now, you stay just like that. Don't move an inch. Don't let your shoulders slouch, or your chin fall, or your spine curve. Don't look around the room." So *of course* Brandon's eyes immediately shifted to the massive reef tank in the wall between the office and the living room. But it seemed an involuntary movement, quickly corrected, and the tank *was* rather hypnotizing, so Jonathan pressed on without calling him on it. "Don't speak. Don't ask for permission to speak. You will be bored. You will get terribly sore. Just focus on me and push through it. And if you lapse?" He tapped the crop ever-so-lightly against Brandon's chest. "I'll correct you immediately. Try not to make me need to; I *do* have work to do, after all."

Surprisingly, it took several minutes before the inevitable fidgeting set in. Just a slight movement, a jerk of Brandon's shoulder, but enough to catch Jonathan's notice. He scooped up the crop and slapped it across Brandon's chest, hard enough to make Brandon clench his jaw. It was such a pleasing sight that Jonathan almost wished Brandon had broken position at the strike so he could hit him again. But Brandon's back remained straight, eyes still focused on Jonathan—albeit with that now-familiar glare. Well, he'd train that out of him soon enough. Give him reasons to smile instead.

Jonathan went back to work. He had to correct Brandon twice more in the next ten minutes, but then not at all for a surprisingly long while. About an hour or so later, he noticed Brandon's gaze taking on a slightly fogged-over look, as if he were about to drift off into that light, hazy trance where time stops dragging and pain falls away. *Good.* He'd not expected Brandon to come anywhere near subspace so soon, but there was no denying the man was one giant mass of untapped potential.

Then Brandon's chin dipped, his head snapping up the moment it touched his chest.

Great. Not subspace, just nodding off. Jonathan snatched up the crop and snapped it hard, twice, over Brandon's left nipple.

Brandon fell right over, one hand braced to the floor, the other hand pressing to the bright red marks blooming on his chest before Jonathan could add another. The crop hit the back of his hand, instead. "Ow, what the f—!"

"That's thirteen. One for falling asleep, one for breaking position so thoroughly, one for speaking out of turn. Would you care to try for fourteen, or would you like to get back into position? And I'll say this now for free and then never again without a demerit: if you *ever* put your hands between yourself and my strike again, I *will* make you sorry."

And he could see it written all over Brandon's face: *Sorrier than I am right now?*

Still, Brandon moved back into position, more or less. His knees weren't spread quite enough, weren't lined up perfectly with his shoulders. Jonathan gave him two hard corrective strikes against the insides of his thighs, and Brandon shouted, doubled over. But he kept his hands behind his back, straightened up quickly—and spread his thighs out.

"It's all right," Jonathan said to the panic writ large on Brandon's face. "I won't fault you for an involuntary reaction. You kept your hands out of the way, and you corrected yourself quickly. That's good enough."

Jonathan went back to work, but it wasn't more than half an hour before Brandon was shaking with the strain of holding position, of holding still, his jaw clenched, his breathing ragged. Truth to tell, Jonathan was surprised he'd lasted this long. Helped to be so fit, he supposed. And that pride and iron will didn't hurt matters either.

"You've done well, Brandon," he said, leaning forward in his chair to smooth a hand over Brandon's trembling shoulder. Brandon's breath hitched, and he tensed like a man fighting himself—likely resisting the urge to jerk away from Jonathan's touch. "Very well for your first day. Why don't you lie down and rest?"

Brandon stared at him as though he thought this was some kind of test, that any second the crop would come out again. But Jonathan shook his head. "I'm serious. You've earned it. Go on, lie down and put your head on the cushion. Stretch those sore muscles; I know you must be aching terribly by now."

Relief swept over Brandon's face—until he started to move, and then it was all clenched eyes and bared teeth and hisses, even a quiet moan that went straight to Jonathan's far-too-long-neglected cock. Good Lord, he couldn't *wait* until tonight when he could let himself go, drive himself over and over into that hot mouth until he *burst* . . .

He cleared his throat, discreetly palmed his aching cock through his pants beneath the desk. Brandon's eyes were jammed shut anyway, though he'd managed to unfold himself, more or less, had slumped onto his side on the floor, cushion wedged beneath one shoulder and his

CAT GRANT · RACHEL HAIMOWITZ

head. He looked absolutely miserable, cold, curled up like a lost child. Jonathan could hear his stomach growling.

He *almost* stood up to get him a blanket. Almost.

CHAPTER 10

ran woke up freezing, hungry, and stiff in a semi-dark room, curled uncomfortably on a hard surface that smelled faintly of lemon. Wood polish? Arrhythmic tapping drifted over his head—fingers on a keyboard. *Jonathan's office.*

Well, he supposed that explained why he was naked.

He wanted to roll over, stretch his aching muscles, curl up tighter to ward off the chill. Felt like he'd been strung up by the wrists and beaten for hours.

Suppose that's not so far from the truth.

But if he moved, Jonathan would know he was awake. And if Jonathan knew he was awake, he'd *want* something from him. And Bran wasn't sure he could handle that right now.

"Good nap?"

Fuck.

The tapping stopped. "Fourteen; I know you're awake."

"I slept like *shit*, Jonathan." He didn't open his eyes—didn't want to look up at Jonathan's infuriating fucking face—but since the jig was up, he rolled onto his stomach, stretched from toes to fingertips—*God, that feels* good—and then curled tight onto his side again, seeking warmth.

"Pity," Jonathan said without an ounce of sympathy. "And goodness, we're going to have to do something about that mouth of yours. Foul language is so . . . *uncivilized.*"

Yeah, well fuck you too, pal.

The typing started up again. "It's nearly eight. Are you hungry?"

He'd slept for over *four hours*? Christ. The last time he'd napped more than fifteen minutes, he'd been too sick to go to work. "You know I am." He drew the pause out as long as he thought he could get away with before adding, "Jonathan."

Tap tap. "Fifteen." *Damn, too long.* "No lip, if you would."

No asking stupid questions, if you would.

Tap tap tap. "Should I even bother offering you supper?"

"Depends, Jonathan. Do I have to eat it from your hand?"

"You know you do." *Tap tap tap.* "Sabrina made a lovely lasagna florentine. Should I only heat a piece for me, then?"

Shit, that sounded good. But he'd eaten at breakfast—admittedly just a piece of toast; he'd been too nervous for anything else—and it's not as if he'd never been hungry before. Hitching from Jersey to California, he'd gone four or five days at a time sometimes without food, *weeks* at a time with nothing more than he could scrounge from truck-stop trashcans or sympathetic passers-by. Hadn't gotten much better when he'd made it to San Fran, either, at least not for a while. If Jonathan thought he could break Bran this way, well, he had another thing coming.

"Sixteen," said Jonathan. Odd, but he sounded weary. Guess it'd been a long day for both of them. Bran kind of liked the idea that he'd worn the little fucker out.

Not so thrilled, though, about the demerits he kept racking up. Better answer the damn question, then. "Yes, Jonathan. Just a piece for you."

In the kitchen, Jonathan made Bran kneel at his feet again. He got it right in one, relieved not to have to endure the wicked little bite of the crop on his nipples or the insides of his thighs—two places, quite frankly, he'd never realized could hurt so much. But holding position for long was not going to be easy. He felt like he'd spent an entire day hauling bricks up a hill; his muscles were protesting to the point of trembling and cramps. And the lack of food wasn't helping. Staying still took all his energy. Staying warm was impossible. At least his ass didn't really hurt anymore, even with his heels digging into it. Which was a damn good thing, seeing as he had a fresh beating coming sometime soon.

Hard to decide which was worse: the thought of suffering that pain on already-abused flesh, or the smell of lasagna wafting down from Jonathan's plate as the man moaned and hummed around bite after bite of hot food.

Of course Jonathan left Bran to do the dishes, and when that was finished, he led Bran back upstairs to his bedroom. Bran half expected the dungeon—okay, more than half, what with *sixteen* hanging over his head—but then, Jonathan hadn't gotten off in a while, so he supposed the bedroom made sense. Especially given the hard-on Jonathan had been sporting all day. If he'd been in Jonathan's shoes, he'd never have lasted this long.

Well, hopefully Jonathan would fuck him *before* he beat him. Bran wasn't looking forward to either, but being used would be ten times worse with a sore ass.

Being used? Two weeks ago, sex with Jonathan would've thrilled you.

Yeah, well, things change.

Speaking of, Jonathan's bedroom was rather conspicuously different than the last time Bran had seen it: a yoga mat lay on the floor at the foot of the bed, complete with pillow and knit blanket. No question of what that was for. He turned his gaze from the rough approximation of a bed to Jonathan's face and said, "Still not treating me like an animal, then?" Why the fuck not—sixteen, seventeen, what difference did it make?

"You don't understand yet," Jonathan said, "but you will. Are you paying attention? What number are you on?"

"Twelve," Bran lied.

Jonathan *tsked*, shook his head. "Oh Brandon, Brandon . . . give me a *little* credit. You know that makes it eighteen, right?"

"Yeah," he sighed. He'd known before he'd opened his mouth. "Jonathan."

"Have a seat." Jonathan waved him to the yoga mat. "Back against the footboard. I'll be tying you up now." Added, clearly tired, "Will you fight me?"

Bran thought about it for a second, but some things just weren't worth the trouble. Besides, the last two times Jonathan had bound him, he'd come out his fucking *ears*. "No, Jonathan."

He sat as directed. The yoga mat wasn't much better than the floor, and for all he'd thought his ass had healed, it reminded him now how unhappy it was. The footboard was wrought iron, black, smooth, shaped into post-modern squares each big enough to put a fist or a foot through. *Or a set of handcuffs.* Shocking cold against his naked back. He let his legs splay out in front of him. The gleaming hardwood was cold against his heels.

Jonathan rummaged in a wardrobe, came back with a red paisley bandana and an armful of smooth black rope. Nylon. Five coils, he realized, when Jonathan shook them out, each no more than a few yards long.

He felt surprisingly calm about the whole thing when Jonathan took his right arm and stretched it all the way out, tied his wrist near head-level. Jonathan didn't put the rope through an O-ring on his cuff, but rather pushed the cuff back as far as it'd go and coiled the rope around

Bran's wrist. He must have raised an eyebrow at that or something, because Jonathan said as he took Bran's left wrist, "You move too much. You'll hurt yourself." A pause, a thumb swiping over the bruising at the base of his thumb. "You already have."

Yeah, and you had nothing to do with that, pal.

Jonathan stretched out Bran's left arm, secured that to the footboard as well. Guess it helped to have a king-sized bed when you were laying out your sex slave for the night.

The next coil of rope went around his waist, not tight enough to dig, but snug enough to feel—and to keep his back and ass pressed firmly to the footboard. Which, he supposed, meant Jonathan planned to use his mouth, since even his hands were unavailable now.

Huh, wonder what he'd do if I bit him . . .

He had to admit, the thought held some appeal.

"Knee up, please," Jonathan said, squatting between Bran's legs and tapping his right thigh. Bran eyed the rope in Jonathan's hand and bit his lip. There was no way this could end well for him, letting Jonathan spread his thighs like that, expose his genitals. But what was he gonna do—kick the guy?

Actually . . .

No, he wasn't that stupid. *Or suicidal.* He pulled his leg up right as Jonathan started to say, "Nineteen." Did that count? Jonathan didn't take it back as he started wrapping rope in a figure-eight around Bran's shin and thigh to keep his knee bent, so he supposed it did.

Jonathan gave the rope a good tug, and Bran tried to straighten his leg out and couldn't. What a strange sensation. Not bad, not even uncomfortable, just . . . *strange.*

And kind of worrisome, quite frankly, when Jonathan pushed Bran's bent leg out to the side and anchored it to the footboard, opening him up wide.

Jonathan's fingers skated over the inside of his thigh, just the barest hint of pressure and fingernails, and Bran jerked, bit back a laugh. He was *ticklish*? When had that happened?

Great. Never gonna live that *down, Bran.*

Jonathan did it again, and that impish fucking grin crawled onto his face. "I see you've been keeping secrets from me, Brandon," he said, bringing both hands to bear now on Bran's unprotected thigh. Bran couldn't hold back the laugh this time, jerked so hard he banged his head on the footboard. "Fuck, please!" he managed between gasps, his one free limb kicking out and accidentally catching Jonathan on the shin—

Oh, shit.

Jonathan stopped, turned to look at him, his face just inches from Bran's own. Bran was panting, desperate to scratch his thigh and, curiously enough, hard again. Even though Jonathan was probably going to kill him for what he'd done.

Jonathan's hands came up to Bran's face, and he flinched away but then caught himself, let Jonathan touch him, fingers curling round his ears, thumbs stroking across his cheeks. "It's okay," Jonathan said. "It's my fault. I should have finished binding you first."

Relieved as Bran was, he couldn't stop thinking, *Please don't fucking tickle me again. Please.*

One of Jonathan's thumbs dipped down from Bran's cheek and swept over his mouth. Bran parted his lips, even though Jonathan hadn't asked him to. Instinct, he supposed.

God, he could smell a faint echo of tomato sauce on Jonathan's skin.

Jonathan left his thumb there, resting against Bran's teeth, and just stared and stared. Okay, this was starting to get weird. Was he gonna say something? Do something? Or just squat here forever?

At last Jonathan stood up, stepped back, grabbed the last coil of rope and wrapped it around Bran's free ankle and foot. The other end he secured to an O-ring that'd been hiding flush beneath the corner of a nearby area rug, pulling Bran's leg straight and open just wide enough to strain a little. Bran tried not to think too hard about the fact that he couldn't turn his foot—that the tender inside of his thigh (and his even more tender cock and balls) was right there for Jonathan to do with as he wished. He also tried not to think too hard about where else Jonathan might be hiding rings and hooks, where else he might be able to bind him. In the kitchen for the maid or cook to see? In front of a window for the whole fucking *world* to see?

Turned out he fucking *sucked* at the whole not-thinking-too-hard thing.

Speaking of too hard . . . his dick was definitely interested in the proceedings, the traitorous thing. It twitched against his thigh—and thank God he was tied up, or he wouldn't have been able to keep from squirming. Didn't stop Jonathan's gaze from zeroing right in on it—or that fucking smug smirk from spreading across his lips as he unzipped his fly and pulled out his own erect dick.

The sight of that single bead of pre-cum pooled at the tip made Bran suck in a breath, his dick growing stiffer.

The little fucker's programmed it to sit up and beg every time he ties you up. Doesn't mean anything.

Jonathan took his own dick in hand, gave it a few quick strokes— not that it needed it. He already looked hard enough to drill concrete. Jesus, had he really been that aroused all day? Then he picked up the bandana off the floor and stuffed it into Bran's right hand. "In a moment you won't be able to speak. This handkerchief means 'red.' Drop it and I'll stop. Do you understand?"

A safeword for a face-fuck. Bran didn't know whether to be worried that Jonathan thought he might need one or impressed at Jonathan's cleverness. Didn't really matter, though, so he just nodded and said, "Yes, Jonathan."

Jonathan nodded back. "Good. Now relax and breathe through your nose. I'm not going to choke you."

Then he sank his fingers into Bran's hair and shoved all the way in his mouth. Bran fought back panic—*the handkerchief, remember you have the handkerchief*—as the tip of Jonathan's dick bumped against the back of his throat, just like that night in the alley. Only this time he didn't have the option of getting up and walking away. Hell, he couldn't even *move*.

Not that he didn't try—twisting his wrists, pulling hard against the rope around his waist. But Jonathan's knots held tight, no give in them at all. Black spots danced in front of his eyes, chest hitching from lack of air, fingers beginning to slacken around the handkerchief—until he remembered what Jonathan had told him. *Breathe through your nose, moron. It's not like you've never done this before.*

True, but it'd been awhile, and he'd never been that good at it. Never really liked it enough to be good at it, and most of his flings had been more than willing to suck him without reciprocation. And he *could* stop this if he needed to. But maybe if he did his best here, Jonathan would take it easy on him when it came time to dish out his next beating.

Jonathan wasn't even that big, but tonight it felt like he was cramming out Bran's fucking teeth. Maybe he could speed this up; he tried to give Jonathan a flick of his tongue, but the man just kept going, stroking in and out in a slow, steady rhythm until Bran's jaw hurt so bad he had to pull away, had to close his fucking mouth, just for a second, just—

Jonathan's fist clenched tight in his hair and gave him a little shake. He cried out, tried to protest, to warn him, to jerk away, but Jonathan just held him fast, fucked him deeper, started gagging him in earnest and he squeezed his eyes closed against the pain and the urge to puke and the need to *breathe*, grunted around Jonathan's dick, then tried to scream around it when Jonathan *wouldn't fucking listen*, and it was, quite frankly, the fucker's own fucking fault when Bran couldn't hold himself back anymore and closed his teeth, just a little, around Jonathan's dick.

Jonathan pulled free of Bran's mouth with a grunt, lips tightening into a scowl. "What did you do that for?"

What the fuck did *he* have to be angry about? Bran just glared at him, dragging in deep breaths. Anything he said was bound to get him in more trouble.

Jonathan glared back. "Is there something you want to say?"

Yellow. Red. What fucking difference did it make? His ass was gonna end up black and blue by the end of the night anyway.

"Fuck. You," Bran rasped.

Jonathan's gaze went stone cold. He grabbed Bran's hair again in one hand, yanked his head as far away from the footboard as his bindings would allow, and smacked him.

The blow rattled his teeth, sheeted his vision. He hadn't been hit like that in years. Hadn't *allowed* it. Not without giving as good as he got. Not without sending the other guy to the fucking hospital. At least Jonathan had pulled his head away from the footboard, or he'd have cracked his skull on it.

He was expecting another strike, but Jonathan just let him go. Hardness in his eyes, but no real anger. Hadn't been, Bran realized, even when he'd struck him, and Bran couldn't decide if that perfect fucking control made things better or worse.

"I told you," Jonathan said, "I'm not going to choke you. If you hadn't tensed up, you would've been fine. You *were* fine; you were hard until a second ago."

Like he needed to be reminded.

He didn't say "fuck you" again—didn't dare with that frigid glint still shining in Jonathan's eyes and the hot imprint of the man's palm on his cheek—but the look he shot Jonathan said it all.

"Fine," Jonathan said. "I was going easy on you, but I can see the effort's wasted. Maybe you'll like it better this way. At least it'll be over faster."

And with that, he twisted his fingers hard in Bran's hair and grabbed him at the pressure points at the hinge of his jaw, forcing his mouth open. Then he shoved his dick back in.

He thrust deep into Bran's mouth and just kept going, kept gagging him, banging over and over into the back of his throat. Hot tears spilled down his cheeks, chest shaking with rage and lack of oxygen.

Serve him right if I puked on him.

His jaw was throbbing, his throat so sore he'd probably lose his voice. All he had to do was drop the handkerchief, and it would stop. But what would Jonathan do to him *then*? How would the man make him pay for quitting on a stupid little blowjob—and worse, for denying Jonathan his orgasm?

Before he could decide whether it was worth finding out or not, Jonathan pulled back until just the crown of his dick remained inside Bran's mouth. "Suck it," he ordered.

Just like that night in the alley, when Jonathan had twisted his wrist until he'd fallen to his knees in that puddle. *When I came in my fucking pants*. He realized that his lips had closed around Jonathan's dick—that his cheeks had hollowed, that he was sucking like a good little sex slave and that he was *aroused* by it, Goddamn it—when Jonathan burst in his mouth.

It was fucking *disgusting*, salty and bitter and slimy, but with Jonathan still clamping onto his jaw, he had no choice but to swallow or hold it in his mouth. And no fucking *way* was he swallowing this asshole's spunk. *Soon as he lets go of me, I'm spitting it all over him.*

Jonathan's fingers dug even tighter into his jaw, pain so sharp he cried out behind closed lips. "Swallow," Jonathan ordered.

Bran glared at him.

Jonathan's hand clenched in his hair with just as much force as the fingers at the hinge of his jaw. He'd have gasped if he could've opened his mouth. Tears pricked at his eyes again. He squeezed them shut, felt wetness track down one cheek. *Fuck,* he really needed Jonathan to let go of his fucking jaw.

"You don't want to eat my food, fine. But you *will* take nourishment from me one way or another. And you will *not* disrespect me by spitting that out. *Swallow*."

Those fingers tightened even more somehow, and the one tear turned into five or six. Bran strained against his bindings so hard he imagined the footboard bending. He couldn't have unclenched his own fists for all the money in the world.

But what did it matter? Nothing he did or didn't do now would erase that look of cold fury from Jonathan's face. Nor could he break Jonathan's icy control any more than Jonathan could break Bran's iron will. Stalemate.

Except for the part where he gets to hurt you until you cry. All you get to do is irritate him.

Hardly seemed fair. Or very smart, quite frankly, and *God* but this spunk on his tongue was getting grosser by the second, collecting there with all the spit he hadn't swallowed either. He turned his eyes up to Jonathan—the only part of himself he could even move right now—and Jonathan flashed him a nasty grin, let go of his hair, and instead pinched his nose shut.

Well, fuck.

"Remember that part where I said I'm not going to choke you?" Jonathan asked. "Well, apologies; it seems I may have been a bit premature in my assessment."

God, who *talked* like that?

"Swallow, and I'll let you breathe."

Bran's chest hitched, muscles spasming. It hurt, fuck, *everything* hurt, his jaw felt broken in a thousand places, and he tried to jerk his head away from that iron grip but couldn't and his vision was starting to swim and he was pretty sure he was wasting his last precious drops of air screaming behind Jonathan's hand—

And then suddenly he was free—had he dropped the handkerchief without realizing?—and he went to hock the glob of cum into Jonathan's smug face and realized it was gone. He'd fucking swallowed it? When had he fucking swallowed it?

"Get away from me," he rasped.

Jonathan leaned in close, swiped a thumb across a drop of cum on Bran's lower lip. Bran snapped his teeth at him, grinned in feral satisfaction as Jonathan snatched his hand away.

"I don't think," Jonathan said as he tucked himself back into his pants, his face and voice gone oddly neutral, "they make numbers high enough to account for your behavior these last several minutes. So I'll ask you once more before we move on to showing you the myriad errors of your ways . . . Would you like to cancel our contract?"

"You're not getting rid of me that easy," Bran growled without hesitation, then wished he hadn't; *fuck*, his throat hurt. Added, since he'd be sticking around to face the music, "Jonathan."

"Very well, then." Calm as ever, Jonathan plucked the handkerchief from Bran's fist—didn't need it anymore now that he could curse at Jonathan out loud, he supposed—turned on his heel, and headed into the wardrobe. He came back a moment later with a riding crop in his hand, smiled and slapped it against his palm, then laid it on the floor near Bran's outstretched leg. Could be worse; Bran had gotten through the croppings this afternoon just fine.

Then Jonathan went back into the wardrobe again. This time he came back with a big-ass wooden paddle. Looked like a fucking boat oar with three Greek letters carved into it. Jonathan had sworn he'd never injure him, but if he hit him with that thing while he was still tied to the footboard . . . He swallowed hard, watched carefully as Jonathan placed the paddle beside the riding crop on the floor.

A Costco-sized pump-bottle of lube came next. Who used *that* much lube? Bran's gaze flicked from the lube to the paddle and crop. What the fuck was going on here?

Jonathan shot him a bemused grin, then disappeared back into the wardrobe.

How much crap did he *have* in there? Thing must've reached right through to fucking Narnia.

What'll he bring out next? A fucking lamppost*?*

Well, that would explain the lube . . .

What Jonathan came back with instead was actually worse. Bran didn't even recognize it for a second, all black and shiny rubber as it was, but then Jonathan gestured toward him with it, grinning wide, and he realized it was a fist. A fucking rubber fist. On an *arm*.

"Calm down before you hurt yourself," Jonathan said, and Bran realized he was struggling, yanking over and over at the ropes around his wrists and outstretched leg. Breathing hard, sweating bullets. Why the hell couldn't Jonathan just beat him and get it over with?

"Why, would that take all the fun out of it for you?"

Jonathan froze, eyes narrowed, then spun around and stalked back to the wardrobe. This time he came back with . . . was that a *Taser*? So much for calming down.

"Hey, man . . ." Bran whispered, licking at frozen lips. "Look, I didn't mean—"

Jonathan flicked the stun gun on, triggered it. Bright blue electricity arced between the contact points. "I know *exactly* what you meant," he said, kneeling between Bran's legs and pressing the contacts to his neck, right below the ear. Bran squeezed his eyes shut, jerked his head away with a whimper, but Jonathan just grabbed him by the hair and held him still.

"Please, Jonathan . . ." God, he could barely get the words out, couldn't suck in air deep enough or fast enough and *Jesus fuck,* Jonathan was gonna *kill* him—

"Shhh," Jonathan said as he ran the stun gun down Bran's throat, along his collarbone, lingered long at his left nipple. "You talk too much, Brandon. You know that, don't you?"

Jonathan let go of his hair, and he nodded his head like a fucking bobble doll. "Please don't do this, Jonathan." A panting rasp, hardly intelligible. He followed the stun gun with his eyes as Jonathan dragged it down his belly. Couldn't help it. Thought he might fucking puke when he realized where it was going, tried to beg again but only managed a whimper.

"Shhh," Jonathan repeated, dragging the contacts down Bran's sweat-slicked skin, down between his legs where his pubic hair used to live, touched the base of his dick with it and Bran jerked, whimpered again, pulled so hard against his bindings that pain flashed bright in his elbows, wrists, and shoulders.

"Easy now." Soothing. Chiding. The contacts slid lower, around the back of his dick, nestled with a gasp-inducing shove against his balls. Jonathan leaned forward, slid his free hand around the back of Bran's neck. Gentle, a lover's touch. So was the kiss that followed, soft, only the faintest hint of tongue, and Bran kissed him back like his fucking life depended on it, then tried to pull away when he ran out of air but Jonathan wouldn't let him. He moaned against those full, demanding lips—*please let me go, please don't do this*—and at last Jonathan pulled away, kissed him on the forehead, and stood.

Bran sagged in his bindings like someone had dropped a brick on his head, relief so strong he might have wet himself if he'd been even a little less attentive. He couldn't catch his breath, could still feel those twin cold contacts between his balls, even though Jonathan had laid the stun gun on the floor beside all the other implements of torture.

Bran had been so fucking scared, it only occurred to him as Jonathan headed back to the wardrobe—*Oh God, what now?*—that he could have, *should* have, said *yellow.*

"Close your eyes," Jonathan called from the wardrobe.

Bran wasn't sure he could right now, no matter how much he didn't want to piss Jonathan off.

Jonathan was shutting the wardrobe doors, something small and black in one hand. "Are they closed?"

Bran shuddered, swallowed audibly. "No, Jonathan," he said, voice shaking as hard as the rest of him. "But I . . ."

Jonathan turned to face him, crossed the room with his hands behind his back. Odd, but he didn't look angry at all, had that same soft-focus look he'd had when he'd pulled back from the kiss. "But you *want* to, yes? You're *trying*?"

Mind reading again. *Thank God.* Bran nodded, simultaneously trying to look at what Jonathan was hiding behind his back and talk himself into closing his eyes. Surprise surprise, neither worked. And Jonathan was *looking* at him, expectant, until he remembered . . . "Yes, Jonathan. I'm trying. I'm . . ."

Fucking terrified.

Jonathan knelt between Bran's thighs and touched the back of one hand to Bran's cheek. "It's all right," he murmured. "Say it. Say the words, and I'll help you."

Bran caught himself leaning into Jonathan's touch—*a kindness, any kindness in this place.* Tried to stop his chest from heaving, tried to gather enough moisture to speak. "I'm . . ." Shit, why was this so hard? Why couldn't he just admit it?

Fucking pride. Keeps getting you into trouble, you dumb fuck.

"Yes?" Jonathan asked, still stroking-stroking at Bran's cheek with the backs of his fingers. "You're strong, Brandon. Stronger than you know. You can say it. It's nothing to be ashamed of."

Bran sucked in a huge breath, and whispered on the exhale, "You fucking *terrify* me."

He half expected Jonathan to hit him for that, but Jonathan's whole face lit up, and he leaned in and kissed him again, all soft and sweet like lovers, and murmured against his lips, "There, that wasn't so hard, now was it?"

Ha.

"Don't you feel better now?"

Oddly? Kinda yeah. "I guess, Jonathan."

Jonathan pulled his other hand out from behind his back, held it up in front of Bran's eyes. He was holding a blindfold—a black leather blindfold. "I promised I'd help you and I meant it." It fastened with a

Velcro strap; Jonathan pulled the ends apart with a ripping sound that cut right through Bran's jagged nerves. Yet despite his panic, he held his head still, let Jonathan fasten it tight without a fight.

"See? Now you don't have to keep your eyes closed." Another brush of lips on lips—this one took him by surprise, he twitched but then caught himself, kissed back like Jonathan no doubt wanted him to. "It'll be over before you know it," Jonathan promised.

The next moments crawled by as Bran listened to Jonathan's footsteps move away and then back. What the hell was he doing? Which instrument of torture had he decided to use first?

God, please, not the fist. Please *not the fist.* It'd be one thing if Jonathan meant to hit him with it, but Bran wasn't stupid enough to believe that. Shoving that thing up his ass would tear him apart, lube or no lube.

But would it really be worse than that fucking stun gun?

Guess he'd find out soon enough.

He whipped his head around at a soft whooshing sound, the slap of leather against skin. Had to be Jonathan smacking the crop against his palm. Well, okay. That much he could take. Couldn't be any worse than Jonathan's hand.

At least that's what he thought until the first finger of fire seared across his nipple, right where Jonathan had smacked him that afternoon. It caught him so much by surprise he actually *forgot* to scream. Then the next blow rained down, this time on the opposite nipple. He groaned and threw his head back, teeth clenched. It was the only way to keep from crying out.

Jonathan worked his way down Bran's torso in tiny increments, painting white-hot agony on his skin, every blow laid down with merciless precision. Chest, belly, tops of his thighs. Insides of his thighs. No fucking way to keep quiet through that. A moment's break in the rhythm, and then three hard raps on the sole of his exposed foot, vicious enough to make his toes curl.

Then the blindfold came off, damp with sweat and tears he hadn't even realized he'd shed. Jonathan knelt beside him and cradled his face in both hands, smoothed back the hair plastered to his forehead.

"You are so beautiful," Jonathan murmured. "And you took that so well. Thank you, Brandon. You've pleased me very much."

Relief blossomed in Bran's chest, right alongside the gallons of adrenaline still making his heart thrash. For several long moments he just tried to remember how to breathe like a normal person, how not to shake apart at the fucking seams.

But then, drawn as if by magnets, his gaze traveled to the collection of toys piled on the carpet. Jesus, what if Jonathan wasn't done yet?

"Don't worry, it's over," Jonathan said, then reached out to loosen the rope around his outstretched leg. God, it felt so damn good to be able to move it again, even if the slight pins-and-needles sensation made him wince.

But that was nothing compared to the cramping in his other leg, the one that'd been drawn up to his chest for the last however long. He couldn't suppress a moan as the blood flowed back into it, or as Jonathan dug strong fingers into his aching quads, kneading out a whole endless day's worth of tension.

"Mmmf," he mumbled, head lolling back against the footboard, eyes drifting closed. "Please, don't stop."

Jonathan chuckled, but still his fingers worked their magic. "You're not two minutes off your last punishment," he said, voice light, filled with humor. "You want to make me start counting again *already*?"

"Sorry, Jonathan," Bran murmured. Hard to be afraid when he was so wrung out. Besides, for once it sounded like Jonathan didn't actually mean it. Still, better not slip again. Not tonight.

Once the ache in his leg subsided to a dull throb, Jonathan moved up to Bran's right wrist. "Brace yourself, this will be a shock."

Understatement of the century. He hadn't been tied cruelly, or at least it hadn't felt that way at the start, but he'd been tied long and he'd struggled hard. When Jonathan freed his hand and the blood rushed back into his strained muscles and bruised wrist, the pain was so intense he hazed out for a second.

He came back to himself with his face buried in Jonathan's throat, Jonathan's hand at the nape of his neck, stroking softly. "It's okay, it's okay," Jonathan whispered. Jonathan's other hand was stroking down his arm, soothing his trembling muscles. *God,* felt like he'd sprained every single one of them, right down to the little ones in the back of his hand.

One more wrist untied, another wave of pain, and Jonathan held him through it until he could breathe without shuddering. Then Jonathan eased him down onto the mat, helped him roll onto his back.

"I'll be right back," Jonathan said, draping the blanket over him. Bran sighed; so soft and warm and fuzzy.

Jonathan reappeared a minute later with a washcloth and a glass of water with a straw. He helped Bran sit, held the water out. Bran didn't hesitate before wrapping his lips around the straw and taking a deep pull.

"Here," Jonathan said, moving the water just out of reach and offering two white pills instead. "Ibuprofen."

Bran didn't need to be told twice. He opened his mouth and let Jonathan place them on his tongue like some fucking baby bird, drank from the straw when Jonathan offered it again. When the glass was empty, Jonathan put it down, picked up the washcloth instead. He wiped Bran down just like that night he'd handcuffed Bran to his bed, except this time he was more careful, what with all the welts he'd left.

"Need to water the grass?" Jonathan asked. A little, but in truth, he couldn't be bothered right now. Wasn't sure he could get his feet under him even with Jonathan's help, and his shoulders and arms still hurt too much to hold himself up. His back teeth would be floating by morning, but that was hours away yet, and he'd deal with it then.

For now, he just shook his head, then mumbled, "No, Jonathan." Added, "Permission to speak?" It came out slurred; he sounded like a fucking drunk.

"Go ahead," Jonathan said, slipping an arm around his shoulders and lowering him back to the yoga mat.

"I just want to sleep, Jonathan. Is that all right?"

Jonathan hovered over him, smiling at him like a favored child. He reached out, brushed the hair from Bran's forehead. "Of course." Jonathan leaned in, kissed the tip of his nose, then pulled the blanket back over him and walked away.

Bran closed his eyes, ready to pass out right there on the hard floor, never mind the lights were still on, never mind he hadn't brushed his teeth, never mind his stomach was grumbling and his bladder wasn't quite comfortably empty and his body was fucking *screaming* at him and this was only his *first fucking day*. But then Jonathan squatted down beside him again and said, "Shoulders up," and Bran opened his eyes to see the man holding out a heating pad.

Oh, fuck *yes.*

He lifted his head, let Jonathan slide an arm beneath his shoulders and ease him off the mat just enough to slide the pad in. It was already warm, big enough to cover half his back and neck, both his shoulders, even bleed heat into his triceps. He may or may not have made a *completely* undignified moan as he settled back against it, but what the fuck. It wasn't as if he hadn't checked his dignity at the door the moment he'd stepped through that fucking elevator.

ran cracked his eyes open, agony slicing through his brain. And his legs. And his arms and back. Hell, every fucking fiber of his body.

All this from a riding crop and a few coils of rope?

The thought of all those other, much scarier-looking "toys" down in the dungeon made him shudder. He rolled over, his bladder aching. Jesus Christ, was there any part of him that *didn't* hurt?

Maybe his hair, but only because most of it was gone. No, wait, that hurt too, where Jonathan had grabbed it. Didn't exactly help his headache. Which, no wonder. He hadn't had any caffeine since yesterday morning, and he was usually a pot-a-day man.

His *one* indulgence. And he was seriously starting to regret it now.

He sat up very slowly, every muscle in his back protesting. The heating pad had shut off during the night, and he couldn't figure out how to turn it back on again. A soft snore floated through the air—a tiny whistling sound. Fucking irritating.

He lifted his head to confirm Jonathan was still asleep, then darted a glance toward the bathroom. Should he risk waking Jonathan to ask permission, or should he just get up and use the toilet? Satisfying as the thought of waking Jonathan was, if it were Bran, he would've preferred to remain sleeping.

Straightening up as gingerly as he could, he tiptoed to the bathroom and closed the door behind him. He didn't even need to turn on the light; there was enough sunshine pouring in through the window. Jesus, what time was it? He wasn't used to getting up after the sun. He took a quick but oh-so-satisfying piss, flushed, and headed back to the bedroom—

Where Jonathan was sitting on the edge of the bed, arms folded over his chest. "You aren't nearly as stealthy as you think you are."

"Um . . . sorry," Bran said. "Jonathan. I didn't think you'd want me to wake you up."

"Actually, I would have preferred you ask permission," he said around a yawn. "I'll let it go this time because I didn't give you clear instructions. But now you know." He pointed at the robe hanging on the bathroom door. Bran handed it to him. "Well, since we're up, follow me."

Bran nearly asked where they were going, but caught himself just in time and followed Jonathan mutely downstairs. For a moment he dared to hope it was just to the kitchen—though he didn't entertain fantasies of either eating with utensils or having a nice steaming cup of black coffee. But they turned right instead of left at the bottom of the stairs, which left only the dungeon.

Bran's feet tried to freeze, and he stumbled over them.

"You all right?" Jonathan asked, eyeing Bran over his shoulder.

Bran nodded, but he was pretty damn sure Jonathan knew better. He was so busy thinking *Not again, not yet, too soon* that he forgot to answer Jonathan out loud.

"One," Jonathan said, yawning again.

What's the matter, Jonathan? Wear yourself out wailing on me yesterday?

"Come on." Jonathan reached back to grab Bran's wrist, and only then did Bran realize he'd stopped moving. "Don't worry, I'm not going to hurt you."

He sure said that an awful lot for a guy who couldn't seem to *stop* hurting him.

Jonathan led him into—and, thankfully, straight through—the dungeon, to the bathroom at the back. "I expect you to groom yourself without any supervision from me. I want you clean inside and out—and that means *two* passes with the shower shot, not the one I let you get away with yesterday, though the second need only be a quick rinse, just a little water and no need to hold it. I also expect you to be clean-shaven on your face, groin, and armpits; and to brush and floss your teeth and comb your hair. No shaving nicks, no missed spots, no stray hairs, no rough patches—you'll be punished for any and all. And the most important rule? Don't you *dare* touch yourself except to wash and groom. Your body isn't yours to pleasure anymore, it's *mine*, and I expect you to be ready to perform for me at all times. Are we clear?"

Truth be told, he was so worn out and fucked out he hadn't even contemplated touching himself. Strange, then, how Jonathan's words— *be ready to perform for me at all times*—sent a little flutter through his stomach, and a not so little flutter that settled in his balls, made his dick twitch. "Yes, Jonathan."

"Good. Lastly, I expect all this done before I wake up each morning. Which is usually no later than seven. And the bathroom had better be spotless when you're done with it. If I come down here and find so much as one hair in the sink, it's coming out of your hide."

Welcome to fucking boot camp, Bran.

Jonathan lifted the enema nozzle from its cradle and thrust it toward him. He shifted from one foot to the other. "Um . . . should I do that now, Jonathan?"

"Yes, since you only have"—Jonathan consulted his watch—"well, you're actually 90 minutes late, but let's say you have until nine. That's half an hour. Which should be at least ten minutes more than you actually need if you stay focused."

Bran turned on the water, his gaze zeroing back in on that damn nozzle Jonathan had shoved up his ass. How the hell was he supposed to use that thing?

"Would you like me to give you a demonstration?" Jonathan asked, once more in mind-reader mode.

When had his life become so fucking absurdly embarrassing? Oh, that's right—yesterday. And fuck Jonathan for it. "Sure, Jonathan," he replied. "Why don't you bend over, and I'll watch?"

"That's two." Jonathan shook his head, mock-sympathetic. "If you've already forgotten how much these demerits hurt, then clearly I haven't been hitting you hard enough. My apologies"—he clasped Bran on one bare shoulder—"I'll simply have to do better next time."

Awake for fifteen minutes and I already *want to strangle him.* Didn't bode well at all.

God, he needed a cup of coffee.

Still, if he didn't want to hurt himself with that nozzle, he was going to need some help. "Yes, Jonathan. I'd like you to show me how to use the . . . shower thing."

Jonathan still had it in his hand, so he merely stepped over to the shower and flipped a switch at the base of the shower head. "You divert the water from the shower head to the nozzle here. Test the water on the inside of your arm before you insert the nozzle, and lube it first as well. Otherwise you'll get a very unpleasant surprise. If the water's too hot, it will burn. If it's too cold, you'll cramp. Do it slowly, or you'll cramp. Don't use too much water, or you'll cramp."

"So what you're telling me is, I'm going to cramp?"

Jonathan chuckled, but that didn't stop him from saying, "Four. What I'm telling you is not to be careless or hasty. You didn't cramp when I did it, right?"

By the end, he'd felt like he was about to, but, "No, Jonathan."

"All right, then." Jonathan handed him the nozzle. "Go ahead."

He took it gingerly between thumb and forefinger. "Uh . . . can I ask you something, Jonathan?"

"Very good. Yes, you may ask."

"You want me to do this now? With you standing here?" He swallowed hard. "Jonathan?"

"Why not? You did it with me here yesterday."

"But . . . but I *didn't* do it yesterday. *You* did."

"Five." Jonathan leaned in, peered at him. "You seem quite out of sorts this morning. What's wrong?"

"I'm sore," he said, then added a hasty, "Jonathan," when he realized he'd nearly gone two in a row on that mistake. "And I'm not used to skipping my morning coffee." His growling stomach added to his list of complaints, but he didn't dare give it voice; Jonathan would just tell him he'd brought that one on himself. "Have a bit of a raging headache, actually," he admitted instead. "Jonathan."

Like a fussy mother, Jonathan pressed the back of his hand to Bran's forehead. After a few moments, he declared, "Probably just need to eat." Did that mean he'd *let* him? No, Bran decided, probably not. "And no coffee until you've earned it, which means no demerits for an entire day." A wan smile, and then, "I suspect your contract will be up before *that* happens. Anyway, take care of yourself. You're down to twenty-two minutes. I'll be in my office. Don't be late."

Then he turned and left, leaving Bran standing there staring at that stupid fucking nozzle.

Bran climbed in the shower, letting out a yell at the first blast of hot water on fresh welts. He nearly slipped and cracked his head on the tile. *What a way to die—on the floor of a dungeon shower with a fucking enema nozzle dangling over my head.* Once the shock wore off, he lathered up with Jonathan's ridiculous organic soap, scrubbing very carefully around the mass of welts his torso and inner thighs had become. The hot water on his unmarked skin actually felt pretty amazing, and he hadn't craved a good wash so much in years. He washed his hair next, rinsed again, scalp still sore where Jonathan had pulled his hair. Which, come to think of it, was pretty much everywhere.

Well, nothing left to do but the damn fucking enema. But . . . would Jonathan even *know* if he skipped it?

He did have his tongue halfway up your colon yesterday, idiot. And fuck Jonathan and fuck his own dick for getting excited at the memory of it.

He sighed. Well, best to get it over with as quickly as he could.

He turned the heat down, tested the temperature on the inside of his arm, just like Jonathan had told him. A little lower, barely lukewarm. That ought to do. He grabbed the tube of lubricant from the soap dish and squirted some on the end of the nozzle, and in it went.

It actually felt pretty good. *Really* good, in fact. Bigger than a thumb, smaller than a dick. Smooth enough not to hurt. He angled it toward his prostate, and damn if his dick didn't stand up and salute. Well, Jesus, no wonder—he hadn't gotten off since yesterday morning, and this entire fucking atmosphere seemed purpose-built to keep him perpetually horny. One little tug—what could it hurt? Jonathan would never know. Might help him *stop* hurting—or at least make him forget how sore he was for a few minutes.

He was already so aroused he nearly came the second he wrapped his fist around his dick. Must be the thrill of being caught, because it sure as fuck wasn't the thought of how he'd spent the night. Or the evening before it.

Although he did have to admit to a certain fondness for the tender Jonathan who'd—

Shit. Please tell me I did not *just come thinking of Jonathan being* tender.

Except for the part where he had, apparently. Splattered the far wall of the shower and everything.

He grabbed the shower head from its cradle and rinsed off the wall, then put it back. Reconsidered and took a long drink from the shower head before re-hanging it. For a second he almost forgot he still had the damn nozzle up his ass. He reached behind him to make sure it was seated properly before flipping the switch to divert the water from shower to nozzle.

It didn't feel so bad at first—a little cooler than he'd have liked, but that was okay. Everything seemed fine, so he turned up the flow—and promptly doubled over, gut cramping. Just like Jonathan had warned him.

He sank to his knees, groaning, until he remembered to turn the fucking water off. Jesus, how the hell was he supposed to do this *twice*? Yanked the nozzle out hard enough to hurt himself, clenching against the urge to let his bowels void right then and there. No fucking way did he want to clean *that* up.

He practically had to crawl to the toilet, but he made it just in time. Never felt such incredible relief in his life. How many more minutes did he have left? Didn't matter—it'd take as long as it took. Jonathan would find some excuse to punish him no matter what he did.

When he was finally done, he staggered to his feet—sighing at the lack of pain in his gut, if not the rest of his body—and climbed back in for a second go. Impatient as he was to get this over with, he went much more slowly this time. Jonathan hurt him plenty; no reason for him to add to the pile himself.

He toweled off, then shaved—and shaved and *shaved*. A week's worth of artful stubble . . . no way was he finishing in half an hour, and of course, Jonathan had to know that. Well, let the little fucker wait.

Pits next—God, he felt like a fucking *girl*; who shaved their *armpits*?—which took longer than he'd have thought. He kept missing bits, and the hair was too long. Clogged the damn razor right up. Hopefully Jonathan would give him a new one before he had to shave his face again, or things wouldn't be pretty.

At last he got around to combing his hair, brushing his teeth, and cleaning up the bathroom—which took for-fucking-ever, with all the hair in the sink—then headed down the hallway, poking his head into the kitchen as he passed.

Damn, the cook was there, kneading dough at the center island. A white-haired, sixtyish lady who reminded him of his grandmother. No way could he sneak past her to grab food, but he might be able to con her into giving him some.

Then she looked up at him and grinned, and that's when he remembered he wasn't wearing a fucking thing. She gave him a long, leisurely look, up and down and back again. Now her grin didn't look *anything* like his grandmother's.

"You must be the new boy. Brandon, is it?"

"Um." He cleared his throat, folded his hands in front of him, for all the good it did. "Bran, actually."

"You're cuter than the last one." Her gaze dropped to his crotch, her grin widening. "And taller too."

Oh, God. Is everybody *in this house a pervert?*

She chuckled, went back to kneading her dough. "You gingers sure do know how to blush," she said as he maneuvered himself behind the island.

"Um, yeah, so . . ." His eyes darted to the muffins cooling on a rack behind her, to the cup of coffee—no longer steaming, but who the fuck cared—resting on the corner of the island, within easy reach. "Is that, uh, yours?" He pointed at the coffee.

"Yes, dear, it is."

Okay, not gonna offer him one of his own then. "So I'll just grab a muffin and go, then. Nice to meet you . . ."

"Sabrina. And nice try, honey. Touch those and I'll crack you with a rolling pin. *And* tell Jonathan."

Shit.

"Do be a dear now and tell him you tried to steal food. I don't much think he'll appreciate hearing it from me."

Shit shit shit. Bran rubbed at his neck, tried on the smile that made every woman he'd met since his days on the streets want to feed him, and said, "Yeah, um, about that . . ." He inched around the island, let her look at him, kept that damn smile pasted on his face. "I didn't know . . . I mean, maybe just this once you couldn't tell him? I won't do it again."

She leaned over, patted him on the arm. "Of course you won't."

"So we're good then?" he asked, hardly daring to hope. It seemed impossible that *anything* could go right for him in this place.

"I'm quite good, thank you, yes. You, on the other hand, won't be good for some time if you don't get on up there and admit the truth. That's a beautiful smile you've got, but you won't be swaying me with it; I know who signs my paychecks, after all. Now off you go."

Jonathan sat at his desk, toggling through the camera feeds from downstairs. Didn't take Brandon more than thirty seconds to sprout wood after he'd stuck the nozzle up his ass. And of course, despite Jonathan's explicit instructions, Brandon didn't waste any time getting himself off.

"Tsk, tsk, Brandon," he muttered to his screen. "Whatever am I going to do with you?" Luckily—for him if not for Brandon—he'd brought a cane along with him from the dungeon. Clearly, it was time to teach Brandon another lesson.

He couldn't help chuckling as Brandon tried to charm a muffin out of Sabrina. That woman had superhuman strength of will—or just a healthy sense of self-preservation. Unlike someone else Jonathan could name.

And speaking of, here he was, still flushed from his shower. At least he'd shaved—kind of a shame Jonathan needed to enforce that rule; he'd rather liked all that ginger scruff. He waited a moment, until Brandon started to fidget, then got up and said, "Stay right where you are. I need to inspect you." As he came around the desk, he added, "If at a loss for instruction, by the way, you should stand as you kneel: feet shoulder-width apart, back straight, shoulders squared, hands clasped behind your back, eyes on me."

Brandon nodded, arranged himself as Jonathan closed the distance between them.

"There's water at the small of your back. You dried yourself off too hastily. See that doesn't happen again."

"Yes, Jonathan."

Jonathan *tsked*. "Don't make that face at me, Brandon. I know this seems silly to you, but there is method to my madness, I assure you. You're always so focused on the rest of the world, on tomorrow. You need to learn to focus on yourself, on today. You need to learn to take care of yourself, take *pride* in yourself. Do you understand?"

Brandon blinked at him, but then nodded and said, "Yes, Jonathan." Even if he probably didn't understand—at least not really, not yet. He would, though. Soon.

"Good. Arms up." Brandon obeyed, and Jonathan ran fingers over the newly-smoothed skin of Brandon's armpits. "Not bad for your first time," he said. Then he slowly circled around to the front, gaze locking on Brandon's as he grasped Brandon's chin in one hand, turned his head this way and that. "You did a decent job here as well. No cuts at all. No rough patches. Very good." He let go of his chin and stood back. "So . . ." he said, "is there anything you'd like to tell me?"

Brandon blinked, shook his head, panic flashing in his eyes as he realized he hadn't answered aloud. "No, Jonathan."

"You're sure?"

"Yes, Jonathan."

"Interesting." Back around the desk, where Jonathan scooped up the thin rattan cane he'd propped against it. He tapped it lightly on his palm as he approached Brandon again. "How many demerits have you earned today?"

A moment's pause, as if Brandon were contemplating another lie. His eyes darted to the cane, stayed there, pupils dilating. *Afraid. Good.* "F—" He stopped, cleared his throat. "Five, Jonathan."

"So *many*?" Jonathan chirped, mock-surprised. "It's so *early* still. You must be terribly misbehaved. Makes me wonder what you might've done while I wasn't looking."

Beads of perspiration were popping up on Brandon's forehead. "Um, well, okay. I tried to get a muffin from the kitchen. But Sabrina wouldn't let me. Jonathan."

"Smart woman. Loyal, too." Another light rap across his palm with the cane, then he ran the tip of it across Brandon's chest, right where he'd struck him with the crop last night. Such lovely red marks. They'd have company soon. "One more chance: is there anything *else* you'd like to tell me?"

Brandon swallowed hard, and Jonathan could practically see the wheels turning in his head. Was he going to admit it? "N-no, Jonathan."

"Very well, then. Lean over the desk—ass out. Prop yourself against it with both hands."

Brandon swallowed again, pulse pounding at his neck and temples, wide eyes discs of bright green with only the smallest dot of black in the center. For a moment, Jonathan thought he might bolt, but then he shuffled up to the desk, pressed his thighs to it, planted his hands on either side of a stack of files and let his arms take his weight.

Now it was Jonathan's turn to swallow. *Good Lord*, Brandon was gorgeous like this. He stepped close, ran a palm down one tense arm, outlining muscle and tendons with his fingertips. He pressed himself up against Brandon's back, murmured in his ear, "Feet apart, shoulder-width." Backed up and watched Brandon force himself to comply, bare toes digging into the area rug and shuffling sideways half an inch at a time.

"That's it," Jonathan said. "Ass out, now." Another second's hesitation, then Brandon bent a little more. "And hold still."

He brought down the first blow with all the force he could muster, snapping the cane across the crease between Brandon's ass and thighs. Brandon let out a cry and slumped against the desk, knees giving out in a single, perfect moment of shock.

Jonathan let Brandon have his moment, then said, "Back up, please. We've only just begun." Brandon trembled, tried to comply, but his arms and legs had already turned to rubber.

With an impatient grunt, Jonathan grabbed him by the elbow and yanked him to his feet. "Brace yourself more firmly this time. I won't stop again."

Then he circled around to the other side, running the tip of the cane along Brandon's ass as he went. Such beautiful, terrified shivers. Too bad he couldn't drag this out for the rest of the morning, but he had work to do.

Another strike, right across the back of Brandon's other thigh, another perfect red welt blooming on that pale skin. Less of a shock this time, but Brandon still let out a shout, arms shaking, head hanging low between tense shoulders.

A third strike, half an inch below the last one. Brandon's cry went straight to Jonathan's cock, and in the window behind his desk he saw a faint reflection of clenched eyes, bared teeth. Shame he hadn't put a mirror up.

Oh well, next time.

He circled back around to the other side and landed the fourth strike right below the first one.

Brandon fell to his elbows with a vicious cry, forehead pressed to clenched fists. His knees had gone again, and he was breathing so loud and fast the sound filled the entire room. Hard as Jonathan was hitting him, he was surprised the man had made it even this far without falling again.

There's something to be said for stubbornness.

"Don't hyperventilate," Jonathan said. Not very soothing, true, but this was a serious lesson Brandon needed to learn. Now was not the time for softness. "And get up. Palms on the desk or you'll earn yourself another strike."

Well, that did the trick. Brandon sucked in a huge, wet gasp—*Crying already? How lovely!*—and levered himself back up. He didn't lift his head, but Jonathan didn't fault him that. He took a moment instead to admire the play of muscle in Brandon's back, the line of his spine, the broad canvas of pale skin his for the marking . . .

One more on this side, another sweet red welt right below the last one. Such gorgeous, perfectly placed stripes. Almost like a candy cane. Brandon gasped, arms shaking, yet managed to hold himself in place. Impressive. But he still had one more left to take.

On the other side this time. Jonathan circled back, running one hand along Brandon's quivering spine, all the way down to the small of his back. He was tempted to give him a word of encouragement, of genuine praise. Not too many subs could take six of his best their first time out. Jonathan had half-expected him to be a blubbering puddle on the floor by now.

Well, maybe this one would put him there. He brought his hand up high, then drove down with enough force to make his own wrist ache. It landed right below the last welt, twice as red. Brandon screamed and slumped against the desk, then slid to the floor as the second wave of pain hit, curled up tight and pressed both fists to the backs of his thighs. Not *on* the marks—he probably couldn't even bear the *thought* of that—but below them, as if that would help. His eyes were open wide, blinking too much, wet with tears.

Jonathan stood there enjoying the show for a long moment, then said, "Get up."

Brandon groaned, whimpered, slowly rolled onto his knees and elbows, hands still fisted, forehead pressed to the rug. *Beautiful* sight. Despite that, Jonathan couldn't afford to indulge him. Not if he intended to make this lesson stick.

"I said, *Get. Up.* Now."

"You also said no blood," Brandon rasped into the rug. "You *promised.*"

Jonathan sighed, squatted beside Brandon and pried one of his hands out from under him. "Here," he said, tugging until Brandon's fist hovered over the welts. "Feel for yourself. I didn't cut you."

Slowly, Brandon's hand unfisted, and his fingers traced ever-so-carefully over a welt, jerking away as if they'd touched something burning before settling back to explore again. Must've hurt like hell.

"See? No blood. Now get up. Don't make me ask you again."

Jaw clenching, Brandon pushed himself up on his palms, grabbed hold of the desk to pull himself to his feet. He stumbled and listed, slumped against the desk a moment before pulling himself upright. His shoulders hitched with the effort of taking in air. A few stray tears still ran down his cheeks, but he wasn't crying so Jonathan could hear.

Too proud. Still too damn proud.

"Look at me."

Brandon lifted his head, swiping at his eyes. Sniffed.

"Hands at your sides."

Brandon obeyed, hands uncurling. He wouldn't be in *too* much pain anymore—at least until he put pressure on those fresh welts.

Jonathan stepped forward, backing Brandon up against the desk, the edge of it biting right into his cane stripes. Another lovely whimper, Brandon's teeth clenching hard. Jonathan kicked Brandon's legs apart and wedged himself between them, grasping the base of Brandon's throat in one hand. "Tell me why I did this."

Another shuddering breath. "Because I tried to steal the muffin." His voice was small, rough with tears. Perfect.

"Yes and no. Because you tried to steal the muffin, and because I had to ask you about it—several times, I might add. Because you were sloppy with your grooming, and took too long." He paused. "And because you touched yourself without permission."

Brandon's eyes widened. "How—?"

Jonathan's hand tightened around Brandon's throat, cutting off the question. "Nothing happens in this house without my knowledge. Think about that the next time you consider touching something that no longer belongs to you." He took a step back and trailed the tip of the cane down Brandon's chest to his crotch, pointing right at his cock. "*That* is mine. I do with it as I please. You only get to touch it if I give you explicit permission. In case I didn't make myself clear enough about that before."

He slid the cane down to Brandon's balls, gave them a gentle tap. Brandon lurched like he'd been wailed on, whimpered softly. "And to be clear now, those six strikes? Were the demerits you'd already earned this morning. You've ten more coming for the muffin, another ten for touching yourself, and another ten for lying. But I can be generous; I'll hold them in reserve for you." Jonathan met Brandon's eyes and said, slow and deliberate, "If you ever do *any* of those things again, you'll be getting all thirty at once."

For a second, Brandon went so white that Jonathan thought he might faint right there. But he recovered himself, swallowed hard—what a lovely sensation beneath Jonathan's pressing hand—and stuttered, "Y-yes, Jonathan."

Jonathan grinned at him, took his hand from Brandon's throat and stroked his damp cheek with it instead. "There's a good boy. Now thank me for correcting you."

With the tip of the crop still resting against Brandon's balls, the man didn't hesitate for a *second*. "Thank you for correcting me, Jonathan," he said. It came out all in a single breathless rush—maybe just terror, but probably some anger in there, too.

"You're welcome. And for my mercy, as well, don't you think?"

Brandon nodded like he couldn't quite figure out how to stop himself. "Yes, Jonathan, thank you for your mercy."

Jonathan stepped away, and Brandon fell to his hands and knees again, breathing hard.

"Now be a dear and get the stool out of that closet." He pointed with the cane to the door in the far corner of the office. Brandon followed warily with his gaze, then climbed to his feet to obey.

Jonathan settled at his desk with a grin, waiting for the moment of realization—

Ah, there it was. Brandon's knuckles went white on the open door. "Don't dawdle," Jonathan warned. "Bring it here."

Brandon grabbed the stool in one hand and put it down beside the desk like it was on fire.

Well, close enough, I suppose, when he plants ass to Astroturf.

"Like it?" Jonathan asked, skimming a hand across the prickly green plastic grass covering the hard wooden seat. "Made it myself."

Brandon shifted from foot to foot, fingers clenching and unclenching by his sides. But he *was* learning; he'd been asked a question, and he replied, "No, Jonathan."

"Sit anyway."

Brandon eyed the stool, bit his lip . . . and sat. Gasped, whimpered, curled in half and grabbed the edges of the seat in two white-knuckled grips. "Yellow," he choked out. "Please . . . Yellow."

Jonathan stood, took Brandon's face in both hands, gently straightened him up and made him meet his eyes. Brandon blinked at him, one tear trailing down his cheek.

"Breathe," Jonathan ordered. "In through your nose, out through your mouth. That's it, good." Brandon blinked away another tear, but did as told, breathing slow and deep. He could do this. He might think he couldn't, but he could. "Better?" Jonathan asked.

Brandon sniffled, shook his head, but he was visibly calmer now. "Don't lie to me," Jonathan warned. Added, softly, "Or to yourself. Better?"

Another sniffle. "A little, I guess. Jonathan."

Jonathan stroked his hair, kissed the crown of his head. "Good boy. You're a tough one, Brandon; you'll be fine. Ten minutes, all right? Then you can have your cushion. Here"—he sat back in his own chair, set the little timer on his desk and turned it so Brandon could see it— "you can peek at it if you want to, but focus on me. On something besides the pain. Learn to push through it, come out the other side. Let the endorphins carry you; you might even find you enjoy it."

The look on Brandon's face said *You're crazy,* clear as day, but he nodded, kept his eyes on Jonathan's face.

"And no squirming," Jonathan warned. "It'll only make you more uncomfortable."

Jonathan tried to work for the next ten minutes, but that perfect picture of suffering beside him made it impossible. At last the timer went off, and Brandon practically oozed off the stool and onto the floor, then scooted gingerly over to the cushion. He knelt, assuming the position Jonathan had shown him the day before, knees and shoulders lined up just about perfectly despite the trembling in his limbs.

"Very good," Jonathan said, genuinely impressed. Brandon really was a quick learner. Now if only he could learn to get out of his own way . . . "Here," he added, taking a stack of papers and a box of envelopes from the far edge of his desk. "Stuff these. If you wish, you may lie down while you do it."

Brandon wasted no time rolling onto his stomach, propping himself on his elbows. Jonathan took the opportunity to admire his handiwork, even reaching out to give those fresh welts a soft pat. The flesh there was still burning hot; he couldn't resist flattening his palm against it. Brandon gasped, shuddered beneath his hand, but managed to pick up his first sheet of paper, fold it in thirds, and seal the envelope. His fingers shook the whole time.

Wonder how he'd take it if I rubbed some menthol into that skin . . .

Jonathan's cock jumped at the thought, but no. Even with the lies, the muffin, the masturbation, he couldn't quite justify that kind of punishment.

Yet, anyway.

But given Brandon's attitude problem? Soon, no doubt. Soon.

n the morning of the fourth day of Brandon's refusal to eat, Jonathan threw his fork down, grabbed Brandon by the arm, and dragged him bodily into a chair. By now Brandon needed the help; he was clearly lightheaded, not quite entirely with it. The weight loss was starting to show—must've been three, four pounds already. Too much for a man who'd started this process whip-lean.

"Brandon, this has to stop. Contract or no contract, I won't allow you to damage yourself."

Brandon's jaw clenched, just like every other time the subject of eating had come up. "I won't eat from your hand like . . . like a fucking *dog*, Jonathan. So you can stop asking me. Or," he added, like he didn't even want to say it, "you can order me."

"I'm not asking, and I won't order you. Not on this; you have to come to it yourself or it doesn't *mean* anything, do you understand?"

Brandon nodded hesitantly, said even more hesitantly, "Pride. Walls. All that. I get it, Jonathan."

"Well, that's something, I suppose. But if you can't let that go, if you insist on doing this to yourself . . . I won't sit by and watch. Two more days. And if you can't make peace with letting me feed you, I'm sending you home."

"But you *can't*—"

"Actually, I can. There's a very clear medical provision in our contract, and you're on the cusp of seeing it breached. Any doctor in the country would agree with me. I told you I'd never harm you and I meant it; nor will I let you harm yourself." He leaned forward in his chair, laid a hand on Brandon's thigh. "Two days, Brandon. Can you do this?"

"Yes, Jonathan." Too quick and automatic for him to have given it any real consideration. He drew himself up, sucked in a breath, almost as if he were bracing himself for a blow. "I just need a little more . . ."

"Patience?" Jonathan prompted. "I've given you plenty. And I have no intention of waiting until you collapse. Now answer me again—and this time *think* before you speak—can you do this?"

Brandon's mouth opened, closed, opened again. He looked *wrecked*—small, frightened, upset, maybe even on the verge of tears. "I don't know," he said at last, voice tiny, cracking in the middle. He shook his head, threw his hands up. "I just . . . I don't know. Believe me, this isn't fun, I don't *want* to be like this, but . . ."

"I understand." Jonathan reached for Brandon's hand; Brandon offered it to him, and he held it in both his own. "I *could* help you. Obviously I haven't done enough, underestimated what you needed. Do you want my help?"

Brandon thought about it for a moment, then said, hesitantly, "This is going to hurt, isn't it."

Jonathan chuffed. "You know it will. But the choice is yours. How badly do you want this?"

Three million dollars flashed clear as day across Brandon's face. Jonathan was no fool; he knew why the man was here. Shame it wasn't more than that—especially when it'd become so clear to him that it *could* be, that Brandon was *built* for this if he'd just *let go*, but he'd take it for now. Who knew . . . maybe after this, after Brandon was eating again, all those walls would be down and they could start to do the *real* work, start to share in pleasures instead of constant punishments. He didn't want to spend the next six months like this any more than Brandon did—frustrated, exhausted, always at odds.

"I want it," Brandon said at last. Added "Jonathan" like the reflex it had become. And then, surprising Jonathan, "Please. Help me."

Bran thought it couldn't get any worse than that fucking cane, but Jonathan proved him wrong within two minutes of dragging him back into the dungeon. Into the bathroom first, then into the shower. Then that fucking nozzle again. Not like he had anything to clean out anyway; he hadn't eaten in days. Yet still Jonathan shoved the thing up so high Bran could almost feel it in the back of his throat.

Then he turned the water on.

It flowed in warm and slow, just like last time. But unlike last time, it didn't stop. Jonathan kept going until Bran felt like he'd fucking *burst*, until cramps set in so bad they sent him to his knees. Still the water flowed, Jonathan's hand warm and forceful at the nape of his neck.

"Almost there," Jonathan said as pain ripped through Bran's gut. He was afraid to even look at himself, sure that much water must have bulged his stomach out. "I'm pulling out the nozzle now. Hold the water in. Trust me when I say you don't want to have to clean this up if you fail."

Bran believed him.

Jonathan made him stay like that long after the nozzle came out, one hand still firm at the nape of his neck, the other pinching his sore ass cheeks together. Only when the cramps had reduced Bran to a quivering, begging mess did Jonathan help him out of the tub, guide him to the toilet and let Bran end the pain. "Water the grass, too. This'll be your last chance for a good long while."

Didn't have to tell Bran twice.

They finished in the bathroom, and Jonathan led him back out into the dungeon. Bran's eyes skipped from one rack of implements to the next. Which would Jonathan use first? He seemed quite fond of the crop, but Jonathan had beaten him with it enough to know it wouldn't break him. Maybe a cane then? One of those fat ones at the end of the rack, maybe. *Shit. Why did I ask for this?*

"Up you go," Jonathan said, patting the padded leather table near the center of the room. "On your belly, legs spread."

Bran let his eyes close for just a moment, took a deep, steadying breath, and resolutely did *not* think of all the things Jonathan might do to him on his belly as he climbed up onto the table. He supposed it was a good sign, at least, that Jonathan didn't restrain him. Meant Jonathan thought he could hold more-or-less still through whatever might come next.

Jonathan walked away for a moment, and came back with something thick and black in his hand, shaped like a spade on a playing card: six inches long, thick as a thumb at the point and twice as wide as a dick— at least—at the bottom before it narrowed to the flange.

Oh my God. That's not what I think it is, is it?

"Open wide," Jonathan said with that infuriating tiny smirk of his. He held the plug to Bran's lips and pushed inside. Bran couldn't even close his teeth around it, much less his lips. Hurt just to try, like his mouth was about to rip at the edges. "Get it good and wet. You know where it's going next."

Bran swallowed hard around the plug and tried very hard not to think about what Jonathan had just said.

Oh, God. It's gonna tear me apart.

So much for not thinking.

He got as much spit on the plug as he could, despite his mouth having gone dry as a fucking desert. Jonathan pulled it out none too gently and moved out of eyesight, one hand skimming down Bran's back. *As if that's gonna make this any easier to take.*

Bran gripped the edge of the table, every muscle tensing against the inevitable breach. But it was only Jonathan's fingers that slid between his ass cheeks, cool and slick with lube, easing inside him. *God, please tell me he's not gonna shove that thing in after all. Please tell me it's just another one of his mind-fucks.*

Shit, no such luck. Jonathan pulled his fingers out, replaced them with the plug. Or the tip of it, anyway, until it could go no further. Probably no more than an inch or two, and Jesus, already the burn was *terrible*, but Jonathan just pushed and pushed some more, slow but inexorable, and said, "Relax, Brandon. We'll be here for *hours* if you don't relax."

Hours? Bran shut his eyes, tried to will himself loose, but he couldn't even pry his fingers from the edge of the table, let alone relax his sphincter. Jonathan pulled the plug out a fraction, jammed it back in, gave it a twist. Out and in again. Fucking him with it. It wasn't pleasant—too big, too unyielding, too much force, nowhere near his prostate. Jonathan wedged his free hand between Bran's cheeks and spread them wide, gave the plug another hard rock; it slipped in a little more, and Bran gasped.

"Try bearing down," Jonathan said, and yeah, he could do that, wanted it *out out out* anyway, so he tensed his abs, pushed. And son of a fucking *bitch*, in the plug went a little further, burning like fucking fire and there was *no fucking way* Jonathan wasn't tearing him, making him bleed—

"Easy," Jonathan said, still rocking the plug, pushing it in and out and in and out in tiny, tiny increments. "You're not tearing, I promise."

Fucking mind reader.

Another hard push—*Jesus, aren't his arms getting tired?*—and in it went a little more, forcing him open a little wider. His toes curled, came up off the table. He was halfway to his hands and knees before he even realized he'd moved, and Jonathan—never easing up on the fucking plug—planted his elbow in Bran's spine and shoved him back down. "I'll restrain you," he warned. "I'd have to let go. We'd have to start again."

Fuck that. Bran held on—just barely—until the damn thing wouldn't go in any further. Felt like a whole *arm* shoved up inside him. Too big. Too much. He couldn't hold it. His whole body had turned into a single throbbing ball of *hurt*. Trembling, panting, cold sweat dripping into his eyes.

One way to make it stop, and the word was out his mouth before he could bite it back: "*Red.*"

Jonathan stopped immediately, and the plug slithered out between his legs. Cold air brushed over his hole. Felt like someone had drilled him open.

Jonathan circled the table, leaned down to look him in the eye. "Will you eat?"

Bran's stomach rumbled. As if he wasn't miserable enough already. But he couldn't, he just *couldn't.* "No."

"Do you want to leave?"

Did he? Could he take much more of this? Or hell, *any* more?

But . . . *three million dollars.* His whole fucking *life,* his *future.* And for what? A few hours of discomfort?

"Discomfort." Hah.

Stop being such a fucking pussy, Brandon. Nobody likes a crybaby.

Great, thanks, Dad. Really helping here.

Suck it up.

"Brandon?"

Bran jumped, nearly launched himself off the table to cringe on the other side. For a moment, just one moment . . .

He's not your father. He's a man of his word; he won't harm you.

Voice soft, face even softer. Hand in his hair, stroking. "Do you want to leave?"

Bran met his eyes and said, "No."

Jonathan's softness faded so fast Bran wondered if he hadn't just imagined it. "Then shut up."

Jonathan walked back around the table. A few seconds later, more lube squirted into his hole—cold and slimy and not the least bit reassuring. Then came the plug again, pain returning in a flash as Jonathan pushed with renewed vigor.

This was really going to hurt him if he didn't find a way to relax.

He sucked in a breath, then another, and bore down like Jonathan had told him to. The plug slid in further, but still not all the way. Jesus Christ, this thing was fucking *endless.*

"That's it, keep going like that. Breathe. We're almost there."

Almost?

"God, you should see yourself," Jonathan said, the plug rocking-pushing-rocking, "all stretched wide around the plug. So hot. Makes me want to shove my cock in there right now."

Just, God, please, not beside the plug.

"Why don't you?" Bran asked. "Please, Jonathan. I want it."

A hard slap on the back of his left thigh, right atop God knew how many marks from Jonathan's various "toys." Bran hissed in a sharp breath, even as Jonathan chuckled and said, "Nice try, Brandon."

Another hard push. Well, hard*er*, anyway; the pressure was unrelenting, the stretch and burn even more so. Jonathan gave the plug a twist, angled it forward and *holy mother of*—

Bran's chest came off the table, mouth open on a gasp, dick suddenly *rock fucking hard* between the leather and his thigh as the plug pressed against his prostate. The pain of it was still huge, but less terrible somehow. Tempered, distant beneath the sudden wash of pleasure.

Until the next hard push, and then it was the other way around as the widest part of the plug forced its way inside, the pleasure (and his erection) fading and distant beneath *too much too full take it out take it out take it* out*!* The muscles in his ass clenched hard around the neck of the plug, which had looked about the width of Jonathan's cock but felt like *nothing* now after the stretching he'd just taken. But the *rest* of the plug, the full heavy length and breadth of it buried inside him like a giant fist . . . He bore down, growl morphing to a closed-mouthed scream as he tried to expel it. Fucking hopeless. It barely even moved.

"If I rolled you over right now and sucked you," Jonathan said, trailing a hand along Bran's sweaty back as he circled round the table to meet his eyes again, "You'd come so hard you'd probably pass out."

Kinda absolutely fucking impossible to believe that, but no point in arguing.

"Hurts something fierce when I'm not touching you though, doesn't it."

That wasn't technically a question, so he didn't feel compelled to reply.

"How long do you think you can bear that, Brandon? Five minutes? Ten? You look ready to cry already."

He grimaced, clenched his teeth, bit back a *Fuck you*.

Jonathan *tsked*. "None of that, now. I'm only doing as you asked."

God, please, not like this . . .

"What about the whole night? Think you could stand it? Think your body would relax, stretch, learn to accept it?"

Fuck, that actually *was* a question. Took him a moment to find his voice, though, to work up enough moisture to reply. "I don't know, Jonathan."

Jonathan's smile had far too many teeth. "I'll tell you a little secret. It won't. You don't get used to something like that, not without practice." He patted Bran on the cheek, so condescending Bran barely resisted the urge to bite him.

"Up you go, then. We've only just begun."

Was he fucking kidding? How was he supposed to walk like this?

"I said *get up*," Jonathan growled, and strange but Bran found himself rolling to his feet before he even had time to contemplate the logistics of it.

Over to the suspension bar again. His wrist cuffs were attached to either end of it, just like that first day. Feet anchored to the floor, only this time Jonathan gave him no slack at all. In fact, he was stretched out so far the muscles in his belly burned and the cuffs bit into his wrists and the tops of his feet.

Jonathan strode over to the wall of toys, fingering various crops and canes. Picked up a massive whip, letting the leather tails tumble through his fingers. Looked like there were a couple dozen of them, all sleek black leather, thick and heavy. Jonathan tried it out on his arm, the smack echoing in the silence.

Bran nearly swallowed his tongue. "N-no blood, Jonathan. You promised."

Jonathan came back to the table, buried his fingers in Bran's hair. Gently, reassuringly. "And I will keep that promise. I won't make you bleed. See?" He draped the whip over Bran's shoulder, let it trail across his skin. The leather was heavy, but supple, with no hard edges.

Jonathan's hand followed where the whip had fallen, smoothing and soothing as he stepped behind Bran and moved back. The leather left his skin. Then came back a moment later, high across his shoulders with a mighty *thwack.*

The sound was almost worse than the strike itself—it didn't hurt that much, at least at first. More thud than sting. Nowhere near as bad as a cane, or even a crop.

But then the pain of the first strike blossomed as the second landed overtop it, deep like a fucking tackle, knocking air from his lungs in a grunting whoosh. The third strike hit before he'd gotten his breath back from the first two, and in the same fucking place. Less force, somehow, but so much fucking sting he couldn't bite back a shout. A mass of fire, a dozen little burning bites of pain, and the next strike fell on top of them before he could even get his head around the last one.

On and on it went, strikes hard and fast and *merciless*, traveling down his back with all the speed of a fucking snail and all the pounding sting of a 2x4 with nails in it. Hard to believe he wasn't bleeding. *Impossible* to believe. But the only thing he felt dripping down his back was sweat—no telltale sting of salt in an open wound.

Like you'd even notice it over the burn of the whip.

The first blow on his ass made him scream loud enough to hurt his throat. Pain layered upon pain of too many other implements, four days' worth of lessons and demerits. And *God,* he didn't think that fucking plug could hurt any worse, but as the whip landed across his ass, it felt like he was being punched from the fucking *inside.* Jonathan aimed the next strike right over the plug's base, driving it forward. Took Bran a second to come back from that, to realize the whip had moved on, lower across his ass, across a constellation of old welts and bruises that hurt so fucking bad he couldn't even *breathe*, couldn't even find the wherewithal to scream, and this was going to fucking *kill* him, he couldn't take it for another *second*, and so fucking what if he *was* a crybaby because—

The flogging stopped, and somehow Jonathan was standing in front of him, stroking a hand down the side of his face, grasping his chin, lifting his head up. "Will you eat?" he asked, infinitely patient.

Bran was so fucking nauseous he didn't think he could right now even if he wanted it more than anything. And he *didn't* want it more than anything. Well, okay, part of him did, but the rest? He shook his head.

"Do you want to leave?"

Yes. "No."

Jonathan's fingers tightened on his chin. "Don't safeword again unless you mean it."

He'd safeworded? *When?*

At least Jonathan was kind enough to switch to the front when he started up the flogging again. His chest this time, tips of the flogger catching across a nipple and *holy fucking shit don't do that again*, but of course he did, again and again, then switched hands and caught him on the *other* one, and he was pretty sure he was screaming with every strike, the fury in his back slowly fading as the fury in his chest built and built. At last the flogger dropped lower, to the straining muscles of his belly, painting bright red stripes across his stomach, masses and masses of them until they all ran together in one bright red ball of fucking *napalm* and he had to squeeze his eyes closed, look away, because not seeing was somehow less awful than seeing.

And then the flogger dropped again, and his eyes flew open as the tails landed with a hard, noisy *thwack* about an inch above his crotch.

You wouldn't dare . . .

He fought to keep his eyes open, to read Jonathan's face, but all he saw there was intense concentration, focus, even a little strain, and no wonder—surely his arm must be tired for as hard as he was hitting Bran. The next strike didn't land *above* his groin, it landed *on* it, and for a second Bran couldn't even find his voice, but a second later he was screaming, thrashing, *make it stop get away get away—*

Another strike right over the last knocked every coherent thought from his head. He thought he might have blacked out for a while, but he was pretty sure unconsciousness wasn't supposed to hurt so much.

When the dungeon and the sound of leather on skin came back into focus, Jonathan was flogging Bran's thighs near the knees. Strange how disconnected he felt from it, like his body wasn't even *his* anymore, and no, the irony of that didn't escape him; God knew Jonathan had been trying to teach him that lesson from the word go. Pain filtered in from somewhere—fuck, from *everywhere*—and his heart thudded in his ears, loud as the thwack of the flogger on his skin, loud as his labored breaths. He licked his lips, tasted salt. Something else, too, something strong and metallic in the back of his throat. Not blood—adrenaline. His head felt enormous, light, ready to pop. *Like a fucking balloon on a string.*

The beating stopped. Maybe had some time ago; the flogger was nowhere in sight and Jonathan had an arm around his waist, was holding him up as he unhooked his hands. His legs were already free, and when the fuck had that happened?

". . . with me now?"

He let his head roll on Jonathan's shoulder and mumbled, "Huh?" Speaking hurt right down to his toes.

"I said, are you with me now?"

Bran shrugged, instantly regretted it, slurred, "Sure, Jonathan," instead.

Jonathan huffed a little laugh, hoisted him higher, and said, "You're one crazy son of a bitch, you know that?"

Pot, kettle.

Jonathan guided him over to the table, let him lean against the edge, but he just slumped over. Felt good, touching that soft, padded leather, cool on his burning skin. He let his eyes drift shut and inhaled. It even smelled good.

"Will you eat?" Jonathan asked again, fingertips trailing along Bran's shoulder, soothing the hurt he'd applied so thoroughly.

Maybe if I say yes, he'll let me stay here for a few minutes.

Then he shifted, and that fucking plug jostled inside him, burning and aching. How the hell could he have forgotten about it? Felt like a fist shoved up there, stretching him wider with every little movement. That pleasant haze of a moment ago disappeared, and no matter how hard he tried, he couldn't get it back, couldn't ignore the pain building and building in waves that never fucking seemed to break. Even Jonathan's fingers dragged like knives over his skin, amplifying every twinge. He tried to shrug out from under them, but didn't have the strength or the coordination to manage more than a twitch.

This is how he helps *me?*

"No," he rasped. And then, to those stroking fingers trailing acid in their wake, "Get off me."

Jonathan moved his hand up, fingers sinking into Bran's hair, hauling him off the table. "Fine. Sounds like you need some time alone."

He was dragged along by his hair, teeth gritted so hard his jaw felt ready to shatter, still in so much pain he had no choice but to follow. A pyramid made of steel bars sat in the corner, maybe three feet tall by a foot and a half at the base. It couldn't *possibly* be what Bran thought it was. How could a human being fit into something that small?

Jonathan left him to contemplate it while he rummaged in a nearby drawer, came out with what looked like a piece of a horse bridle. "Mouth open," he said, and *no fucking way* flashed through Bran's head before he realized he didn't actually have the strength to stop Jonathan right now. He stood still as Jonathan stepped behind him and brought the gag up to his face, but made Jonathan wedge his teeth apart with the rubber bit. Jonathan tightened the gag until it pushed against the corners of Bran's lips and his back teeth—he fought the urge to puke he always got when something touched his tongue that far back—and buckled it into place.

Thank God there were no mirrors in here, because he was pretty sure he'd die of shame if he had to look at himself right now.

Done, Jonathan turned back to the pyramid and undid a latch at the top. One whole side of the thing swung out on a hinge at the floor. "In," he said, gesturing toward the cage. When Bran only looked at him like he was out of his Goddamned mind, he jerked his thumb toward the dungeon door. "Or out. Your choice."

He'd come this far. No way was he chickening out now. But first he had to figure out how to get *in* the fucking thing.

"Sit with your back to the door." Fucking *mind reader.* "Pull your knees up to your chest, hunch over them, and scoot back slowly. Watch your head. Wedge your arms wherever there's room."

Wedge is right. He sat down on the open flap and nearly lurched right back to his feet; between the pain of flogged skin to metal bars and that *fucking plug* tunneling up to his fucking throat as he sat on the flange, he actually forgot for a second what he was supposed to be doing.

Oh. Right. Midget cage.

There was barely enough space for him to squeeze through the door. He banged his head on one of the bars scooting in, then inched over and tried to sit up. A child—or maybe *Jonathan*—might've managed it better, but Bran was stuck hunched over his folded knees, his shoulders scraping the sides of the cage, and *ow holy fuck* did that hurt. He grunted around the gag, found himself oddly grateful for something to bite down on when the pain crested clear into agony as the bars dug into freshly flogged skin. God only knew how Jonathan was going to shut the door. Maybe if he could fit his feet through the bars . . .

But he couldn't. The door banged into his knees when Jonathan tried to close it, and Jonathan barked "Back up" like it was *Bran's* fault he was too big for the fucking pyramid. Bran wiggled a little, pulled his knees in tighter to his chest, his muscles already starting to scream along with his beaten skin. Jonathan leaned hard against the door to close it the last quarter-inch and locked it shut.

For one panicked second, Bran couldn't breathe.

"Easy," Jonathan said. "You have room. You may not feel like it, but you do." Jonathan squatted down low enough to catch his eyes despite his chin resting on his folded knees. "Look at me. Very slowly now, take a nice deep breath. Through your nose, remember?" Bran stared into that blue blue gaze—*wide ocean, open skies*—and sucked in air. His chest expanded. Expanded some more. Nearly filled all the way before the tightness of the space stopped it.

Okay. I can do this.

His lower back twinged hard, and he reached for it and banged his elbow on a bar before he'd moved his hand half an inch.

"I know, it's miserable." No sympathy at all. No pleasure either, though, oddly enough. What, too sadistic even for *him*? "Here," he said, picking up a little plastic handle-shaped thing from the floor. It was attached to a wire, and Bran jerked, expecting . . . well, he didn't know *what* he was expecting, and it's not like he could've gotten away from it anyhow. Jonathan held it in front of his eyes, flipped up the top with his thumb—a little cover on a hinge. Beneath the cover lay a little red button.

He closed the cover back over the button and wedged the contraption through the cage bars and into Bran's hand. "This is a panic button—an electronic safeword for when you're ready to come out. Do it once. Show me you can."

It was a bit awkward, working it with a hand wedged in so tightly he could barely move his fingers, but he managed it. Pushed until he heard a click.

"Good, that's good." Jonathan walked out of sight for a moment, then something beeped and a cold blast of air washed over the cage. *Air conditioning. I'm right under a fucking vent.* "I'll be in my office. When you push that button, an alarm will go off up there, and I'll be down in no more than a minute."

Bran nodded, shivered violently, tried to slurp some drool up from the corner of his chin. *Fucking gag.*

"I can see you at all times." He pointed, and Bran tried to follow the line of his finger with his eyes. Tough when he couldn't lift his head, but he caught sight the camera, a black glimmer of glass on a black wall, up near the ceiling.

"I'm sure this goes without saying, but just in case: don't safeword unless you mean it. Call me to feed you or to send you home. Nothing else, or that flogging you just had? Will seem like tickles. Clear?"

"Hhhhhh," Bran said around the gag. Wow, yeah, real intelligible. He tried nodding instead, but couldn't move his head. Shit, his neck was cramping. *Ow.*

"Good enough," Jonathan said round a tight grin. "I'll be back at . . ." he peeked at his watch, shrugged one shoulder, "Oh, let's say bedtime."

Bedtime? Jesus *fuck,* wasn't it only, like, early afternoon? "Ngggh!" he shouted, trying to shake his head, trying to say *Please, please don't do this* with his eyes. But Jonathan just stood, turned around, and walked away. Bran tried to throw himself against the cage, but of course there was no leverage and *holy fuck* it hurt, and anyway he was pretty sure the fucking thing was bolted to the floor. "Hhhhhhhgh!" he screamed, screamed again, but then the dungeon door closed, and Jonathan was gone.

CHAPTER 13

Jonathan tried to work, but his attention kept wandering. He couldn't help flipping back to the dungeon's camera feed, watching as Brandon screamed and shivered and struggled as best he could inside the tiny cage. Half an hour he'd been in there. About twenty-five minutes longer than Jonathan thought he'd last. Another ninety minutes, and Jonathan would go let him out one way or the other. No doubt he was in enough agony already.

Come on, Brandon, push the bloody button. Let it go, all right? Just take the bloody food from my hand.

He'd never had to push any submissive this far before, and honestly, it was exhausting. Every day another power struggle, every day another doubt—was he pushing too hard, too far, being too strict, too unfair? But no . . . in the end, he'd heaped patience upon patience on the man, maybe let more slide than he should have. In truth, he wasn't sure how much longer *he* could keep it up before he just said *screw it* and stopped bothering to try to make it good for Brandon.

The galling part was, he *knew* Brandon would enjoy it—in fact, *had* enjoyed it—when he stopped fighting with himself long enough to relax. To let go of his damn stubborn pride. All those erections and orgasms didn't lie.

He turned back to the screen, watched Brandon trying to shake the cage apart. *What I wouldn't give for that kind of energy . . .* Surely he'd wear himself out soon, no? Jonathan turned the dial on his speakers, and the sounds of Brandon screaming around his gag filled the office. His voice was half gone, but that didn't stop him from trying.

Nothing *stops him from trying.*

And damn but if that wasn't half of what made him so intriguing.

Half an hour later, Brandon went so suddenly still and silent Jonathan worried he'd passed out. But no—a close look at the monitor revealed slow, heavy blinks. *Just exhausted, then.* And the panic button was still clutched in one fist. Small tremors wracked his frame, but it was only 55 degrees in there right now, and the vent was right on top of him. No way he'd make it another hour. And Jonathan was glad of that for more reasons than one. This was starting to wear pretty hard even on his ice-coated sense of sympathy.

Jonathan went back to work, one eye on the video feed, one eye on the timer. He left the sound on, just in case. But Brandon wasn't shouting anymore. Just the occasional moan or whimper—involuntary, or maybe self-comfort. It was patently absurd how badly Jonathan wanted to go down there and wrap him in a blanket.

Come on, come on, push the bloody button. Let me take care of you.

Thirty minutes left. Twenty-five. Twenty. Jonathan gave up all pretense of accomplishing a thing and just stared at his reef tank between glances at the video monitor, watching the fish dart in and out of the coral. Ten minutes. Five.

Shit. He's not going to push the button, is he.

The timer buzzed. Jonathan smacked it rather harder than was necessary, took one last look at the monitor—Brandon was still force-huddled in his tiny cage, shivering and blinking but otherwise still—and headed downstairs with a sigh. Guess it was time to put him in an even unfriendlier cage.

The dungeon door opening jarred Bran from the not-quite-*so*-agonizing haze into which he'd managed to settle. Had Jonathan come to goad him some more? Well, fuck that. He wasn't eating from Jonathan's fucking hand, and he wasn't leaving. He *wasn't*.

The air conditioner kicked on again, and he tried to burrow tighter into his knees. Not happening. Nowhere left to go, and trying hurt so bad it brought tears to his eyes. *Again.*

Then Jonathan unlocked the cage, one side falling open like a drawbridge. "Come on, climb out."

Was it bedtime already? It'd felt like fucking *ever*, but surely he hadn't been stuck in here for eight hours.

. . . Had he?

Which could only mean . . . "Wwwww," he moaned into the gag, shaking his head as Jonathan squatted down and touched his forearm. Holy shit, his fingers felt hot.

Jonathan wedged his hands around behind Bran's head and unbuckled the gag. Good God, shutting his mouth had *never* felt so good, but he worked up enough spit to swallow and opened it again to say, "No, wait." When had his teeth started chattering so hard he could barely speak? "I didn't—" Shit, his jaw hurt. *Just like every-fucking-thing else.* "I didn't press the butt—"

"Shhh." Hot fingers pressed to his lips. "I know. But I don't suppose you'd like to eat anyway?"

"*No*," Bran practically spat. Should've. Fuck Jonathan anyway for thinking he'd suffer through all this for *nothing*.

"Well, just a change of scenery then. Come on, out you go."

Took Bran several seconds to unclench his arms from around his knees enough to straighten his legs out. He stretched maybe an inch before pain slammed into him like a fucking eighteen-wheeler—his back, his shoulders, every inch of his skin, the muscles in his still-folded legs. Jonathan, the little shit, just watched him impassively, let him struggle, didn't help. Didn't even flick so much as a sympathetic blink when Bran managed to get a leg straight in a burst of effort so costly it left him panting and sniffing back tears.

The other leg next, and then he sat there wondering, *What now?* There wasn't enough room to work his hands behind him to push himself forward, wasn't enough strength or feeling in his legs to use them to pull himself out.

In the end, Jonathan solved the problem by wrapping burning-hot hands around his ankles, and with a soft admonition to "Watch your head," dragged him by the feet right out of the cage.

He probably screamed, if the pain in his throat was any indication. When he came back to himself, he was curled into a tight little ball on the floor—and wasn't *that* ironic—clutching with one hand at the inferno in the small of his back.

No Jonathan-massages this time to help him through it. "Get up," Jonathan said, and when Bran didn't—*couldn't*—move, Jonathan thrust fingers into Bran's hair and just started dragging him. Best incentive he'd ever known to scramble up onto hands and knees, even if he couldn't quite get them to hold his weight.

At least they only went eight or ten feet. *Change of scenery*, Jonathan had said. Bran looked up from where Jonathan had dropped him, saw a clear plastic box on the floor.

Like a fucking coffin. Smaller than. Tapered like a sarcophagus. Well, at least it had air holes.

"I'm guessing you can't stand, and I can't lift you, yes?"

Bran didn't bother to answer, just rolled onto his back, then his side, then his back again, trying to get comfortable. Fuck comfortable; he'd settle for even just a *little* less cramping in his legs and shoulders and back.

"All right. In through the side, then."

Bran rolled his head just enough to watch Jonathan undo a series of latches on the little clear plastic coffin, push the lid back, and then unhinge the long side facing Bran.

Bran blinked at it, wondering if Jonathan really meant for him to go in there.

Of course he does.

He might have fought it if he were capable of moving anything more than his toes and fingers without making himself cry.

Coffin. It's a fucking coffin . . .

Jonathan knelt down beside him and log-rolled him right into the box. Shit, the plastic was cold. Fucking miserable for his chattering teeth, but it felt kinda good against the skin of his back—all smooth and chilly against spasming muscle and eleven million whip marks.

Jonathan closed up the side of the box, and suddenly it was *seriously* fucking cramped in there. Better than the pyramid cage—he was lying stretched out flat, after all—but both walls touched his shoulders. Like it'd been made for him.

Probably was. What else does a wealthy sadist do with his heaps and heaps of money? Swim in it?

Jonathan leaned into his field of vision with a long-suffering sigh. "You know the routine, yes?" He placed the panic button in Bran's hand. Thought about it for a second and then wrapped the cord three times around Bran's wrist. Making sure he couldn't drop it, he supposed. "Yes?"

Bran tried to nod, and a tendril of pain shot up his neck and settled behind both eyes. God, all he wanted to do was sleep. At least he probably could in this contraption.

Jonathan stood, took two steps to the ends of the box, and wrapped a hand around one of Bran's ankles. Bran tensed, expecting pain—he hadn't answered a direct question, after all—but nothing happened. Or rather, nothing bad. Just felt like Jonathan had clipped his ankle cuff to the side of the box. Then Jonathan reached over and clipped the other cuff, leaving his legs a little spread, but certainly not enough to expose bits and pieces he'd rather protect right now. Okay, so he'd have a little less range of motion than he'd expected. Still no biggie—it was a miracle just to be able to stretch out.

"I asked you a question, Brandon. You know what to do?"

Bran sighed, but answered. Stupid to make Jonathan angry now. "Push the button when I'm ready to eat from your hand or end the contract. Nothing else." His voice was raw to the point of barely audible, but Jonathan seemed to get the gist, at least.

"There's a good boy," Jonathan said, straightening to his feet. "Watch your face, now; I'm afraid there's only a couple inches of clearance."

He let the lid drop closed, and Bran felt the whisper of air against his forehead and cheeks as it clunked into place.

Shit. *Shit.* He lifted his head and promptly banged his nose against the lid. Jonathan hadn't been kidding about the low clearance. Bran had never been claustrophobic before, and the fucking lid was *see-through*, for fuck's sake, but there was no denying the urge to rattle the box, pound and rage against the lid until it popped. Not like he could've though, even if he'd thought it worth the strain; there wasn't enough room in here to move his arms like that.

Jonathan stepped over him again, leaned in close. Bran stared up at his slightly-blurred form through the thick Plexiglas lid. "Plenty of air holes, so don't worry about that. One thing, though—no sleeping, all right?"

Yeah, *fuck* that. No way Jonathan would be able to stay up long enough to police him.

But he kept that to himself as Jonathan walked away.

Despite being a mass of pain, he managed to drop off for a few seconds—until something buzzed, and suddenly it felt as if a ring of fucking fire ants had bitten his ankles. His calf muscles spasmed and he jerked his legs back the inch or two the cuffs allowed. What the *fuck*? Was he so far gone he was starting to hallucinate? Dream of Jonathan beating his feet?

Great. Cos he doesn't torture me enough in real *life.*

He tried to settle back down, close his eyes, find sleep again. If he could just stop shivering, even for a *second . . .*

He squirmed a little, tried to find some small measure of comfort or warmth. That fucking monster plug in his ass wiggled along with him, and he tried, for the thousandth time, to force it out. Wouldn't budge. And he could've sworn it bit him for trying.

At least the air conditioning didn't blow quite so hard in here. And there was plenty of air wafting in through those holes. Even his back had stopped spasming. It wasn't so bad compared to the other cage. All he had to do was relax, ignore the pain of the flogging, let himself drift off again . . .

And then that fucking buzz came back and brought the fire ants along with it. No sleep-dulled sensation this time; the pain was *huge*, and his calves cramped and his legs jerked and the monster plug shifted in his ass and he hit his nose on the lid again. A fucking *electric shock.* That had to be it. Was Jonathan watching him through the camera, hitting the button every time he started to fall asleep?

Probably stroking a fucking white cat while he does it.

"Yeah? Well *fuck you too!*" he shouted, braced himself for a shock that didn't come. Maybe there was no sound on the camera system? Or maybe Jonathan was just fucking with his head again. Certainly seemed to be the fucker's favorite pastime.

He risked closing his eyes again, clenched jaws and teeth against the inevitable—

Huh. Not so inevitable after all.

Maybe Jonathan really wasn't watching.

Or maybe he was just waiting for Bran to get comfortable again, let his guard down before he pounced.

Well, not like he had anything better to do down here anyway. And both mind and body were pulling him toward sleep by the roots of his hair. This time when his eyes slipped closed, it wasn't on purpose.

He'd nearly drifted off when the pain hit again, there and gone in an instant like it'd never even happened. Except for the part where he was wide awake again. And he'd banged his elbow on the wall of the box, right on that awful spot that makes you nauseous. And the damn plug had shifted again, and Jesus, Jonathan hadn't been kidding when he said you never got used to it. If anything, it hurt more now than it had at the beginning. His muscles wouldn't stop clenching against it, trying to expel it, even though they'd gone so far past strained that the effort hurt more than the plug did.

He dug his shoulders and heels in and tried to arch his hips up off the ground. Made it an inch or two before his pelvis hit the lid of the box. Felt better not to be lying on the plug, but no way could he hold this position for more than a few seconds. He was trembling already. Hey, at least it kept him warm. Ish. Well, at least not *totally* freezing.

He fell back, panting and exhausted and totally determined not to close his eyes.

Except the shock still came. And then again what felt like five or so minutes later, and again five or so minutes after that.

No Jonathan watching. No white cat. Just a timer.

Jonathan was probably asleep in his big comfortable bed, happily dreaming of Bran's suffering. Did that mean he planned to leave him in here *all night?*

God, fuck him. Fuck him with a rusty fucking spike.

Bran's stomach cramped. Again. Empty. So empty it felt like it was touching his spine. Every part of him ached, burned. Screamed. For hours.

He clamped his mouth shut, tried not to let it out. He couldn't anyway. He was all screamed out, his throat raw from it. Didn't matter if he didn't—no, *couldn't*—move. Every last inch of his skin had been scoured with Jonathan's whip.

He lifted his head as far as he could without bumping his nose, breath hitching, shuddering in his chest. Couldn't even close his eyes without bracing himself for the next shock. Without seeing a fist coming toward him. Without tensing for the blow.

Without being too small again to fight back any other way.

A tear crawled down his temple, the only warmth he'd felt in forever. Cold and wet a moment later. Couldn't even wipe it away.

And then he couldn't stop. Jesus *fuck*, was he *sobbing?*

Suck it up, sissy. Don't be such a fucking baby.

Zzzzt! "Fuck!" he shouted—tried to, anyway; had no voice left—body jerking like it did every time, knees and elbows hitting the coffin like they did every time, pain chasing every thought from his head and bringing tears back to his eyes. The hurt was already gone by the time he'd stopped moving—at least *that* hurt, anyway, blessedly residue-free, as awful as it was when it happened—but the tears weren't leaving so easy.

He couldn't stop. He couldn't *do* this anymore. Why had he even bothered trying? What was worth so damn fucking much?

Strange how calm he felt as he went to flip the lid of the panic button with cold, cold fingers . . . Until he realized it had slipped from his hand.

Oh shit oh shit, where is it? He scrabbled at the side of the box, grabbing the wire still attached to his wrist. Horrible relief as he pulled it into his palm, thumb flicking at the cap.

It didn't open.

For one awful moment, his breath froze, but then he flicked it again with a trembling hand and the cap popped open, the button smooth against his thumb. Another breath, another shudder—*You sure you want to do this?*—and he punched it.

Jonathan seemed to materialize at his side, just *there* between one blink and the next, opening the lid. "I'm here, Brandon, I'm here," he said, voice as warm and soothing as the hand he stroked across Bran's cheek, wiping at tears. "Can you sit up?"

He couldn't. Not without help. Was all he could do to shake his head.

"It's all right, I'll help you." Jonathan opened the side of the box, slid his hand under Bran's shoulder and let him roll out onto the floor. Weirdly soft. Fucking *freezing*.

And then suddenly he wasn't so cold anymore. A blanket over him, Jonathan's arms wrapped around him, rubbing up and down his own. Bran let out a pathetic little moan and leaned into it, head pushing into the solid warmth of Jonathan's chest.

Jonathan's heart beat calm and strong. He radiated heat like an oven. Bran pressed closer and soaked it in like a lizard on a rock. Wished he could stop crying.

For a second, he almost forgot how hungry he was. How angry he was. He knew he was supposed to be, but like the pain toward the end of the flogging, everything was hazy, distant, happening to someone else. He couldn't quite seem to get himself past *warm-free-youcameforme-you*came*forme*, even as his teeth still chattered and his limbs refused to move and Jonathan had only come for him because he'd *put him there in the first place*. Because Bran had wussed out and pushed the fucking button.

Didn't matter. None of it mattered. Jonathan was here, holding him. Asking if he needed help.

"Can you stand?"

Bran shook his head. Then realized the clock was ticking, ticking, the timer was counting down and those cuffs were still locked around his ankles and there was *no fucking way* he could go through that again, he'd *pushed the fucking button*, and he clutched at the front of Jonathan's shirt and begged, "Take them off, please, take them off!"

Jonathan looked down at him, their foreheads just inches apart. "Take what off?"

"The . . . the—" Jesus, he couldn't even *say* it, they scared him so fucking bad. "Please, I can't . . ." He tucked a knee tighter to his chest, gripped his calf beneath the blanket in a shaking hand. It wouldn't help. Jonathan looked on patiently, brow furrowed with concern or perhaps just confusion, and Bran finally spat out, "The *shocks*. Take them off, please."

"Oh." Relief broke across Jonathan's face, and he brushed Bran's sticky hair back from his forehead, replaced it with a warm press of lips. "It's all right. You're not hooked up to the machine anymore. It's just your cuffs."

Jonathan's logic asserted itself for about two-tenths of a second before the fear came rushing back in. Just the *feel* of those things around his ankles . . .

"Please," he said again, and Jonathan kissed him and murmured "okay" and took a little key from a chain around his neck and unlocked the cuffs from Bran's ankles.

Bran felt so relieved when they were gone he could scarcely credit it.

He felt, strangely, *naked.*

Probably because you are, moron.

Which reminded him of something else he needed off him—or rather, *out* of him. He rolled onto his side, moaning as the plug inside him shifted. Jonathan nodded, immediately taking the hint—*thank God*—then pulled it out as gently as he could. It slid free a lot easier than it had gone in, leaving Bran moaning again, this time in relief. Still, he had to suck in a few deep breaths to process the lingering ache.

"So, am I taking you to the kitchen, or upstairs?" Jonathan asked.

Bran's stomach lurched, the mere thought of food making him dizzy. How long had it been since he'd had anything but water? Five days? Six? Couldn't even remember what having anything in his mouth felt like. *Well, anything besides Jonathan's dick.*

"Kitchen," Bran huffed, stomach cramping, roiling again. Jesus, could he even eat now? Fuck it, he had to at least try. "Please, Jonathan."

Except he couldn't get up, even with Jonathan's help. His legs had gone all boneless and rubbery, flopping under him like dead fish. A hot flush of humiliation crawled up the back of his neck.

Jonathan's hand came up to rest there for a moment, lips brushing against Bran's forehead, his cheek. He gently laid him on the floor, smoothed the blanket over him. "Wait here, I'll be right back."

Bran hugged the blanket tighter to himself—fleece, down, all softness and warmth and *it smells like Jonathan*, earthy and clean and crisp—and fell dead asleep.

He lurched himself awake some moments later, phantom shocks shooting up his legs. Jonathan was back, holding a steaming mug in both hands.

"Here," he said, resting the mug on the floor and sitting down, his back pressed to the coffin that had broken Bran into a million blubbery pieces, his legs spread in a V. He slid an arm round Bran's shoulders, hoisted him upright and arranged him, still cocooned in the blanket, with his back to Jonathan's chest. Jonathan took the mug in one hand, curled his other loose but steady around Bran's chest to stop him from listing sideways. Bran blinked, must've fallen asleep again—next he knew, the mug was at his lips, sweet mouthwatering steam wafting over his face, and Jonathan was coaxing him to "Drink, come on, open up."

Bran parted his lips, let Jonathan tip a small splash of *oh sweet God in heaven what* was *that?* over his tongue. Rich, sweet, creamy, thick. A second later his sense of taste kicked in—hot chocolate, and not the shit that came in powder form. Easily the best hot chocolate he'd ever tasted—fuck, easily the best *anything* he'd ever tasted, and he swished it around before he swallowed it down, coating his mouth with it, and then tried to nudge the bottom of the cup through the blanket, to make Jonathan pour faster—

Ambrosia, it was fucking *ambrosia,* but then nausea surged and he had to turn his head away, clamp his teeth together and suck in deep breaths through his nose until his stomach settled round the first sip he'd taken.

"Easy, easy, you'll make yourself sick," Jonathan admonished, his voice a gentle rumble against Bran's back. "Can I get you some broth instead?"

Bran shook his head vehemently—or at least as vehemently as he could manage right now, which was admittedly kind of pathetic—and mumbled, "S'okay. Better now."

"Good." Jonathan gave him another sip, pressed his lips to Bran's temple again. Strange how normal it felt. How right. How much Bran craved the heat of his body, melted into his tender touch. Same hands that had beaten the ever-loving shit out of him . . . when was it, exactly? Yesterday?

Jonathan's sleeve brushed against the blanket, smooth blue silk nearly the same shade as his eyes—his robe instead of his usual sweater. His tousled hair tickled Bran's cheek. Jonathan had climbed out of bed to rush down here and take care of him. Just like he'd promised.

They sat there on the floor until Bran had finished the cocoa, until his eyes drifted shut again and he let himself relax into the calm, patient rhythm of Jonathan's breathing. At last Jonathan chuckled and gave Bran a tiny shake. "Come on now, don't nod off on me. We'll both end up stiff if we spend the night down here."

What'd he mean, end up?

Bran groaned as Jonathan shifted him forward a bit and stood. He set the mug on the nearby table, then held out his hand to Bran. "Let's try getting your legs under you."

Muscles still protesting, Bran rolled onto his knees and pushed himself up with both hands. Shoulders, back, and legs all screamed in unison, but he gritted his teeth and slowly straightened. Well, at least he was standing, which was more than he could have done a few minutes ago. However, something told him putting one foot in front of the other would be a different story.

Sure enough, he only made it a couple of steps before he faltered, slumping over, fresh pain hitting him from all sides. Jesus, wasn't there even one fucking *tendon* Jonathan had managed to miss with that flogger?

"Put your weight on me," Jonathan said, his arm sliding around Bran's waist. Bran couldn't help stiffening, though the added tension flooding his body made him bite back a groan. Jonathan was half a foot shorter than him. How the hell was he supposed to get them both up that staircase?

Bran pulled away, lurching ahead a step or two, until he had no choice but to grab hold of the wall. Breath coming in ragged gasps, he almost tumbled to the floor.

"Still so stubborn," Jonathan murmured, sidling up to wrap his arm around Bran's waist again. "Lean on me, Brandon. I promise you, I will *not* let you fall."

Jonathan had done a lot of awful things, but he'd *never* reneged on a promise. He'd come down in the middle of the night to take Bran out of that fucking box, hadn't he? Besides, there was no way Bran could make it any further on his own; his legs were shaking just with the effort to stay upright.

So he nodded and let Jonathan lead him out of the dungeon. He started to veer toward the staircase, but Jonathan shook his head, led him past it, to the kitchen. Correction, to the elevator across from the kitchen. How had he forgotten about that?

He felt kind of silly taking an elevator one floor, but honestly, there was no way he'd ever have managed the stairs. He barely managed the elevator; two steps into the upstairs foyer, he had to press a shoulder to the wall and just breathe for a minute. Jonathan waited patiently, hand rubbing up and down Bran's back, a warm, reassuring touch he could feel even through the blanket. "Almost there, Brandon."

Jonathan helped him along to the bedroom. God, that fucking yoga mat looked so damn good right now, but when he started to lower himself onto it, Jonathan shook his head and gestured toward the bathroom.

His *private* bathroom. Which Bran hadn't used since the morning after he'd arrived.

"Come on," Jonathan said. "You look like you could use a good long soak."

Jonathan's hand at his elbow, Bran managed to stagger into the bathroom, then plopped down on the toilet lid while Jonathan ran him a bath. Half zoned-out, he stared off into nothing for God knew how long, until Jonathan's hand on his shoulder jerked him back to the present.

Bran reluctantly gave up the blanket and stepped into the tub, wincing as he sat down. Jesus, the water was barely lukewarm, and it still made every mark on his skin scream afresh.

"Sorry about that," Jonathan said, "but you'd hurt worse if I'd made it any hotter. And cold water would make your muscles cramp. Give it a few minutes and the smarting should subside."

Smarting? Is that what you call it?

Bran squeezed his eyes shut and leaned back against the smooth enamel, trying to relax. He'd just about managed it when Jonathan tapped him on the arm and said, "Scoot up a bit."

He's gonna climb in with me?

Robeless and naked, Jonathan did just that, sliding in behind Bran and then pulling him close, Bran's back to his chest, just like downstairs a few minutes ago. Then he reached for a washcloth, wetted it down, and started running it over Bran's chest.

It stung at first, just like when he'd sat down, but then the warm water started to feel damn good. He'd been a soggy, sweaty mess for so long, he'd forgotten what it felt like to be clean. He would've preferred to wash himself, but he was too fucking exhausted to put up a fight.

So he didn't even give a token protest when Jonathan nudged him forward, making him sit up straight so Jonathan could wash his hair. He sighed and relaxed into it, not caring anymore that Jonathan was treating him like a damn baby. Not when Jonathan's fingers felt so fucking amazing massaging his scalp.

Jonathan grabbed the showerhead to rinse him off, and then Bran eased himself back, resting against Jonathan's chest, the slow, steady thump of his heart seeping into Bran's skin.

He'd come close to nodding off again when Jonathan's lips brushed his temple. "Water's getting cold. High time we were both in bed, don't you think?"

God, you mean I'm supposed to get up and walk *after this?*

For a second, Bran considered asking Jonathan if he could just sleep in the tub, but Jonathan stood and stepped out, ignoring the fact that he was dripping all over the bathmat while he held his hand out to Bran.

Bran made it as far as the toilet lid before his muscles, now relaxed but still aching, gave out on him. He sat there watching as Jonathan dried himself off, then grabbed a fresh towel and began doing the same for Bran.

Soft as the cotton—and Jonathan's touch—was, the nap of the terrycloth grated over Bran's welted skin. Jonathan murmured soothing nonsense as he dried him—*There now* and *It's okay* and *Almost done*—and helped him lean against the vanity while he wiped his back, between his ass cheeks, down his legs, even the soles of his feet. When Jonathan was finished, he opened the medicine cabinet, grabbed a bottle of lotion, and began massaging it into Bran's skin.

God, it smelled great. Vanilla and something flowery he couldn't identify. Any other time, he would've balked, but not tonight. Not with Jonathan's hands moving all over him, soothing where he'd brought the hurt before.

Why was he doing *that?*

Too many contradictions, and Bran's brain was still too scrambled to ponder them all. He didn't want to think anymore. He wanted his yoga mat and his blanket, and he wanted them *now*.

But Jonathan took him by the arm and steered him over to the bed. The bed Bran hadn't slept in since that night Jonathan had handcuffed him to it.

Bran took one look at the rumpled blue sheets and froze. *Oh, God.* Jonathan wasn't planning to fuck him now, not after everything else he'd put him through. Was he?

"I don't want anything from you tonight, Brandon. Except to see to your comfort." Jonathan smiled and patted the edge of the bed. "Come on, climb in so we can both get warm."

The room was a bit chilly, but after the freezing dungeon, Bran barely registered it. Still, the sheets felt like heaven, sleek cotton sateen floating over his skin. Jonathan slid in beside him, then tugged the comforter up to their chins.

He instinctively tensed as Jonathan scooted closer. If he didn't want sex tonight, what *did* he want? What price would Bran have to pay for spending the night here instead of huddled on his yoga mat?

"Easy," Jonathan murmured, lips at Bran's shoulder, fingertips trailing down his arm. Maybe it was that soft, sexily liquid tone in his voice, maybe it was the touch of his hand, maybe it was simply being *comfortable* for the first time since he'd arrived here . . . For whatever reason, Bran found himself instantly hard.

Of course, Jonathan knew it practically the moment it happened. *As if the tent over your crotch wasn't his first clue.* Down came his hand, his fingers closing around Bran's dick, giving it a quick tug.

"Would you like this tonight?" Jonathan asked. "No reciprocation expected."

God, he was too fucking tired to get off—and too fucking tired, apparently, to maintain his erection. Too fucking tired to even be embarrassed about it. "I. . . I'd just like to sleep, Jonathan." He licked his lips, hoping Jonathan wouldn't be disappointed.

And where the hell did that *come from?*

Jonathan's grin spread wide as he leaned in to give Bran a kiss. "Sleep then," he murmured against Bran's lips. "Sleep as long as you like."

ran woke, still exhausted, to the pain of a shock shooting up his ankles. Took him a second to register that he was alone in Jonathan's bed, not back in the coffin. No shocks. Not even any cuffs. Just a nightmare.

He squinted at the clock: 11:07 AM. He had to pee, but fuck it; he was too sore to move, and Jonathan *had* said to sleep as long as he liked. Or had he dreamed that part too? Whatever. Jonathan wasn't here, wasn't bothering him, so he decided to go with it, imagined or not, and closed his eyes again.

He next woke just after three in the afternoon to the same jolting sensation as before, and this time his bladder would brook no argument. He felt pretty rested now, anyway. How long had he slept? Ten hours? Twelve? *When did I get out of that box?*

Rolling out of bed was an exercise in strict self-control, and somehow he still ended up on his hands and knees instead of his feet, forehead pressed to the floor, head spinning and body so far past aching he couldn't even catalog his individual hurts. For one terrible second, he found his mouth forming Jonathan's name, but he bit that bullshit back—no fucking way he'd call the man for help right now.

He crawled to the bathroom instead.

It'd been a damn long time since he'd had to sit to piss, but he was pretty far past pride at this point, and hey, congrats to Jonathan for finally managing that, the little fuck.

Bran's fingers clenched. *So easy. You gave it up so easy. A day, maybe? Half the night? You barely made him work for it.*

God, why had he *asked* for that?

And why did it feel so easy to live with now?

His stomach rumbled. Had been for almost a week; he barely even felt the pain anymore. But after that taste last night, that hot blissful rush of fat and sugar, it'd gotten greedy again. He shook off, levered to his feet with the help of the vanity and the wall, reached down to pull his pants up and remembered he wasn't wearing any. Hadn't been for a week.

He went to wash his hands, a bit steadier on his feet now, and caught sight of that massive bathtub. Fuzzy memories of last night, of Jonathan climbing in with him, washing him, drying him . . . so very gentle, so kind and attentive. Almost like love.

But it's not. He was just patching his broken toy back up, and don't you forget it.

. . . Yet he took you to bed like a lover.

Nothing had happened, though. Had it? He'd been so tired. Was *still* tired. Thought of crawling back into that big soft bed, but thoughts of food won out.

He staggered halfway down the hall to Jonathan's office, but by the time he got there, he'd loosened up enough to stop holding onto the wall. Jonathan glanced up and smiled as Bran came in.

"Well, you look rested. Would you like something to eat?"

It took all Bran's willpower not to say, "God, yes!" Instead, he forced a smile of his own and came over, kneeling down on the cushion beside Jonathan's desk. Landing ass to heels with all those aches and pains shooting up his legs and back nearly made him groan aloud, but he bit it back. He'd let Jonathan hear enough of his screaming this week.

"Yes, Jonathan," he replied. "I'd like some breakfast."

"More like lunch," Jonathan said, reaching for the house phone. "But I'll have Sabrina bring something up."

She showed up with a tray several endless minutes later, Bran's roiling stomach on the verge of eating itself while he waited. Fruit, toast squares with jam, a small pot of tea. No coffee, of course. He hadn't earned it yet.

A whole day without demerits before I get so much as a fucking sip. Might as well be a million years.

Jonathan plucked a grape from the tray and popped it into Bran's mouth. Sweet, moist, absolute *heaven*. Best fucking grape he ever ate. So was the next one. And the piece of melon that followed, the bite of toast, buttery and delicious. What kind of jam was it? Blackberry? Homemade? God, he'd never tasted anything so good.

He sucked on Jonathan's fingers even as shame burned his cheeks—not enough to stop him, though, not at all—trying to get every last crumb of toast and drop of jam. So fucking *hungry*. Hungry enough to take whatever Jonathan gave him without hesitation.

Enough to rest his cheek on Jonathan's knee when directed by a stroking hand, butt his head into Jonathan's palm like a fucking dog. Was this really all it took? A rumbling stomach, a little pain and fear, and he was on his knees eating out of Jonathan's hand?

I can't go back in that box again.

Just the *thought* of it was so fucking terrifying he almost lost his appetite.

Almost.

Another grape, and this time Jonathan's thumb lingered, teasing Bran's bottom lip until Bran let the tip slip inside. It still tasted like jam. Jonathan thrust it gently in and out, and another part of Bran's body responded in spite of himself. Was all he could do to keep from reaching down and palming his stiffening dick. Must be the good sleep, the good food. Jonathan had *tortured* him, *broken* him—no way could he still want to fuck the guy.

Or be fucked, more like. He'd never let you top.

That questing thumb went a little deeper, and Bran closed his lips around it, breathed hard through his nose. So, okay, irritating as it was, Jonathan was damn fucking attractive. Pheromones, maybe. Just chemistry.

In fairness, you did ask him to break you.

Strange how knowing that didn't seem to make a damn bit of difference, though. So why was he sucking around Jonathan's thumb? Why had he just let out a little moan? Why was his dick so fucking hard?

"More?" Jonathan asked, and for a second, Bran wasn't sure which appetite Jonathan was offering to sate. But then the finger was gone and a little triangle of toast—God, Sabrina had even cut the fucking crusts off, like he was some kid or something—was hovering at his lips. He ate it down in one big bite, and like the fucking dog he'd sworn upside down and sideways he wasn't, he opened his mouth for another.

Fuck Jonathan for that. Seriously. Fuck *him.*

Jonathan popped a slice of kiwi in his mouth, and for a moment, as the tangy sweetness burst on his tongue in a nearly orgasmic rush, he forgot to be angry.

Forgot a second time when Jonathan's bare foot inched up the inside of Bran's spread thighs and curled around his erection.

God, he has really soft feet.

Bran leaned into that touch despite himself, amazed that the soles of anyone's feet could feel so good.

He probably gets fucking pedicures or some bullshit.

Jonathan's own erection bulged against his fly, the heat of it seeping into Bran's skin from nearly a foot away. His thumb pushed into Bran's mouth again, and Bran dragged his teeth along the pad, Jonathan's hiss making him realize, too late, that he'd bitten down a bit too hard.

Bran flinched and drew back, half-expecting Jonathan to smack him. But Jonathan just cupped his chin and smiled.

"Still hungry, I see." He leaned down, brushing those red lips over Bran's mouth, darting his tongue inside. He tasted like berries and melon and buttered toast and—*oh sweet God*—fresh black coffee. The same thing he'd served that morning after he'd taken Bran to bed.

After he'd cuffed you and made you come so hard you hit yourself in the chin.

The memory made Bran's dick stand straight up, every spare drop of blood in his body pulsing between his ears.

"You want this?" Jonathan asked, catching hold of Bran's hand, bringing it up to cup his erection. So stiff it was practically bursting through his zipper. How the hell did he keep from coming right then and there?

Did he want it? His body certainly seemed to—he could practically feel it already, hot and heavy on his tongue. And he'd been attracted to this kinder, gentler version of Jonathan from nearly the moment he'd laid eyes on the man. So hard to forgive him for what he'd done, though. To forgive him for being so fucking *edible* all the time, even when he was a total ass, infuriating, heartless and cruel.

So hard to forgive *himself* for wanting the little shit anyway. Maybe that's what happened when you broke.

"One," Jonathan said, his hand still stroking Bran's where it lay pressed to Jonathan's crotch. Bran had to fight the urge to clench his fingers; Jonathan would *not* appreciate that. "It's all right." Jonathan's free hand came up to stroke Bran's cheek. Warm. So, so gentle. Why did he have to be like that? Why did he have to make it so hard to hate him? "It won't be like yesterday. You might even find yourself *enjoying* these demerits. Now answer the question." His hand tightened over Bran's, pressing Bran's fingers to Jonathan's straining dick. "Do you want this?" Jonathan's foot stroked over Bran's dick; Bran gasped. "And this?"

Fuck it. He *did* want it, and if it was just one more way Jonathan had fucked him up, well . . . at least he'd stop hurting for a little while. "Y-yes, Jonathan."

Jonathan gave his shoulder a gentle push, until Bran lay flat on his back on the carpet. Felt good to unfold himself from that awful kneeling position and stretch out, though the nap of the rug bit into his sore back and ass. Jonathan followed him down, waited for him to make himself comfortable—*relatively, anyway*—then turned to face him.

"Unzip me," he said, and Bran didn't need to be asked twice. Jonathan's hard-on popped out, tapping Bran's chin, and he scooted down instantly, sliding the tip between his lips.

Hot. Salty. Firm. A perfect mouthful. This time he remembered to breathe through his nose, braced himself for Jonathan to start thrusting. But to his surprise, Jonathan didn't. He just slung a leg over Bran's chest, turned himself to face Bran's feet, and began kissing his way down Bran's belly.

Oh, Jesus. As if I don't have enough to distract me.

Bran tried to keep his mind on the dick in his mouth, swirling his tongue around the crown. At least Jonathan wasn't pushing him to take more than he could comfortably handle. No face-fucking this time. He was actually being *gentle*. What the fuck was going on?

Bran nearly lost it—nearly forgot himself and bit down—as Jonathan swallowed his dick. He had to pull back a second for the shock to pass, to let himself breathe.

What the hell was Jonathan doing with his tongue? Wrapping it along the length of Bran's dick, flicking it, sucking. Jesus, where had he learned to *do* that? Bran had never had head this good, not in any seedy back alley, not in any filthy bar bathroom. Not even in his fucking fantasies.

He wasn't anywhere near this good at giving it, either. No wonder Jonathan would rather grab hold of his hair and plow his mouth. Would he even be able to get Jonathan off? He sucked harder, grabbing the root of Jonathan's dick with one hand. Maybe he couldn't fit the whole thing in his mouth without being forced, but at least he could do this much.

He sucked and stroked, and Jonathan shifted his weight to one hand and wrapped the other one around the base of Bran's dick as well, so that their motions almost mirrored. Such a strange, delicious sensation, and who knew, maybe he could learn a thing or two. Jonathan swirled his tongue around the crown of Bran's dick as he twisted his wrist to match, and Bran copied the movement, tore a little moan from Jonathan. How strangely satisfying that was, to know he'd done that himself, wobbled Jonathan's composure, even if he had done it by copying the guy.

He tried it again, and then dipped his tongue in Jonathan's slit when Jonathan did the same to him and made him gasp so hard he nearly choked. Again Jonathan moaned, easy and wanton, and the vibration shot right through Bran's dick and up to his balls, his lower belly, the base of his spine. Fucking *amazing*. He hummed around Jonathan's dick in return, fingers tightening around the base as he pumped him, pumped him, and Jonathan's hips jerked once, twice, his mouth coming off Bran, his fingers going slack around Bran's dick. Bran had one second to think *Selfish bastard* before he felt the telltale rush of blood beneath his fingertips, heard Jonathan's breath go shallow and fast, and he gave one last hard suck before pulling Jonathan's dick from his mouth and jacking him to completion, letting him come all over his chest.

Jonathan had barely stopped spurting before he buried his face in Bran's groin again, swallowing him right down to the root, free hand rolling his balls before it slipped back further and a single spit-coated finger plunged inside him. Damn good thing Jonathan's dick wasn't in Bran's mouth anymore; Bran rocked his head back, shouted through gritted teeth at the pain and the pleasure of the rough penetration, his ass so sore from yesterday's monster plug, but Jonathan's finger so sweet against his prostate. The pain faded almost instantly beneath the onslaught of *pressure-pleasure-relief,* and he bucked his hips up into Jonathan's willing mouth, drove his cock down Jonathan's willing throat, squeezed his eyes closed and grappled at Jonathan's head with both hands as the man hollowed his cheeks and stroked his tongue across Bran's shaft and worked his throat around Bran's head as Bran came and came and came.

Took a little while before he floated back to earth with Jonathan curled up beside him, fingers playing with his hair, lips pressed to his temple. *Like a lover. Like he actually* cares.

Bran rolled over, head still spinning, blinking against the haze clouding his eyes, body still abuzz with the force of his orgasm, and good God, how the hell did they keep getting more intense when the last one had nearly blown the top of his fucking head off?

Was it him? Was it Jonathan? Was it just the fact that his body had never felt more alive, more on fire, even if most of the time it hurt like hell?

His rumbling stomach jarred him from his blissed-out haze. Jonathan must've heard it too, because he sat up, grinning, and said, "Want to finish breakfast, then?"

"Yes, Jonathan," Bran replied, dragging himself back into the kneeling position Jonathan expected of him. He hurt less on the endorphin high of that orgasm, but seemed to have less control over his body now, too. Took him a while to lever himself back into position. And, *fucking ewww,* he felt Jonathan's cum dribbling down his chest when he sat. Shit. When was Jonathan gonna say something about that?

After all, Jonathan had swallowed for Bran, and he'd made such a huge fucking deal about it last time, had nearly *suffocated* him to force it down.

Bran tried very hard not to draw any attention to the cum as he met Jonathan's easy gaze and waited for the man to say, "Two."

But he didn't. Just leaned forward, still grinning, and kissed Bran. On the lips. With *tongue.* And the taste of Bran still in his mouth, slimy and disgusting. Bran tried to pull away, but Jonathan held him there for a second more before letting go. Just to make his point.

Bran had to suppress the urge to spit out even that much, until his gaze landed on the cane lying on the edge of Jonathan's desk. A chill shot straight through him. Was Jonathan going to punish him for jerking him off instead of swallowing? For hesitating before answering him earlier?

Please, no. Not now.

"Don't worry," Jonathan said. He'd been saying that a lot this morning; did he really think Bran was that fragile right now? *Was* Bran really that fragile right now?

. . . 'Fraid so, pal.

"You're afraid I'll punish you for not swallowing." Bran nodded, and Jonathan—who'd already thrown Bran off his game half a dozen times this morning—threw him again by just handing him a wad of tissues. "I won't, not now. Later, when you can take it again. But you *are* at two."

Great. Something else to look forward to. How had he forgotten, even for a second, how much power he'd let Jonathan hold over him? How much Jonathan enjoyed wielding said power?

Jonathan held up another grape, pressed it against Bran's lips. Bran didn't open his mouth—not at first, anyway—as the wheels turned in his head. Sure, he could resist. He could take things back to the way they were a day or so ago, force Jonathan to force him again. Maybe even force Jonathan to drag him back down to the dungeon and—

No. No. He couldn't win in the end anyway, not against *that*, so what was the point in fighting? He was tired of hurting. He was tired of being afraid. And he *liked* nice-Jonathan. Liked the things nice-Jonathan did for him, liked the way nice-Jonathan could make him feel. So what if he didn't particularly like *himself* under nice-Jonathan's thumb? So what if he felt weak there, childish, helpless, needy, *hungry*, ashamed of his urges? What was any of that compared to another night in the fucking coffin?

He opened his mouth, and let Jonathan put the grape on his tongue.

CHAPTER **15**

"It's been going well these past couple of days," Jonathan said as Sabrina carried a covered tray onto the balcony. A stainless steel carafe and two plates. One fork, of course, since Brandon wouldn't need one for himself. Jonathan reached down to stroke Brandon's cheek, thumb teasing his lower lip. "You've done such a good job grooming yourself today, too. I'm quite pleased."

Brandon flashed him a shaky smile and bowed his head for a moment, until Jonathan tipped his chin back up. "Close your eyes."

More than a touch of apprehension flashing across those striking features, but Brandon did as told, his chest rising and falling a bit more rapidly than before. He'd been doing that a lot over the past two days. What did he have to be afraid of now? Jonathan hadn't taken him down to the dungeon in all that time. Kept him in bed with him every night, made sure he got off first. Fed him from his hand several times a day, waiting for his stomach to recover from five days of not eating at all. He'd never been this patient with any other submissive.

Jonathan lifted the lid off the first plate, scooped up his fork, sliced off a bite of the omelet Sabrina had made. Cheese, mushrooms, spinach, tomato. After days of starvation followed by two days of bland rations, this was bound to be a treat.

He held the fork under Brandon's nose, waved it back and forth. Brandon leaned forward, opening his mouth.

"Ah ah ah, not yet," Jonathan admonished. "Smell it first. Good, isn't it?"

Brandon took a deep breath through his nose, let it out through his mouth. He was practically drooling already and he hadn't even tasted it yet.

"I'm not teasing you for my sake, or to be cruel," Jonathan added. "You haven't taken much time to enjoy your food, have you? Well, I intend to correct that. Eating is about much more than chewing and swallowing. Food is more than just fuel. There's a sensuality to eating, and it's high time you learned to indulge in it."

Jonathan pushed the fork toward Brandon's lips. "Lick your lips. Then open your mouth, but only a tiny bit."

The pink tip of Brandon's tongue darted out, slowly, hesitantly, parting his teeth. Jonathan slid the bite of omelet between them, waiting for the tiny whimper he knew was coming. "I told you it was good, didn't I?"

Brandon had to pull back, dislodging the bite of omelet from his lips. Was Jonathan imagining it, or was that the world's faintest groan he heard? Well, no wonder. Sabrina's omelets could make even the most dedicated epicurean weep. And he still hadn't let Brandon fully savor his first taste yet.

Brandon licked his lips, his closed eyes fluttering. "Y-yes, Jonathan." Brandon's stomach punctuated that reply with a growl.

Well, maybe he was being a *bit* cruel. But then, he had to get some fun out of this too, didn't he? "All right, open wide." He let Brandon take the bite of omelet off the fork. "But chew *slowly*. Savor all the flavors. That's aged gruyere cheese, shiitake mushrooms, tomatoes and spinach grown here, picked fresh this morning. Eggs from free-range hens. Fresh butter. And a splash of the very best homemade pancake batter in the world, whipped in with the eggs to give them body and air and just a hint of starchiness. All the best ingredients prepared to perfection, all meant to be enjoyed like the luxuries they are. So *enjoy* them."

Brandon started to chew, and yes, this time that *was* a groan, and nothing the least bit faint about it. His eyelids fluttered again, and he breathed deep, as if trying to get himself through athletic sex. "It's good, isn't it?"

"God, yes . . . Jonathan."

Jonathan could practically hear the unuttered *Please, give me some more*. Could see the muscles bunch in Brandon's arms and shoulders, the barely-leashed urge to keep from grabbing the plate off the table and gobbling everything down. And yet, Brandon held himself in check, kept his eyes closed, kept his hands behind his back. A few days ago, such control would've been beyond him.

Another bite, slid off the fork into those moist, pink lips, then Jonathan took the cover off the other plate, sliced off a bite of Sabrina's famous chocolate chip pancakes, drenched in butter and whipped cream. Waved it under Brandon's nose, just like before. Brandon swayed, leaning back on his heels with a groan, shoulders jerking, breath coming even faster. His cock twitched up proud and neglected between his spread thighs, but Jonathan doubted he even noticed right now.

"See, it's much better when you take your time, isn't it?" Jonathan asked.

"Yes, Jonathan. Can I . . .?"

"Yes, go ahead."

"Can I open my eyes now?"

"Absolutely not. This is about the feel of the food on your tongue, the texture and the heat of it, the scent of it in your nostrils, the taste of it—salty, savory, sweet. While Sabrina's arranged it all quite beautifully, I know you well enough to know that if you're busy looking, you'll be too busy to remember to taste and smell and feel. Keep your eyes closed and engage your other senses." Jonathan nudged Brandon's parted lips with the bite of pancake, a blob of homemade whipped cream dripping onto the cushion beneath Brandon's knees, and said, "Slowly now. Just lick first. Tell me what you taste."

That agile tongue again, so much promise, poking hesitantly from between his lips. Swiping sweet cream and butter and a smudge of chocolate. Brandon sighed, shuddered, pulled his tongue back and ran it all along the inside of his mouth. "*God,*" he whispered, so softly Jonathan didn't have the heart to call him on speaking out of turn. Another pass of tongue across the inside of his cheek, and then, "Um, whipped cream, Jonathan?"

"Yes, very good, and not the stuff from a can, either. What else?"

"Butter. Real butter." Probably not a standard on Brandon's shopping list. Too extravagant. Brandon took another sniff of the bite still hovering before his lips, and smiled. "Chocolate."

"70% dark. The finest from Switzerland." Another thing Brandon was unlikely to indulge in often, even the Hershey's variety.

"Pancakes?" Brandon asked, hesitant again, like he thought he might be wrong. Like he was *afraid* of being wrong.

Jonathan brushed fingertips across Brandon's cheek and tried not to be bothered by Brandon's flinch before he went still. He just hadn't seen it coming, was all; it had surprised him. "You tell me," Jonathan whispered, and put the bite on Brandon's tongue.

Brandon's teeth closed around the tines of the fork, and Jonathan slid it out from between pursed lips, reminding him, "Slowly now," when Brandon chewed like he thought the pancakes might escape before he could swallow them. Brandon immediately complied, head tilted back, chewing through a moan and a smile, chewing and chewing and chewing before finally swallowing.

Jonathan took mercy and didn't make Brandon wait for the next bite. The whipped cream was melting, anyway. He snuck his own bites in between, eyes drifting again and again from the rapturous enjoyment on

Brandon's face to the very erect expression of said enjoyment between Brandon's legs. He licked his lips, found the air in the greenhouse suddenly quite thick.

Patience yourself, Jonathan. Dessert comes after *the meal.*

Time to give him something to drink—and Jonathan knew exactly what Brandon had been waiting for. Over a week without so much as a drop of coffee. Jonathan poured a fresh cup from the stainless steel carafe and carried it to Brandon's lips.

Brandon's back and shoulders went straight the moment the aroma wafted into his nostrils. "I promised you coffee if you went a day without demerits," Jonathan said. "Here, have a sip—you earned it. But be careful, it's hot."

He tipped the cup toward Brandon's mouth, heard the soft slurp as Brandon sucked it down. A tiny sip, then another, accompanied by a not-so-soft moan. Jonathan pulled the cup away for a moment, not terribly surprised when Brandon leaned in after it, following the scent even with his eyes closed.

"Want more?" Jonathan teased. Oh, why not? He'd been waiting for Brandon to let him do this ever since he'd arrived. It was so much better being playful than cruel. But there was a way to accomplish both at the same time.

Jonathan took a long sip but didn't swallow, relishing the sharp, bold taste for a moment before leaning down, cupping the back of Brandon's head with one hand. That same familiar touch that said, "You're *mine*, you're safe, just let it go." And was it his imagination, or did Brandon do just that, moving forward, pressing his lips to Jonathan's. Opening his mouth as Jonathan did the same, groaning at the taste of hot coffee as it spilled from his mouth to Brandon's.

Their lips remained locked long after Brandon had swallowed the coffee, tongues tangling, until Brandon gave a tiny groan and tried to pull back. Jonathan held him there for a few more seconds, sucking Brandon's lip between his teeth. After all, he needed breakfast too.

"Have you learned your lesson?" Jonathan asked, lips still hovering right over Brandon's.

Brandon leaned forward to close the distance between them, pressing his tongue between Jonathan's lips and tasting, exploring, moaning into Jonathan's mouth. God knew how he managed to keep his hands behind his back all this time; Jonathan's own wandered back up to Brandon's hair, gripping and tangling as the kiss drew on. At last Brandon pulled back—Jonathan let him this time; he'd started it, after all—and murmured, "To savor, Jonathan."

Jonathan almost, *almost* fooled himself into believing Brandon had said, *To savor Jonathan.*

After breakfast, Jonathan took Brandon back to his office and set him to stuffing envelopes again. This time he gave Brandon a small, low table to work from, with a cup of tea to wet his whistle after licking all those envelopes. Which was possibly not the best idea, since he couldn't help stealing glances whenever Brandon took another sip, cradling the hot cup in both long-fingered hands, liquid sliding down that sleek, smooth throat. Couldn't tear his eyes from that pink tongue lapping at the envelope flaps. By mid-afternoon, Jonathan had a hard bulge in his pants that wouldn't go down no matter how much he stared at the foundation's latest grant proposals.

Part of today's lesson was teaching Brandon to maintain his posture and position while he worked. And, to Jonathan's surprise and delight, Brandon didn't break form very often. Every now and then his shoulders would move out of alignment, and Jonathan would scoop up the crop from the edge of his desk and tap him with it, just hard enough to make him wince and pay attention. He'd straighten up without any coaching—or complaining or back-talk—which was far better than he'd done a few days ago.

Around four, Jonathan had had enough. Standing up, he took a long moment to stretch his cramped muscles, then gestured for Brandon to do the same. "Why don't we take a stroll downstairs?"

Brandon's eyes went wide. "Uh . . . did I do something wrong, Jonathan?"

Jonathan just smiled. "No, of course not. Did you hear me counting up today?"

"N-no, Jonathan, but . . ."

"Come along. It's time for another lesson." A hand on the back of Brandon's neck again, rubbing and soothing. Shame he still tensed at every touch. After all the orgasms, all the meals he'd fed Brandon with his own hands . . . Surely by now Brandon should have realized it wasn't all about pain or humiliation or being shoved in a cage.

Brandon trailed him wordlessly down the staircase to the dungeon, though he held the railing so tightly his fingers looked about to shatter. Sabrina poked her head out as they walked by, her gaze raking Brandon from head to toe. Curiously, Brandon didn't even seem to notice until she chirped, "Well, hello, you two. If you're off to play, I'll be sure to make extra portions tonight."

Jonathan stopped only just long enough to say, "Thank you, Sabrina, that'd be lovely," before guiding Brandon into the dungeon. He didn't want to risk Brandon falling out of the quiet headspace he'd found today. Not with what they were about to do.

Brandon's gaze zeroed right in on the two cages as they entered the dungeon, and he started to shake.

"I'm not putting you in there today. In either of them, or any of the others. You've done well the last two days—you've pleased me tremendously. You deserve a reward." Jonathan waved Brandon over to the leather-covered St. Andrew's cross along the far wall. Brandon's eyes widened again, his mouth dropping open. "Remember that night I put you up on the suspension bar, and you came so hard you nearly fainted?"

Brandon nodded slowly. "Yes, Jonathan. But I . . ."

"It's not all about pain, or fear. Or being cold or uncomfortable. In fact, it's not even *mostly* about that—not unless you make it be. I told you this room was a chamber of delights. It's about time you saw the truth in that."

Brandon swallowed hard, but walked over to the cross and stood in front of it.

"It's all right to touch it if you want," Jonathan said. "Feel the textures, press yourself against it. Stretch your arms above your head and feel the solidity of it beneath you. Don't be afraid to put all your weight on it."

Or sniff it, drinking in the scent like it was his favorite leather jacket. Brandon inhaled, rubbed his cheek against the smooth upholstery. Let his fingertips drift along the length of one strut until he touched the steel O-ring at the end of arm's reach. Went up on his tiptoes to curl his fingers into it, did the same with the O-ring on the opposite strut, and pulled himself a few inches off his feet. Strangely enthralled—like Jonathan was by the sudden play of muscles in Brandon's back, shoulders, and arms—or maybe just trying to figure out how Jonathan might use a device right out of some medieval torture chamber to tease out Brandon's pleasure. Or maybe he just appreciated the craftsmanship, fellow builder that he was. It, like most everything else in this dungeon, had been retooled just for Brandon, after all.

Jonathan went over to the nearest rack, picked up a pair of suspension cuffs, then slowly walked over to the cross. Laid one hand on the back of Brandon's neck, felt the muscles there tense before Brandon turned around.

"Hold out your hands," Jonathan ordered.

Brandon bit his lip, but immediately obeyed, questions in his gaze as Jonathan began to unlock the steel cuffs from his wrists.

"You're not going to give me trouble when I go to put these back on later, will you?"

Brandon shook his head. "No, Jonathan."

"Because I want you to be comfortable tonight, and God knows the leather's much softer than the steel."

Brandon looked a bit confused by Jonathan's statement, but seemed sincere enough when he said, "I promise I won't give you trouble, Jonathan."

It'd been over two days since Jonathan had used the cuffs around Brandon's wrists as actual restraints, but still the skin beneath them was a mass of bruising. Too much struggling in cuffs that simply weren't kind enough for that. Jonathan winced at the sight of it, lifted Brandon's left hand and brushed lips across the skin there. Maybe he shouldn't rush to put the steel cuffs back on, after all. Brandon had been so pliant these past two days, leather would suffice. And give him a little time to heal. Only the most hardcore masochists among his prior subs would have appreciated this kind of constant pain.

He buckled on the leather suspension cuffs, first onto Brandon's right wrist, then his left. "Turn back around. Face the cross," he said. "Lift your arms."

Brandon did as ordered, and Jonathan snapped the end of the cuffs to the steel O-rings on either strut. Poor Brandon was already trembling, and not from the cold this time. Jonathan pressed his lips to the nape of Brandon's neck, smoothed a hand down his back. "Have I *ever* lied to you, Brandon?"

A pause, then, softly, "No, Jonathan."

"Do you trust me, then?"

Another pause, much longer than the first. And, even softer than before, "I don't know, Jonathan."

Jonathan stroked circles across Brandon's back, letting him know he wasn't mad at that answer. Disappointed, maybe, but even he had to admit he'd expected a *no*. "Do you trust me at least not to hurt you tonight if I promise you I won't?"

This time the pause went on so long Jonathan nearly had to prompt him. "I'm afraid your definition of 'hurt' is not the same as mine. Jonathan."

He stroked another circle across Brandon's back, leaned in close enough to brush a kiss across his shoulder. "Your definition, then. I promise I won't hurt you. Trust me."

It wasn't a question, exactly, and Brandon didn't answer. But nor did he protest. Good enough.

Jonathan went to fetch a set of padded leather ankle cuffs, then knelt to fasten them. Brandon gave a tiny jerk when the first one went on, then went perfectly still. Almost *too* still. "Relax," Jonathan said. "I'm just going to secure you to the bottom struts. No electricity, I promise. Okay?"

A hitch in his breath, then, "Could . . . um, could you loosen the cuff a little? My ankles really hurt, Jonathan."

Not surprising; they were in worse shape than his wrists. All that time raging in the Plexiglas cage. "Of course." They were mostly for insurance tonight anyway. He doubted he'd really need them.

He straightened up once he was done, then rubbed his hands over Brandon's shoulders, down his arms. Brandon really was cold. Jonathan murmured, "I'll turn the heat up," then went over to the thermostat to do just that.

After a few seconds, the heater clicked on, blowing warm air into the dungeon. Almost uncomfortably warm. Might as well take advantage. He stripped out of his clothes, folded them and placed them on the nearby table, then ambled over to the toy rack to pick out his implement of choice for the evening.

Didn't take him long to select the perfect flogger—that soft, supple suede one he'd noticed Brandon fingering the night he'd left him alone down here. Sensual enough to bring a nun to tears. It didn't escape Jonathan's notice, either, that Brandon was ever-so-unsubtly watching him from the corner of his eye, trembling a bit. Even after all that soothing and reassuring, Brandon still didn't believe him. Well, it wasn't as if Jonathan had given him much reason to—at least, not before tonight. Time to correct that.

He let the soft tresses pour through his fingers, savoring the weight and the texture as he approached Brandon. "I told you I wouldn't hurt you, and I meant it." He draped the falls over Brandon's shoulder, let them trail down his back. This time Brandon's shiver was most definitely *not* from the room's temperature. In fact, it was positively decadent.

The lesson was off to a good start. "Does this feel like something that will hurt you, Brandon?"

Another shiver. "No, Jonathan."

"Good." With a smile, Jonathan trailed the falls over Brandon's other shoulder, along his arm, down his back, to the base of his spine. Brandon gave a little ticklish start, then settled. "See? I told you this wasn't all about pain." A hand on the nape of his neck again, waiting for Brandon to steady, to stop shivering. The room was certainly warm enough by now. Jonathan was already sweating, and he hadn't taken a single swing yet. "Let yourself go, just like this morning. Let yourself revel, savor, drift. No thinking. Let your senses be your world."

Then he stood back and gently swung the flogger. It landed on Brandon's left shoulder with a soft thump, the falls slithering down to the center of his back. Brandon lurched, landing against the front of the cross, let out a surprised whoosh of breath.

"See?" Jonathan asked. "No pain, right?"

Brandon shook his head. "No, Jonathan."

"Actually feels kind of nice, doesn't it?"

Interesting that Brandon could manage to shrug with his hands cuffed above his head. "Feels . . . okay," Brandon conceded.

It'd feel a lot better than okay once Jonathan got going. He pulled back his arm and landed a firmer but still gentle blow on Brandon's right shoulder. Not even enough to turn his skin pink. Brandon gave another start, then let out a breath, his hands tightening around the tongue of leather running up his palm.

Jonathan came over, skimming a hand up Brandon's arm. "Did that hurt? You seem to be bracing yourself."

"N-no, it didn't hurt, Jonathan. But . . ."

But he was still waiting for it to. What could Jonathan do to convince him otherwise? Nothing, except carrying through with what he'd promised.

He retook his position, drew the flogger back, landed another soft stroke on Brandon's shoulder. And another, and another. Over and over with the same light touch, the same gentle pace, until Brandon finally stopped flinching, stopped holding the cuffs in a death grip. Started to slump against the cross's soft leather upholstery, head bowed, finally letting himself enjoy the massage-by-flogger. Relaxing at last.

Jonathan slowly worked his way down Brandon's back, pinking up the skin from shoulder blades to ass cheeks. The sounds Brandon made deepened from whuffs of air to bone-deep sighs and groans of pleasure.

The way he'd sounded that first night they'd fucked in Jonathan's bed. No doubt he was enjoying it just as much now.

He continued on, all broad strokes, avoiding using the tips of the flogger. Brandon was already bruised, and Jonathan truly didn't want him to feel an ounce of pain tonight.

Sweat was pouring off of Jonathan by the time he stopped, every inch of Brandon's shoulders, back, and ass a lovely pink. He sidled up to Brandon, laid a hand on his shoulder. Brandon's skin radiated heat, and he moaned and shuddered as Jonathan ran his fingertips along his back. "That doesn't hurt, does it?" Jonathan asked gently.

Brandon just moaned again, then, "Feels . . . good. I-I like it." A puffed breath. "Jonathan."

Halfway to subspace, and he'd only just finished the warm-up. This looked promising. "I'm going to go a little harder now. All right? You'll tell me if I hurt you, even a little bit."

"All right, Jonathan."

"Good." He stole a quick moment to wipe his face on his discarded shirt, then turned back to the task at hand. Down came the flogger with a bit more force, enough to knock Brandon against the cross. Brandon grunted, but his fingers didn't tighten around the cuffs like before. His head was bowed now, resting against one of the struts. Letting the cross bear his weight. As relaxed as if this actually *were* a massage of the more traditional sort. Absolutely *beautiful*. The man took to pleasure as exquisitely as he suffered.

Jonathan indulged in a single press of his free hand to his straining cock, then pulled his arm back and laid the flogger down hard, over and over, until he'd reached Brandon's ass again. Groans and grunts, but not a word of protest. Not a single signal that he'd gone too far, pushed Brandon too hard. After all, he'd given Brandon license to let him know if he was hurting him—and based on past experience, Jonathan had no doubt he would.

Jonathan kept swinging until his arm felt ready to fall off, then dropped the flogger to the floor and stepped forward, pressing his sweaty torso to Brandon's hot, reddened back. Stood there a moment savoring the feel of Brandon's body against his, hanging in his restraints. To Jonathan's delight, Brandon pushed into his touch, pressing against him as if he craved it. As if he couldn't get enough.

He draped a hand on Brandon's neck, fingers sliding up into Brandon's hair to draw his head back. Not a hint of resistance. Not a hint of iris left, either, pupils blown beneath the endorphin rush. Lost in subspace. Flying. *Finally.*

"See how easy?" Jonathan whispered. "How *good* it can be when you don't fight it?"

Brandon's head rolled on Jonathan's shoulder, face turning in toward Jonathan's neck. Parted lips and a hint of tongue against his pulse were the only reply. Past talking for once. Maybe even past thinking. *Good.*

He cupped Brandon's head a moment, then slid his hand around to Brandon's sweaty throat, down to his chest, feeling his heart thump, his lungs work. Down further, to the lax muscles in his belly, to the flat of his pelvis . . . to the one part of Brandon not rendered loose and liquid beneath the falls of a suede flogger. Jonathan wrapped his fingers around that impressive erection, and Brandon moaned against his neck, wanton and wasted, too far gone to even remember there was such a thing as pride or shame.

"Do you want me inside you?" Jonathan murmured, and Brandon hummed against his neck again, made a half-successful effort to lift his head, to nod, to beg with those big black eyes. Still no words. No need of them, either.

Jonathan kept slick in nearly every drawer in the dungeon, but he couldn't reach any without stepping away, even if just for a moment. How cold the room suddenly seemed when he did—to Brandon, as well, if his sad little moan as Jonathan pulled away, the way he tried to follow Jonathan with his body, was anything to go by. Jonathan considered telling him he'd be right back, but truth was, he was loath to break the spell, and God knew what might do it. Brandon *seemed* down pretty deep, but it was his first time, and he was a skittish thing.

Jonathan snatched up a bottle of lube and rushed back to Brandon, pressed his chest against all that flaming skin again and worked a slicked-up hand between Brandon's spread legs. Two fingers, no resistance. None *at all.* So loose the prep wasn't even called for. Still, no pain—he'd promised no pain.

Not that Brandon would feel it now anyway, even if you shoved your whole hand up there.

Tempting as the thought was, he settled for three fingers instead. A few quick strokes to spread the lube, and then he pulled out his fingers and thrust in with his cock, taking Brandon's own in his slick fist.

Even loose as Brandon was, that first thrust nearly undid Jonathan. He'd been waiting for this since breakfast—heck, since the moment Brandon had walked through his door—waiting for this willing, pliant body beneath him, this needy, tactile creature. Waiting for these moans, these quickened breaths, these thrusts back onto his cock and forward into his fist, all these miles and miles of whip-kissed skin, hot and red and burning just for him . . .

Jonathan sank his teeth into the meat of Brandon's shoulder as he came, not hard enough to break skin but hard enough to mark, and for one panicked moment through the bright blast of pleasure that was his orgasm too long denied, he worried he'd hurt Brandon, broken his promise, but then Brandon gave his own cry—loud, drugged, utterly unrestrained—and came all over Jonathan's fist.

It took Jonathan a few moments to come down, and even then he clung to Brandon, pressing soft kisses to his reddened back. All that heat felt incredible against his lips, and if Brandon's drunken little purr was anything to go by, Jonathan's lips felt incredible too. Loath as he was to let go, he had no choice. Brandon was going to collapse when he took him down, but at least he was so far gone his arms wouldn't hurt.

Jonathan unsnapped the ankle cuffs from the cross first, then reached up to unsnap Brandon's wrists. Brandon's arms slumped, but Jonathan caught hold of one, tugged it over his shoulder and slung an arm around Brandon's waist, and together they staggered over to the table.

Brandon needed no more than the tiniest nudge to flop down on his belly, one leg and one arm dangling over the edge. Jonathan grinned at the boneless sprawl, carefully arranged Brandon's wayward limbs and took the opportunity to plant fresh kisses across Brandon's skin.

He worked his way up Brandon's arm, to his shoulder, his neck, tasting salt and heat and a heady buzz of pleasure. "Do you want to talk about it?" he whispered in Brandon's ear when he reached the lobe with his lips. Brandon just blinked, once, sluggishly, then gave a tiny shake of the head. That was fine; whatever he needed, whatever he wanted, it was his.

CHAPTER 16

Bran woke to the first hint of pre-dawn lightening the shadows in Jonathan's room. Earlier than he needed to be up—earlier by an hour, at least—but he couldn't bring himself to care; for the first time in five days, he hadn't woken from a nightmare of being shocked.

He thought about going back to sleep, but frankly, the yoga mat wasn't comfortable enough to stay on without the aid of exhaustion. He'd thought he might get used to it with time, or at least less bothered by it as the welts and bruises faded, but no. Still miserable. Why had Jonathan kicked him out of the bed again anyway? He hadn't done anything wrong. Had been desperately careful, in fact, to do everything right.

Cowering like a kicked dog. Disgusting.

The thought made him flinch. His stomach rumbled. Did that a lot these days. Not that Jonathan didn't feed him, but he was still gaining back the weight he'd lost last week, and it turned out that holding a kneeling position for hours and coming two or three times a day actually burned quite a lot of energy. He felt as sore at the end of a "training session," as Jonathan called all those hours on his knees with his thighs spread and his back straight and his shoulders squared, as he often felt at the end of a long day of construction.

Shit, I miss making stuff.

Didn't miss his crappy apartment, though. Or his fresh-from-a-can cooking. Fact was, a guy could get used to a place like this. To Sabrina's meals. To the housekeeper—*What's her name again? Jenny? Jeanie?*—washing his bedding, keeping the place spotless.

To Jonathan's mouth on your skin, hands on your dick—

"Stop it," he scolded himself—very, very quietly. Fuck-all only knew what Jonathan would do to him if he woke the guy too early.

Well, best to get out of here then. He had to get ready anyway.

He rolled onto his hands and knees and pushed himself to his feet, keeping the blanket wrapped around his shoulders for just another moment. Cold in here—always too cold for a guy without clothes. Comfortable for Jonathan, no doubt. *Everything* was comfortable for Jonathan. Look at him, sleeping away the morning in his big soft bed, cocooned in a fine down blanket, head propped on two gigantic pillows.

While I sleep on the floor like a fucking animal.

With a sigh, Bran shucked his blanket and crept into the hall. Down the spiral staircase. Turned right to the dungeon . . . stopped, looked left, to the kitchen. Still dark. Sabrina wasn't up yet. His stomach rumbled again.

Jonathan's sleeping. He'd never know.

Fucking ridiculous he couldn't feed himself anyway. Fucking ridiculous he had to wait for Jonathan to wake up, for Jonathan's *permission*, to do something as basic and fundamental as fuel himself.

Food isn't just fuel. He could practically hear the smug little fuck in his head. *A luxury. A banquet of the senses. Savor. Enjoy.*

Fuck you, you fucking rich asshole. You can afford *to savor your aged gruyere and your fresh fruit and your fucking chocolate pancakes. To linger for an hour over your gourmet coffee beans shit from a civet and your copy of the* Wall Street Journal. *The rest of us have to make do with whatever's on sale at the local Safeway, scarf it down on the way to work. The rest of us can't afford to buy people to do our cooking and cleaning for us.*

Or live-in whores to fuck. Don't forget that one, Brandon.

Yeah, well fuck you too, Dad.

And fuck all of this. He was *so done* with this shit. Jonathan wanted him to savor his food? Fine, he would. "Without you shoving it down my fucking throat, *Jonathan.*"

Felt good to make the decision for himself. Hell, felt good to *speak* for himself, without waiting for Jonathan's permission for that, either. Without waiting to be asked a question. Like he was some fucking kid again.

The kitchen was dim, even with the light spilling in from the hall. And though it wasn't likely anyone would notice if he turned on the light in here, just the *thought* of getting caught curbed his appetite. Not worth the risk. He fumbled his way past the center island, stubbed his toe on the edge, cursed a blue streak beneath his breath and limped over to the fridge. Had a moment of paranoia strong enough to make him check for a hair or a piece of tape or some bullshit that would let Sabrina see the door had been opened by someone other than her. Jesus, was this what his life had come to?

Nothing. He was being ridiculous anyway; Jonathan hadn't alarmed his fucking fridge.

. . . Had he?

Eh. Fuck it. There was fruit on the counter—he'd take that instead. His mouth watered at the sight of it. Apple or banana? He kind of wanted the pear, but there was only one left. Someone might miss it. Five bananas, a couple already missing from the bunch by the looks of it. No way anyone would notice. He snatched one, peeled it, wolfed down half of it in one gigantic bite when he realized . . . *Shit. What do I do with the peel?*

Where was the fucking trash in this place? He chewed, chewed some more—*I'm* savoring, *Jonathan, so fuck you*—swallowed down the bite he'd taken as he very quietly opened and closed cabinets, looking for the garbage can. Finally found it—three of them, actually—in the cabinet beneath the sink: one for trash, one for recycling, and one that looked suspiciously like compost. *Fucker probably makes his own fucking* soil *for the vegetables he grows out on his balcony.* He popped the rest of the banana free and dumped the peel in the compost bin. Closed the cabinet softly and crept, banana-prize in hand, down the hall to the dungeon.

It hadn't been a very big banana, but he managed to make it last until he'd crossed through the dungeon and into the bathroom. Licked the last sweet remnants off his fingers. *Fuck*, it was good. But then, anything probably would be, seasoned with the delicious taste of feeding-yourself-like-a-fucking-adult. Not that he'd know these days.

He turned the shower on steaming hot and stepped beneath the spray. Felt *amazing*. Usually he was too damned welted and bruised for anything more than a lukewarm wash, but he'd been so careful since he'd come out of that fucking coffin, and Jonathan had been so oddly gentle. No new bruises in four days, and the old ones had begun to fade, didn't really hurt anymore. Even his wrists and ankles were healing up nicely. Strange that Jonathan hadn't tried to put those steel cuffs back on him, but he certainly wasn't gonna look a gift horse in the mouth. It was too fucking nice not to look—and feel—like a battered spouse or some fucking crash-test dummy anymore.

You know, it's actually pretty nice here when he's not hitting you. Apartment was gorgeous, food was great. And the sex . . . fuck, it was *mind-blowing.*

Bran snorted. *Yeah. Keep telling yourself that and you'll have no one to blame when you* do *look like a battered spouse again.*

He scrubbed the thought away with an actual sea sponge and a bar of soap that was probably made from, like, free-range cashmere goat milk and the first baby petals of some rare flower that only grew on a unicorn's ass. Washed his hair with equally rich shampoo that came in bar form for some fucking reason. Probably had a smaller carbon footprint that way. *Yeah, assuming Jonathan doesn't make that in his garden too.* His hair was just beginning to grow out a bit on the back and sides, starting to curl over the tips of his ears again. He felt a little more like himself this way, hoped Jonathan wouldn't make him shave it again. He rinsed the shampoo from it and just stood there under the spray, reveling in the pounding heat, the steam, the white noise, the privacy. Strange how he'd come to like this morning ritual, take comfort in it, even. Despite the shaving-every-day bullshit. Despite the *enema.* It was his own little quiet corner of space. His chance to be good to himself. Even better this morning for not needing to rush.

He turned his face into the spray, closed his eyes and opened his mouth. He always drank in the shower now—made him less thirsty later, less liable to have to cave to drinking from Jonathan's hand. Besides, he was in no rush to use the fucking enema. Bad enough—way *beyond* bad enough; downright fucking *mortifying*—that it'd started turning him on once he'd learned to go slow enough. Even worse that he couldn't do anything about it, couldn't even touch himself, let alone relieve himself.

Except . . . *Jonathan's still asleep. He'd never know.*

Bran grabbed the nozzle, lubed it up, slid it inside himself. Closed his eyes at that first fresh rush of pleasure, the gentle stretch, the not-quite-burn, the sense of full but not nearly full enough. His dick, as always, got very interested in the proceedings. He angled the nozzle to hit his prostate, thrust it in and out ever so slightly, just a few times. Let his forehead thunk against the tiles and leaned his weight there, eyes closed, hot spray running down his back like fingers. *Like the falls of a suede flogger.*

Shit. Where had *that* thought come from?

He let his hand wander down his belly. To his navel. Beneath it. Rasped fingertips over the hint of stubble where his pubic hair used to be. Clenched his hand into a fist before he did something even dumber than steal food and pried it away from his body. Turned down the water temperature, turned down the flow, and flipped the toggle on the shower shot. Closed his eyes again as that first warm trickle of water pushed up inside him.

More, and more, and more still, slowly, sensuous—a careful, aching, *teasing* build. Like that fucking bite of pancake in front of his lips: scent, a dab of whipped cream, a hint of chocolate, then texture, warmth, an explosion of flavors, fucking *orgasmic* . . .

Shit. He yanked his hand from his dick with a mean pinch, half punishing himself for having slipped so badly, half hoping to make his erection go away. Not a fucking chance, though, not with all that warm water filling him up, pressing against him so deliciously all at once, creeping into places dick and fingers could never reach . . .

Jonathan's sleeping. He'd never know . . .

"He knows *everything*, asshole," he whispered between clenched teeth. *Don't be an idiot. Not worth the risk. He'll get you off soon enough anyway.*

And like one of Pavlov's fucking dogs, he'd salivate at the mouth for the mere *chance* of it, beg and writhe and come out his fucking *ears* for Jonathan, and just why did he let the man do that to him anyway? Why was Jonathan the one who got to decide when he could and couldn't have some fucking fun?

Three million dollars, remember? It's not like you didn't know what you were signing on for.

Except, he supposed, for the part where he really actually kinda *hadn't* known.

Whatever. These thoughts were bad news. The whole fucking *thing* was bad news. He flipped the water off. Pulled the nozzle out. Voided his bowels and did it again. Faster this time—fast enough to cramp. Better that than tempt himself with things he could no longer have. Even if he had signed them away willingly.

Even if he was, quite frankly, having the best fucking sex of his entire fucking life, Jonathan's terms or no.

And just why was he thinking about sex so much, anyway? Never had before. He stepped out of the shower, emptied himself again, wrapped a towel around his waist and scrubbed another through his hair. Slung it around his shoulders and shaved. Carefully as always here—nice and slow, no missed spots, no nicks. Against the grain so as not to leave the slightest hint of stubble. Shaved his crotch, too. Balls were a little tough to reach, but fuck knew he didn't want to cut himself there, and that had nothing to do with Jonathan's threats. Finished up, rinsed off, smeared rich scentless lotion from head to toe. He was losing the calluses on his hands. Ran a fingertip across the top of his palm and shivered at the sensation—so odd to have *any* sensation there from such a light touch. He felt . . . pampered. No. *Foppish.*

He sighed, scrubbed his hands through his hair. No real need to comb it yet, not as short as it still was, and anyway Jonathan seemed to like it undisciplined, loose with its hint of curl. *Not like he's not gonna fuck it all up within the hour anyway.* The man seemed incapable of keeping his fucking hands to himself. Or at least out of Bran's hair.

One last careful inspection in the mirror—he found a few beads of moisture at the small of his back that he toweled away—before cleaning up the bathroom and creeping back upstairs. He'd have stayed in here a while yet, but he really had no idea what time it was, and didn't plan to start his day with fresh cane welts across his ass.

He found Jonathan out on the balcony, sipping tea and reading the paper. Bran came in and knelt on the cushion at his feet, eyes straying to the table. No food yet; just Jonathan's teapot and favorite green ceramic mug. Jonathan didn't say a word to him, just kept turning the pages of the financial section. Didn't even offer Bran the front page to read, like he usually did when he was done with it himself. So was Jonathan just ignoring him on principle, or . . .? No, he couldn't know. If he did, he'd be beating Bran black and blue by now.

. . . Wouldn't he?

Bran's back went rigid, but he kept his eyes straight ahead, focused on Jonathan. After a few minutes, Sabrina came in with a tray. Only one covered plate on it this morning. More pancakes? Maybe an omelet? Bran's nostrils flared, trying to figure out what she'd made.

Jonathan's eyebrow quirked up as she set the tray down and lifted the cover. "Only enough for one?" he asked.

Sabrina flashed Bran a wide slice of teeth. Not the least bit grandmotherly. *No, more like the wolf who ate her.* "Brandon's already had his breakfast."

Bran's gut went ice cold, every part of him starting to shake.

"There was a banana missing this morning. And I *was* planning to use them to make muffins. For you *both*," she added, that last bit directed straight at Bran.

"Oh, *really?*" Jonathan turned his own very calm, extremely fucking alarming gaze on Bran. Whenever he got that cool, unflappable look, Bran knew he was in for some *serious* hurt. "And he'd been doing so well these past few days." A tiny sigh, and he put aside his paper. "Thank you for telling me, Sabrina. I'll take care of it from here."

Bran almost called out, begging her not to go, but it wouldn't make one bit of difference. Jonathan would beat him with or without her in the room. The bitch would probably enjoy watching. That gray hair didn't fool him anymore.

"Well, Brandon, what am I going to do with you?" Jonathan sounded more disappointed than angry, but that didn't fool Bran either. "You do realize you have thirty cane strokes in store. Remember what I told you last time?"

Oh God. Oh fucking fuck. No. He couldn't do it. Couldn't take thirty cane strokes. It'd drive him out of his fucking mind.

Without thinking, he broke position, grabbed Jonathan's ankle and bent his head, pressing his lips to Jonathan's plaid flannel slipper. "Please, Jonathan, please don't. I'll do *anything*, just please please fucking *please* don't do that . . . Red, okay? Red!"

Jonathan's fingers slid into Bran's hair, curled around a rough handful, jerked him back up. "I haven't even touched you yet, and you're already safewording? No, I'm afraid that will not do."

So even his fucking safeword wasn't gonna get him out of this? What the fuck was it for, then? "Y-you're gonna punish me anyway? Even though I said I was sorry?"

"Actually, you didn't say you were sorry. You asked me not to hit you. Not the same thing." Jonathan pushed back in his chair and stood up. "If you'd like to apologize, I won't stop you. But it won't affect your punishment."

Maybe not a chance to get out of this, but maybe he could . . . make it less painful? Less humiliating? Fat fucking chance, but he had to try. "I-I'm sorry, Jonathan. It'll never happen again."

"Then why did it happen this time? Don't I feed you enough? What's it been . . . six, eight times a day? You need only *look* at me and I drop everything to satisfy you. You know that."

"I . . . I don't know, I was just . . . I woke up really hungry, and I . . . I didn't want to wake you, and—"

"And I don't believe you for a moment. You're making this up as you go, aren't you? You do realize you'll get an additional demerit for every lie or prevarication."

"It's the truth! I was hungry, a-and I was afraid you'd get mad at me if I woke you—"

Jonathan's mouth tightened, his eyes going icy. *Shit.* "You obviously have no regard for my rules. Or for me." He gestured for Bran to rise. "Get up. We're going to the dungeon."

Bran's knees shook as he rose, but somehow he managed to follow Jonathan to the staircase. He shot Sabrina a dirty look as they passed by the kitchen. She caught his gaze, and returned it with a sardonic grin. *Fucking bitch.*

Jonathan opened the door and gestured Bran ahead of him. Bran *never* got to walk ahead of him, but maybe Jonathan just wanted to give him a little extra time to look at all these implements of torture before he strapped Bran into one.

Maybe if I don't fight him . . .

Bran forced himself to walk to the suspension bar hanging in the middle of the dungeon, even though every single step was like trudging uphill, backwards, barefoot over broken glass. He looked up at it, closed his eyes for a moment and imagined himself hanging there, bloody and in fucking tears because what if Jonathan wouldn't believe him when he safeworded and *six* strikes with the cane had felt like dying and how the fuck was he going to make it through *five times* that?

He jerked around at the sound of Jonathan rummaging through a drawer. Things clinked and rattled against each other. Jonathan snagged something, turned around—

Fuck. The steel cuffs. *So he means to beat my ass* and *make me break my wrists? Fuck that.*

"Hands out," Jonathan said, and only then did Bran realize he'd folded his arms across his chest, tucked his hands and wrists beneath his armpits. Somehow he managed to pry them free, though, and offer them to Jonathan. He didn't want to wear those fucking things again, but they'd hurt less than fighting.

"Going without these," Jonathan said, circling his fingers around Bran's wrist, "was a privilege. A reward. A show of trust. Which"—a twist of Jonathan's wrist, and suddenly Bran found himself on his knees, gasping at the pain shooting up his arm—"you've betrayed." Jonathan took his hand away, but Bran left his arm in the air; no fucking way was he moving without permission. One steel cuff closed around his wrist, then Jonathan gestured for the other one. "You're going to struggle. These will hurt you when you do. Bruise you. A reminder to think on later. It seems you need one."

Jonathan turned back to the drawer, returned a moment later with the ankle cuffs. Bran swallowed so hard he coughed. Couldn't take his eyes off them. He wasn't going to . . . Was he?

"Get up." Bran stumbled to his feet. "Put these on." He handed Bran the ankle cuffs and folded his arms across his chest, scowling. Waiting. Bran bent down and fastened the fucking things, even though his hands were shaking hard enough to make clicking them together difficult, even though he could practically feel the charge, the there-and-gone agony of the *zap* running through the steel and up his legs.

When he finished and straightened up, Jonathan hooked a finger through an O-ring on his wrist cuff and dragged him over to that low bench contraption he'd examined the day Jonathan had made his cursed offer. Jonathan pointed at it and said, "Down." One-word commands. Like he was some fucking dog again.

And here he was cowering with his tail between his legs, because he got down on that bench so fast he hurt his knees. Jonathan manhandled him into position, clipping his wrist cuffs to the ring by the grab-handles, then pushing his legs onto the shin pads and locking his ankle cuffs down. Leather straps went around his biceps and thighs, too, holding him well and truly in place, ass in the air, junk exposed. Inner thighs bared too, and though it'd been a week or more, he hadn't yet forgotten the pain of a crop landing there. *Beyond* pain. And that'd just been a little strip of leather, not a cane.

He found himself opening his mouth to beg again, and shut it. Jonathan wouldn't care and Bran saw no reason to humiliate himself further. At least Jonathan didn't close the strap over his neck. Still, not a whole lot of wiggle room. Not enough to get away from the cane.

Not enough to get away from the hand Jonathan stroked down his spine, either. "I know I promised you thirty cane strokes," Jonathan said, rocking up to his heels and walking somewhere behind Bran, where Bran couldn't see no matter how far he tried to turn his head. He heard a drawer open, close. Jonathan came back, but his hands were empty. Something in his pocket, though. "But you lied to me, Brandon. You stole food, and then you looked me right in the eye and lied about it. You also touched yourself in the shower this morning," he added, perfectly casual, and all Bran could think was *thank God I didn't go through with jacking off* because Jonathan had seen him, of *course* he had, never mind that he was supposed to be asleep.

"I've told you before," Jonathan went on, pulling a leather glove from his pocket and tugging it over his right hand, "nothing happens in this house that I don't know about. And I don't think a mere caning, however severe, will suffice to get that through your head this morning. Nor would it knock the attitude problem away, or your propensity toward fibbing, or theft. You know . . ." He paused, smoothed his gloved hand over Bran's left ass cheek, then the right one, then gave it a squeeze. "When I was on the commune, we didn't own very much. None of us did—*commune*, after all. But what little we did have? Was sacrosanct.

Thieves were banished. I remember that vividly, the first one I saw. I was seven, friends with his little girl. His wife chose not to leave with him. Kept his daughter. He lost *everything*, and for 'what?"

Was this Jonathan's way of saying *Get out?* Well, good luck with that. He wasn't going anywhere without his fucking money.

"I can't banish you quite so easily, but I *can* make you regret what you've done. Maybe, in time, you'll even understand why it matters so much. Maybe you'll actually be sorry. And not just because you were caught. Look at you"—another leather-gloved touch, down the backs of his thighs, across his arms—"you're trembling. Am I so frightening to you now?"

"No, Jonathan," Bran said. Pure bravado. *And stupidity. Stop lying, you idiot.* He sighed, met Jonathan's steady gaze. "Yes." Fucking talk of banishment . . . what was he, Amish?

Jonathan just raised an eyebrow, like he wanted more. Waited. Well, he'd wait for fucking ever if he didn't ask a question; no way was Bran speaking out of turn right now.

At last Jonathan said simply, "Why?"

Was he *kidding*? "I dunno, maybe because you're about to *torture* me?" *Asshole.* "Jonathan."

A tiny smile flitted across Jonathan's lips, and he shook his head. "Try again. Or rather, try harder."

What the fuck did he *want* from him? What else was there to say? He turned away from that deep blue gaze, rested his chin on the bench. Jonathan seemed to want the truth—might as well keep letting him have it. "Because you're so fucking *sure* of yourself, Jonathan. Because you're not the first man who thought he could control me, and it didn't end so fucking well the last time. Because I can't fucking figure you out; one second you're beating me, the next you're fucking me, and you know what? Sometimes I'm not sure which is worse . . . Jonathan."

Silence. He dared a glance back—nothing subtle about it, he had to move his head to meet Jonathan's eyes, sure he'd find fury, maybe even hatred. Found instead . . . amusement? Contemplation? Confidence, for sure. So much fucking *confidence*. Like Jonathan had known exactly what Bran was gonna say before he'd even said it.

Jonathan reached out, took Bran's chin between thumb and forefinger. No force, just heat and a little pressure. "I'm not your father," Jonathan said, and suddenly it was all Bran could do not to jerk his chin from Jonathan's fingers. "His control came from a place of anger, insecurity, immaturity. He broke you down to build himself up, to make his life easier. *My* control? Is a gift, as surely as your submission is. I break you down to build *you* back up, to make *your* life better. Do you think it's easy for me, having you here? Fighting all the time? Do you think I *want* this?" He actually sounded sincere—desperately so—his grip tightening on Bran's chin. "I may be a sadist, but it loses a lot of its fun when the man on the receiving end doesn't want it too. I don't *like* to punish you so often, Brandon. I want you to be happy. I want you to *get out of your own way*. And when I try to help you do that, you spit in my face. You think I don't know what stealing that banana meant? You think I didn't hear that giant *fuck you*?"

Did Jonathan just *curse*? Shit, he really *was* in trouble. And yet, the man still sounded so calm . . . so fucking *calm*.

"I get it, I do," Jonathan said. "Children need discipline, routine. They're grateful for it later, but at the time?" A wan smile, which Bran would have punched right off his face if his hands weren't bound. He was *not* a child. "Not so much. I recall being angry with my parents sometimes. But look what they gave me. Look what I was able to accomplish because of their guidance, their firm hands. But you? The last twenty years, you've known only cruel hands, or greedy ones. I mean to fill that gap."

Jonathan let go of Bran's chin, reached into his pocket with his gloved hand and pulled out a little squeeze-bottle of lube. So, what, he meant to fill that gap with his dick? *Somehow, I don't think it works that way, pal.*

But Jonathan just squirted some lube into his ungloved hand, reached under the bench, and grabbed hold of Bran's flaccid dick.

"You're going to come for me this morning," Jonathan said, starting up a rhythm with his hand, half stroke, half twist, squeezing at the head. And despite the situation, the discussion, the fear, the fact that he was *shackled to a fucking bench on his hands and knees*, Bran felt himself hardening in Jonathan's hand. "You're not going to want to. You'll be angry." *Stroke.* "Ashamed." *Stroke.* "Conflicted. Somehow you've gotten it into your head that submission is weakness, that you're not allowed to enjoy these things. That you can't let someone else take control, take care of you. That pleasure and pain are mutually exclusive. That *wanting*—wanting *anything*, let alone *these* things—is disgraceful, degrading. But it's not."

God, didn't he ever *shut up*? This was the last fucking thing in the world Bran wanted to hear with that hot slick fist on his dick, with the first tight coils of pleasure curling his fingers and toes. He laid his cheek on the bench, closed his eyes. Thrust his hips as best he could into Jonathan's hand, just to prove him wrong—*See? No shame here.* Jonathan chuckled, kept up that maddening rhythm—

And *spanked* him? His left ass cheek stung, and he clenched and unclenched it, letting the sensation sink in. Not pain, not really. Heat. Tingling. He was hard as a fucking I-beam in Jonathan's hand. Another stroke of those magic fingers, another twist . . . and another spank, much, much harder than the first.

"Ow, what the hell!" he shouted, jerking in his restraints, then remembered to add "Jonathan" before the fucker hit him again.

Jonathan chuckled, still jacking him at the same steady pace, and said, "You do recall this is a *punishment*, right?"

You talked so fucking much I forgot. Seemed like a bad idea to say that out loud, though, so he settled for, "Yes, Jonathan."

And was rewarded with another slap, and another, and then four more in rapid succession, all on the same tender spot where ass met thigh until he was shouting, squirming, desperate to get away. But of course the restraints held, and so did Jonathan's fucking fingers, still fisted and twisting slick around his dick, which had flagged at the pain but was perking up again now that Jonathan had stopped.

"I'm going to keep hitting you until you come," Jonathan said, and for a second Bran wasn't sure he'd actually heard him right because, seriously, how did Jonathan think the first thing could ever lead to the second?

Or maybe he doesn't. Maybe he's just planning to beat your ass until he can see his reflection in it.

Jonathan smirked at him. So fucking smug and condescending and *amused.* "You think that's impossible." Another hard smack, at least to somewhere new this time, thank God. The blow drove Bran's hips forward into Jonathan's slick, waiting fist, and a sharp bolt of pleasure dulled the pain. "You're wrong."

Another blow, another thrust into Jonathan's fist, and Bran's brain didn't know *what* to feel, what to think, except that maybe, just *maybe*, the smug fucker was right. Maybe he *could* come like this. God knew he'd been hungry enough for it this morning, and the spanking didn't hurt *that* bad.

But it will. You know *it will.*

And if he *did* come? He'd never hear the end of it. Jonathan was right about that too: he didn't *want* to come like this. Not at all, even if it really was the only way to stop the beating. Felt his face heat at just the *thought* of it, and *fuck* Jonathan anyway for trying to force this on him.

Another smack, and then another and another, and he shouted again, tried to slide sideways off the bench or even just close his legs or get Jonathan to *stop jacking him off*, but of course he couldn't do any of those things. All he could do was sit there squirming and just *take* it, and he supposed that was the fucking point.

"You could enjoy this, Brandon, if you'd just let yourself," Jonathan whispered in his ear, lips brushing over the lobe so softly it made Bran shiver. *Fucking hell.* It took every last shred of Bran's willpower to keep from head-butting Jonathan in the face. "You *do* enjoy it. Or rather, your cock does." Another long, slick stroke, followed by another smack on his ass. The sting was starting to fade, replaced by a lingering sensation of heat. Bran's skin felt like an overinflated balloon, thin and sensitized and ready to burst. Jonathan's fingertips skimmed over his left cheek, five red-hot matches fanning the flame even higher. Worse than any cane.

A hundred times worse, because it's his hand. *Both hands. Exactly where I* don't *want them, no matter what he says.*

His erection shriveled again, and again Jonathan stroked him harder, got him to stand up in his fist. Slapped his ass again as he did it, driving his hips forward. His knees ached, and so did his arms, his wrists, his ankles. Those fucking cuffs were going to mark him badly. How the hell could they feel so *cold* when the rest of him was on fire? For a second, Bran flashed back to that horrible night in the coffin, the electric shock buzzing through his body. Was this really any better? At least the shock was over with in a second, but this . . . this went on and on and *on.*

The next few blows came easier, thudding down on desensitized skin. He breathed deep through his nose and closed his eyes, willing himself to calmness. Which meant the following smack rained down twice as hard as any before, hard enough to wrench a raw cry from his throat, to leave him gasping.

"Can't have you getting complacent, can we?" Jonathan said, jerking him again. Sliding his hand back, sliding the tip of his thumb into Bran's ass. Wiggling it around until all Bran could do was groan. Jonathan pulled his thumb out, rubbed it right over Bran's hole. "Maybe I should use a cane *right here.*"

Bran jolted out of his floaty little half-stupor as Jonathan got up and moved toward the toy rack. *Oh fucking hell. Is he really going to cane me on my* asshole? Too terrified even to squeak, he sucked in a breath, squirming and struggling, hoping he could loosen one of the straps. *Good luck with that.* He'd just end up hurting himself.

Jonathan's fingers sank into his hair, stroking and petting. Trying to soothe him, when there was no fucking way he was going to calm down, not now. Not with the thought of what Jonathan was about to do slicing through his brain like a fucking ax. Which, come to think of it, would probably hurt less.

Jonathan circled back around, ran his gloved hand over Bran's flaming ass. Bran squeezed his eyes shut, bracing himself for the cane. A whimper escaped his lips as Jonathan parted his ass cheeks . . .

Then pulled back his hand and smacked him again, right on his asshole. The force of the blow sent Bran scraping along the top of the bench, every inch of skin on his chest and belly as on fire as the rest of him.

Before he even had a chance to recover, Jonathan had taken Bran's dick in his fist again. Freshly slicked—*so that's what he was really doing when he turned his back on me, the sneaky little fucker*—and so *warm* Bran nearly groaned at the sensation. Can't have been regular lube. That fancy shit that heated up. He had to stop himself from thrusting forward into it. Not that he *wanted* it, just . . . the pleasure was the only way to dull the pain.

Jonathan's hand dipped down, stroked over his balls, rolled them in slick, expert fingers. The heat was incredible. Dick, balls, ass, all one red-hot, pulsing knot of *feeling*. He slumped against the bench, let it take his weight. Fuck *let*; no choice at all as Jonathan's lubed hand worked Bran's dick and balls and his gloved hand stroked up and down Bran's sweaty back, tugged gently at his hair, scraped back down to the sensitized skin of his ass and kneaded gently, slipping a thumb into his crack, rubbing at his hole before pressing inside. Bran gasped, fought the urge to thrust into Jonathan's fist. He didn't want to come. Not like this.

Except you'll be stuck on this bench the whole fucking day if you don't.

Jonathan did something absolutely spectacular with his hand, and for one teetering second, it seemed Bran wouldn't have any say in the matter after all. His balls tightened, pulled up high as the muscles in his ass clenched and the pleasure built and built and built until it almost *hurt*—

Smack! Jonathan's gloved hand thwacked hard across his ass and knocked Bran's looming orgasm back two states. Hurt so much he bit his tongue.

And a good thing for it, because if he hadn't, he'd have cursed at Jonathan for pulling a stunt like that, the teasing little fuck.

Another smack, and another and another and another, and before long that orgasm he absolutely didn't want to have was starting to look like a pretty fucking nice alternative to the thrashing he was enduring now. Jonathan's slicked-up fist was still around his dick, still stroking and twisting and squeezing and pulling, but he was losing his hard-on despite that, the pain too big, his skin too small, the heat and thud and sting too strong, obliterating everything until all he could do was shout and writhe and pull at his restraints, frantic to *make it stop, get away,* and those distant, faded flashes of pleasure from Jonathan's other hand had no hope of competing and he was never going to come like this and this was never going to fucking *end* if Jonathan didn't—

"Stop fucking hitting me! Please! I can't . . . I *can't* . . ."

There was some very important way to finish that sentence, he was sure, but he couldn't think of it for the life of him.

"Yes, you can," Jonathan said, "and believe me, you will." Another smack, another brutal twist of his wrist, and he pushed two slippery fingers inside Bran's ass, found his prostate and *thrust*, and those faded flashes leaped to the fore and lit his whole world in a shower of sparks, raw electric (pain) pleasure erupting from his dick and balls and ass and every last inch of his too-hot skin as he spurted so hard his vision sheeted white.

The second it was over, he hurt again. Fucking everywhere. Amazing how fast the buzz faded, how profoundly *un*-good he felt. How jittery. How *furious.* How fucking *dirty.*

Too exhausted to do a damn thing about it, though. Couldn't have taken his own weight if Jonathan had threatened him with the shock coffin. And to think that until now, he'd thought that was the worst thing Jonathan could ever do to him.

How wrong he'd been. How unbelievably fucking wrong.

Jonathan caught the cold, furious look Brandon threw him—how could he not, when it was tantamount to having a brick hurled in his face?—as he knelt to unfasten him from the bench. "Can you stand?" he asked, holding out a hand to help Brandon up.

Of course Brandon shrugged him off. He swayed, stumbled, until Jonathan caught him under the arm and hauled him up, dragged him toward the back of the dungeon. To the door right beside the bathroom.

Brandon didn't put up a struggle until he realized they weren't going into the bathroom. When Jonathan reached for the other door, Brandon started to squirm, but it was too late. He already had the door open and was shoving Brandon inside.

Not that he thought Brandon would mind all that much once he saw it. True the room was tiny—just four feet by eight—but whatever dark terror Brandon had expected to find in there was supplanted by the vision of a camping pad, a sleeping bag, and the two things he'd brought with him from his apartment: a dog-eared old copy of *Huck Finn* and a photo of his mother.

Brandon stood frozen just inside the doorway, lips parted slightly, eyes wide, taking in the space. Jonathan might have laughed at the man's surprise if he weren't feeling so irritable himself.

"This is where you go when I can't be bothered with you."

He could see the response writ large on Brandon's face: *Well, beats the sarcophagus cage.*

"It's not a punishment, *per se.* At least, not always. Today, though? Consider it a time-out in the corner to think about what you've done." Jonathan shouldered past Brandon, giving him a hard knock on the way, then bent down to scoop up the thin little air mattress, the sleeping bag, the book and the picture. Brandon looked appropriately crestfallen at seeing those luxuries taken away—exactly why Jonathan had left them there for him to see in the first place.

He turned back to the door with a sharp, "Stay." Brandon didn't try to follow; Jonathan hadn't expected he would. Arms full with bedding, Jonathan used his chin to point toward the grate in the floor. "If you need to water the grass," he said. The connecting door to his left led to the bathroom, but Brandon didn't know that, and Jonathan meant to leave it locked today anyway. "I'll come get you when I think you've had enough time to ponder your *issues.*"

Brandon glared at him from where he'd propped himself against a corner. He looked very, very tempted to say something, but held his tongue. Fuming, but not enough to be stupid. He nodded at Jonathan instead, a disrespectful little jerk of the chin, a silent *Fuck off, and I won't miss you for a second.* Jonathan turned back to the door, grinning a little despite himself. Brandon might think that *now*, but he'd be ready for Jonathan to rescue him by evening. Hunger, cold, and boredom would see to that.

Jonathan left the cubby, stuffed the bedding and Brandon's effects in a nearby cabinet, and then locked the door from the outside. Flipped off the light, plunging the windowless little closet into total darkness. And then, for the final touch, pushed the air conditioner in the cubby down to a nippy 60 degrees.

"What am I going to *do* with you?" he mumbled, shaking his head as he left the dungeon.

He trudged upstairs to his office, started checking his email. But after what'd just happened, it shouldn't have come as a surprise that he couldn't keep his mind on work. Everything skated past his eyeballs, barely making an impression. When he realized he'd just read a sentence for the third time, he picked up his phone and dialed the one man who might be able to help him, the man whose feet he himself had trained at. Devon Turner, Dom extraordinaire.

"Hey, Waveboy, what's up? Everything— Yeah, I know." Devon's voice faded; talking to someone else? "I'm not messing it up, I promise. I'll be careful." Speaker back to his mouth now. "Sorry Jonathan, they just spent half an hour making today's fake blood on the side of my head match yesterday's fake blood. Didn't want me putting phone marks in it."

Jonathan grimaced. "If this is a bad time . . .?"

"Nah, we're in between setups. I've got . . . fifteen? Fifteen. New boy still not eating?"

"No, he's eating. I finally had to put him in the sarcophagus and shock him on a timer. He still lasted half the night."

Devon whistled. "Stubborn son of a bitch. Sounds more and more like Nicky every time we talk. You *sure* he's not a hardcore masochist? Certainly seems to *invite* pain."

Jonathan shrugged. "Doesn't seem to be. Not from the way he reacted to the spanking I just gave him."

"He come?"

"Eventually, when I stopped hitting him and started fingering him, but . . ." He sighed. "He's exhausting me. Every time I think he's getting it, he pulls back. I'm not sure how much more of this either of us can take."

"You know how it is sometimes when you're breaking a boy fresh. Nicky was a *disaster*. Just out there punishing himself. Sounds like maybe Brandon's doing the same. In a different way, maybe, but from what you've told me? Guy like that's too proud to lay it down. Can't admit it to himself. Growing up in his house? Probably learned never to show an ounce of weakness. Never to give in, show emotion, indulge himself or anyone else. So what you've got to ask yourself now is, is he worth it? A road like that, it's a long one." A pause—Jonathan could practically hear him shrugging. "But hey, I found my husband at the end of my road. Worth every exhausting, blister-inducing step. And *he* found *him*self, too. Just needed a guiding hand."

If only it were that simple. "But you *knew*. You looked at Nicky and you *knew*. He *craved* it. He *asked* for it. All Brandon's ever done is fight me."

"You're telling me you don't know if he's submissive?"

Jonathan slumped forward, leaned his forehead on his palm. "I'm telling you I may have . . . misjudged the situation. May have made a terrible mistake."

"I—" A scuffling noise on the other end of the line, and Devon said, "Thank you, five," to someone. "Sorry, gotta run soon. But look, I think you know better than that. That night in the alley? That first night with the cuffs? He may not realize he wants it, may not be strong enough yet to *admit* he wants it, but he wants it. And maybe you and he need to sit down and *talk* about that, yeah?"

Jonathan cracked a brittle smile; hard to talk to Brandon when the only two words he seemed to know were "fuck" and "you."

"No roles, no pretense, no fear. I realize it may be too late to renegotiate your contract, but it's not too late to open a dialog, right?"

"I suppose it's worth a try," Jonathan conceded. They'd found each other so fascinating once upon a time. He still wanted that. Perhaps, somewhere deep down, Brandon did too.

"And if you two can't find a way to make things work, well, then maybe it's time to part ways, no hard feelings. Listen, I've gotta go, man, but you call me back anytime. If I'm shooting, Sarah will take a message and I'll get right back to you."

"Thank you, Devon."

"Like I said, anytime. Oh, hey, I have next Friday and Saturday off, and Nicky's coming out to LA this week to shoot a guest spot on *Show Choir.*"

"Really? That's fantastic!"

"I know! He's very excited. Anyway, look, we could come visit next weekend if you think that'd help. Maybe let Brandon see what it *could* be. He and Nicky have a lot in common; I bet they'd get along great."

Not such a great idea—at least, not now. Brandon wasn't ready for that yet. Maybe not ever, if Jonathan were being honest with himself.

"We'll see. Give me a call when Nicky arrives. Maybe I can come meet you for lunch."

"Okay man, will do. Off to go get my ass kicked by a girl now. No stunt double; pray for me."

Jonathan laughed despite himself. "Admit it, you love it."

"Not a chance. See you later, Waveboy!"

The phone went dead before Jonathan could tell him to *stop calling me that*, though he supposed it was at least slightly less embarrassing than his *actual* name. He clicked off the line, then turned back to his computer and flicked on the infrared camera feed inside the cubby. Brandon was huddled in the middle of the room, arms wrapped around his drawn-up knees. His face was turned away from the camera, but Jonathan could hear the soft sound of his breathing, the tiny hitch that might have been cold shivering or might have been crying. For a second, Jonathan was tempted to get up, go down there and let him out. But then he'd have to deal with Brandon's sullenness and bad behavior for the rest of the day, and he most definitely was not up for that right now.

Truth to tell, he wasn't sure he was up for it anymore, full stop. Was Brandon really worth it? Last week Jonathan would have said yes without hesitation, but today . . . today he was just plain *tired*. Tired of fighting an endless battle of wills with a submissive he wasn't entirely sure *was* submissive. Maybe he really had misread Brandon, despite Devon's certainty. But then, Devon had never met Brandon. He didn't know how bad things could get. How bad they were right now.

Somehow, he didn't think a mere talk was going to fix this. But he supposed he had to try.

ran's eyes squeezed shut instinctively as the door creaked open, a faint sliver of light leaking in from the hallway. Dread twisted through him, tension bunching up his muscles as he skittered away, putting his back to the wall. The shadow in the doorway looked . . . not as familiar as he was expecting. Shorter. Thinner.

Then the light overhead flicked on, and he flung an arm over his eyes.

"Come on," Jonathan said, stepping inside, holding out his hand. Bran's vision finally adjusted to the sudden burst of light, but still he blinked, gazing at what looked like a terrycloth robe in Jonathan's other hand.

What the fuck?

"Dinner's ready. You haven't eaten all day." A blazing hot hand on Bran's shoulder now, under his arm, helping him up. His legs were still stiff and shaky, mostly from the fucking cold in here. Jonathan pulled him up, strangely gentle, held out the robe for him. Bran slipped his arms into the sleeves, shivering at soft fabric on sore skin. When was the last time he'd had on more than a pair of fucking cuffs? A week? Two? Three? He'd lost all track of time since he'd arrived.

The robe covered him from neck to mid-calf. He tucked it tightly around himself, but when he went to knot the belt, his fingers wouldn't cooperate. They felt like frozen sausages, too clumsy to do any good. Jonathan reached over and did it for him, then patted him on the shoulder again. "Let's go upstairs."

Jonathan led them to the elevator—*probably because he's afraid I'll fall and break my fucking neck on the stairs*—a hand under his arm to steady him. When the doors opened, he guided Bran into the dining room.

Bran's gaze locked immediately on the dining room table. Two places set. And no cushion on the floor by Jonathan's chair.

"Have a seat," Jonathan said, gesturing toward the chair opposite him. Bran sat gingerly, his tender ass sending up a protest as he did. Still, it hurt less than kneeling on the fucking floor.

Jonathan lifted the covers on the serving dishes and began spooning food onto Bran's plate. Whatever it was, it smelled good—even for vegetarian crap. Something with stir-fried veggies and tofu. Something else with greens and fruit and nuts, like a Waldorf salad. He put his nose closer to the plate, inhaling with lust. He was hungry enough to eat with his fingers, but thankfully there was a fork right there.

"Um . . . may I ask something, Jonathan?"

Jonathan finished fixing his own plate and sat down. "Go ahead. But if you're wondering if you can feed yourself, that's why I gave you the fork. And if you're wondering why I've dressed you and let you sit at the table, well, I'd like to discuss some things with you tonight, and I want you to feel free to speak your mind, as an equal, without fear of reprisal." He pulled a familiar key from his pocket, slid it across the table. Bran snatched it up and unlocked his wrist and ankle cuffs before Jonathan changed his mind. "Just you and me as two . . ." He bit his lower lip, an irritatingly sexy little quirk of his. "As two friends," he offered hesitantly, like maybe he worried Bran would contradict him.

Actually . . . no fear of reprisal? In that case, "We're *not* friends."

Jonathan winced, nodded. "I rather thought you might say that. But we were once, weren't we?"

Bran glanced up at him, rubbing at the bruising on his left wrist. The marks went so deep it hurt to move his fingers. "We were two guys fucking in an alley," he said, cold as he knew how to make it.

Jonathan winced again. There'd been more between them than just that and they both knew it, but no way was Bran admitting that now.

"I do . . ." Jonathan began, then stopped. What'd happened to all his fucking *confidence*? "I do *care* for you, Brandon. I think I have from the moment I met you. And I would very much *like* to be your friend again."

Bran picked up his fork, stabbed angrily at a perfectly-cooked, perfectly-seasoned crown of broccoli and said around it, "You have a funny way of showing it." Speared a potato and added, "You could start by using my actual fucking *name*, you know. Or maybe I should start calling you *Ocean Windsong*?"

Another wince, this one more self-conscious than the ones before. Was he *blushing*?

"Yeah, you're not the only one who can use Google, you smug little fuck."

Jonathan's jaw clenched and his hand tightened around his fork— as yet unused; he hadn't touched his food—but all he did was duck his head and say, very softly, "I suppose I deserve that."

"Oh, you *suppose*, do you?" There was something very satisfying about getting this all out of his system. In knowing he could speak freely and not be fucking flogged or caned or spanked for it. Or put in a motherfucking *coffin.*

"But you have to understand, being a Dominant . . ." Jonathan shook his head. "It's not about *smugness.* It's about *steadiness.* It's my job to understand you, inside and out. It's my job to know things, to be able to act on them with confidence. To be your anchor when you fly. To be the rock you can depend on when the ground tilts beneath your feet. It's my job to take care of you, just as surely as it's your job to take care of me. And you've not permitted me to do *any* of that. You've not *trusted* me. Even though I've never lied to you. Even though I've never indulged my own desires ahead of yours, never beat you just for my own pleasure, never set you to tasks you can't accomplish. Even though I've held you when you've cried, and cared for you when you've suffered, and tried with all I have to open your eyes to the wonders of this world, to show you the pleasures inside yourself. And I think . . ." Another sexy lip-bite; Bran very seriously considered punching him in the mouth just to make him *stop that.* "I think that if you're going to continue refusing these things—the most valuable, precious things I know how to give—if you're going to keep insisting you don't want them, then it's time I start believing you. Time for you to leave."

What? After all he'd been through—the punishments he'd taken, being stripped naked and treated like a fucking *animal*—Jonathan intended to toss him aside like he was nothing? Like he was some kind of whore?

And not even a well-paid one. Sure, his rent was set for the year, and he had the thirty grand Jonathan had promised him from the start, but he'd quit his fucking job over this. Dropped out of the world, put his entire life on hold for six months. And what whore in the world would let someone do what Jonathan had done to him, for *any* amount of money?

He'd given up *everything.* He had no power here—except the power to say no to this. To make Jonathan hold to their contract whether he wanted to or not. He was in for the duration. They both were.

And besides, he wanted his fucking *money.*

He looked Jonathan dead in the eye and said, "Fuck you." And then, "No, I'm not going anywhere."

Jonathan didn't look surprised by that, but he did look pretty distraught. "Brandon— *Bran*, please, I'd urge you to reconsi—"

"Look at you," Bran snorted. "You're like some spoiled child. Like no one's ever said no to you before. Like you've never had to spend a single fucking day of your life *without*, like you don't even know what it *means* to be disappointed." He stabbed a piece of tofu, kind of irritated that he actually liked it, and then thrust his empty fork at Jonathan's chest. "Well, I've got news for you, pal. The world *sucks*. It *hurts*. It swallows you fucking whole, pukes you back up and does it again. Maybe it's time you fucking *learned* that. *You're* tired? *You're* unhappy? Well boo fucking hoo. *You're* not the one being tortured and molested every fucking day. I've got no fucking sympathy for you at all. And I'm not leaving until this contract is up, so pull up your fucking big-girl panties and *deal* with it."

Amazing as it felt to say all that out loud, he had to admit some disappointment at how fucking unflappable Jonathan seemed. Disappointed, sure, and maybe a little shocked, but mostly he just sat there letting Bran yell, face unmoving, almost blank. He blinked at Bran, folded his hands very primly on the table in front of his still-untouched plate, and said, voice level, "Are you finished?"

Bran took the time to eat another piece of tofu, chew thoroughly, swallow. Let the fucker wait. "Yeah, why not. Actually, you know what? No. Since this is probably the last time you'll ever let me speak for the next five and a half months? Let me just leave you with one more *Fuck you.*" He smiled—nothing friendly about it, the mouthful of teeth that scared the neighbor's kids. "To remember me by."

Jonathan nodded like he'd expected that, like he'd have been disappointed by anything less, then very calmly reached across the table and took Bran's fork right from his hand. Plate next. Then he pointed at those cursed fucking steel cuffs, sitting on the table by Bran's left hand, and said, "Fine, then. In that case, the rules haven't changed. Put those on, take that off"—he pointed at the robe now—"and kneel."

"There's no cushion."

Jonathan's hand lashed out, struck him across one temple, then back across the other. Somehow, Bran ended up on the floor, ears ringing.

"One for speaking out of turn, one for not addressing me properly. Now shall I fetch a cane, or will you obey me?"

Once Bran's ears stopped ringing, he gave Jonathan a long, cold stare. No pity, no mercy in those bright blue eyes. Not that he'd expected any. In fact, he was amazed Jonathan hadn't dragged him back to the dungeon by his earlobe and locked him in that fucking cage again.

Slowly, he rose, unknotted the robe, slid it off, let it fall to the rug. The cool air wafted over his bare skin, but he suppressed his shiver. No fucking way was he letting Jonathan see that. No way was he giving him one fucking ounce of satisfaction. Maybe Jonathan thought he was being bullheaded, but fuck him for that. Fuck him with that fucking cane he kept threatening Bran with. If Jonathan thought he could intimidate him with the promise of more pain, he'd be waiting a long fucking time. Another five and a half months, to be exact.

Bran picked up the cuffs, one by one, and locked them around his limbs. The cold weight of the steel immediately sent a bone-deep ache shooting up his arms and legs. Wasn't as if he hadn't gotten used to it, though. Two steps, three, and he was at Jonathan's side, sinking to his knees. The hard floor and rough nap of the rug bit into his kneecaps. Felt like he was kneeling on broken glass, but he bit back the grunt that rose to his lips. If Jonathan wanted him to make noise, he'd have to beat it out of him.

Jonathan stared down at him, very coldly, fingering his fork. "Beg me to feed you the rest of your dinner."

Bran's gaze didn't waver, but he didn't reply.

"That was *not* a request. Beg me, or face those thirty cane strokes you still have on account."

Fuck. He'd forgotten about that. Besides, he really was hungry— had eaten nothing but a banana and a few bites of stir-fry all day. "Jonathan," he ground out between gritted teeth, "would you *please* feed me?"

Jonathan speared a piece of tofu and a tiny slice of carrot and held out his fork. Bran took the proffered bite, chewed slowly. It really was good. Sabrina might be a stone cold bitch, but she sure could cook. A few more bites, then Jonathan set down the fork and snagged a plump blueberry from the fruit bowl. "Open," he said, leaning forward to drop it into Bran's mouth.

Too tempting to resist. Bran lifted his head slightly, just enough to catch Jonathan's fingers with the edge of his teeth. Just enough to make Jonathan yank his hand back with a small yelp of pain. Enough to make Jonathan's eyes narrow. Just like they did when the fucking cane was about to come down.

"You did that on purpose," Jonathan said, staring at the tips of his reddening fingers. *Huh.* Bran had given him quite a nip. Better than he'd been aiming for.

Didn't throw off Jonathan's aim, though; the fucker seized him by the chin and planted another smack across Bran's right cheekbone. Hard enough to rattle his teeth and make his vision swim momentarily, the chandelier dancing before his eyes like a thousand candles.

Jonathan's hand sank into his hair, grabbing hard. "Since you seem to be so fond of the dungeon, perhaps it's time you spent the night there."

Jonathan dragged him to his feet before he had a chance to panic or argue or talk back, which was probably a good thing, because scared as he was, he was way, *way* more pissed. Tempted even now, bent over while Jonathan dragged him down the hallway by his hair, to say, *Better to spend the night in the dungeon than spend it with* you.

Back downstairs, through the dungeon, back into the cubby. The bedding hadn't magically reappeared, sadly, but hey, at least this was better than a cage. It'd be a long, cold, hungry, uncomfortable night on the hard floor in the pitch black, but there'd be no shocks, no claustrophobic confines, no eyes on his every breath. All he'd have to do was try to sleep, and try not to wake up thinking he was somewhere—some*when*—else again.

How hard could that be?

Jonathan shut the door to the cubby and rubbed a hand over his face. Luckily, Brandon didn't fling himself against the door or start screaming, but he could still hear him on the other side, bare feet slapping the linoleum, breathing hard enough for the sound to carry into the dungeon. Angry, frustrated. Scared.

Good. Maybe Jonathan was finally getting somewhere—but whether toward convincing Brandon to leave or to accept the spirit of the contract, he had no clue. Of course, by tomorrow they could be right back where they started. *Again.*

Best to just let him stew. Jonathan stifled a sigh and headed upstairs to his office. Sat down at his desk, drummed his fingers on the blotter for a few seconds, then dialed Devon.

"Devon Turner's phone."

His assistant. Damn. "Hello, is Devon busy?"

"Being violently murdered, last I checked. Can I take a message?"

"Please. Tell him Jonathan Watkins called, if you would."

Paper rustling in the background as the assistant mumbled, "Jonathan . . . W-a-t-k-i-n—"

"Hey, is that Waveboy? I'm here, I'm here." A scuffling noise, and then Devon's voice got much louder and clearer. "We're in between takes. You've got five minutes. What can I do you for?" Shouting in the background, something banging. Then . . . chewing? "Sorry, at the craft table. Turns out getting shot in the face works up quite an appetite. Don't mind me."

Jonathan sighed. "I don't know what to do with him. I tried to talk to him like a regular person tonight, and he told me to fuck off." Devon laughed. "Several times, actually. Then when we stepped back into role, he *bit* me."

Devon laughed again, gasped, coughed. Was it mean to hope he was choking on his coffee?

"Nicky did that to me our very first time."

"What'd you do?"

"Pinned him down and fucked him dry." This time the cough in the background wasn't Devon's. "Kidding, kidding," he said to someone, then, to Jonathan, "He was looking for it. If you're sure Brandon isn't . . .?"

"As sure as I reasonably can be."

"I take it you want him gone, then?"

Jonathan picked up the cane that lived on his desk—the same one he used to correct Brandon's posture when the crop didn't leave enough of an impression—and ran it between his fingers, not sure how to answer. He'd had such high hopes for Brandon, but he'd given their arrangement more than enough time and energy. "I can't see any other way for it to end. I can't call a halt to it, and he knows it. Right now all he's doing is making me as miserable as I'm making him. He won't leave."

"I kinda hate to suggest rewarding bad behavior here, but have you considered just giving him the money anyway?"

Jonathan shook his head. "He'd never take it. Too proud. In fact, I'd bet another three million that if I did offer, he'd just dig his heels in twice as hard. Accuse me of trying to buy him, of thinking I have the right to."

"Then you need to chase him out," Devon said, all his usual good humor evaporating from his tone. "Let your freak flag fly, man. Get medieval on his ass."

Jonathan fingered the cane again, tapped it desultorily against his thigh. "I don't just want to *torture* the man . . ."

Devon snorted. "Sure you do. I've only seen pictures of him with his clothes *on*, and *I* want to torture him. And I'm happily married."

"He'll just safeword anyway. You know I have to respect that."

"Of course you do. But if he safewords too early, you can kick him out. If he gives you shit about bending over for the cane or getting into the sarcophagus or whatever else you decide to do to him, you can kick him out. So he's got to endure it until he can't. Do that three, four, fuck, six or eight times a day? He'll run screaming within the week."

"Or my arm will fall off."

Another snort. "Nah. Look, you've got *leverage*. So use it. Knock him off his game. Don't let him sleep. Don't *ever* let him feel safe, not even at night. Where is he now?"

"In the cubby."

"Dark? Cold?"

"Yes."

"So set your alarm for, oh, 2 a.m. or so, go down there and wake him with a leather strap. Don't say a word. Don't stop until he calls red. Then lock the door and go back to sleep. You'll see—it'll throw him hard." A pause; Jonathan could practically hear the smile. "And who knows, you might even get a kick out of it."

"Maybe," Jonathan said, but somehow, he doubted it. This whole thing had moved way past fun the moment Brandon had bitten the hand that fed him.

Jonathan set his alarm for 2 a.m., but when it went off, he nearly stayed in bed. The room seemed oddly cold and weirdly silent without Brandon's soft snoring punctuating the air. But eventually he climbed out and wandered over to the small desk in the corner to check the camera feed from downstairs.

Brandon was curled up in a little ball in the center of the cubby. He was shivering, but his eyes were closed. Looked like he'd managed to fall asleep—out of sheer exhaustion, no doubt. Jonathan rubbed his eyes, flung a wistful gaze at his own warm bed, and reached for his robe.

The dungeon made him shiver as he strode through, snagging a long thin strap from the toy rack before continuing on to the cubby. No sounds from the other side, other than Brandon's tiny wheezing snore. Sounded like a kitten Jonathan had had as a child. Almost made his hand falter on the doorknob. *Almost.*

Get it over with. We'll both be better off.

He shouldered open the door and burst in, swinging the strap in front of him. The first strike landed hard across Brandon's flank before the sound of the slamming door had faded. Brandon jerked awake with a panicked shout, and Jonathan landed the second strike before Brandon could get his hands beneath him to skitter away. A third strike, and a fourth—Brandon gave up trying to escape and just curled in on himself, hands protecting his head, ragged breaths ripped from his chest as Jonathan struck him again with as much force as he could muster.

Brandon finally managed to roll onto his knees and forearms, presenting a much cleaner target; Jonathan laid four good stripes across Brandon's back before he pressed himself into the corner, head still buried in his arms, and good lord, was he *crying*? It couldn't possibly hurt that much. At least not yet.

Another strike, this one landing square across Brandon's forearms, the noise making even Jonathan wince.

"Dad, please! Don't! I'm sorry, I'm *sorry!*"

Shock stayed Jonathan's hand mid-blow. The strap slipped from his fingers. Thumped to the floor. Brandon whimpered another apology, and Jonathan stumbled away so fast he nearly tripped. Fumbled behind himself for the door. Backed through it and all but slammed it shut.

Jesus Christ . . . What had he *done*?

ran woke to pain, every frozen muscle protesting as he sat up. The light had come on overhead, bright enough to make his eyeballs ache. Fuck, what an *awful* dream he'd had last night. He pulled his knees up to his chest to conserve heat, chafed his hands across his arms. Shit . . . It'd been years since he'd felt that kind of fear, years since he'd let his father have that kind of power over—

Bran stared at his forearms. At the fresh red welts across them. More on his shins, his chest, his sides. He could feel them across his back and shoulders, too. And there, near the door, a leather strap like a fucking belt without a buckle.

Not a dream. Not a dream at all.

Fury drove him to his feet, bunched his hands at his sides, sent him flying toward the door. He pounded on it with both fists. "Get down here, you little fuck! Face me like a—!"

The door clicked open.

What, the little fucker hadn't even bothered to lock him in?

He half-expected to find Jonathan waiting for him in the dungeon, but instead all he found were his things sitting on the leather-upholstered table. His duffel bag, his clothes, his shoes. The key to his cuffs. His copy of *Huck Finn*, and the picture of his mother Jonathan had taken away from him yesterday. Bran ran his fingertip along the edge of the frame, then quickly turned it over.

Don't want her to see me like this. Even if it was fucking stupid.

He unlocked the cuffs, threw them on the floor. Picked up his jeans. They felt . . . softer, smelled like sunshine. Jonathan must've had his maid wash them. His T-shirt, plain old white cotton, had had a tiny rip in one armpit, right on the seam. It was mended now.

He dragged the shirt over his head, his shoulders and back sending up a screech as the material chafed like sandpaper on his welted skin. He'd just stepped into his jeans when he caught sight of the damn toy rack, his gaze lingering on the soft suede flogger Jonathan had used on him a week or so ago. The day he'd eaten from Jonathan's hand for the first time.

What the hell had happened between then and now? Could he find his way back to it?

Did he *want* to?

No. Not even a little. He'd never traded his self-respect for comfort before, and he wasn't about to start now. He finished pulling his jeans up, buttoned and zipped them. Shit but it felt good to be warm.

One other way to never go cold again. Just walk out of here. Fuck Jonathan and fuck his bullshit abuse and his even more bullshit pop psychology about what you supposedly really want and just leave.

Jonathan obviously wanted him to. Why else would he have left all his stuff down here? Fucking coward couldn't even face him to say goodbye.

But if you leave, he wins. You walk out on your whole future. You walk out beaten. Weak. The coward, the loser Dad always said you were.

Shit. He really fucking needed to stop thinking about his dad so fucking much. And fuck Jonathan for *that*, too. For reminding him of it. No doubt he'd done it on purpose. Crossed a fucking *line* there.

He didn't even want to think about how hard he'd fallen for it. Of what he'd said to Jonathan last night in the heat of his half-asleep disorientation. Of how he'd *begged*. Cried like some little fucking kid. Of how terrified he'd been, how he'd thought—

Stop it. Big-girl panties, Bran.

Or, in this case, no panties at all. With a sigh, he unbuttoned his jeans, slid them off, stepped out of them. Took off the shirt as well. Stuffed both back in his duffel, along with *Huck Finn*. Naked again but for those fucking steel cuffs he scooped up off the floor and locked back on. He picked up the photo of his mother, brushed his fingers across her soft smile. So lovely she'd been, even when she'd lost all her hair, her eyebrows, even when she'd gotten skinny enough for his twelve-year-old arms to lift her. She wouldn't have wanted this for him—any of this. But she'd always taught him to stand by his principles, to follow his heart. She'd never doubted him when he'd told her he'd go to UC Berkeley, become an architect. Never mind that he'd been eight years old at the time. He'd hung on to that dream through all the shit life had thrown at him. Had it in his reach now. He wasn't going to quit. He *wasn't*.

He brought the photo to his lips, kissed his mother on the forehead and then laid it very carefully inside his duffel. Sniffed back the urge to cry. No time for this sentimental bullshit; he had to get ready to face his day.

He went into the bathroom to groom himself, then headed upstairs. He hesitated a moment as he reached the top of the staircase before stepping into the living room. Jonathan was sitting on the balcony, reading the paper, as usual. Little fucker hadn't even come down to check on him. Or maybe Jonathan thought he'd already left?

Time to give him a shock, then. Straightening up as best he could, he marched over to the balcony. Slid open the door, stepped out, knelt on the cold paving stones at Jonathan's feet. No cushion this time, but then, he hadn't expected one. The pavers bit into his knees, nearly forcing a grunt out of him, but he bit it back, assumed the correct posture. Looked up to meet Jonathan's gaze, defiant as ever.

Jonathan folded the paper back and said, casually dismissive, "You're still here, eh?"

"Damn straight, Jonathan. And if you *ever*—" He broke position when Jonathan cast his gaze back to the newspaper, reached up to grab the fucker's wrist and squeezed until Jonathan met his eyes. "If you *ever* cross that line again, *I will fucking kill you.* Do you understand, Jonathan?"

Jonathan's gaze was bright blue in the early morning sun, steady, endless, not cold like Bran had expected. Completely opposite, in fact: Repentant? Guilty? Fuck that; Bran wasn't buying that for a second.

At last Jonathan nodded. Said softly, "Yes, I understand."

Then he extricated his wrist from Bran's hand—carefully, no force—and went back to his paper. Whatever permissiveness, whatever understanding had passed between them, the moment was gone. Bran folded his hands behind his back again, content to have said what needed saying, content Jonathan had listened. Surprised, though, at the lack of demerits. Was that Jonathan's way of apologizing?

Bran remained in position, watching Jonathan thumb through the financial section as his hollow belly rumbled. Finally Jonathan set aside the paper and reached for his fork, speared a fat red strawberry off his plate and held it out to Bran. Their gazes locked as Bran accepted it, a hot flush creeping up the back of his neck when he realized how eagerly he was chewing. How good one small bite of food could taste after a whole day and night of going hungry.

"I want you to stop shaving every day," Jonathan said as he fed him another strawberry. "You obviously have no regard for yourself, no respect for discipline or routine, and I like you better scruffy anyway."

That was Jonathan's plan to run him out of here? Insult him to death? Turn him into a yeti?

"And you won't be joining me in my office anymore. You've not earned the right to kneel at my feet."

Then what am I doing here now?

"In fact, don't come upstairs at all anymore. Sabrina will see you fed."

You. Have. Got. To. Be. Fucking. Kidding. *Me.*

"Bite *her* and she's like as not to emasculate you with one of those exquisitely sharp knives of hers."

Bran resisted the very strong urge to press his knees together.

Jonathan spooned up a blob of oatmeal and shoved it at Bran so hard he knocked the spoon against Bran's teeth. *Ow.* "I plan to mark up every inch of you, and see to it you stay that way for the next five and a half months."

Lovely. But it ain't gonna work, you little shit; I'm not going anywhere.

"Since nothing about our arrangement interests you in the slightest, at least one of us should enjoy themselves, don't you think?"

Was that a rhetorical question or an actual one? Actual, he realized, when Jonathan's slippered foot flicked out and caught him in the nuts, more nudge than kick but still painful enough to double him over. He didn't even realize he'd scraped his knees on the pavers until the pain in his nuts had faded.

"Break position again and I'll correct you with *this*," Jonathan said, not even looking at Bran as he picked up a . . . What the fuck was that? Bran squinted, leaned forward for a closer look, and Jonathan casually reached down and touched it to his thigh. Next Bran knew, he was curled over himself screaming, the pain of the shock so big he couldn't even wrap his head around it for a good ten seconds. That fucking *stun gun*, the one Jonathan had teased him with that night he'd tied him to the footboard, ten times as bad as the shock cage and not nearly so quick to fade. Was that thing even *legal*? His thigh muscle twitched uncomfortably, twitched again, then settled. He clenched his hands behind his back, desperate to rub at his still-throbbing leg, terrified that Jonathan would zap him again if he did.

"When we're done with breakfast, you'll be getting to know this toy *very* well. If you're prone to vomiting, perhaps you'd like to wait to eat until later."

Prone to *vomiting*? What did that even *mean*? And why the fuck wouldn't Jonathan even *look* at him?

"In fact, I think you've had enough breakfast for now." Two strawberries and a spoonful of oatmeal after a 24-hour fast was enough? Apparently, because Jonathan stood, dragging Bran up by his hair, shoving him out the door ahead of him. Down to the dungeon they went, his heart thudding so hard he felt dizzy. Amazing—*no, shameful*—how fast the bravado cracked when fucking *stun guns* came into play. He stumbled inside, and Jonathan quickly grabbed his arm, yanking him over to the suspension bar. "Stay here."

Jonathan went over to the toy rack and came back with the leather cuffs he'd used that time he'd flogged him. With the suede flogger. The one thing in this motherfucking room that had actually felt good.

No such luck today.

It took every last shred of will to keep from bolting at the thought of that stun gun zapping him again. Fortunately, he had a lot of fucking will; he stood there quietly, biting his lip so hard he was surprised he didn't make himself bleed while Jonathan removed the painful steel cuffs and replaced them with the leather, then gestured for him to reach up and grip the bar.

Jonathan clipped the leather cuffs to either end of the bar, then bent down to attach the leather ankle cuffs to the chains in the floor. Pulled the chains taut, and in doing so pulled his legs wide apart, almost uncomfortably so. No fucking slack at all.

No room to struggle.

Back to the toy rack. This time Jonathan returned with a long leather strap with a buckle on the end and a dick-thick, black rubber bit in the middle.

"Since I've heard quite enough lip from you this morning, you can wrap your smart mouth around this." Jonathan shoved the bit between Bran's teeth and buckled the strap at the back of his neck, so tight the bit hurt the corners of his mouth. Left his hand there for a fraction of a second, lightly teasing Bran's hair. The way he used to at the beginning, before everything had gone to hell.

Bran jerked his head away.

Jonathan clenched his fingers in Bran's hair and yanked his head back. "Don't even think about pulling away from me again. I'll touch you if I damn well please." He tugged Bran's head back even further—felt like he was pulling the hair out at the fucking roots; Bran's eyes watered and he clenched his teeth around the bit.

Jonathan's lips brushed his ear, hot breath and a flash of tongue. "Or maybe I'll just *fuck* you." Another tug, accompanied this time by a thrust of hips against him. "Right here, right like this." Jonathan's free hand came down in a hard slap across his ass, then parted his cheeks. One finger stabbed dry inside him and he barked a cry around the gag, squeezed his eyes shut. Couldn't even close his legs. Couldn't even *safeword.*

Jesus fuck, was Jonathan gonna rape him dry?

"Breathe," Jonathan said, stepping back a little, fist still in Bran's hair. He gave Bran's head a hard shake, said, "Breathe," again. Bran sucked in a deep, shaky breath through his nose, felt his thrashing heart begin to settle, just a little, down to beats he could distinguish one from the next. "Here." Jonathan reached up, stuffed something soft into Bran's right hand, turned Bran's head by the hair until he could see it. The red paisley handkerchief?

"That's red, remember?" Jonathan said, giving his hair another tug, and holy fuck how had it not all just ripped in his hand already? *Shit,* his scalp hurt. "Drop that and I stop. Drop it before you need to and you give me grounds to void the contract, understand?"

Jonathan's fingers loosened just enough for Bran to nod his head. Fuck, Bran even believed him. He'd *know* if Bran were faking. He *always* knew.

Jonathan circled around to face him. Curled one hand behind Bran's neck, lifted the stun gun in the other. He pressed it to the hollow between Bran's collarbones, dug in hard. Bran tried to jerk away, couldn't with Jonathan holding him like that. Fuck, but the thing was cold. Jonathan dragged it down his sternum, leaned in and pressed his mouth to where the stun gun had been—a hot, soft contrast to the cold hard steel of the contacts. He licked, sucked, and if Bran hadn't been so fucking disgusted he supposed it would've felt pretty nice . . . until Jonathan *bit* him hard enough to leave a mark.

He cried out around the gag, tried again to pull away, got nowhere. Jonathan's teeth were still latched to his skin, still biting-digging like he was trying to *eat* him, and there was no fucking way *anything* could hurt that much and not draw blood and he'd *promised*—

Jonathan let go, stepped back. Bran looked down at the bruise Jonathan had raised near the top of his sternum. Jesus, it looked nasty, but much to his surprise, it wasn't bleeding. *At least not openly. Plenty of blood* beneath *the skin, though.*

Jonathan grinned like a shark and dug the pad of his thumb into the teeth marks until Bran whimpered, squeezing tears from the corners of his tightly clenched eyes—

Which flew open really fucking fast when Jonathan jammed the stun gun low on his left hip and pressed the trigger.

Jonathan had to admit to a little thrill as Brandon screamed around the bit gag, jerking and writhing in his bonds. He was chained via spreader bars to the floor and ceiling, but that didn't stop him from thrashing around like he was dying. "What's the matter?" Jonathan drawled, lifting the stun gun to Brandon's tearing eyes and triggering it a few inches from his face. Brandon's eyes widened and his head snapped back. "Did that *hurt*?"

Those green eyes narrowed dangerously, lips peeling back from around the bit to bare two endless rows of teeth.

"What's that? You want another?" Brandon's glare could've flayed the skin off Jonathan's face. He trailed the stun gun down Brandon's chest, belly, pelvis, teased the length of his cock with it. Brandon's chest heaved and his thigh muscles bunched into sharp relief, fighting the spreader bar, but of course the restraints held. The urge to shock his genitals was strong, but he didn't want to push that hard unless he had to, so he slid the stun gun back, to Brandon's balls, his ass, pressed the contacts firmly to one cheek and said, "Since you asked so nicely," then pulled the trigger.

Another muffled scream that surged through him like a lightning bolt, heading straight for his cock. Not what he'd intended, but good Lord it was hot watching Brandon struggle. Every muscle in that lean body clenched, sweat dripping down his chest, teeth sinking harder into the bit, breaths so ragged and rapid he wondered if Brandon wouldn't pass right out. Such exquisite suffering. Why hadn't he thought to do this before?

Oh, yes. Because you were trying to be nice.

He slid his hand—and the stun gun—back between Brandon's legs, caressed Brandon's inner thigh with it, then drifted round to the back of Brandon's left leg. Dragged the contacts over the long muscle there, which was trembling hard enough to feel right through the stun gun. He glanced up, saw Brandon's head tipped back, eyes fixed on the ceiling, cheeks streaked with sweat and at least a few tears. He looked . . . terrified. Resigned. And yet, somehow, *defiant*. Braced to take whatever Jonathan could dish out. His hand was fisted so tight around the handkerchief his knuckles were white. He clearly had no intention of dropping the thing anytime soon.

Come on, you bloody fool. Just end it and go home.

Jonathan pressed the stun gun to the hollow of Brandon's left knee and squeezed the trigger again.

Chains rattled hard as Brandon screamed, jerked. Jonathan stumbled back on reflex, getting his face out of the way of Brandon's kicking leg, but of course the chains caught before the man could move more than an inch or two. Muscles twitched all up and down Brandon's leg, just for a moment, then settled. His chin fell against his heaving chest. Even the fingers of his free hand had gone slack.

Jonathan gritted his teeth and jammed the stun gun into the crease between pelvis and thigh, triggered it again. Best not to let Brandon catch his breath. It'd be over faster this way. Another zap on the opposite side, another writhing scream, yet still the stubborn fool held onto the handkerchief, clung to it like he couldn't unclench his fist even if he wanted to.

Bloody hell. Jonathan reached up, grabbed at the hankie, gave it a tug. Brandon's fingers clamped down tighter. "Let go. I'm just switching hands."

Good, Brandon could still unclench those fingers after all. Jonathan stuffed the hankie in Brandon's opposite fist and turned his attention back to that long lean body hanging at his mercy.

Or rather, his *lack* of it. He almost smiled at the thought, but arousing as this was, he wanted it done with, and the sooner the better.

One sure way to manage that . . .

He wedged the stun gun between Brandon's cock and balls, wrapped hard fingers around the back of Brandon's neck, and whispered in his ear, "Had enough yet?"

Fine tremors beneath his fingers were Brandon's only response. The man didn't even look at him. He let go of Brandon's neck, grabbed him by the chin instead. Gave in to the impulse to lean in and lick the tears off one cheek. "Mmm," he hummed into Brandon's ear, long and leering. Brandon shuddered, tried to turn his face away. Jonathan let him, but only because he didn't want his hands on Brandon's body as he pulled the trigger again.

The scream this time went on *forever*, and when Brandon ran out of air, he sucked in a new breath and screamed all over again. Jonathan took advantage, depressing the trigger once more, the contacts still wedged up between Brandon's cock and balls. Brandon's scream trailed off into a sob, and he shook his head, shook his whole body, trying to escape the agony. Another zap, and the scream didn't even make it out this time—just a cracked, broken whimper, Brandon's trembling body slumping in his restraints as the handkerchief, *at last*, fluttered to the ground.

Strange to be so sickened and so relieved and so bloody *aroused* all at the same time.

Jonathan laid the stun gun on a nearby table, fighting the desire to take Brandon down from his chains, hold him and kiss him and praise him and wipe away his tears. "Have you had enough?" he asked instead. "Do you want to go home?"

Brandon made no reply, just hung in his chains, chin to his chest, panting fit to hyperventilate.

Jonathan made himself cross back over, grab Brandon by the hair and jerk his head up. His face was streaked with tears, his lips slack around the spit-soaked gag. "Answer me."

Ever so slightly, Brandon shook his head.

"Then you'll be taking care of *this* for me now," Jonathan said, shoving Brandon's chin down with one hand and freeing his painfully hard cock with the other. Brandon's eyes widened, and the slight headshake turned into a forceful one; Jonathan let go of him to pick up the dropped handkerchief, stuffed it back in Brandon's hand. "You know the rules."

Brandon's fingers fisted tight around the cloth again, but he hadn't stopped shaking his head.

"You know what?" Jonathan said, grabbing Brandon by the chin. "I've spent the last two weeks fretting over how to make it good for *you*, and you spit in my face. So now it's *my* turn. You don't want this? *Go home.*" He spat into his hand. "Speaking of . . ."

Brandon's jaw tightened as Jonathan thrust a spit-slicked finger inside him and twisted it. So tight he could barely move it, but he pulled out and shoved back in with two fingers, purposely avoiding Brandon's prostate as he stretched the man. If Brandon was determined not to enjoy this, Jonathan was happy to oblige him.

Tempted as he was to force his cock in with no further lubrication, Jonathan wasn't all that keen on causing *himself* pain—and besides, he'd promised Brandon no blood. He spat into his palm again, quickly coated his cock with it, and pressed the tip to Brandon's hole. "*Sure* you wouldn't rather go home?"

Brandon wagged his head, grunting and thrashing in his chains. For all the good it would do him.

"Fine." Jonathan wrapped an arm around Brandon's waist to hold him still. "Then this one's for me."

In he thrust, balls-deep, with one merciless push. Brandon immediately tensed, clenching so hard Jonathan felt it down to the root of his cock. Brandon let out a tiny strangled noise as Jonathan grabbed his hips and started to move, slamming into him hard enough to rattle his chains. Every last drop of blood in Jonathan's body rushed to his cock, but still he glanced up, keeping an eye on the handkerchief clutched in Brandon's fist.

"Had enough now?" he whispered. "Or do you like it after all? Like my cock in your ass, like my chains around your wrists. Like it when I *hurt* you"—he pulled out to the tip, thrust back in again hard enough to slap skin against sweaty skin. Brandon cried out around his gag, shook his head. "Like it when I use you like some cheap whore, when I don't even *touch* you, give a *shit* about your pleasure. Like you're just some collection of *holes* for me to come in."

Another thrust, two, and the telltale pull of his balls told him he was close. "On second thought, you're not even good enough for that." One more deep stroke before he yanked his cock free, jacked it in his fist—

And came all over Brandon's back.

The rush made his head spin, made spots dance in front of his eyes. He stepped back on unsteady legs, pulled up his zipper. Went over to a toy rack to grab a rubber plug half again the size of his cock.

"So you won't get lonely while I'm gone," he said, giving it a quick swipe through the jizz trickling down Brandon's ass crack, then shoving it deep inside him. Brandon groaned and shook his head, but still the handkerchief didn't fall. "You really are determined to make this hard on yourself, aren't you?"

When Brandon said nothing, Jonathan tracked behind him again, touched the stun gun to Brandon's ass. Brandon jerked as if he'd pulled the trigger, but he hadn't, not yet. Slid the stun gun down to the plug, instead . . . *Shame it's not a metal one.* Slid it further yet, to that tender patch of skin between Brandon's hole and his balls, and said, "One for the road, then?"

He supposed it should've come as no surprise that Brandon lacked the energy to protest, but the man's plaintive, high-pitched whimper tugged at his heart much more than he'd thought it would. He'd only meant to frighten Brandon, anyway, not actually shock him again.

He suppressed the urge to grimace as he circled back to Brandon's front, laid the stun gun very deliberately on a shelf in Brandon's direct line of sight, and went to fetch a panic button and a roll of tape.

When he returned, he tried to tug the handkerchief from Brandon's hand, but the man didn't want to give it up again. "Look," he said, and had to lift Brandon's chin from his chest before he could hold up the panic button in front of him. "You'll be spending some quiet time here today. I won't. I can't hear the handkerchief drop from my office. I *can* hear this."

Brandon blinked at him, long and slow, eyes heavy and glazed, but his fingers loosened around the handkerchief. Jonathan replaced it with the panic button, taped it right to Brandon's hand so he couldn't drop it and made him press the button once while he was standing there. He might want to chase Brandon out, but he wasn't willing to do it on the back of the man's incapacity to consent. Not even now.

"Good boy," he said, patting Brandon twice on the cheek. "Now you take some time to think about what you really want. Sabrina will come in later to feed you. All that screaming you'll be doing takes energy, after all."

Jonathan turned away then, the dark cold weight of Brandon's glare square between his shoulder blades as he let himself out of the dungeon and shut the door.

ran and the dungeon became close personal friends over the next week or so. He and the cubby got practically intimate. Cold, hunger, and constant pain joined in the fray. He'd thought Jonathan had been sadistic before. He'd been *wrong*.

And truthfully, he didn't know how much more of this he could endure. Morning, noon, night . . . he could barely even sleep for fear of waking to a flogger or a shock prod, the cubby floor cold and hard as a fucking ice rink, the stifling confines of Jonathan's various cages even less forgiving than his live-in closet. And Jonathan had been true to his word: he'd marked up every inch of Bran, and when he'd run out of fresh inches to mark, he just started working his way back over the old ones. Bran couldn't even scream out his pain anymore; he'd lost his voice so completely he could barely even whisper.

Strange, then, how hard it was to hold on to his fury. Maybe he was just too worn out to waste what little energy he had on shit like that.

Or maybe you brought this on yourself and you know it.

"Shut up," he croaked, a scratchy near-whisper that tore at his throat like Jonathan's favorite cat-o-nine-tails. He hugged his knees closer to his chest, rocked a little to conserve heat. Thought about maybe doing some sit-ups and push-ups, jogging in place, but really, he'd hurt too much for any of that for at least four days now. Or was it five? Six? Fuck-all knew how long he'd been down here. How long since he'd even been able to look out a window, see the sun.

He must've nodded off a sec, because next he knew he was jerking his chin up, thrusting out a hand to stop himself from toppling sideways. He'd been doing that a lot lately. What'd they call that . . . micro-sleep? Something like that.

Who the fuck cares?

His stomach growled. Might've been the middle of the fucking night, though, for all he knew. Probably was, or he'd be in chains or a cage instead of the cubby. Sabrina came in pretty often, seemed to get quite the kick out of making him beg to eat, and truth was, right now he'd have done it happily. At least he didn't feel quite so cold right after he'd eaten. At least it was easier to sleep, then.

And just how had his life gotten miserable enough for him to find patterns in the misery? Hadn't been like that in over a decade, barely surviving like some half-drowned little street rat scampering around, praying no one would step on its tail. Why was he *doing* this to himself?

So much for never trading your self-respect, Bran. Fuck, even three million dollars wasn't worth this kind of misery.

. . . Was it?

Who knew. Hard to think now about anything, let alone something as big as that.

A door opened somewhere beyond the cubby, and the sharp dry taste of adrenaline flooded his mouth. He hugged his knees tighter, squeezed his eyes closed. Could be food, but could be pain, too. He wasn't sure he wanted to find out. Just wanted to curl into a little ball in the corner, disappear right through the fucking floor and sleep and sleep and sleep until this all went away.

No choice, though. Never any choice.

Not true. You can stop this. You know how to stop this.

He started bodily as the cubby door opened, but didn't back away. Too tired, and anyway, what was the point? If Jonathan wanted to hurt him, he'd hurt him no matter where he was.

Just Sabrina, though, carrying a tray. She flipped on the overhead light, and Bran buried his face in his knees, blocking out the shock. Relieved. So fucking *relieved*. Too much to feel even the slightest hint of shame as he curled his arms tight round his head and wept into his knees.

Jonathan kept toggling between his quarterly report and the camera feed from downstairs. Brandon had held out far longer than he'd expected. Days of torture—canings, floggings, a variety of difficult confinements and cages. Back to the stun gun, which invariably got him to safeword, but not leave.

Truth to tell, Jonathan admired his tenacity, even though it made him grind his teeth. Just how far would he have to go to make Brandon finally say *enough*?

Devon had told him to go medieval on his ass. Maybe it was time to take that literally.

He watched as Sabrina entered the cubby, flicked on the light, set down the tray. Usually Brandon put up a token protest before he took food from her hand, but this morning he practically crawled into her lap when she offered him a strawberry. As hungry as that, or just desperate for human contact that didn't hurt, some hint of kindness? And was it Jonathan's imagination, or were those *tears* rolling down Brandon's scruffy cheeks?

Perhaps he was finally ready.

Jonathan watched as Sabrina finished feeding him and sent him to the bathroom for his morning ritual. He waited the thirty minutes Brandon was permitted for washing, then stood from his desk and headed downstairs. He heard a muffled bumping noise on the other side of the cubby door as he opened it. Brandon was over in the far corner, hunched down on his knees.

"Get up," Jonathan snapped. It didn't take more than a second for Brandon to comply. It never ceased to amaze him how pliant continual misery could make a man, even one as bullheaded as Brandon. He gave Brandon a push as he came through the door, shoving the man ahead of him into the dungeon.

Then he gestured toward the leather sling over by the cross. One of the few items in the dungeon Brandon hadn't yet had the pleasure of experiencing. Shame his first time in it would be so negative, but alas, the Fun Ship Sex-Swing had sailed long ago.

"Climb in," Jonathan said. Brandon just looked at it sideways, likely trying to figure out how. "It's just like a swing." He patted the thick rectangle of leather that would support Brandon's back. "Hop up here. Then lie back and lift your legs, feet in the stirrups."

Brandon's eyes narrowed, but he did as told, grabbing hold of the chains supporting the lower end of the sling and boosting himself up. He winced, swallowed back a gasp as his welted backside planted on the leather, winced again as he laid back. Jonathan could physically see him psyching himself up to put his feet in the stirrups. He had to be wondering what Jonathan was going to do to him, had to figure it was sexual. Certainly figured—if his expression was anything to go by—that he wasn't going to enjoy it at all.

Yet still he lifted his legs into the stirrups. He knew by now: better to do it himself than make Jonathan shock him into submission with the stun gun.

"Scoot down," Jonathan said, "so your ass is half off the sling."

Brandon obeyed with hesitance but not hesitation, and Jonathan clipped his ankle cuffs to the stirrups, then buckled leather straps around his calves and thighs, keeping his knees raised and his legs spread wide. Two more straps around Brandon's hips and chest, taking away his

CAT GRANT · RACHEL HAIMOWITZ

ability to squirm. Brandon's arms, however, he left slack, bent at the elbows, wrist cuffs snapped to the back support chains. Plenty of room for him to struggle there, for all the good it would do him.

Jonathan turned back to the toy rack, watching Brandon watching him out of the corner of one eye as he reached for a bottle of lubricant and a pair of latex gloves. Snapped the gloves on, one by one, while panic chased the near-constant haze from Brandon's wide green eyes. He started squirming, setting the whole contraption to rattling, but that thing could hold a full-grown bear—no pun intended—and Brandon was no match for it.

Still, it was a fun mind-fuck—and from the look on Brandon's face, it seemed to have done the trick. Start out with him frightened, and it would only get more effective from there.

Brandon's fear seemed to settle into apprehension as Jonathan flipped open the cap on the lube and squeezed some into his hand. More than he'd ever used when they'd fucked—enough to soak his whole hand and drip-drip-drip onto the dungeon floor. Probably more than he needed to begin with, since he'd taken to keeping Brandon plugged more or less 24/7 these past days.

Sure enough, when he removed the cock-sized plug, his first two fingers replaced it without any trouble. So he added a third, and got a stifled groan—but was it pleasure, or pain?

Normally he would've worked his way in slowly, but today he didn't intend for this to be pleasurable in the slightest. So he brought the tips of all four fingers together and *pushed*. They slid to the first knuckle before he encountered resistance. Then he folded his thumb in and pushed some more.

Brandon cried out, bit his lip, gripped the chains so hard the entire swing shimmied.

"Relax," Jonathan singsonged, "or this is really going to hurt." He punctuated his taunt with a hard thrust, working his fingers in to the second knuckle. Brandon did the exact opposite, of course, bucking up beneath him, trying—and failing—to get away from Jonathan's invading hand.

"This is going inside you one way or the other, so you might as well stop fighting me."

Brandon lifted his head just long enough to glare at Jonathan, but he said nothing. Had gotten very, very good at saying nothing this past week, in fact. Still, shame colored his cheeks, and pain tightened the lines around his eyes and mouth. Such a pretty picture; too bad Jonathan felt like too much of an ass to enjoy it.

But Brandon was ripe for the pushing, Jonathan was sure of it. One more little fist-shaped nudge and he'd be out of here. He'd safeword for the last time, and he'd leave.

Jonathan forced said fist in a little deeper, halfway to the third knuckle, and smiled placidly at Brandon's bared teeth.

"I think when I've got my whole fist in there, I'll shove my cock in beside it. Think you'd like that, Brandon?"

It was a direct question, and Brandon knew better than not to answer those now. In fact, Jonathan knew how close to breaking Brandon had come by his answer: a plaintive "Please don't, Jonathan." No heat, no fury . . . and no safeword.

At least not yet.

Jonathan sighed and wedged his hand in further with a swift, brutal thrust. Right up to the third knuckle, and Brandon's own knuckles went white around the swing's chains, head rolling back against the leather to bare his sweaty throat. Tempting to bite it, but he'd have to pull his hand out, and he wasn't willing to give Brandon the respite. He twisted his wrist instead, right and left and right again, forcing his knuckles up against Brandon's hole, making every effort to keep his scrunched-up fingers away from Brandon's prostate. Brandon coughed out a cry, groaned deep in his chest, the ring of muscle clamping tight around Jonathan's fingers.

"You're not doing yourself any favors," Jonathan said, twisting his hand back and forth again, again. He paused to squirt on more lube, not that he thought he needed it, but still . . . Brandon was *fighting* him, and he didn't want to tear the man.

He kept going, rocking his hand back and forth, trying to ease in a bit further, but the base of his thumb proved tricky. And with Brandon resisting him, getting in all the way was going to be tough. Jonathan's wrist and triceps already ached with the effort of holding himself steady. He pulled out, removed his thumb from the equation and pushed back in with four fingers. They slid in up to the third knuckle, but Brandon still whimpered like he'd been rammed with a mace. Was this as far as he could go? As far as Brandon would let him go? Was Brandon *ever* going to safeword, or did he need to switch tacks?

He let his hand slide free, then turned to the toy rack. Picked up his violet wand and an intimidatingly large attachable glass probe with a bulbous head.

"Would you prefer this?" he asked, plugging in the wand and waving it, sparking electric purple like a Tesla coil, in front of Brandon's face. He dipped the probe below Brandon's navel, held it an inch or so above the freshly shaved skin there and let the electricity arc in a bright, noisy, tortuously painful spark. Brandon yelped, jerked, face twisting with panic as the swing rocked and Jonathan lowered the probe again. He didn't let it arc this time, just took hold of the swing to steady it, leaned into Brandon's line of sight, and said, "Just for clarity? This goes *inside* you."

Brandon swallowed hard, his Adam's apple bobbing. Shivering in the swing.

"So," Jonathan said, "Would you prefer this inside you, or my hand?"

Brandon licked his lips. "Y-your hand, Jonathan."

"What *about* my hand?"

Yes, I really am *going to make you say it. So* say it, *you mulish ass.*

Brandon's face went the color of rice paper, but for two hot splotches of pink on his cheeks. "I . . . I want your hand inside me . . . Jonathan."

"There's a good boy." Jonathan unplugged the violet wand and laid it aside, reached for the lube. Made a long, leisurely show of slicking up his hand again, then slid it between Brandon's cheeks. Went all the way in, thumb included, up to the third knuckle before he met serious resistance. The base of his thumb was still being stubborn, and this time it wasn't because of Brandon. Or at least, Brandon wasn't *deliberately* fighting him anymore.

So he pushed again. And again. Brandon groaned and whimpered, still grabbing the chains so hard Jonathan was surprised he hadn't taken all the skin off his palms. Another push, and he earned another quarter inch, the base of his thumb now lodged halfway inside Brandon. It looked exquisitely painful, clearly was by the sounds Brandon was making, the rapid hitching of his shoulders and chest.

And would the man please hurry up and safeword before Jonathan's arm gave out?

"Just a little further," Jonathan said, and then, lest Brandon think the ordeal was nearly through, "And then I'll work my cock up right up next to it, fuck you and my own fist at the same time."

He had to admit, the idea held appeal. Except for the part where he was fairly certain Brandon's muscles would shear his cock clear off if he tried to wedge it in there beside his hand.

Well, what he doesn't know won't soothe him.

He gave another hard shove, forced his hand in nearly to the base of his thumb. Brandon cried out, arched up beneath him, arms and legs spasming, chest pressing up against the strap that held him. "Fuck!" he shouted, voice watery and cracked and so far past broken Jonathan just wanted to wrap him in a blanket and feed him soup. But he kept pushing, gave his hand a little twist, and Brandon cried out again, rasped, "Stop! Fuck! You're fucking ripping me in half!" Not quite, no, but Jonathan could imagine how it might feel that way. He grabbed the strap around Brandon's hips with his free hand, used it to leverage Brandon forward onto his fist as he tried to muscle it deeper, and the next fraction of an inch earned him a scream, and finally, *at last*, "Red! Fuck, please, *red*!"

Jonathan slid his hand out as gently as he could, but still Brandon choked back a sob. He thought about fucking that loosened hole, but he'd lost his erection at some point in this whole mess and didn't much care to coax it back. Maybe he'd just leave Brandon in the swing a while. Maybe he'd—

"Let me up," Brandon said, his voice so rough it came out barely audible. Jonathan met his eyes, and Brandon added, "I mean it. Let me out of this thing."

No *Jonathan* at the end of either of those demands. Dare he hope . . .? "Are you ready to go home, then?"

Brandon held his gaze a long, weighted moment, the muscles in his jaw clenching. "Yes."

Thank. Fucking. God.

CHAPTER **20**

Brandon trudged up the five flights of stairs to his apartment, his legs screaming with each step. His whole body screaming. There wasn't an inch of skin below the neck Jonathan hadn't marked. Even the soles of his feet were bruised. He couldn't wait to take some aspirin, sleep in his own bed, eat a meal with his own two hands. Even cold ravioli out of a can sounded pretty fucking good right now.

He fumbled his keys out of his pocket with rubbery fingers. God, was he ever gonna stop shaking? His wrists ached down to the bone, deep purplish marks peeking out from the sleeve of his jacket.

He'd just managed to wrestle the key into the lock when the door across the hall swung open. "Bran, where have you been?" Mrs. Chan's face lit up with a smile. "You left without saying a word, and—" Her gaze dropped to his exposed wrist, and her eyes went wide. "Are you all right?"

"I am now," he replied, forcing a thin smile. "Thanks for asking."

She still looked . . . apprehensive, or was it scared? Bran figured he probably looked like he'd just staggered away from a car wreck. Or a gang fight.

Well, at least she didn't bolt back inside and lock her door.

"I have noodles I could bring you," she said. "If you're hungry."

Bran's stomach growled so loud he was amazed every door on the floor didn't fling open. "Um, yeah. Thanks, Mrs. Chan. I'd appreciate that."

They exchanged nods, and Bran let himself in, let the door swing shut behind him. God, the place smelled like . . . well, like it hadn't been aired out in three weeks. He strode over to his one working window and opened it, eardrums freshly assaulted by the screeches of bus brakes and people yelling from the street. Funny, he'd learned to tune all that shit out a long time ago, but after weeks living in the fucking sky (not to mention in a dark silent closet), he must've lost his tolerance.

He stripped off his clothes as gingerly as he could, threw everything in the hamper, and headed in for a shower. Dialed the water down to lukewarm—he'd learned his lesson about hot water on fresh welts that first week at Jonathan's—and stepped under the anemic spray. It still hurt as the water poured down his skin, but he gritted his teeth and got through it, grabbing a bar of soap to wash his face and hair. Couldn't wait to get the stench of Jonathan's dungeon off him. Of *Jonathan* off him. He still smelled like leather from that fucking sling. Still had lube in his ass. Jonathan had offered him the use of the shower—his upstairs shower, in fact—but Bran couldn't wait to get out of there. Couldn't wait to get Jonathan's face out of his head.

Good luck with that, pal.

He dried off, tied the towel around his waist. Padded into the kitchen to see what—if anything— was left in the fridge. A battered old gallon jug of tap water, a jar of kosher dills, and a whole lot of frost.

Better than nothing, he supposed.

He poured himself some water, grabbed a pickle, and flopped onto the edge of the bed. Bad idea—his ass was still way too sore. Stifling a groan, he rolled onto his side—which hurt just as bad—and bit into the pickle. Dripped all over the damn bedspread, but he was too fucking tired to care. Finished the whole thing in three bites, rolled over on his stomach, and fell into a coma.

He wasn't sure how long he slept, but there was sunshine pouring in through the open window when he opened his eyes. Every joint felt rusted together, but finally he managed to roll to his feet. The place hadn't looked so bad in the dark, but now he could see the film of dust coating everything, the holes in the carpet and curtains. The crappy kitchen linoleum he'd patched with fucking duct tape.

This is your life, Brandon McKinney. And welcome back to it.

So, what would he do now? Jonathan's thirty grand in the bank, plus the four he'd managed to save on his own, and this shithole was paid up for the next eleven months. Whoop-dee-fucking-doo.

Although, you could *afford to go back to school now . . .*

Could maybe even afford to take a year off to do it right. Enroll at Berkeley full time. But it was barely April now, and he couldn't start until September—assuming it wasn't too late to apply. And he'd gotten tired of sitting (kneeling) around doing nothing all day after just three weeks. Might as well call his boss and see if he could get his job back.

He picked up the phone, dialed the office number. The secretary answered: "Sung Integrated Design, how may I help you?"

"Hey Jen, it's Bran. Is Mr. Sung around?"

"Bran, hi!" God, *way* too chipper. His head hurt too much for her brand of flirty-friendly today. "Are you— is everything okay?"

He'd left without much explanation to his co-workers, but the central staff was tight-knit enough that Mr. Sung might have spread his sob story. Hopefully not; he'd felt bad enough lying to *one* person who'd been good to him. "Yeah, everything's fine. Back a little sooner than I thought I'd be. Boss there?"

"Sure, sure, hang on one sec." A click, and then the spiel Mr. Sung had programmed into their phone system in mildly accented English. *At Sung Integrated Design, we'll help you realize your dream from start to finish. From conception, to planning, to nailing the last shingle on the roof . . .*

"Bran, how are you?"

He snapped himself out of his hold-talk-induced stupor and tried not to sound too needy when he said, "Fine, fine. My dad's responding really well to treatment. Told me to go home, get back to work. So, uh, here I am."

A sucked-in hiss of air between teeth, and then a long, drawn-out, "Yeeeeeeah. Look, about that. I'm sorry, Bran, but we won the bid for the Hillside Home and I needed a full crew right away. I couldn't be down a foreman."

Bran closed his eyes, dropped his head into his hand. Sure, Mr. Sung had warned him he might have to replace him, but it'd only been three weeks. Three lousy weeks! "Are, I mean, isn't there *anything* I can do?"

"Well, we do need day labor. We're running two shifts at Hillside; I'm picking guys up at Home Depot twice a day."

Migrant workers earning $8 an hour. How the fuck was he supposed to live on that?

"Look, I could give you as much time as you wanted. Well, 60 hours a week, anyway; more than that and the client won't sanction the overtime. But, like I said, we're running two shifts, six days a week. And who knows . . . we cycle through people all the time. Maybe something more permanent will open up soon."

"Yeah, maybe." Except they both knew that was bullshit. No one in their right mind left a good construction job in this economy.

So what does that make you, moron?

"I'm sorry, Bran. I didn't want to have to do this, but you said you might be gone half a year."

"It's all right, Mr. Sung."

"Tomorrow at six, then?"

God, to be *useful* again. To work with his hands again, do something he enjoyed again . . . So fucking tempting. But ready as his mind was, his body still needed time to heal. No way he could spend all day in a harness right now. And how the fuck would he explain all the bruises when it got sweaty enough to force him out of his jacket?

"Yeah, uh, I actually could use a few days, if that's okay. Just got back today, have some errands to run, have to make a few calls for my dad. Insurance bullshit, you know how it is."

Mr. Sung chuckled. "Okay, Bran. Monday, then?"

What the fuck day was it today? How did he not *know* that? Couldn't be any later than Thursday with a 6 a.m. pickup tomorrow; the weekend crews didn't start running 'til 8. Which gave him at least three days. It'd be enough. "Yeah," he said. "Monday's fine. Thanks, Mr. Sung."

"Anytime." A pause, long enough for Bran to start to hang up, and then, "Bran? I'm glad your dad's okay. It's good to have you back."

I hope he's dead. "Thanks, Mr. Sung."

He stared at the phone for a long moment after he hung up, a weird, empty feeling coming over him. He'd better get dressed, go out and buy some food. And yet he didn't move. At last he tossed the phone on the bed and stood, wincing as his body protested. Jesus, was he *ever* going to stop hurting? Every welt and bruise felt like it'd been branded into him. Sure, they'd fade in time, but the memory of how he'd gotten them wouldn't.

Or who'd put them there . . .

He shook his head, trying to dislodge Jonathan's image from his brain. That smug, smirking little fucker who'd thought he could break him.

He did *break you. More than once.* All it'd taken was some pain and discomfort—

And shoving his whole fucking hand up my ass. And putting a fucking stun gun to my balls.

Whatever. He'd dealt with his dad for *years.* And yeah, okay, his dad had never tried to shove *anything* up his ass, but he'd spent plenty of drunken rages beating Bran with the wrong end of his belt. He'd made Bran *bleed.* Had even sent him to the emergency room a couple times. And Bran hadn't given up then. Hadn't given up later, either, after the old man had kicked him out, after he'd run out of friends' couches to crash on, not even after social services had started sniffing around with the threat of foster care. He'd spent months cold and hungry and broke, hitching across the country eating food from trashcans and sleeping under bridges. Still hadn't quit when he'd gotten to San Fran, when all anyone wanted to pay him for was his ass or his mouth, when he'd told them all to fuck off and managed to find real work, a place to stay, a shot at a better future . . .

You got soft, you little sissy. Weak. Just like I always knew you were.

He scrubbed his hands across his face, sat back on the bed. "Thanks, Dad. Real helpful."

You don't deserve help. God helps those who help themselves, not whiny little faggots like you.

"There *is* no God, Dad." *God wouldn't have taken Mom and left me with* you.

Or maybe there was a God, and he just had a fucking mean streak. Dangled the carrot out in front of Bran and then snatched it away. Made it impossible to chase.

Well, maybe not impossible, but at least harder than he was willing to try. Maybe that was God's way of telling him he didn't want it bad enough, after all. That maybe, like his father always said, he deserved what he got.

Turned out it was Tuesday, and Bran spent the next five days doing nothing but eating, sleeping, and watching TV, cocooned on the couch in every spare blanket he could find. The apartment wasn't *that* cold, but it felt so damn good to be warm again, to sprawl out how he wanted to instead of kneeling on a hard floor, to sleep in his own bed, to take long hot baths in his shitty cracked tub and not have to shave his fucking nuts every day. The hair itched as it grew back in, and he scratched with pure pleasure, reveling in the ability to touch himself without being punished.

And, okay, maybe he touched himself a *lot* for a guy his age, but Jesus, he couldn't get sex off the brain. Couldn't turn his libido down. It was like Jonathan had chemically *changed* him somehow, jacked into something raw and primal and *needy* that'd clung to him after he'd left that nightmare of a place. He wouldn't admit it out loud for a million bucks, but he even kind of missed the shower nozzle. Closed his eyes as he washed and jacked himself, imagining how it'd feel if he were full of warm water, letting the pressure in his ass and gut build and build along with the pressure in his dick and balls . . .

Jonathan had never let him do that. But Jonathan was gone, for good, for *ever*, and good riddance anyway, and Bran would do as he damn well pleased.

He fell into bed around 8:30 Sunday night, decked head to toe in flannel pajamas so old and soft he couldn't remember what color they'd once been. He'd eaten enough to make him sleepy, and yeah, it wasn't exactly Sabrina's cooking—hell, it wasn't even *McDonalds* cooking—but even five days on, he still got a kick out of choosing his own meals and feeding his fucking self. His bed was a little on the lumpy side—he'd had the same one for over a decade now—but it beat the shit out of a yoga mat, or worse, the floor. Or a damn fucking cage.

He woke up at 2 a.m., for once not from a nightmare, but shit, this was worse. He'd woken thinking of *Jonathan*. That pretty mouth, those talented hands on his dick, that slim little plug up his ass, the one just small enough to cause more pleasure than pain. His balls were aching. He was hard enough to pound nails. He slid his hand beneath the waistband of his pajama pants and grabbed himself. Not too rough—not like Jonathan would've done. Just warm, firm pressure, a steady rhythm, meant to get the job done.

Except . . . he didn't want it to end so fast. Wanted to—*Goddamn it*—*savor* it. He arched his hips up, shoved his pants down, kicked them off. Pulled his shirt off too, after a moment's thought. Rubbed a hand up his chest, gave one nipple a light pinch. Pressed gentle fingers to the fading bruises—a moment's pain, hardly worth noting. His dick twitched.

He'd be damn fucking glad of it when all these fucking marks went away. When he wasn't reminded of Jonathan every time he looked in the mirror, every time he looked down at himself, every time he touched himself.

And yet here you are, touching yourself just like Jonathan did.

Well, he supposed he could concede that Jonathan had taught him a new trick or two. Like this one: he sucked two fingers into his mouth, then let them trail down behind his dick, fondle his balls a moment, then rub over his hole, pressing gently. He pushed one finger inside to the first knuckle, then added the second finger. Worked them in as far as he could, found his prostate and rubbed at it with gentle little rocking motions. Didn't touch his dick, though it practically wept for attention. If Jonathan had done this to him, he'd have raged at the man for teasing, but in his own hands, under his own control . . .

(It feels better when he does it and you know it.)

Under his *own* control, it was absolutely fucking amazing. He let his legs splay open, canted his hips up, spat into his free hand and gave his dick a single hard tug. He didn't have lube, didn't even have hand lotion, but spit would do. Had a nice little edge of roughness to it, actually, and—

And where the fuck did that *come from? Since when do you like edges?*

Since the night Jonathan fucked your mouth in a dirty back alley.

"Shut *up!*" he growled, jacking himself harder, thrusting his fingers in and pressing with purpose against his prostate. He tilted his head back, drove his fist faster and faster over his dick, thrust his hips up into it, all thoughts of savoring gone. He just wanted to come, just wanted to relieve all that *pressure* and be done with it and go the fuck back to sleep for an hour or two before he had to get up for work.

His orgasm slammed into him with all the force of a full-body tackle, left him drained and sore and *hollow* somehow as he pulled his fingers from his ass with a hiss, wiped the cum off his belly and chest with the T-shirt he'd left on the floor before bed. He closed his eyes, let his breathing steady, and fought the absolutely fucking insane urge to go again. He wasn't seventeen anymore; he probably couldn't get it up again tonight even if his heart was really in it. Which it wasn't. Not even a little.

Bran's alarm went off what seemed like five minutes later. Four thirty, and it was still pitch black out. He rolled out of bed with a groan and headed in for a quick shower. Fought the urge to jack off again—just barely—dried off, went into the kitchen for coffee. The cheap stuff he still had in the cupboard, tasted like battery acid. But hell, it was *his*, and he could drink the whole damn pot if he wanted to.

It was freezing outside, but at least he had his clothes on. Which didn't make waiting for the bus any more fun. Or strap-hanging, because the fucking bus was already full. He got off a few blocks from the job site and walked the rest of the way, hands shoved in his pockets against the morning chill. Tomorrow he'd have to remember his gloves.

Mike flagged him down as he walked up the unfinished driveway, came over to slap him on the back. Bran flinched, but recovered quickly and flashed a smile. "Looks like you losers survived without me," he said.

Mike laughed, slapped him on the back again. "You're a real Goddamned sweetheart, you know that? Come on, the boys all pitched in and bought you breakfast." Mike led him to the construction trailer, gestured him through with an exaggerated bow. About half the regular crew was there already, lounging around the coffee pot and the drafting tables. They stood when he walked in, clapped. Someone handed him a cup of coffee and a donut with a candle in it. Wasn't even lit.

"Um."

"Welcome back, buddy." More back slaps, and okay, yeah, these guys were all right, but could they please stop fucking touching him so much? He sat down in the first open chair—a decent barrier between himself and all the friendly hands. Mike sat down next to him, whispered sidelong, "New foreman's a real hardass."

"Yeah," said Pete, breaking a bite off Bran's celebratory donut without asking. "Fucking slave-driver." He winked at Mike, popped the bite of donut in his mouth.

Bran took a big bite of what remained before anyone else could steal it from him, and turned to Mike, wide-eyed. "You? Mr. Sung gave *you* my job?"

Mike looked like he didn't know whether to keep smiling or apologize. He settled for a shrug and said, "Sorry man, but I got three kids, you know? Besides, we thought you were gonna be gone for a while. So . . . how's your dad?"

Bran pasted on a smile and took a long drag on his coffee. Really, if anyone was going to take his place, and of course someone was going to, no one deserved it more than Mike. At least the mood on the job site wouldn't change. "He's doing really well," he said. Felt the smile slip and covered it with another sip of coffee; he hated lying to people he liked. "So well he told me to go home, stop putting my life on hold."

Mike grinned, checked his watch. Bran had tried to put his own on this morning, couldn't quite bear the feel of the strap around his wrist. "That's good, man, that's good. Real glad to hear it. And you? You all right?"

How the fuck was he supposed to answer that? Didn't seem like one of those polite "How you doings"; seemed like Mike really wanted to know. And he supposed Mike was his boss now, after a fashion. He took another long pull on his coffee, and Mike's gaze zeroed in on his hand.

Shit. Not his hand; his wrist. His still-very-bruised wrist.

"Dude, what the hell? Nurses couldn't bear to let you leave?"

Before he could stop himself, he said, "Actually, some rich guy chained me up in his basement."

For a second Mike looked like he wasn't sure if Bran was joking, but then he burst out laughing and slapped him on the back again. "Well, you do kinda look like hell. Finish your donut, slave-boy, and let's get to work."

The rest of the day went on the way they usually did on a work site—lots of fetching and carrying, good, physical work with results he could see unfolding before his eyes, joking around with the guys, stealing Mike's lunch out of the fridge. Before he knew it, the three o'clock whistle rang, and the first shift filed out as the second filed in.

Mike came up and laid a hand on his neck—way too damn close to where Jonathan used to put his—and said, "Hey, you wanna come have a beer with me and some of the guys? I know it's not your usual thing, but what the hell. Our treat?"

Bran thought about saying yes, but the word wouldn't come. He'd never made a habit of going out drinking with the guys before, mostly because . . . well, he used to be their boss, and the idea of socializing with guys he had to supervise made him uncomfortable. But that wasn't a problem anymore, so . . . why was he hesitating?

Truthfully, all he wanted was to go home and fall into bed. Couldn't face the thought of having to make small-talk for the next hour or two. Besides, he was still pretty sore, and all the lifting and carrying today hadn't helped. Felt good to use his body for something practical—that satisfying good-day's-work kind of sore—but sore nevertheless.

"Mind giving me a rain check? I'm still pretty wiped."

Mike's cheerful expression fell, but he nodded. "Sure, man. I get it. Maybe on Friday, huh?"

Bran nodded back and started off for his bus stop. "Sure."

And yet, when he got off the bus, he found himself walking toward Jian Li's, right around the corner from his apartment. Wasn't terribly crowded yet, so he slid onto a stool at the bar.

Jian Li's eyebrows shot up the second he saw him. "I saved your stool for you all month. You were missed, Mr. Bran."

His way of saying *What happened* and *Are you okay?* Bran smiled as Jian Li drew him a beer and slid the glass over with a respectful nod.

Bran nodded back, took a sip. "As were you, Jian Li." He'd spoken in Chinese without even realizing until he'd finished. Felt good.

So he sat and drank his beer, casting a glance around the bar. A familiar sea of Asian faces, though he found himself looking at the door, half-hoping, half-dreading to see someone else. Never used to bother him that the only person who ever talked to him in here was Jian Li. He used to like this place for exactly that reason; nobody ever hit on him here. He could sit quietly, drink his warm beer, and head on home.

But tonight, for some reason, he longed for a little conversation. A little banter, a little flirting with someone fun. The people here respected him—he was a *Gweilo* who'd taken the time to learn their language and culture—but he wasn't one of them. Seemed like he wasn't one of anything, these days.

And really, wasn't that his own damn fault? The guys at work kept inviting him out, and he kept saying no. Kept making excuses—he had nothing in common with them, he couldn't afford the bar bill, he was their boss—but that's all they were. *Excuses.* Real reason was, he didn't like letting anyone in. Didn't trust people. It always ended badly.

So here he was, exactly where he'd been a month ago. Sitting in a bar by himself, going home to his shitty apartment alone. Nothing had changed.

I don't know how to fix this.

He sighed, dragged the tip of his finger through the foam of his beer. Had he really been lonely so long he couldn't even *tell* anymore? And why did it suddenly hurt so fucking bad? After fifteen fucking *years*?

Jonathan. Fucking *Jonathan*. Making Bran *savor* life. All that did was make the shithole that was reality all the more shitty when he had to go back to it. He wasn't a gazillionaire. Couldn't spend his life living in a fucking bubble like Jonathan did. Guy had no right to do this shit to him. To open all those old wounds, leave him so raw, feeling so fucking much.

Bran propped his chin in his hands, closed his eyes. Felt, for an instant, the brush of Jonathan's fingers on the back of his neck, so fucking *real* he spun around, heart pounding—

Didn't know whether to be relieved or disappointed when Jonathan wasn't actually there. Hated not knowing just as much as he hated what Jonathan had done to him.

Fucked you up worse than your dad did, Bran.

Yet he was also the first person to lay selfless hands on Bran since his high school boyfriend. First person since he was fourteen to touch him out of kindness, be *gentle*, who didn't want to hit or hurt him or just get their rocks off and leave.

Well, sometimes, *anyway.* Bran snorted into his beer, took a mouthful and swooshed it around before swallowing. Maybe if he finished it, and then drank another one or two, he'd stop being so fucking maudlin. Stop fucking thinking of Jonathan.

He could help you.

"Shut up . . ."

He tried to help you. You wouldn't let him.

"Shut *up*!" He chugged his beer, hoping to drown that stupid little voice. Didn't work. Thought back at it, *He* hurt *me. Humiliated me. Used me. Treated me like a fucking* whore.

Because you goaded him. Fought him every step of the way. Admit it—you liked him. You liked what he made you feel. You liked the way he made you think. You liked the way he opened your eyes.

So what if he did? Didn't change how Jonathan had hurt him.

And what about how you *hurt* Jonathan*?*

Jesus Christ, this was fucking ridiculous. He was *not* going to sit here having a fucking argument with himself over warm beer.

Just go talk to him. You know you want to.

No, he didn't. Not even a little. Never wanted to see the smug little shit again.

. . . So then why did he keep glancing at the door, hoping Jonathan might come through it?

I thought I taught you better than that, you worthless little shit. Either pull on your big-girl panties or don't, but stop the damn whining before I shut you up myself.

Bran drained his beer and plunked the glass on the bar. "Never thought I'd say this, Dad, but you're right." He stood, shrugged his jacket on. This wasn't gonna fix itself. Only one way to make things right: suck it up and face them.

onathan's intercom buzzed around eight, and he leaned forward in his chair to answer it. "Yes, Joel?"

The doorman cleared his throat. "There's a Mr. McKinney here to see you, sir. Shall I send him up?"

Brandon? What the hell was he doing here? Jonathan sat back, rubbed a hand over his chin. *Probably came back to punch you in the nose.* And why should he give him the opportunity? Hadn't he put up with enough of Brandon's childishness and fits of temper?

Still . . . he was curious. Maybe Brandon had finally come to his senses. Well, only one way to find out. "Go ahead, Joel."

He flicked off his computer and headed into the living room. Waited by the elevator until the doors opened. Brandon glanced at him as if he thought Jonathan might have the stun gun ready to go.

"Well, are you coming in?" Jonathan demanded. "Or did you just drop by to tell me to go fuck myself again?"

Brandon shuffled in, hands in his pockets. Looked around as if he'd never seen the place before. As if Jonathan's penthouse hadn't been his home for the past month. "Y-you got some of that good scotch on hand?"

Jonathan stiffened, his mouth tightening. *You scorned every kindness I tried to show you over the past three weeks, and now you saunter in asking for a* drink? It took him a moment to conquer the impulse to toss Brandon out on his highly presumptuous ear before he led the man over to the couch.

The steel cuffs were still on the coffee table, right where Brandon had left them last week. For some reason, Jonathan couldn't bear the thought of putting them away just yet. Brandon looked surprised when he saw them, but sat down nonetheless, his gaze glued to them for a long moment. Something else flickered across his face—a touch of regret?—but it was gone too quickly to be sure.

Jonathan poured them both doubles, handed Brandon his, and sat down. Leaned back in his chair, crossed his legs, waited for Brandon to tell him why he'd come.

Brandon peered at his drink, swirled and sniffed it, but didn't actually take a sip. So this was serious, then, if he wanted to be sober for it?

"You—" Brandon began, then changed his mind and tasted his scotch after all. He kept his gaze locked on his drink as he spoke. "I think maybe we fucked up."

We? Jonathan uncrossed his legs, fought the urge to lean forward. "Explain," he said when the silence stretched. He had his own ideas about this, but was suddenly very intrigued to hear Brandon's. Not that he was about to let Brandon know that. He set his drink on the side table and pasted on a neutral expression while he waited for Brandon to continue.

"When I came here . . ." Another tiny sip of scotch, glass twirling round and round in his nervous fingers. "I thought, well, this guy's fucking infuriating, but he's also *fascinating*. And hot. Seriously fucking hot. I liked you. I liked talking to you. I liked . . ." He finally glanced up from his drink, squeezed now in tense fingers. "I liked the way you made me *feel*."

"Well, you certainly had a strange way of showing it. Fighting me. *Biting* me. Making me punish you every day, making me break you just to get you to eat—"

"I know, I know, and . . . I'm sorry. I didn't understand what it all meant. Didn't know what I . . ."

Silence again.

"What you *wanted*?" Jonathan said finally. "That was apparent from the very first day."

"Look, I know, and I'm sorry, I really am, just . . . Let me finish. Please."

Jonathan gave a grudging nod. After all, if Brandon meant to ask Jonathan to take him back—and that certainly seemed to be where this was going—then he had a lot more explaining to do. And a lot more apologizing, frankly.

Maybe, just maybe, it'd be good enough.

"When I first got here, well . . . Okay, I'm not gonna lie and say the money didn't matter, because of course it did. I've worked and scraped and *worked* for every fucking thing I've ever had in this world, and the chance to just . . . to see my whole future laid out ahead of me like that, everything I ever dreamed of . . ."

Ah, yes, the *money*. The only reason Brandon had agreed to this in the first place. *And now here you are, about to beg me to take you back so you can collect your three million? Not bloody likely—but I'll still listen to you grovel.*

Brandon put his drink down, barely touched, on the coffee table, right near the steel cuffs. Scrubbed both hands through his hair and then folded them in his lap, fingers tangling. "But I told myself it was more than that, you know? That I would've spent the next six months sleeping with you anyway. And I *meant* it. But then I get here, and suddenly we stop talking. You stop asking me questions. You don't let *me* say a fucking thing at all. Everything I know about you I learned from fucking *Google*, for fuck's sake. I felt like . . ." He swallowed, flushed clear to the tips of his ears. "You made me feel like a *whore*, Jonathan," and thank God he was still staring at his hands, because Jonathan flinched at that like Brandon had hit him. "Like the one fucking thing I'd never, *ever* sunk to, even when I was living on the streets. Like a . . . what'd you say to me that last day? Like a hole to fuck. Like a thing to be used."

Jonathan pushed back in his chair, gripping the arms as the shock— and the truth—of Brandon's words sank in. Not what he'd meant to do. Not *at all*. Good God, he really had messed this up right along with Brandon, hadn't he? "Oh, *Brandon*, I never—"

"Please," Brandon said, holding a hand up. "Just . . . just let me finish."

Jonathan swallowed back his protest and nodded. He owed him that much. More. Maybe if he'd let the man speak his mind three weeks ago . . .

"I couldn't . . . I couldn't *deal* with that, you know? Couldn't *hear* you when I felt like that. So all that shit you said, all those things you did and all your reasons for them . . ." Brandon huffed, shook his head, the corners of his mouth lifting ever so slightly. "In one ear and out the other. But now I've had some time to think, and some time to realize how much truth there was in all that. I'm . . ." He shook his head, hands once again scrubbing at his hair. "*Different* now. You've *changed* me somehow, and I can't . . ." He shrugged, finally looked Jonathan in the eye, plaintive and desperate, confused and naked, totally *naked*, for the first time ever in Jonathan's presence. "And I don't understand it. I don't know what to *do* with myself, with my feelings, with these . . . these *things* I want now, these things I think about. I don't . . . I don't want to be alone anymore, and I'm tired of fighting all the time. And so I thought . . ."

This time, as the silence stretched on, cautious hope built so strongly in Jonathan's chest he couldn't stop himself from saying, "So you thought you'd come back."

Brandon nodded ever so slightly, like a man convinced he couldn't possibly have what he was asking for. *Could* he, though? Brandon had never said so much to Jonathan. He hardly knew what to do with it all—the long-overdue revelation, the stirrings of self-awareness, the pseudo-admission of responsibility for their separation.

Hardly knew what to do either with *You made me feel like a whore.*

Had he? He'd been so careful—or so he'd thought—to care for Brandon, to not dehumanize him, not objectify him, not dismiss or ignore his pleasure, not oversexualize his suffering.

And yet he *had* stopped talking to Brandon, hadn't he? Or rather, stopped talking *about* Brandon. About himself, too. Had been so focused on the man's training, on breaking through the stubbornness and the pride and that thick wall of shame to coax out the submission lying beneath that he'd forgotten to focus on *them*, on what had drawn them to each other in the first place, on their pasts, their present . . . maybe even their future. In that, he'd been just as culpable as Brandon. More, even.

He took a long sip of his own drink, then put it down. Now was not the time for tipsiness. "When I was eight, I got into my first and last fistfight with another boy. Over something ridiculous, I don't know, I don't even remember anymore why we were fighting. What I *do* remember is the thrill of wrestling him to the ground. Of how satisfying it felt to make him cry. And of how *horrified* I was by that satisfaction, that pleasure, that desire I couldn't even name. I fled. I left him bleeding in the dirt, and I fled right back to Mum and Dad, where I promptly confessed everything in a fit of tears, right down to how good it had felt to hurt him."

Brandon blinked at him, opened his mouth, closed it, opened it again. Said, finally, "What'd they do?"

"They made me apologize to the boy *and* his parents, and then they grounded me for a week. But they also told me it was all right to feel that way. That there was nothing wrong with me, that I wasn't a bad person. That as long as I felt too guilty to do it again, the good guys were winning and all would be well."

A hesitant smile curled one corner of Brandon's lips. "The origin of a sadist, huh?"

Jonathan smiled back. "It was quite the relief, you understand, to grow up and find others like me. Find men who *wanted* to be hurt, who *liked* to cry at my feet."

"I bet. And those other men? Did you tell *them* stories about your childhood?"

Touché. "I'm man enough to admit when I've made a mistake, Brandon. I held us back. I won't— I *wouldn't* do it again."

Brandon met his gaze, quite serious of a sudden. "You promise?"

Jonathan nodded. "I promise."

Brandon nodded back. Then his gaze fell away from Jonathan's, went back to his drink. His hand followed, and he gulped down half the glass before slamming it on the table, standing suddenly, and . . . leaving?

Jonathan's first instinct was to call after him, but he bit it back, watched him disappear down the hall, into his study. Watched him come back a moment later, eyes widening as he saw what Brandon was carrying: the cane that lived on his desk.

Brandon was blushing clear to the roots of his hair as he laid the cane in Jonathan's lap and knelt, with perfect posture, at his feet.

Oh really?

"So tell me then," Jonathan said, picking up the cane and tapping Brandon on the shoulder with it, "how things would be different on *your* end this time."

The question seemed to stump Brandon. "I don't know, Jonathan. I don't even know if I *want* a 'this time.'"

Yes, you do. He was strong enough to admit it, too; he just needed a little help.

Jonathan tipped up Brandon's chin with the point of the cane. "Pretend you do. Now convince me you deserve a second chance."

Brandon sucked in a deep breath, blew it out, looked like he might be considering a protest. But he left his pride behind and said, "Well, I know what I'm getting into this time."

Even he seemed to know how weak that was. Jonathan shook his head, poked him in the chest with the cane. "You knew what it was when you left, too. That hasn't changed."

Brandon bit his lip, nodded. "I, uh, I realize now what you . . . well, what you were trying to do for me. How hard it was for you. How much of yourself you gave to me." His eyes darted up to Jonathan's, dropped back to the carpet. "How dismissive I was. How resistant. And I don't . . . ." He hunched in on himself for a moment, hands fisting at the small of his back. "I don't know if I'll ever be the man you think I am. I don't . . . I don't *like* it when you hurt me. I wish you wouldn't. But I *do* know I've had the best sex of my life here. That I like the way you make me feel when you're good to me. That I like . . ." God, he was blushing again so hard he looked feverish. "That I like how you make me forget to be ashamed. That you make me feel like maybe it's okay to want this, to want"—he broke position to gesture with both hands, a floppy, helpless toss that seemed to encompass the whole world— "*anything*. Everything. To stop living like such a damn monk. To . . . to maybe trus—" He cut himself off, reached over to the coffee table to finish his scotch, did *not* finish his sentence.

But that was okay, because clearly, Jonathan had gotten through to him after all. Brandon had been so raw, so emotional, so angry all the time, no wonder he'd needed a week to decompress and process everything he'd been through here. No wonder the realization of what he'd walked away from had left him aching, longing for more.

The question was, could Jonathan give it to him? He was so tired, so drained himself. Another five months of this would probably do him in. Except . . . well, except that he too was aching, longing for more. Three weeks with this man . . . three trying, difficult, *stressful* weeks, and yet he'd not been able to get Brandon out of his head. Hadn't even been able to bring himself to put the man's cuffs away, and if *that* wasn't him trying to tell himself something, he didn't know what was.

"There will be questions if you stay," he said. Brandon perked up, just a little, looking as cautiously hopeful as Jonathan had felt before. "We'd talk. Every night. You would be *honest*. Can you handle that?"

There followed a long enough pause to make clear that Brandon was honestly considering the question. Finally, he said, "I'd do my best, Jonathan."

God, so easy. Slipping right back to where they'd been. Jonathan's heart twitched along with his cock. This might really work. They might really be able to have this.

"And this cane would still have your name on it."

Brandon swallowed, bit his lip again, but he nodded. "I'd try not to make you need it, Jonathan."

Jonathan quite appreciated that, but decided to test Brandon all the same: "Sometimes I'd use it whether I needed it or not."

Another hard swallow, but Brandon said, "I understand, Jonathan. You, uh . . . you deserve your pleasure too."

"And we'd need to do something about that filthy mouth of yours. Cursing is so *crass*."

Was that a smile playing at Brandon's lips? "I'd do my best, Jonathan."

"And don't think I'd count the week you've been away toward your six months."

"Of course not, Jonathan."

Jonathan felt a smile playing at his own lips, and wiped it clean. Stood up, squatted in front of Brandon, and laid his hand on the nape of Brandon's neck. Took Brandon's chin with his free hand and lifted it, gentle as could be, until their eyes met. "This won't be easy. You know that, right?"

Brandon blinked at him with those big green eyes, so full of hope, of fear, of affirmation. "I know, Jonathan," he said softly. Added, almost as if to himself, "But I want this. I do." He met Jonathan's eyes again and said, quite emphatically this time, "I *do*. And I know it won't be easy"— one corner of his mouth quirked up—"for either of us, I suppose. But if I've learned anything in life, it's that nothing worth having comes easy, and you've gotta be willing to fight for what matters to you."

Wise man, that.

"So please, Jonathan, I want to come back."

Jonathan rubbed his thumb over Brandon's gently parted lips, then leaned in to taste, his kiss soft, nearly chaste. "Yes, well," he murmured against Brandon's mouth, breath passing warm and moist between them, "just do be a dear and try not to fight me *too* hard."

Brandon laughed, rubbed his cheek against Jonathan's palm and then ducked out from beneath it, leaning sideways toward the coffee table. Before Jonathan realized what he was doing, Brandon had one cuff already locked around his wrist and was halfway to fastening on the other one. "I won't, Jonathan," he said. "Or"—another quirk of the lips into that painfully adorable lopsided smile of his—"at least, I promise to *try* not to. I don't discount the possibility you'll have to, um, help me break a few bad habits."

Just a *few*? Jonathan grinned; he had a feeling the next five months were going to be very . . . *educational.* But satisfying, too. Deeply so.

For both of them.

ACKNOWLEDGMENTS

A special thank-you to our betas, Heidi Belleau and Alex Whitehall, and to everyone on Twitter and Facebook and Goodreads who cheered us on so heartily. Also to Oleg, for the muse-food gif—yeah, you know which one. Gratitude to our editors, of course: Tal Valante for the World's Most Insightful Fix on the last scene, Carole-ann Galloway for the ever-important (and repeated) sanity checks, and Aleks Voinov for being his regular BAMFy self. Lastly, our eternal devotion to Imaliea, our stunningly brilliant cover artist, who plucked Jonathan and Brandon from our heads and rendered them so exquisitely on paper.

ALSO BY CAT GRANT

The First Real Thing (Icon Men, #1)
Appearing Nightly (Icon Men, #2)
A Fool for You (Icon Men, #3)
Entangled Trio
Sonata Appassionata
Allegro Vivace
Once a Marine

Priceless (Irresistible Attraction #1)
Doubtless (Irresistible Attraction #2)
Fearless (Irresistible Attraction #3, Coming Soon)
Power Play: Awakening, with Rachel Haimowitz

ALSO BY RACHEL HAIMOWITZ

Counterpoint (Song of the Fallen, #1)
Crescendo (Song of the Fallen, #2)

Master Class (Master Class, #1)
SUBlime: Collected Shorts (Master Class, #2)

Anchored (Belonging, #1)
Where He Belongs (Belonging, #2)

Break and Enter, with Aleksandr Voinov

Power Play: Awakening, with Cat Grant

The Flesh Cartel, Season 1: Damnation, with Heidi Belleau
The Flesh Cartel, Season 2: Fragmentation, with Heidi Belleau

ABOUT THE AUTHORS

Cat Grant lives by the sea in beautiful Monterey, California with one persnickety feline and entirely too many books and DVDs. In her spare time, she reads (mostly for research), goes to the movies and opera a lot and fantasizes about kinky sex with Michael Fassbender.

You can find Cat at catgrant.com.

Rachel Haimowitz is an M/M erotic romance author, a freelance writer and editor, and the Managing Editor of Riptide Publishing. She's also a sadist with a pesky conscience, shamelessly silly, and quite proudly pervish. Fortunately, all those things make writing a lot more fun for her . . . if not so much for her characters.

When she's not writing about hot guys getting it on (or just plain getting it; her characters rarely escape a story unscathed), she loves to read, hike, camp, sing, perform in community theater, and glue captions to cats. She also has a particular fondness for her very needy dog, her even needier cat, and shouting at kids to get off her lawn.

You can find Rachel at her website: rachelhaimowitz.com, at her blog: rachel-haimowitz.blogspot.com, and on twitter @rachelhaimowitz. She loves to hear from folks, so feel free to drop her a line anytime at metarachel@gmail.com.

Enjoy this book? Find more hot kink at RiptidePublishing.com!

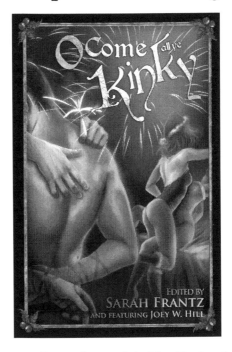

Christmas is a time of love and joy, and the New Year is a time of renewal. But they are also times of stress and strife, family drama, pressure and heartache—a potent mix of high expectations and conflicted emotions. Add in power exchange relationships, kinky gift swaps, and unconventional love in a sometimes unforgiving world, and you have a formula for a sizzling anthology of stories that tug at your heart.

Whatever your desires, we invite you to explore new fantasies and old with these eight kinky tales of holiday happy endings.

www.riptidepublishing.com/titles/o-come-all-ye-kinky
ISBN: 978-1-937551-51-3

Printed in Great Britain
by Amazon.co.uk, Ltd.,
Marston Gate.